STEPHEN JONES is the winner of two World Fantasy Awards, the Horror Writers of America Bram Stoker Award, and nine-time recipient of the British Fantasy Award. A full-time columnist, book and film reviewer, television producer/director and genre movie publicist (all three *Hellraiser* films, *Nightbreed*, *Split Second* etc.), he is the co-editor of *Horror: 100 Best Books*, *The Best Horror from Fantasy Tales*, *Gaslight & Ghosts*, *Now We Are Sick* and the *Best New Horror*, *Dark Voices: The Pan Book of Horror* and *Fantasy Tales* series. He has also compiled *Clive Barker's The Nightbreed Chronicles*, *The Mammoth Book of Terror*, *Clive Barker's Shadows in Eden*, *The Hellraiser Chronicles*, *The Mammoth Book of Vampires*, *James Herbert: By Horror Haunted* and *The Illustrated Vampire Movie Guide*.

RAMSEY CAMPBELL is the most respected living British horror writer. After working in the civil service and public libraries, he became a full-time writer in 1973. He has written hundreds of short stories (his latest collection, *Alone With the Horrors*, commemorates thirty years of chilling spines) and the novels *The Doll Who Ate His Mother*, *The Face That Must Die*, *The Parasite*, *The Nameless*, *Incarnate*, *Obsession*, *The Hungry Moon*, *The Influence*, *Ancient Images*, *Midnight Sun*, *The Count of Eleven*, *Night of the Claw* and *The Long Lost*. A multiple winner of both the World Fantasy Award and British Fantasy Award, he has also edited a number of anthologies, broadcasts weekly on Radio Merseyside as a film critic, and is President of the British Fantasy Society. He especially enjoys reading his stories to audiences.

BEST NEW

HORROR 3

BEST NEW
HORROR 3

Edited by
STEPHEN JONES
and
RAMSEY CAMPBELL

Carroll & Graf Publishers, Inc.
New York

First published in Great Britain in 1992 by Robinson Publishing.

First Carroll & Graf edition 1992

Carroll & Graf Publishers, Inc.
260 Fifth Avenue
New York, NY 10001

ISBN: 0-88184-858-1

Typeset by Hewer Text Composition Services, Edinburgh.

Manufactured in the United States of America

ACKNOWLEDGEMENTS

We would like to thank Kim Newman, Jo Fletcher, Peter Coleborn, Richard Dalby, Neil Gaiman, Humphrey Price, David Sutton and Ellen Datlow for their help and support. Thanks are also due to the magazines *Locus* (Editor & Publisher Charles N. Brown, Locus Publications, P.O. Box 13305, Oakland, CA 94661, USA) and *Science Fiction Chronicle* (Editor & Publisher Andrew I. Porter, P.O. Box 2730, Brooklyn, NY 11202–0056, USA) which were used as reference sources in the Introduction and Necrology.

CONTENTS

Introduction: Horror in 1991
THE EDITORS
1

True Love
K.W. JETER
15

The Same in Any Language
RAMSEY CAMPBELL
27

Impermanent Mercies
KATHE KOJA
35

Ma Qui
ALAN BRENNERT
53

The Miracle Mile
ROBERT R. McCAMMON
71

Taking Down the Tree
STEVE RASNIC TEM
75

Where Flies Are Born
DOUGLAS CLEGG
85

Love, Death and the Maiden
ROGER JOHNSON

97
Chui Chai
S.P. SOMTOW

111
The Snow Sculptures of Xanadu
KIM NEWMAN

117
Colder Than Hell
EDWARD BRYANT

129
Raymond
NANCY A. COLLINS

143
One Life, in an Hourglass
CHARLES L. GRANT

155
The Braille Encyclopedia
GRANT MORRISON

167
The Bacchae
ELIZABETH HAND

183
Busted in Buttown
DAVID J. SCHOW

189
Subway Story
RUSSELL FLINN

201
The Medusa
THOMAS LIGOTTI

221
Power Cut
JOEL LANE

229
Moving Out
NICHOLAS ROYLE

235
Guignoir
NORMAN PARTRIDGE

259
Blood Sky
WILLIAM F. NOLAN

279
Ready
DAVID STARKEY

289
The Slug
KARL EDWARD WAGNER

301
The Dark Land
MICHAEL MARSHALL SMITH

321
When They Gave Us Memory
DENNIS ETCHISON

337
Taking Care of Michael
J.L. COMEAU

341
The Dreams of Dr Ladybank
THOMAS TESSIER

339
Zits
NINA KIRIKI HOFFMAN

403
Necrology: 1991
STEPHEN JONES & KIM NEWMAN

For
HUGH B. CAVE
Here's to many more rounds
at the Gray Toad Inn

INTRODUCTION: HORROR IN 1991

Despite many predictions that the horror genre would collapse in 1991, there were only slightly fewer titles published in the field than in the previous year. However, although the market looked as healthy as ever, the overall quality of much of the material being published left a good deal to be desired.

Not that this affected the bestsellers. Dean R. Koontz began and ended the year with new novels: *Cold Fire* was a psychic thriller in his usual mould, while *Hideaway*, about near-death experiences, was more of a welcome departure. Dan Simmons strayed into Stephen King territory with his bulky *Summer of Night*, a coming-of-age novel set in a small town beset by evil forces, while Robert R. McCammon took the same route, though with less emphasis on the horror, in *Boy's Life*. King's own *Needful Things* was billed as "the last Castle Rock story", as the author finally destroyed his own small town. He also published the third volume in his offbeat "Gunslinger" series, *The Dark Tower III: The Waste Lands*, which was another sure-fire hit.

Clive Barker demonstrated at length what he means by the *fantastique* with his immense novel *Imajica*, which was joined on the bestseller lists by the first separate English-language edition of *The Hellbound Heart*. Peter Straub brought out the complete version of his story "Mrs God" (abridged in *Houses Without Doors*) as a short novel, and another tale which finally saw solo publication was L. Ron Hubbard's 1940 novel *Fear*, packaged with an enthusiastic quote from Stephen King.

Whitley Streiber returned to form with *The Wild*, a down-to-earth werewolf novel, and Dennis Danvers' *Wilderness* was an acclaimed first novel about a female werewolf falling in love. Brian Stableford's

The Angel of Pain was a nineteenth-century sequel to his *The Werewolves of London*. Michael Cadnum published *Saint Peter's Wolf*, an exultation of the Lycanthropic state (as well as *Sleepwalker*, an atmospheric tale in which a bog man is revived, and *Calling Home*, a young adult mystery novel).

It was more the year of the psychopath and in particular the vampire, however. Brian Lumley concluded the adventures of vampire hunter Harry Keogh in *Deadspawn*, the fifth in his bestselling "Necroscope" series, while the fifth volume in Les Daniels's chronicles of vampire Don Sebastian was *No Blood Spilled*. P. N. Elrod continued the "Vampire Files" series with *Art in the Blood* and *Fire in the Blood*, the fourth and fifth books to feature Jack Fleming, an undead reporter and private investigator, pursuing vampires in prohibition Chicago, and Tanya Huff's *Blood Prince* varied the theme by teaming a female private investigator with a vampire in contemporary Toronto. Brian Aldiss's *Dracula Unbound*, like his earlier treatment of Frankenstein, was what used to be called science fantasy, and had Bram Stoker trying to destroy a race of time-travelling vampires. *In the Blood* was Nancy Collins's eagerly awaited sequel to *Sunglasses After Dark*. T. M. Wright set his *The Last Vampire* after the holocaust, while Jeffrey N. McMahon's *Vampires Anonymous* was a black comedy about a hip, gay vampire. Counteracting all this interest was a revised edition of *The Highgate Vampire* by the Reverend (now Bishop) Sean Manchester.

The literary fashion for serial killers gained Thomas Harris's *Red Dragon* and *The Silence of the Lambs* a belated and entirely deserved success, but *Sliver* marked a disappointing return to the theme by the author of *A Kiss Before Dying*, Ira Levin. In a year which saw the unexpurgated Marquis de Sade in British paperback, it seemed appropriate that Bret Easton Ellis's *American Psycho* sneaked the prose equivalent of the worst of the video nasties onto the mainstream fiction shelves. Pretty nearly as explicit, though less widely discussed, was Dennis Cooper's *Frisk*, about a gay serial killer. The author of *Dirty Weekend*, Helena Zahavi, apparently saw a serial killer as a role model for her female readers. Ramsey Campbell's *The Count of Eleven* was published as horror, but was at least equally a comic novel, featuring what one reader described as "the most sympathetic serial killer in fiction".

Other books were published on the fringe of the field. Elizabeth Engstrom's *Lizzie Borden* added an occult twist to the famous case. Mark Jacobson's *Gojiro* (the Japanese name that is translated as "Godzilla") was inspired by comic books and that jolly green monster that keeps stomping Tokyo. *Outside the Dog Museum* showed that Jonathan Carroll's imagination still knows no bounds. Thomas M.

Disch's *The M.D.* twisted the scalpel nicely, though we gather that even if the book's subtitle was "A Horror Story", the author objected to being reviewed by Gahan Wilson. The introduction to *Secrets of the Morning* admitted that the late V. C. Andrews didn't write her latest family saga, but it failed to mention that Andrew Niederman did. Theodore Roszak's *Flicker* was one of the more challenging horror novels of the year, a book about the occult power of movies which raised moral and aesthetic issues which most horror writers appear to prefer to ignore.

Joe R. Lansdale gave the Dark Knight an even darker twist when he pitted him against Indian magic and a killer car in the original novelization *Batman: Captured by the Engines*. An Ouija board set evil in motion in *Darkness, Tell Us* by Richard Laymon, who also came up with a rain that drives people insane in *One Rainy Night*. Steve Harris achieved the same results with a hybrid cattle disease in *Wulf*. *The Fetch* was a superior new horror novel by Robert Holdstock, and *NeverLand* added to Douglas Clegg's growing reputation. Pulp veteran Hugh B. Cave returned to the voodoo theme in *Lucifer's Eye*, and Robert Weinberg kept the pulp tradition alive with *The Armageddon Box* and *The Black Lodge*. Garry Kilworth's *The Drowners* was a haunting ghost story for young adults. Charles L. Grant entered the young adult market with the psychic thriller *Fire Mask*, and chilled his older readers with *Something Stirs*. The underrated Bernard Taylor published a welcome new novel, *Charmed Life*. *The Burning* (aka *The Hymn*) and *Black Angel* (aka *Master of Lies*) all appeared by Graham Masterton. Stephen Gallagher's *The Boat House* featured psychological terrors, and Peter James's *Twilight* again reflected that author's fascination with the supernatural.

Mark Morris consolidated his growing reputation with a second novel, *Stitch*, as did Kim Newman with his latest and biggest novel *Jago*. Graham Joyce's first novel, *Dreamside*, also made quite an impact. *Reprisal* was F. Paul Wilson's sequel to *Reborn*, itself a sequel to *The Keep*. *Helltracks* proved that Willaim F. Nolan has lost none of his energy as a novelist. An evil mailman with psychic powers attacked an innocent family in Bentley Little's *The Mailman*, and the inmates of a county jail were made away with by monstrous plants in J. N. Williamson's *The Night Seasons*. Ecological horrors ran wild in *The Bridge* by John Skipp and Craig Spector, the first horror novel to come equipped with its own soundtrack album! Ray Garton's *The New Neighbor* and *Lot Lizards* both appeared in specialist editions. Also worth noting were *House Haunted* by Al Sarrantonio, *Dark Twilight* by Joseph A. Citro, *Dark Lullaby* by Jessica Palmer, *Captain Quaid* by Sean Costello, *Wurm* and the novelization of *Child's Play 3* by Matthew J. Costello, and *Cold Whisper* by Rick Hautala.

John Saul gave his readers what they expected with *Darkness*, about an unpleasant swamp-horror, and the same reliability might be claimed for Guy N. Smith (*The Black Fedora* and *The Resurrected*) and Shaun Hutson (*Renegades* and *Captives*, which once again proved that you can't judge a book by its cover).

Dell's "Abyss" line enlivened the horror field with several standout novels during its first year, including *The Cipher* by rising star Kathe Koja, *Nightlife* by Brian Hodge, and *Prodigal* by Melanie Tem.

Waking Nightmares collected nineteen tales by Ramsey Campbell. *Grimscribe His Lives and Works* was a fix-up of short stories by Thomas Ligotti. Robert Holdstock returned to the mysteries of Mythago Wood in *The Bone Forest*, a collection of eight tales, and ten recent stories were included in *Night of the Cooters*, subtitled "More Neat Stories", by the unclassifiable Howard Waldrop. *Sexpunks & Savage Sagas* was a self-published collection of fourteen tales by Richard Sutphen, whose Spine-Tingling Press also released a number of audio tapes based on his own and other authors' work.

While the number of collections may have been down, the anthology market was as crowded as ever. Byron Preiss *et al* tried to edit by numbers three anthologies loosely linked to vague anniversaries of movies, but *The Ultimate Werewolf*, *The Ultimate Dracula* and *The Ultimate Frankenstein*, despite their titles, weren't. Ellen Datlow chose eighteen tales of a wide range of vampirism for *A Whisper of Blood*, the superior successor to her *Blood Is Not Enough*, while *Under the Fang*, edited by Robert R. McCammon and set in a world overrun by vampires, consisted of seventeen stories by members of the Horror Writers of America.

Borderlands 2 wasn't quite the cutting edge anthology claimed by editor Thomas F. Monteleone, but it did include some fine fiction, as did Tim Sullivan's anthology *Cold Shocks* and Gary Raisor's *Obsessions*. *Final Shadows*, the twelfth and last anthology of the series edited by Charles L. Grant, was as high-grade as ever. Mystery and horror climbed into bed together in Richard Chizmar's first book as anthologist, *Cold Blood*, while Paul F. Olson and David B. Silva concentrated on urban horror in *Dead End: City Limits*. J. N. Williamson's fourth *Masques* anthology appeared only in a limited edition. *Night Visions 8* featured John Farris, Stephen Gallagher and Joe R. Lansdale, with an afterword by Robert R. McCammon, and F. Paul Wilson introduced *Night Visions 9*, which showcased work by Thomas Tessier, James Kisner and Rick Hautala.

Amy Myers' long-delayed *Fifth Book of After Midnight Stories* appeared from a new publisher and turned out not to be worth the wait. The man who has done so much to promote water conservation in the bathroom, Robert Bloch, proved to be a wise choice to edit *Psycho-Paths*, which featured seventeen stories about psychotic killers. *Chilled to the Bone* contained fifteen stories on a gaming concept, edited by Robert T. Garcia.

Dark Voices 3, edited by David Sutton and Stephen Jones, continued the *Pan Book of Horror* series, and the same team was responsible for two more volumes of *Fantasy Tales*. Jones also collaborated with Neil Gaiman on an anthology of Nasty Verse, *Now We Are Sick*, and was sole editor of *The Mammoth Book of Terror*, which mixed new tales with classic reprints.

Other mixtures of new and reprint material included *I Shudder At Your Touch*, twenty-two stories of sexual horror collected by Michele Slung, and *The Mammoth Book of Ghost Stories 2*, edited by Richard Dalby, which boasted more than 650 pages and an introduction by Christopher Lee. Dalby also compiled *Tales of Witchcraft*. Another veteran anthologist, Marvin Kaye, gave us forty-eight tales in *Haunted America: Star Spangled Supernatural Stories*. *Gaslit Nightmares 2* featured stories from the Victorian and Edwardian period, expertly selected by Hugh Lamb.

The indefatigable Martin H. Greenberg and Charles G. Waugh included twenty-one zombie stories in *Back from the Dead*, and teamed up with Frank D. McSherry, Jr. for *Civil War Ghosts*. Greenberg and Jane Yolen introduced young adult readers to thirteen stories of *Vampires*, and Greenberg alone showcased all-new stories of the world's most popular child molester in *Nightmares on Elm Street: Freddy Krueger's Seven Sweetest Dreams*.

The reprint anthology offering the best value for money was probably *Famous Fantastic Mysteries*, an instant remainder collection of the best stories from the classic pulp magazines *Famous Fantastic Mysteries* and *Fantastic Novels*, edited by Stefan Dziemianowicz, Robert Weinberg and Martin H. Greenberg. *The Complete Masters of Darkness* edited by Dennis Etchison was a doorstep-size omnibus of three anthologies and (despite its renaming one of its contributors "Brain Lumley") one of the most beautifully produced volumes of the year.

Ellen Datlow's and Terri Windling's *The Year's Best Fantasy and Horror: Fourth Annual Collection* was another 500-plus pages of the finest material being published in those fields. Karl Edward Wagner's always dependable *The Year's Best Horror Stories: XIX* continued to mine some of the more obscure sources. *The Best of Pulphouse: The Hardback Magazine* edited by Kristine Kathryn Rusch contained a mixed bag of twenty-five stories. *The Best of the Rest 1990* edited by Steve Pasechnick and Brian Youmans showcased stories from the small presses, and we hope that our own *Best New Horror 2* filled in the rest of the gaps.

After less than a year, the much-troubled British newsstand magazine *Skeleton Crew* finally ceased publication, while *Fear*, and its short-lived fiction sister *Frighteners*, both disappeared following the collapse of their publisher and the banning by the bookshop chains of the first issue of the latter. Horror fans were left with *The Dark Side*, which was saved by an editorial buy-out when the original publisher decided to drop it, and a new but undistinguished title, *Terror*.

Despite the appearance (and in some cases non-appearance) of several alleged rivals, *Interzone* continued to publish some of the best fiction in the UK or indeed anywhere else, and it was joined by a companion journal, *Million*, devoted to popular fiction and featuring a regular horror review column by Mark Morris. Kristine Kathryn Rusch moved from *Pulphouse* to *The Magazine of Fantasy and Science Fiction* and breathed new life into its contents.

Among the the semi-professionals, *Midnight Graffiti* managed just one issue, two issues of *Iniquities* appeared, and the award-winning *Cemetery Dance* looks set to turn professional soon. Chris Reed's *Back Brain Recluse* made the mistake of aiming for newsstand distribution too soon and quickly floundered.

One of the best new fanzines of the year was *Tekeli-li! Journal of Terror*. Its first two issues were devoted to Les Daniels and Douglas Clegg respectively. Another excellent newcomer was *Necrofile: The Review of Horror Fiction*, published quarterly by leading genre commentators Stefan Dziemianowicz, S. T. Joshi and Michael A. Morrison.

Robert Price's *Crypt of Cthulhu* (still subtitled *A Pulp Thriller and Theological Journal*) and S. T. Joshi's *Lovecraft Studies* continued to dissect Lovecraft minutiae. Of wider interest was Joshi's *Studies in Weird Fiction. Eldritch Tales* continued in "the *Weird Tales* tradition", while *Weird Tales* itself managed two more excellent issues.

There were new issues of *After Hours, Deathrealm, Forbidden Lines, Grue, Haunts: Tales of Unexpected Horror and the Supernatural, The Scream Factory, 2AM* and *Weirdbook. The New York Review of Science Fiction* presented the results of a survey on contemporary horror. *Pulphouse: A Fiction Magazine* was a new bi-weekly featuring an interesting mix of stories and non-fiction. Horror also turned up in *Alfred Hitchcock's Mystery Magazine, Mystery Scene*, and specialist booklets produced by Roadkill Press, Necronomicon Press, Chris Drumm, Haunted Library, The British

Fantasy Society and Pulphouse, the last in a bewildering variety of formats.

It was Clive Barker's turn to get the non-fiction treatment, with no less than three volumes devoted to his career: *Clive Barker Illustrator*, edited by Fred Burke, contained plenty of Barker's artwork—sixteen pages in full-colour—and an introduction by Stephen R. Bissette. *Pandemonium*, a collection of interviews, was less satisfactory, though it did contain the complete text of Barker's play *The History of the Devil*. By far the most substantial was *Clive Barker's Shadows in Eden*, edited by Stephen Jones, which ran to nearly 500 pages of articles and interviews by and about Barker, along with hundreds of illustrations and an extensive working bibliography.

Katherine Ramsland wrote *Prism of the Night*: *A Biography of Anne Rice*. George Beahm proved you could still get blood out of a stone with *The Stephen King Story*: *A Literary Profile*, and Stephen Spignesi managed to fill 800 pages of *The Shape Under the Sheet*: *The Complete Stephen King Encyclopedia*. *How to Write Horror Fiction* was the work of someone who should know, William F. Nolan, but the *Horror Film Quiz Book* was a sloppy piece of work by Shaun Hutson, someone who should know better.

Martin Tropp's *Images of Fear*: *How Horror Stories Helped Shaped Modern Culture* did nothing to help the horror genre. Worse still was Walter Kendrick's *The Thrill of Fear*, a superficial study of horror fiction (or rather, "horrid fiction") which received a depressing amount of praise from mainstream book reviewers. The American publishers McFarland continued to specialise in books on horror films: Dennis Fischer's *Horror Film Directors 1931–1990* offered useful interviews among tedious synopses and opinions dully expressed. John McCarty's *Official Splatter Movie Guide Vol.II* offered another superficial overview for movie fans, who were much better served by *Shock Xpress 1*, subtitled *The Essential Guide to Exploitation Cinema*, edited by Stefan Jaworzyn.

DC's *Mister E* was a novel-length comic in four parts written by K. W. Jeter, and Faye Perozich recreated Anne Rice's *The Vampire Lestat* for the graphic novel format. Michael H. Price and Todd Camp adapted the 1962 cult movie in *Carnival of Souls*, the full impact of David J. Schow's script for *The Texas Chainsaw Massacre III* was finally revealed in the *Leatherface* comic, and Steve Niles adapted Richard Matheson's classic vampire dystopia, *I am Legend*, in a four-part graphic format for Eclipse.

For the same company, Niles also adapted Clive Barker's *Son of Celluloid*, ably illustrated by Les Edwards, followed by *The*

Yattering and Jack, with art by John Bolton, and *Revelations*. Indeed—with a special *Hellraiser* companion, *Clive Barker's Book of the Damned*; *Jihad*, a two-part cross-over between his regular *Hellraiser* and *Nightbreed* series; a three-part adaptation of his novel *Weaveworld*, and *Clive Barker's Hellraiser Poster Book*, featuring perforated pin-ups for easy removal and a foldout poster by John Bolton—Barker rather dominated the comics field.

Tundra's *From Hell*, illustrated by Eddie Campbell, was an epic eight-volume examination of the Jack the Ripper murders by Alan Moore, aimed at conspiracy buffs. Also from Tundra, Stephen Bissette's *Taboo* continued to stir up controversy; the fifth issue is unavailable in the UK, S. Clay Wilson's "This is Dynamite . . ." and Michael Zulli's adaptation of Ramsey Campbell's "Again" having proved too strong for the British Customs and Excise.

When not creating shared-world anthologies, Neil Gaiman continued to shake-up the comics industry with his award-winning *Sandman*. DC Comics issued volumes 1–8 and 17–20, titled *Preludes & Nocturnes* and *Dream Country* respectively, as a handsome boxed set of graphic novels, and also reissued Gaiman's collaboration with artist Dave McKean, *Black Orchid*, as a graphic novel. For lovers of macabre humour, *The World of Charles Addams* was a splendid collection of classic Addams cartoons in black and white.

The top film in our field on both sides of the Atlantic last year was *Terminator 2: Judgment Day*, earning over $200 million at the box office and with plenty more to come from ancillary markets (in Britain it was just beaten into the top slot by *Robin Hood: Prince of Thieves*). A close runner-up was the multiple-Oscar winner *The Silence of the Lambs*. Drawn from somewhat older material, both *The Addams Family* and Martin Scorsese's most overt horror film so far, *Cape Fear*, did very well, as did *Bill and Ted's Bogus Journey*, and a surprise success was Kenneth Branagh's derivative hotchpotch *Dead Again*.

Hugo Award winner *Edward Scissorhands* more than doubled its 1990 total. *Freddy's Dead: The Final Nightmare* proved more popular than recent entries in the series, and given its (in one sense of the word) healthy box office, it would come as no surprise if the exploits of Freddy Krueger were further prolonged. Wes Craven returned to form with *The People Under the Stairs*—Frank Capra with cannibalism—and demonstrating that sequels are still in favour, *Child's Play 3* raked in the dollars.

The alleged comedy *Drop Dead Fred* was another surprise hit, while the mega-successful *Ghost* added an extra $11 million to its 1990 total of $20 million-plus. Delayed for a few years in America, *Warlock* finally opened to respectable returns. Also making a reasonable showing were *Body Parts* and the art-house release *Truly, Madly, Deeply*.

Down among the losers were *Predator 2*, barely adding to its disappointing 1990 total; *The Unborn, Poison, Meet the Applegates, Scanners II: The New Order, Firehead* and *The Borrower*.

On video, *The Pit and the Pendulum* was a darkly comic reworking of Poe that marked a return to form for director Stuart Gordon, and *Maniac Cop 2* turned out to be nearly as good as the original. However, Charles Band's long-awaited *Trancers II* was a major disappointment, as was *Whispers*, based on the novel by Dean R. Koontz. We could also do without *Ghoulies Go To College*, the third in the rubber puppet series, and *Shock'em Dead* starring Traci Lords and Aldo Ray. Best titles of the year had to be *Chopper Chicks in Zombietown* and *A Nymphoid Barbarian in Dinosaur Hell* . . .

Undoubtedly one of the treats of the year for horror fans was the HBO television movie *Cast a Deadly Spell*, which starred Fred Ward as down-at-heel private eye H. Phillip Lovecraft, tracking down a stolen copy of the *Necronomicon* in a 1940s Los Angeles where magic works.

The overlong Stephen King mini-series *Golden Years* received mixed reviews, but perhaps more indicative of the network mentality were the redundant and inept sequel, *Omen IV: The Awakening*, and the equally unnecessary remakes of *What Happened to Baby Jane?* and *Night of the Hunter*; *Not of This World*, which had nothing to do with the 1956 Roger Corman movie with a similar title; Charlton Heston playing Sherlock Holmes in *Crucifer of Blood*; the comedy *Frankenstein: The College Years*, and *Blood Ties*, a family saga about vampires.

One of the year's big disappointments was Joe Dante's weekly show *Eerie, Indiana*, which suffered from low ratings and a lack of imagination. Nor did the much-hyped revival of *Dark Shadows* last long, despite the presence in the cast of Ben Cross and Barbara Steele.

Robert Bloch was presented with the first World Horror Award when the World Horror Convention made its debut in Nashville, Tennessee, at the end of February.

The winners of the Bram Stoker Awards, presented at the Horror Writers of America's annual gathering, held in June at Redondo Beach, California, were *Dark Dreamers: Conversations with the Masters of Horror* by Stanley Wiater in the Non-Fiction category; *Four Past Midnight* by Stephen King in the Collection; "The Calling" by David Silva in Short Story; "Stephen" by Elizabeth Massie in Novelette. *The Revelation* by Bentley Little was honoured as First Novel, *Mine* by Robert R. McCammon as Novel. The Life Achievement Award was presented to Hugh B. Cave and to Richard Matheson.

The 1991 World Fantasy Awards were presented in November at the World Fantasy Convention in Tucson, Arizona. The Special Award—Non-Professional went to Richard Chizmar's *Cemetery Dance*, while book designer Arnie Fenner received the Special Award—Professional. Dave McKean was voted Best Artist, Carol Emshwiller's *The Start of the End of It All and Other Stories* was awarded Best Collection, and "A Midsummer Night's Dream", from the DC Comics *Sandman* by Neil Gaiman and Charles Vess, was the surprise choice for Best Short Fiction. Pat Murphy collected the Best Novella Award for "Bones", and Best Novel was a tie between *Only Begotten Daughter* by James Morrow and *Thomas the Rhymer* by Ellen Kushner. Ray Russell was given the Life Achievement Award, and we are proud to announce that the Best Anthology was found to be the first volume of *Best New Horror*.

Also in November, we made it a rare double by winning the same category in the British Fantasy Awards, presented at Fantasycon XVI in London. Michael Marshall Smith's "The Man Who Drew Cats" was chosen as Best Short Fiction, and the author also received the Icarus Award for Best Newcomer. Les Edwards was Best Artist, and *Dark Dreams*, edited by David Cowperthwaite and Jeff Dempsey, was voted Best Small Press. Agent Dorothy Lumley was presented with the Special Award for her services to the genre. Ramsey Campbell was given the August Derleth Award for Best Novel (*Midnight Sun*) and also the Dracula Society's Bram Stoker Award for *Ancient Images*.

Santa Monica bookseller Barry R. Levin announced that Dan Simmons won his Collectors Award for 1991 as the Most Collectable Author of the Year, and the Most Collectable Book of the Year was the Charnel House lettered state of *The New Neighbor* by Ray Garton.

In an overview of 1991, one of the reviewers for *Locus* magazine wrote: "For someone whose love of science fiction and its possibilities runs deep, the growth of the horror field is perplexing, to say the least. In the main, a body of literature that explores the farthest reaches of the *outré*, or wallows in gratuitous gore, would seem to be limited in its relevance to anything." This, from someone who should know better.

Such attitudes kept science fiction restricted to a publishing ghetto for more than four decades, and anyone who seriously believes that the horror field is "limited in its relevance to anything" (a difficult feat to achieve, one might think) obviously has little knowledge of the way the genre has developed in recent years. Good horror, like any other branch of serious fiction, has the ability to reflect and comment on the basic issues of contemporary life. At its best it can make us think about our situation, perhaps even change it.

Best New Horror does not purport to be a collection of the year's best horror stories. Instead, we hope to present a varied selection of fiction—loosely connected by various notions of horror—that illustrates the range of themes and ideas currently being explored in the genre, by top names in the field and exciting newcomers. Only you, the reader, can decide if we have been successful . . .

The Editors
April, 1992

K. W. JETER

True Love

ONCE AGAIN K. W. Jeter leads off a volume of *Best New Horror* with a study of dark sexuality.

Described by Ramsey Campbell as "one of the most versatile and uncompromising writers of imaginative fiction", Jeter began his career as a novelist writing such science fictional books as *Morlock Night*, *Dr Adder*, *The Glass Hammer* and *Farewell Horizontal*. However, more recently, he has gained a reputation as a writer of disturbing horror fiction, with such novels as *Soul Eater*, *Dark Seeker*, *Mantis*, *In the Land of the Dead*, *The Night Man*, *Madlands* and *Wolf Flow*, and short fiction appearances in the anthologies *Alien Sex* and *A Whisper of Blood*.

"I don't know what this story means," admits the author, "other than it's a story about love and happiness. I don't have much more to say about it, except . . .

1. The words *victim* and *victimizer* are not easily defined. People who do have easy definitions for those words are lying to you, for reasons of their own; and

2. Martyrdom is a seductive endeavour, but then, it should be. After that, there's only silence."

T HE BROWN LEAVES COVERED THE SIDEWALK, but hadn't yet been trodden into thin leather. She held the boy's hand to keep him from slipping and falling. He tugged at her grip, wanting to race ahead and kick the damp stacks drifting over the curbs. The leaves smelled of wet and dirt, and left skeleton prints on the cement.

"Now—be careful," she told the boy. What was his name? She couldn't remember. There were so many things she couldn't forget . . . Maybe her head had filled up, and there was no more room for anything else. The mounded leaves, slick with the drizzling rain. Her father scratching at the door, the word when there had been words in his mouth, the little word that used to be her name . . . The boy's name; what was it? She couldn't remember.

The boy had tugged her arm around to the side, not trying to run now, but stopping to press his other hand against one of the trees whose empty branches tangled the sky.

"You don't want to do that." She pulled but he dug in, gripping the tree trunk. "It's all dirty." His red mitten was speckled with crumbling bark. A red strand of unraveled wool dangled from his wrist.

You do want to . . . That was her father's voice inside her head. The old voice, the long-ago one with words. She could have, if she'd wanted to—she'd done it before—she could've recited a list of sentences, like a poem, all the things her father had ever said to her with the word *want* in them.

"There's something up there."

She looked where the boy pointed, his arm jutting up straight, the mitten a red flag at the end. On one of the wet branches, a squirrel gazed down at her, then darted off, its tail spiked with drops of rain.

The boy stared openmouthed where the squirrel had disappeared. The boy's upper lip was shiny with snot, and there was a glaze of it on the back of one mitten, and the sleeve of the cheap nylon snow jacket. She shuddered, looking at the wet on the boy's pug face. He wasn't beautiful, not like the one before, the one with the angel lashes and the china and peach skin.

"Come on." She had to bite her lip to fight the shudder, to make it go away, before she could take the boy's hand again. "It's gone now. See? It's all gone." She squeezed the mitten's damp wool in her own gloved hand. "We have to go, too. Aren't you hungry?" She smiled at him, the cold stiffening her face, as though the skin might crack.

The boy looked up at her, distrust in the small eyes. "Where's my mother?"

She knelt down in front of the boy and zipped the jacket under his

2

chin. "Well, that's where we're going, isn't it?" There were people across the street, just people walking, a man and a woman she'd seen from the corner of her eye. But she couldn't tell if they were looking over here, watching her and the boy. She brushed a dead leaf off the boy's shoulder. "We're going to find your mother. We're going to where she is."

She hated lying, even the lies she had told before. All the things she told the boy, and the ones before him, were lies. Everything her father had ever told her had been the truth, and that was no good, either.

Her knees ached when she stood up. The cold and damp had seeped into her bones. She squeezed the boy's hand. "Don't you want to go to where your mother is?"

Now his face was all confused. He looked away from her, down the long street, and she was afraid that he would cry out to the people who were walking there. But they were already gone—she hadn't seen where. Maybe they had turned and gone up the steps into one of the narrow-fronted houses that were jammed so tight against each other.

"And you're hungry, aren't you? Your mother has cake there for you. I know she does. You want that, don't you?"

How old was he? *His name, his name* . . . How big, how small was what she really meant. If he wouldn't move, tugging out of her grasp, wouldn't come with her . . . She wanted to pick him up, to be done with saying stupid things to his stupid little face, its smear of snot and its red pug nose. Just pick him up and carry him like a wet sack, the arms with the red-mittened hands caught tight against her breast. Carry him home and not have to say anything, not have to tell lies and smile . . .

She had tried that once and it hadn't worked. Once when there hadn't been any other little boy that she could find, and the one she had found wouldn't come with her, wouldn't come and it had been getting dark, yet it had been all light around her, she had been trapped in the bright blue-white circle from a street lamp overhead. And the boy had started crying, because she had been shouting at him, shouting for him to shut up and stop crying and come with her. She had picked him up, but he'd been too big and heavy for her, his weight squirming in her arms, the little hard fists striking her neck, the bawling mouth right up against one ear. Until she'd had to let him go and he'd fallen to the ground, scrambled to his feet and run off, crying and screaming so loud that other people—she had known they were there, she'd felt them even if she couldn't see them—had turned and looked at her. She'd scurried away and then started running herself, her heart pounding in her throat. Even on the bus she'd caught, she'd known the others were looking at her, even pointing at her and whispering to each other. How could they have known? Until she'd felt a chill kiss under the collar of her blouse, and she'd touched the side of her face and her fingers had come away touched with red. The boy's little fist, or a low branch clawing at her as she'd run by . . . The tissue in her purse had been a wet bright rag by the time she'd reached home.

That had been a bad time. The little boy had run away, and she'd been too frightened to try again, scared of people watching when it had gotten so dark, so dark that she couldn't see them looking at her. She'd had to go home to where her father was waiting. And even though he couldn't say the words anymore, to say what he wanted, she knew. One or the other, and the little boy had run away.

She'd stood naked in her bathroom, the tiny one at the back of the house, her face wet with the splashed cold water. She'd raised her arm high over her head, standing on tiptoe so she could see in the clouded mirror over the sink. A bruise under one breast—the little boy had kicked her; that must've been where she'd got it, though she couldn't remember feeling it. Her father couldn't have done that, though her ribs beneath the discolored skin ached with a familiar pain. He wasn't strong enough, not anymore . . .

"Where are we?"

The boy's voice—this one, the little boy whose mittened hand she held in her own—brought her back. They were both walking, his hand reaching up to hers, and the streetlights had come on in the growing dark.

"This isn't my street. I don't live here."

"I know. It's okay." She didn't know where they were. She was lost. The narrow, brick-fronted houses came up so close to the street, the bare trees making spider shadows on the sidewalk. Light spilled from the windows above them. She looked up and saw a human shape moving behind a steam-misted glass, someone making dinner in her kitchen. Or taking a shower, the hot water sluicing around the bare feet on white porcelain. The houses would be all warm inside, heated and sealed against the black winter. The people—maybe the couple she had seen walking before, on the other side of another street—they could go naked if they wanted. They were taking a shower together, the man standing behind her, nuzzling her wet neck, hands cupped under her breasts, the smell of soap and wet towels. The steaming water would still be raining on them when he'd lay her down, they'd curl together in the hard nest of the tub, she'd have to bring her knees up against her breasts, or he'd sit her on the edge, the shower curtain clinging wet to her back, and he'd stand in front of her, the way her father did but it wouldn't be her father. She'd fill her mouth with him and he'd smell like soap and not that other sour smell of sweat and old dirt that scraped grey in her fingernails from his skin . . .

The boy pressed close to her side, and she squeezed his hand to tell him that it was all right. He was afraid of the dark and the street he'd never been on before. She was the grown-up, like his mother, and he clung to her now. The fist around her heart unclenched a little. Everything would be easier; she'd find their way home. To where her father was waiting, and she'd have the boy with her this time.

Bright and color rippled on the damp sidewalk ahead of them. The noise of traffic—they'd come out of the houses and dark lanes. She even knew where they were. She recognized the signs, a laundromat with free dry, an Italian restaurant with its menu taped to the window. She'd seen them from the bus she rode sometimes.

Over the heads of the people on the crowded street, she saw the big shape coming, even brighter inside, and heard the hissing of its brakes. Tugging the boy behind her, she hurried to the corner. He trotted obediently to keep up.

The house was as warm inside as other people's houses were. She left the heat on all the time so her father wouldn't get cold. She'd found him once curled up on the floor of the kitchen—the pilot light on the basement furnace had gone out, and ice had already formed on the inside of the windows. There'd been a pool of cold urine beneath him, and his skin felt loose and clammy. He'd stared over his shoulder, his mouth sagging open, while she'd rubbed him beneath the blankets of his bed, to warm him with her own palms.

Warm . . . He had kissed her once—it was one of the things she couldn't forget—when she had been a little girl and he had been as big as the night. His eyes had burned with the wild rigor of his hunt, the world's dark he'd held in his iron hands. The kiss had tasted of salt, a warm thing. Long ago, and she still remembered.

She took off the boy's jacket in the hallway. Her shoes and his small rubber boots made muddy stains on the thin carpet runner. Her knees were so stiff now that she couldn't bend down; she had the boy stand up on the wooden bench against the wall, so she could work the jacket's zipper and snaps.

"Where's my mother?" Coming in to the house's warmth from the cold street had made his nose run again. He sniffed wetly.

"She'll be here in a minute." She pushed the open jacket back from the boy's shoulders. "Let's get all ready for her, and then we can have that cake."

The boy had just a T-shirt on underneath the jacket, and it was torn and dirty, with a yellow stain over some cartoon character's face. The boy's unwashed smell blossomed in the close hallway air, a smell of forgotten laundry and milk gone off. She wanted that to make her feel better. The boy's mother was a bad mother. Not like that other boy's mother, the one three or four times ago. She remembered standing by the greasy fire in the backyard, turning that boy's clothing over in her hands, all of it clean-smelling, freshly washed. Inside the collar of the boy's shirt, and in the waistband of the corduroy trousers, little initials had been hand-stitched, his initials. That was what she'd do if she'd had a child of her own; she would love him that much. Not like this poor ragged thing. Nobody loved this little boy, not really, and that made it all right. She'd told herself that before.

"What's that?" He looked up toward the hallway's ceiling.

She pulled his T-shirt up, exposing his pink round belly. His hair stood up—it was dirty, too—when she pulled the shirt off over his head.

"Nothing." She smoothed his hair down with her palm. "It's nothing." She didn't know if she'd heard anything or not. She'd heard all the house's sounds for so long—they were all her father—that they were the same as silence to her. Or a great roaring hurricane that battered her into a corner, her arms over her head to try to protect herself. It was the same.

She dropped the T-shirt on top of the rubber boots, then unbuttoned the boy's trousers and pulled them down. Dirty grey underwear, the elastic sagging loose. The little boy's things (*little . . . not like . . .*) made the shape of a tiny fist inside the stained cotton. (*Great roaring hurricane*) (*Arms over her head*) She slipped the underpants down.

The boy wiggled. He rubbed his mouth and nose with the back of his hand, smearing the shiny snot around. "What're you doing?"

"Oh, you're so cold." She looked into his dull eyes, away from the little naked parts. "You're freezing. Wouldn't a nice hot bath . . . wouldn't that be nice? Yes. Then you'd be all toasty warm, and I'd wrap you up in a great big fluffy towel. That'd be lovely. You don't want to catch cold, do you?"

He sniffled. "Cake."

"Then you'd have your cake. All you want."

His face screwed up red and ugly. "No. I want it now!" His shout bounced against the walls. The underpants were a grey rag around his ankles, and his hand a fist now, squeezing against the corner of his mouth.

She slapped him. There was no one to see them. The boy's eyes went round, and he made a gulping, swallowing noise inside his throat. But he stopped crying. The fist around her heart tightened, because she knew this was something he was already used to.

"Come on." She could hear her own voice, tight and angry, the way her father's had been when it still had words. She tugged the underpants away from the boy's feet. "Stop being stupid."

She led him, his hand locked inside hers, up the stairs. Suddenly, halfway up, he started tugging, trying to pull his hand away.

"Stop it!" She knelt down and grabbed his bare shoulders, clenching them tight. "Stop it!" She shook him, so that his head snapped back and forth.

His face was wet with tears, and his eyes looked up. He cringed away from something up there, rather than from her. Between her own panting breaths, she heard her father moving around.

"It's nothing!" Her voice screamed raw from her throat. "Don't be stupid!"

She jerked at his arm, but he wouldn't move; he cowered into the angle of the stairs. He howled when she slapped him, then cried openmouthed as she kept on hitting him, the marks of her hand jumping up red on his shoulder blades and ribs.

She stopped, straightening up and gasping to catch her breath. The naked little boy curled at her feet, his legs drawn up, face hidden in the crook of his arm. The blood rushing in her head roared, the sound of a battering wind. The saliva under her tongue tasted thick with salt.

For a moment she thought he was still crying, little soft animal sounds, then she knew it was coming from up above. From her father's room. She stood for a moment, head tilted back, looking up toward the sounds. Her hair had come loose from its knot, and hung down the side of her face and along her back.

"Come on . . ." She kept her voice softer. She reached down and took the boy's hand. But he wouldn't stand up. He hung limp, sniffling and shaking his head.

She had to pick him up. She cradled him in her arms—he didn't feel heavy at all—and carried him the rest of the way up the stairs.

Her father was a huddled shape under the blankets. He'd heard them coming, and had gotten back into the bed before she'd opened the door.

She knew that was what he'd done. A long time ago, when he'd first become this way—when she'd first made herself realize that he was old—she had tried tying him to the bed, knotting a soft cord around his bone-thin ankle and then to one of the heavy carved lion's paws underneath. But he'd fretted and tugged so at the cord, picking at the knot with his yellow fingernails until they'd cracked and bled, and the ankle's skin had chafed raw. She'd untied him, and taken to nailing his door shut, the nails bent so she just had to turn them to go in and out. At night, she had lain awake in her room and listened to him scratching at the inside of his door.

Then that had stopped. He'd learned that she was taking care of him. The scratching had stopped, and she'd even left the nails turned back, and he didn't try to get out.

She sat the little boy at the edge of the bed. The boy was silent now, sucking his thumb, his face smeared wet with tears.

"Daddy?" She pulled the blanket down a few inches, exposing the brown-spotted pink of his skull, the few strands of hair, tarnished silver.

"Daddy—I brought somebody to see you."

In the nest of the blanket and sour-smelling sheets, her father's head turned. His yellow-tinged eyes looked up at her. His face was parchment that had been crumpled into a ball and then smoothed out again. Parchment so thin that the bone and the shape of his teeth—the ones he had left, in back—could be seen through it.

"Look." She tugged, lifted the little boy farther up onto the bed. So her father could see.

The eyes under the dark hood of the blanket shifted, darting a sudden eager gaze from her face to the pink softness of the little boy.

"Come here." She spoke to the boy now. His legs and bottom slid on the blanket as she pulled him, her hands under his arms, until he sat on the middle of the bed, against the lanky, muffled shape of her father. "See, there's nothing to be afraid of. It's just nice and warm."

The shape under the blanket moved, crawling a few inches up to the turned-back edge.

The boy was broken, he had been this way a long time, it was why she'd picked him out and he'd come with her. Nobody loved him, not really, and that made it all right. He didn't fight as she laid him down, his head on the crumpled pillow, face close to her father's.

A thing of twigs and paper, her father's hand, slid from beneath the blanket. It cupped the back of the boy's head, tightening and drawing the boy close, as though for a kiss.

The boy struggled then, a sudden fluttering panic. His small hands pushed against her father's shoulders, and he cried, a whimpering noise that made her father's face darken with his wordless anger. That made her father strong, and he reared up from the bed, his mouth stretching open, tendons of clouded spit thinning to string. He wrapped his arms around the little boy, his grey flesh squeezing the pink bundle tight.

The boy's whimpering became the sound of his gasping breath. Her father pressed his open mouth against the side of the boy's neck.

The jaws under the translucent skin worked, wetting the boy's throat with whitespecked saliva.

Another cry broke out, tearing at her ears. She wanted to cover them with her hands and run from the room. And keep running, into all the dark streets around the house. Never stopping, until her breath was fire that burned away her heart. The cry was her father's; it sobbed with rage and frustration, a thing bigger than hunger, desire, bigger than the battering wind that shouted her name. He rolled his face away from the boy's wet neck, the ancient face like a child's now, mouth curved in an upside-down U, tongue thrusting against the toothless gums in front. His tears broke, wetting the ravines of his face.

He couldn't do it, he couldn't feed himself. She knew, it had been that way the last time, and before. But every time, hope made her forget, at least enough to try the old way. The way it had been years ago.

She couldn't bear the sound of her father's crying, and the little boy's fearful whimper. She knew how to stop it. On the table beside the bed was the knife she'd brought up from the kitchen—that had also been a long time ago—and had left there. Her hand reached out and curled around the smooth-worn wood. Her thumb slid across the sharp metal edge.

She brought her lips to the boy's ear, whispering to him. "Don't be afraid, it's all right . . ." The boy squirmed away from her, but she caught him fast, hugging his unclothed body against her breast. "It's all right, it's all right . . ." He saw the knife blade, and started to cry out. But she already had its point at his pink throat, and the cry leaked red, a drop, then a smearing line as the metal sank and cut.

The red bloomed on the sheets, the grey flooded to shiny wet. The boy's small hands beat against her, then fluttered, trembled, fell back, fists opening to stained flowers.

He didn't fight her now, he was a limp form in her embrace, but suddenly he weighed so much and her hands slipped on the soft skin that had been pink before and now shone darker and brighter. She gripped the boy tighter, her fingers parallel to his ribs, and lifted him. She brought the bubbling mouth, the red one that she had pulled the knife from, up to her father's parted lips.

The blood spilled over her father's gums and trickled out the corners of his mouth. The tendons in his neck stretched and tightened, as though they might tear his paper flesh. His throat worked, trying to swallow, but nothing happened. His eyes opened wider, spiderwebs of red traced around the yellow. He whimpered, the anger turning to fear. Trapped in the thing of sticks his body had become, he scrabbled his spotted hands at her face, reaching past the boy between them.

She knew what had to be done. The same as she'd done before. Her father's bent, ragged nails scraped across her cheek as she turned away from him. She nuzzled her face down close to the little boy's neck. She closed her eyes so there was only the wet and heat pulsing against her lips. She opened her mouth and drank, her tongue weighted with the dancing, coiling salt.

She didn't swallow, though her mouth had become full. Her breath halted, she raised her face from the boy's neck and the wound surging less with every shared motion of their hearts. A trickle of the warmth caught in her mouth leaked to her chin.

A baby bird in its nest . . . a naked thing of skin and fragile bone . . . She had found one once, on the sidewalk in front of the house, a tiny creature fallen from one of the branches above. Even as she had reached down, the tip of her finger an inch away from the wobbling, blue-veined head, the beak had opened, demanding to be fed . . .

The creature's hunger had frightened her, and she'd kicked it out into the gutter, where she wouldn't have to see it anymore. That had been a baby bird.

This was her father. She kept her eyes closed as she brought herself down to him, but she could still see the mouth opening wide, the pink gums, the tongue in its socket of bubbled spit. She lowered her face to his, and let the lips seal upon her own. She opened her mouth, and let the warmth uncoil, an infinitely soft creature moving over her own tongue, falling into his hunger.

The little boy's blood welled in her father's mouth. For a moment it was in both their mouths, a wet place shared by their tongues, his breath turning with hers. She felt the trembling, a shiver against the hinges of her jaw as his throat clenched, trying to swallow. She had to help even more, it had been this way the last time as well; she pressed her lips harder against her father's mouth, as her tongue rolled against the narrow arch of her teeth. The warmth in their mouths broke and pushed past the knot in her father's throat. He managed to swallow, and she felt the last of the blood flow out of her mouth, into his and then gone.

She fed him twice more, each mouthful easier. Between them, the little boy lay still, beautiful in his quiet.

The boy's throat had paled, and she had to draw deep for more. The sheets were cold against her hands as she pushed herself away from him.

Her father was still hungry, but stronger now. His face rose to meet hers, and the force of his kiss pressed against her open lips.

The blood uncoiled in that dark space again, and something else. She felt his tongue thrust forward to touch hers, a warm thing cradled in warmth and the sliding wet. Her throat clenched now. She couldn't breathe, and the smell of his sweat and hunger pressed in the tight space behind her eyes.

His hands had grown strong now, too. The weak flutter had died, the palms reddening as the little boy had become white and empty. One of her father's hands tugged her blouse loose from the waistband of her skirt, and she felt the thing of bone and yellowed paper smear the sheet's wet on her skin. Her father's hand stroked across her ribs and fastened on her breast, a red print on the white cotton bra. He squeezed and it hurt, her breath was inside his hand and blood and the taste of his mouth, the dark swallowing that pulled her into him, beat a pulsing fist inside her forehead.

She pushed both her hands against him, but he was big now and she was a little girl again, she was that pale unmoving thing rocking in his arms, playing at being dead. She was already falling, she could raise her knees in the dark wet embrace of the bed, she could wrap herself around the little blind thing at the center of her breasts, that just breathed and stayed quiet, and that even he couldn't touch, had never been able to touch . . . the little boy was there, his angel face bright and singing, her ears deafened, battered by that song that light that falling upward into clouds of glory where her mother in Sunday robes reached for her, her mother smiling though she had no face she couldn't remember her mother's face—

She shoved against her father, hard enough to break away from him, his ragged fingernails drawing three red lines that stung and wept under her bra. She fell backward off the bed, her elbow hard against the floor, sending numb electricity to her wrist.

Another shape slid from the edge of the bed and sprawled over her lap. The little boy, naked and red wet, made a soft, flopping doll. She pushed it away from herself and scrambled to her feet.

The bed shone. From its dark center, the depth of the blanket's hood, her father looked out at her.

She found the doorknob in her hands behind her back. Her blouse clung to her ribs, and had started to turn cold in the room's shuttered air. The door scraped her spine as she stepped backward into the hallway. Then she turned and ran for the bathroom at the far end, an old sour taste swelling in her throat.

In the dark, between the streetlights' blue islands, she could feel the leaves under her feet. They slid away, damp things, silent; she had to walk carefully to keep from falling.

There was work to be done back at the house. She'd do it later. She would have to change the sheets, as she always did afterward, and wash the stained ones. She used the old claw-footed bathtub, kneeling by its side, the smell of soap and bleach stinging her nose, her fingers working in the pink water. He let her come in and make the bed, and never tried to say anything to her, just watching her with his blank and wordless eyes, his hungers, all of them, over for a while.

And there were the other jobs to be done, the messier ones. Getting rid of things. She'd have to take the car, the old Plymouth with the rusting fenders, out of the garage. And drive to that far place she knew, where these things were never found. She would come back as the sun was rising, and there would be mud on the hem of her skirt. She'd be tired, and ready to sleep.

She could do all that later. She'd been brave and strong, and had already done the hardest jobs; she could allow herself this small indulgence.

The cold night wrapped around her. She pressed her chin down into the knot of the scarf she'd tied over her hair. The collar of her coat had patches where the fur had worn away. The coat had been her mother's, and had been old the first time she'd worn it. A scent of powder, lavender and tea roses, still clung to the heavy cloth.

At the end of the block ahead of her, the Presbyterian church hid the stars at the bottom of the sky. She could see the big stained-glass window, Jesus with one hand on his staff and the other cupped to the muzzle of a lamb, even though there were no lights on in the church itself. The light spilling over the sidewalk came from the meeting room in the basement.

She went down the bare concrete steps, hand gripping the iron rail. And into the light and warmth, the collective sense of people in a room, their soft breathing, the damp-wool smell of their winter coats.

Where she hung her coat up, with the others near for the door, a mimeographed paper on the bulletin board held the names for the altar flowers rotation. Sign-ups to chaperone the youth group's Christmas party. A glossy leaflet, unfolded and tacked, with pledges for a mission in Belize. Her name wasn't anywhere on the different pieces of paper. She didn't belong to the church. They probably wouldn't have wanted her, if they'd known. Known everything. She only came here for the weekly support group.

There was a speaker tonight, a woman up at the front of the room, talking, one hand gesturing while the other touched the music stand the church gave them to use as a podium.

She let the speaker's words flutter past as she sat down in one of the metal folding chairs at the side of the room; halfway down the rows, so she only had to turn her head a bit to see who else had come tonight. She had already counted close to twenty-four. There were the usuals, the faces she saw every week. A couple, a man and a woman who always held hands while they sat and listened, who she assumed were married; they nodded and smiled at her, a fellow regular. At the end of the row was somebody she hadn't seen before, a young man who sat hunched forward, the steam from a Styrofoam cup of coffee rising into his face. She could tell that he was just starting, that this was a new world for him; he didn't look happy.

None of them ever did, even when they smiled and spoke in their bright loud voices, when they said hello and hugged each other near the table with the coffee urn and the cookies on the paper plates.

They had another word for why they were here, a word that made it sound like a disease, just a disease, something you could catch like a cold or even a broken arm. Instead of it being time itself, and old age, and the grey things their parents had become. Time curled outside the church, like a black dog waiting where the steps became the sidewalk, waiting to go home with them again. Where the ones who had known their names looked at them now with empty eyes and did not remember.

She sat back in the folding chair, her hands folded in her lap. The woman at the front of the room had the same bright, relentless voice. She closed her eyes and listened to it.

The woman had a message. There was always a message, it was why people came here. The woman told the people in the room that they had been chosen to receive a great blessing, one that most people weren't strong enough for. A chance to show what love is. A few years of grief and pain and sadness and trouble, of diapering and spoon-feeding and talking cheerily to something that had your father or your mother's face, but wasn't them at all, not anymore. And then it would be over.

That was a small price to pay, a small burden to carry. The woman told them that, the same thing they'd been told before. A few years to show their love. For these things that had been their parents. They'd be transfigured by the experience. Made into saints, the ones who'd shown their courage and steadfastness on that sad battlefield.

She sat and listened to the woman talking. The woman didn't know—none of them ever did—but she knew. What none of them ever would.

She looked around at the others in the room, the couple holding hands, the young man staring into the dregs of his coffee. Her burden, her blessing, was greater than theirs. and so was her love. Even now, she felt sorry for them. They would be released someday. But not her. For them, there would be a few tears, and then their love, their small love, would be over.

She kept her eyes closed, and let herself walk near the edge of sleep, of dreaming, in this warm place bound by winter. She smiled.

She knew that love wasn't over in a few sad years. Or in centuries. She knew that love never died. She knew that her love—real love, true love—was forever.

RAMSEY CAMPBELL

The Same in Any Language

IT HAS ALMOST become a tradition in *Best New Horror* to include a story with a Mediterranean setting. In this volume it is the turn of co-editor Ramsey Campbell to chill our spines in a warmer climate . . .

Campbell has been described as "perhaps the finest living exponent of the British weird fiction tradition", and in 1991 he was voted the Expert's Expert in a poll conducted amongst his peers in the *Observer Magazine*.

Since first being professionally published in 1962 (at the age of sixteen), Campbell's numerous books, stories, reviews and articles have revealed him to be a unique voice in horror fiction.

His recent novels include *Ancient Images, Midnight Sun, The Count of Eleven, The Long Lost* and a welcome reissue of *Night of the Claw* (originally published under the alias of "Jay Ramsey"). In 1992 he celebrated thirty years as a horror writer, and a bumper collection of his best short fiction, *Alone With the Horrors*, commemorates the event.

The story which follows is based on a visit to Spinalonga, and the final paragraph is meant as a tribute to Stephen King.

THE DAY MY FATHER IS TO take me where the lepers used to live is hotter than ever. Even the old women with black scarves wrapped around their heads sit inside the bus station instead of on the chairs outside the tavernas. Kate fans herself with her straw hat like a basket someone's sat on and gives my father one of those smiles they've made up between them. She's leaning forwards to see if that's our bus when he says, "Why do you think they call them lepers, Hugh?"

I can hear what he's going to say, but I have to humour him. "I don't know."

"Because they never stop leaping up and down."

It takes him much longer to say the first four words than the rest of it. I groan because he expects me to, and Kate lets off one of her giggles I keep hearing whenever they stay in my father's and my room at the hotel and send me down for a swim. "If you can't give a grin, give a groan," my father says for about the millionth time, and Kate pokes him with her freckly elbow as if he's too funny for words. She annoys me so much that I say, "Lepers don't rhyme with creepers, Dad."

"I never thought they did, son. I was just having a laugh. If we can't laugh we might as well be dead, ain't that straight, Kate?" He winks at her thigh and slaps his own instead, and says to me, "Since you're so clever, why don't you find out when our bus is coming?"

"That's it now."

"And I'm Hercules." He lifts up his fists to make his muscles bulge for Kate and says, "You're telling us that tripe spells A Flounder?"

"Elounda, Dad. It does. The letter like a Y upside-down is how they write an L."

"About time they learned how to write properly, then," he says, staring around to show he doesn't care who hears. "Well, there it is if you really want to trudge around another old ruin instead of having a swim."

"I expect he'll be able to do both once we get to the village," Kate says, but I can tell she's hoping I'll just swim. "Will you two gentlemen see me across the road?"

My mother used to link arms with me and my father when he was living with us. "I'd better make sure it's the right bus," I say, and run out so fast I can pretend I didn't hear my father calling me back.

A man with skin like a boot is walking backwards in the dust behind the bus, shouting "Elounda" and waving his arms as if he's pulling the bus into the space in line. I sit on a seat opposite two Germans who block the aisle until they've taken off their rucksacks, but my father finds three seats together at the rear. "Aren't you with us, Hugh?" he shouts, and everyone on the bus looks at him.

When I see him getting ready to shout again I walk down the aisle. I'm hoping nobody notices me, but Kate says loudly, "It's a pity you ran off like that, Hugh. I was going to ask if you'd like an ice cream."

"No thank you," I say, trying to sound like my mother when she was only just speaking to my father, and step over Kate's legs. As the bus rumbles uphill I turn as much of my back on her as I can, and watch the streets.

Agios Nikolaos looks as if they haven't finished building it. Some of the tavernas are on the bottom floors of blocks with no roofs, and sometimes there are more tables on the pavements outside than in. The bus goes downhill again as if it's hiccuping, and when it reaches the bottomless lake where young people with no children stay in the hotels with discos, it follows the edge of the bay. I watch the white boats on the blue water, but really I'm seeing the conductor coming down the aisle and feeling as if a lump's growing in my stomach from me wondering what my father will say to him.

The bus is climbing beside the sea when he reaches us. "Three for leper land," my father says.

The conductor stares at him and shrugs. "As far as you go," Kate says, and rubs herself against my father. "All the way."

When the conductor pushes his lips forwards out of his moustache and beard my father begins to get angry, unless he's pretending. "Where you kept your lepers. Spiny Lobster or whatever you call the damned place."

"It's Spinalonga, Dad, and it's off the coast from where we're going."

"I know that, and he should." My father is really angry now. "Did you get that?" he says to the conductor. "My ten-year-old can speak your lingo, so don't tell me you can't speak ours."

The conductor looks at me, and I'm afraid he wants me to talk Greek. My mother gave me a little computer that translates words into Greek when you type them, but I've left it at the hotel because my father said it sounded like a bird which only knew one note. "We're going to Elounda, please," I stammer.

"Elounda, boss," the conductor says to me. He takes the money from my father without looking at him and gives me the tickets and change. "Fish is good by the harbour in the evening," he says, and goes to sit next to the driver while the bus swings round the zigzags of the hill road.

My father laughs for the whole bus to hear. "They think you're so important, Hugh, you won't be wanting to go home to your mother."

Kate strokes his head as if he's her pet, then she turns to me. "What do you like most about Greece?"

She's trying to make friends with me like when she kept saying I should call her Kate, only now I see it's for my father's sake. All she's done is make me think how the magic places seemed to have lost their magic because my mother wasn't there with me, even Knossos where Theseus killed the Minotaur. There were just a few corridors left that might have been the maze he was supposed to find his way out of, and my father let me stay in them for a while, but then he lost his temper because all the guided tours were in foreign languages and nobody could tell him how to get back to the coach. We nearly got stuck overnight in Heraklion, when he'd promised to take Kate for dinner that night by the bottomless pool in Agios Nikolaos. "I don't know," I mumble, and gaze out the window.

"I like the sun, don't you? And the people when they're being nice, and the lovely clear sea."

It sounds to me as if she's getting ready to send me off swimming again. They met while I was, our second morning at the hotel. When I came out of the sea my father had moved his towel next to hers and she was giggling. I watch Spinalonga Island float over the horizon like a ship made of rock and grey towers, and hope she'll think I'm agreeing with her if that means she'll leave me alone. But she says, "I suppose most boys are morbid at your age. Let's hope you'll grow up to be like your father."

She's making it sound as if the leper colony is the only place I've wanted to visit, but it's just another old place I can tell my mother I've been. Kate doesn't want to go there because she doesn't like old places—she said if Knossos was a palace she was glad she's not a queen. I don't speak to her again until the bus has stopped by the harbour.

There aren't many tourists, even in the shops and tavernas lined up along the winding pavement. Greek people who look as if they were born in the sun sit drinking at tables under awnings like stalls in a market. Some priests who I think at first are wearing black hat boxes on their heads march by, and fishermen come up from their boats with octopuses on sticks like big kebabs. The bus turns round in a cloud of dust and petrol fumes while Kate hangs onto my father with one hand and flaps the front of her flowery dress with the other. A boatman stares at the tops of her boobs which make me think of spotted fish and shouts "Spinalonga" with both hands round his mouth.

"We've hours yet," Kate says. "Let's have a drink. Hugh may even get that ice cream if he's good."

If she's going to talk about me as though I'm not there I'll do my best not to be. She and my father sit under an awning and I kick dust on the pavement outside until she says, "Come under, Hugh. We don't want you with sunstroke."

I don't want her pretending she's my mother, but if I say so I'll only spoil the day more than she already has. I shuffle to the table next to the one she's sharing with my father and throw myself on a chair. "Well, Hugh," she says, "do you want one?"

"No thank you," I say, even though the thought of an ice cream or a drink starts my mouth trying to drool.

"You can have some of my lager if it ever arrives," my father says at the top of his voice, and stares hard at some Greeks sitting at a table. "Anyone here a waiter?" he says, lifting his hand to his mouth as if he's holding a glass.

When all the people at the table smile and raise their glasses and shout cheerily at him, Kate says, "I'll find someone and then I'm going to the little girls' room while you men have a talk."

My father watches her crossing the road and gazes at the doorway of the taverna once she's gone in. He's quiet for a while, then he says, "Are you going to be able to say you had a good time?"

I know he wants me to enjoy myself when I'm with him, but I also think what my mother stopped herself from saying to me is true—that he booked the holiday in Greece as a way of scoring off her by taking me somewhere she'd always wanted to go. He stares at the taverna as if he can't move until I let him, and I say, "I expect so, if we go to the island."

"That's my boy. Never give in too easily." He smiles at me with one side of his face. "You don't mind if I have some fun as well, do you?"

He's making it sound as if he wouldn't have had much fun if it had just been the two of us, and I think that was how he'd started to feel before he met Kate. "It's your holiday," I say.

He's opening his mouth after another long silence when Kate comes out of the taverna with a man carrying two lagers and a lemonade on a tray. "See that you thank her," my father tells me.

I didn't ask for lemonade. He said I could have some lager. I say, "Thank you very much" and feel my throat tightening as I gulp the lemonade, because her eyes are saying she's won.

"That must have been welcome," she says when I put down the empty glass. "Another? Then I should find yourself something to do. Your father and I may be here for a while."

"Have a swim," my father suggests.

"I haven't brought my cossy."

"Neither have those boys," Kate says, pointing at the harbour. "Don't worry, I've seen boys wearing less."

My father smirks behind his hand, and I can't bear it. I run to the jetty the boys are diving off, and drop my T-shirt and shorts on it and my sandals on top of them, and dive in.

The water's cold, but not for long. It's full of little fish that nibble you if you only float, and it's clearer than tap water, so you can see down to the pebbles and the fish pretending to be them. I chase fish and swim underwater and almost catch an octopus before it squirms out to sea. Then three Greek boys about my age swim over, and we're pointing at ourselves and saying our names when I see Kate and my father kissing.

I know their tongues are in each other's mouths—getting some tongue, the kids at my school call it. I feel like swimming away as far as I can go and never coming back. But Stavros and Stathis and Costas are using their hands to tell me we should see who can swim fastest, so I do that instead. Soon I've forgotten my father and Kate, even when we sit on the jetty for a rest before we have more races. It must be hours later when I realise Kate is calling, "Come here a minute."

The sun isn't so hot now. It's reaching under the awning, but she and my father haven't moved back into the shadow. A boatman shouts "Spinalonga" and points at how low the sun is. I don't mind swimming with my new friends instead of going to the island, and I'm about to tell my father so when Kate says, "I've been telling your dad he should be proud of you. Come and see what I've got for you."

They've both had a lot to drink. She almost falls across the table as I go to her. Just as I get there I see what she's going to give me, but it's too late. She grabs my head with both hands and sticks a kiss on my mouth.

She tastes of old lager. Her mouth is wet and bigger than mine, and when it squirms it makes me think of an octopus. "Mmm*mwa*," it says, and then I manage to duck out of her hands, leaving her blinking at me as if her eyes won't quite work. "Nothing wrong with a bit of loving," she says. "You'll find that out when you grow up."

My father knows I don't like to be kissed, but he's frowning at me as if I should have let her. Suddenly I want to get my own back on them in the only way I can think of. "We need to go to the island now."

"Better go to the loo first," my father says. "They wouldn't have one on the island when all their willies had dropped off."

Kate hoots at that while I'm getting dressed, and I feel as if she's laughing at the way my ribs show through my skin however much I eat. I stop myself from shivering in case she or my father makes out that's a reason for us to go back to the hotel. I'm heading for the toilet when my father says, "Watch out you don't catch anything in there or we'll have to leave you on the island."

I know there are all sorts of reasons why my parents split up, but just now this is the only one I can think of—my mother not being able to stand his jokes and how the more she told him to finish the more he would do it, as if he couldn't stop himself. I run into the toilet, trying not to look at the pedal bin where you have to drop the used paper, and close my eyes once I've taken aim.

Is today going to be what I remember about Greece? My mother brought me up to believe that even the sunlight here had magic in it, and I expected to feel the ghosts of legends in all the old places. If there isn't any magic in the sunlight, I want there to be some in the dark. The thought seems to make the insides of my eyelids darker, and I can smell the drains. I pull the chain and zip myself up, and then I wonder if my father sent me in here so we'll miss the boat. I nearly break the hook on the door, I'm so desperate to be outside.

The boat is still tied to the harbour, but I can't see the boatman. Kate and my father are holding hands across the table, and my father's looking around as though he means to order another drink. I squeeze my eyes shut so hard that when I open them everything's gone black. The blackness fades along with whatever I wished, and I see the boatman kneeling on the jetty, talking to Stavros. "Spinalonga," I shout.

He looks at me, and I'm afraid he'll say it's too late. I feel tears building up behind my eyes. Then he stands up and holds out a hand towards my father and Kate. "One hour," he says.

Kate's gazing after a bus that has just begun to climb the hill. "We may as well go over as wait for the next bus," my father says, "and then it'll be back to the hotel for dinner."

Kate looks sideways at me. "And after all that he'll be ready for bed," she says like a question she isn't quite admitting to.

"Out like a light, I reckon."

"Fair enough," she says, and uses his arm to get herself up.

The boatman's name is Iannis, and he doesn't speak much English. My father seems to think he's charging too much for the trip until he realises it's that much for all three of us, and then he grins as if he thinks Iannis has cheated himself. "Heave ho then, Janice," he says with a wink at me and Kate.

The boat is about the size of a big rowing-boat. It has a cabin at the front and benches along the sides and a long box in the middle that shakes and smells of petrol. I watch the point of the boat sliding through the water like a knife and feel as if we're on our way to the Greece I've been dreaming of. The white buildings of Elounda shrink until they look like teeth in the mouth of the hills of Crete, and Spinalonga floats up ahead.

It makes me think of an abandoned ship bigger than a liner, a ship so dead that it's standing still in the water without having to be anchored. The evening light seems to shine out of the steep rusty sides and the bony towers and walls high above the sea. I know it was a fort to begin with, but I think it might as well have been built for the lepers. I can imagine them trying to swim to Elounda and drowning because there wasn't enough left of them to swim with, if they didn't just throw themselves off the walls because they couldn't bear what they'd turned into. If I say these things to Kate I bet more than her mouth will squirm—but my father gets in first. "Look, there's the welcoming committee."

Kate gives a shiver that reminds me I'm trying not to feel cold. "Don't say things like that. They're just people like us, probably wishing they hadn't come."

I don't think she can see them any more clearly than I can. Their heads are poking over the wall at the top of the cliff above a little pebbly beach which is the only place a boat can land. There are five or six of them, only I'm not sure they're heads; they might be stones someone has balanced on the wall—they're almost the same colour. I'm wishing I had some binoculars when Kate grabs my father so hard the boat rocks and Iannis waves a finger at her, which doesn't please my father. "You keep your eye on your steering, Janice," he says.

Iannis is already taking the boat toward the beach. He didn't seem to notice the heads on the wall, and when I look again they aren't there. Maybe they belonged to some of the people who are coming down to a boat bigger than Iannis's. That boat chugs away as Iannis's bumps into the jetty. "One hour," he says. "Back here."

He helps Kate onto the jetty while my father glowers at him, then he lifts me out of the boat. As soon as my father steps onto the jetty Iannis pushes the boat out again. "Aren't you staying?" Kate pleads.

He shakes his head and points hard at the beach. "Back here, one hour."

She looks as if she wants to run into the water and climb aboard the boat, but my father shoves his arm around her waist. "Don't worry, you've got two fellers to keep you safe, and neither of them with a girl's name."

The only way up to the fort is through a tunnel that bends in the middle so you can't see the end until you're nearly halfway in. I wonder how long it will take for the rest of the island to be as dark as the middle of the tunnel. When Kate sees the end she runs until she's in the open and stares at the sun, which is perched on top of the towers now. "Fancying a climb?" my father says.

She makes a face at him as I walk past her. We're in a kind of street of stone sheds that have mostly caved in. They must be where the lepers lived, but there are only shadows in them now, not even birds. "Don't go too far, Hugh," Kate says.

"I want to go all the way round, otherwise it wasn't worth coming."

"I don't, and I'm sure your father expects you to consider me."

"Now, now, children," my father says. "Hugh can do as he likes as long as he's careful and the same goes for us, eh, Kate?"

I can tell he's surprised when she doesn't laugh. He looks unsure of himself and angry about it, the way he did when he and my mother were getting ready to tell me they were splitting up. I run along the line of huts and think of hiding in one so I can jump out at Kate. Maybe they aren't empty after all; something rattles in one as if bones are crawling about in the dark. It could be a snake under part of the roof that's fallen. I keep running until I come to steps leading up from the street to the top of the island, where most of the light is, and I've started jogging up them when Kate shouts, "Stay where we can see you. We don't want you hurting yourself."

"It's all right, Kate; leave him be," my father says. "He's sensible."

"If I'm not allowed to speak to him, I don't know why you invited me at all."

I can't help grinning as I sprint to the top of the steps and duck out of sight behind a grassy mound that makes me think of a grave. From up here I can see the whole island, and we aren't alone on it. The path I've run up from leads all round the island, past more huts and towers and a few bigger buildings, and then it goes down to the tunnel. Just before it does it passes the wall above the beach, and between the path and the wall there's a stone yard full of slabs. Some of the slabs have been moved away from holes like long boxes full of soil or darkness. They're by the wall where I thought I saw heads looking over at us. They aren't there now, but I can see heads bobbing down towards the tunnel. Before long they'll be behind Kate and my father.

Iannis is well on his way back to Elounda. His boat is passing one that's heading for the island. Soon the sun will touch the hills. If I went down to the huts I'd see it sink with me and drown. Instead I lie on the mound and look over the island, and see more of the boxy holes hiding behind some of the huts. If I went closer I could see how deep they are, but I quite like not knowing—if I was Greek I expect I'd think they lead to the underworld where all the dead live. Besides, I like being able to look down on my father and Kate and see them trying to see me.

I stay there until Iannis's boat is back at Elounda and the other one has almost reached Spinalonga, and the sun looks as if it's gone down to the hills for a rest. Kate and my father are having an argument. I expect it's about me, though I can't hear what they're saying; the darker it gets between the huts the more Kate waves her arms. I'm getting ready to let my father see me when she screams.

She's jumped back from a hut which has a hole behind it. "Come out, Hugh. I know it's you," she cries.

I can tell what my father's going to say, and I cringe. "Is that you, Hugh? Yoo-hoo," he shouts.

I won't show myself for a joke like that. He leans into the hut through the spiky stone window, then he turns to Kate. "It wasn't Hugh. There's nobody."

I can only just hear him, but I don't have to strain to hear Kate. "Don't tell me that," she cries. "You're both too fond of jokes."

She screams again, because someone's come running up the tunnel. "Everything all right?" this man shouts. "There's a boat about to leave if you've had enough."

"I don't know what you two are doing," Kate says like a duchess to my father, "but I'm going with this gentleman."

My father calls to me twice. If I go with him I'll be letting Kate win. "I don't think our man will wait," the new one says.

"It doesn't matter," my father says, so fiercely that I know it does. "We've our own boat coming."

"If there's a bus before you get back I won't be hanging around," Kate warns him.

"Please yourself," my father says, so loud that his voice goes into the tunnel. He stares after her as she marches away; he must be hoping she'll change her mind. But I see her step off the jetty into the boat, and it moves out to sea as if the ripples are pushing it to Elounda.

My father puts a hand to his ear as the sound of the engine fades. "So every bugger's left me now, have they?" he says in a kind of shout at himself. "Well, good riddance."

He's waving his fists as if he wants to punch something, and he sounds as if he's suddenly got drunk. He must have been holding it back when Kate was there. I've never seen him like this. It frightens me, so I stay where I am.

It isn't only my father that frightens me. There's only a little bump of the sun left above the hills of Crete now, and I'm afraid how dark the island may be once that goes. Bits of sunlight shiver on the water all the way to the island, and I think I see some heads above the wall of the yard full of slabs, against the light. Which side of the wall are they on? The light's too dazzling; it seems to pinch the sides of the heads so they look thinner than any heads I've ever seen. Then I notice a boat setting out from Elounda, and I squint at it until I'm sure it's Iannis's boat.

He's coming early to fetch us. Even that frightens me, because I wonder why he is. Doesn't he want us to be on the island now he realizes how dark it's getting? I look at the wall, and the heads have gone. Then the hills put the sun out, and it feels as if the island is buried in darkness.

I can still see my way down—the steps are paler than the dark—and I don't like being alone now that I've started shivering. I back off from the mound, because I don't like to touch it, and almost back into a shape with bits of its head poking out and arms that look as if they've dropped off at the elbows. It's a cactus. I'm just standing up when my father says, "There you are, Hugh."

He can't see me yet. He must have heard me gasp. I go to the top of the steps, but I can't see him for the dark. Then his voice moves away. "Don't start hiding again. Looks like we've seen the last of Kate; but we've got each other, haven't we?"

He's still drunk. He sounds as if he's talking to somebody nearer to him than I am. "All right, we'll wait on the beach," he says, and his voice echoes. He's gone into the tunnel, and he thinks he's following me. "I'm here, Dad," I shout so loud that I squeak.

"I heard you, Hugh. Wait there. I'm coming." He's walking deeper into the tunnel. While he's in there my voice must seem to be coming from beyond the far end. I'm sucking in a breath that tastes dusty, so I can tell him where I am, when he says, "Who's that?" with a laugh that almost shakes his words to pieces.

He's met whoever he thought was me when he was heading for the tunnel. I'm holding my breath—I can't breathe or swallow—and I don't know if I feel hot or frozen. "Let me past," he says as if he's trying to make his voice as big as the tunnel. "My son's waiting for me on the beach."

There are so many echoes in the tunnel I'm not sure what I'm hearing besides him. I think there's a lot of shuffling; and the other noise must be voices, because my father says, "What kind of language do you call that? You sound drunker than I am. I said my son's waiting."

He's talking even louder as if that'll make him understood. I'm embarrassed, but I'm more afraid for him. "Dad," I nearly scream, and run down the steps as fast as I can without falling.

"See, I told you. That's my son," he says as if he's talking to a crowd of idiots. The shuffling starts moving like a slow march, and he says, "All right, we'll all go to the beach together. What's the matter with your friends, too drunk to walk?"

I reach the bottom of the steps, hurting my ankles, and run along the ruined street because I can't stop myself. The shuffling sounds as if it's growing thinner, as if the people with my father are leaving bits of themselves behind, and the voices are changing too—they're looser. Maybe the mouths are getting bigger somehow. But my father's laughing, so loud that he might be trying to think of a joke. "That's what I call a hug. No harder, love, or I won't have any puff left," he says to someone. "Come on then; give us a kiss. They're the same in any language."

All the voices stop, but the shuffling doesn't. I hear it go out of the tunnel and onto the pebbles, and then my father tries to scream as if he's swallowed something that won't let him. I scream for him and dash into the tunnel, slipping on things that weren't on the floor when we first came through, and fall out onto the beach.

My father's in the sea. He's already so far out that the water is up to his neck. About six people who look stuck together and to him are walking him away as if they don't need to breathe when their heads start to sink. Bits of them float away on the waves my father makes as he throws his arms about and gurgles. I try to run after him, but I've got nowhere when his head goes underwater. The sea pushes me back on the beach, and I run crying up and down it until Iannis comes.

It doesn't take him long to find my father once he understands what I'm saying. Iannis wraps me in a blanket and hugs me all the way to Elounda, and the police take me back to the hotel. Kate gets my mother's number and calls her, saying she's someone at the hotel who's looking after me because my father's drowned; and I don't care what she says, I just feel numb. I don't start screaming until I'm on the plane back to England, because then I dream that my father has come back to tell a joke. "That's what I call getting some tongue," he says, leaning his face close to mine and showing me what's in his mouth.

KATHE KOJA

Impermanent Mercies

KATHE KOJA is one of the rising stars of horror fiction. After a number of stories in *Isaac Asimov's Science Fiction Magazine*, *The Magazine of Fantasy & Science Fiction*, *Pulphouse*, *Jabberwocky*, *Critical Mass* and such anthologies as *Dark Voices 3* and *A Whisper of Blood*, she created quite a stir with her first novel, *The Cipher*, which launched Dell's cutting-edge horror imprint, Abyss, in 1991. She has followed that with two more books, *Bad Brains* and *Skin*.

To attempt to describe the story that follows would serve little purpose. Let's just say that it's unclassifiable yet is guaranteed to get under your skin. Where it ends up you must find out for yourself.

"OK," ELLIS SAID. "NOW PICK UP the dog."

"True," the boy said. His name was Andy. Ellis had met him at the 7–11.

"OK, pick True up," and Andy did, smiling, sun in his eyes, summery squint and the dog almost smiling too in that half-asinine way of the quintessential mutt; a boy and his dog, shit yes it was cute. Shot after shot after shot, as sweet a stock photo as anyone could want, head a-tilt and happy sweat on his back, OK, uh-huh, and behind the boy the long stretch of railroad tracks, summer and infinity, the beginning of boyhood's journey; you bought it, you name it. "OK, great." Shot and shot, enough. "I think we're done here." Kids were such great models. Cheap too.

Walking back, Andy's questions—little-boy gory, you ever take any pictures of dead stuff? Any dead people?—high voice punctuated by the low gaining sound of a train, infrequent on these tracks. Ellis looked over his shoulder: almost too far away to see, there it was. True ran a loping zigzag on the tracks, Andy on the slope beside glancing up at the dog from time to time.

"You ever *seen* any dead people?"

The train was closer now. "You better call your dog," Ellis said.

"True, c'mere," pausing, one bare foot on the gulley's rise. "True." True paused too, looked at Andy with what seemed to Ellis a particularly stupid grin, snuffle snuffle along the steel of the tracks, lift of small scrawny leg.

"True, come *on*," voice raised in the louder pitch of the train, approaching now as the boy approached the slope, Ellis' hand a warning on his shoulder. "True!" Andy's voice very high, he seemed to lose years in his sudden fear, a littler boy than he had been and *"True!"* Ellis' bellow, best man-to-mammal voice, pure authority that True chose, in his pure doggy way, to ignore. Snuff snuff, yum, more pee.

"True!" And Andy broke for the tracks, almost too fast to stop but Ellis did, startled reflex grab of the skinny elbow, yanking him back as the train ran on, and all at once True turned his head, the look on his face the essence of surprise: *What is that?* and off, four legs in quantum motion, running down the centre of the track, Andy jerking and bucking in Ellis' grip, Ellis yelling something, who knows what into the vortex of the train's momentum, gaining and gained all in a second and True disappeared beneath, now you see him, now you don't. Ellis yelling still, how if True stays still, he's a small dog, if he only doesn't move and in the speaking the word's negation for, without any blood at all, a small round rolling thing spat out from under and down the slope as neatly as a softball. True's head.

Man and boy and silence, the sun all at once so hot and a fullborn headache springing free and Ellis thought, illogical inner laughter, Now True he's got the big headache; what a shitty thought. Funny though. "Stay here," he said to Andy, who stood as if he might never move again, and up the gulley Ellis went, to stand in the train's far away wake and bend to the small headless body. As he picked it up air rushed into the body cavity with a bizarre sucking sound, ugly, he almost dropped it. Back down, and Andy was gone. The head was gone too, presumably with Andy, wasn't going anywhere itself now was it, stop it where's the kid. Ellis saw weeds, dipping and parting, called a few times but no reply; he gave it up, found he was still holding the body, let it fall beside the warm wood of the tracks which he walked beside, but studiously not on, all the way back to his car.

The pictures came out great.

Smoking the last of his cigarettes, coming out of the 7–11 with a new pack in hand and "Hey." Andy. Trueless Andy, not smiling. Ellis stopped, stepped back, false guilty smile on his face which he at once replaced with some other kind of look, who knew. "Andy," he said. "Where'd you go, that day? I was worried about you."

"I took True home." Small bare feet, so bottom-black they left sidewalk prints when he shifted. "Want to see?"

Want to see. Hell no, I don't want to see. "What—you mean his, where you buried him?" Little boy grieves at doggy grave. Poignancy of collision, youth with death, innocence with sorrow. How much film did he have. "All right."

Home wasn't far, befitting a boy on foot, lucky Ellis had stopped again at that particular 7–11. Shitty little ranch house, flats of flowers wilting in their plastic containers, oil spots all over the driveway. No car. Andy led him through the back gate into the yard, more sagging flowers, somebody at least was trying, and into the house through an unlocked screen door. The house was hotter than the day outside. "Where's your folks?" Ellis asked, suddenly uneasy at being here, alone with the boy in an empty house.

"My mom's not home," Andy said in that same flat voice. "He's back here," down the skinny hall, he who. Oh shit, not the dog, the dog's head in all this heat, seeing without noticing the badly framed snapshots, Andy and little Andy and baby Andy, one or two with presumably Mom. And True. The *before* pictures.

"Here," in Andy's bedroom, unmade bed hand-me-down to death, and beneath it, oh shit. A saltine box. A *wet* saltine box. Ellis took a big step backwards, hand on the doorframe. "Andy," reasonable adult voice thinned a little by possible pukedom, "maybe I should just— "

"What's the matter, motherfucker? Squeamish?"

From inside the box.

Oh come on, come on this is *not* happening, the kid's a pissed-off ventriloquist, and Andy said, "I told you he wouldn't like it," and at the same time that deeper voice, "Oh he likes it all right. Hey you," and the box rocked, just a little, just enough to make the first hot pissy dribble squirt onto Ellis' jeans. "Take a picture, it'll last longer." Everybody but Ellis laughed.

"You thought he was just a dog," Andy said, and smiled, thin proud stretch as he patted the box. "He's not. He can do stuff. He always could."

"Like talk?" He hadn't meant it as a question but the quaver was there.

"No," shaking his head. "Not out loud."

"But I can now," from the box, and a sudden booming laugh, incredible TV voice: "And it was *worth it!*"

That's it, that's it right there, I'm out of here and he was, pushing the door so hard it nicked the wall, True's voice yelling after him, "But what are you going to tell Sheila?" and he was out of the house and the driveway and down the street, shaking at the stop sign and grabbing for his cigarettes when the words took hold and he cracked the cigarette in two. Sheila, right, Sheila his ex-wife, hide nor hair for what, eight months, even though he'd stopped sending the cheques. Sheila, hell of a guess. By the time he got home he had persuaded himself that it was all so very improbable that it was probably stupid to even believe it had happened, and the ringing phone was a pleasant diversion, he picked it up before the machine could, let's have some human contact, hallo.

"El, it's me."

His first black thought was that it was somehow the fucking dog, and Sheila's voice, hallo, hallo until he finally spoke and yes indeed it was the genuine article, just calling to ask if he would get that box of camping stuff out of the garage, she and Richard were going to Padgett Park and they needed the Coleman and it would be nice if he could see his way to a cheque or two. Thanks, and bye, and Ellis there with hands too cold to sweat, wondering if, there had to be, a way to find the house again. The 7–11, of course, and of course Andy was there, sucking on a slurpee, the unbearable smugness of a child in the right. "Hi," he said before Ellis could speak, and when Ellis did a cool moment of silence, letting Ellis know that he stood on the sufferance of a nine-year-old boy, and that he, Andy, knew it too. But he was nine, after all, there was no way he could say no.

"He told me a bunch of stuff about you," Andy said, matter-of-fact swing of bare ankles, Nikes worn white over the toes. "Some other stuff too."

"Will he," very careful, now, "let me take his picture?"

"I don't know. Ask him."

Say cheese, Mr Dog Head. Pulling into the afternoon driveway, empty as before. "Does your mom know?"

"Know what," but with indifference, no leverage there; apparently Mom was no mover and shaker in Andy's world. "I clean my own room, and besides she's hardly ever home anyway. Come on," pushing in the screen, you always leave the house wide open, kid? Oh, that's right, you have a watchdog.

The bedroom had a ripe odour that was suspiciously free of decay, but the saltine box was wet to the trademark, wet too the worn yellow carpet beneath. Andy handled the box with priestly care, turned it so the open edge faced Ellis. The damp grey flaps peeled open, and True, big doggy grin, tongue twisted the way no dog's ever should: "How was Sheila?"

"Not funny," forgetting everything but the face before him, Andy behind him, hands clasped in happy calm. True, speaking, a bunch of stuff indeed; they used to call it prophecy. Not so much world "events", stock market tips or sports bullshit, but things in Ellis' own daily life: the guy from *Watersports* will call, the woman from the Sunday supplement won't, your air conditioner's going to hell and it'll get there a week from Wednesday, and Ellis mesmerized by the inscrutable flow, his day-to-day laid bare, so weird and oh, so compelling. Finally True stopped, made a sound it took a second to recognize as a bark.

"I'm thirsty," rolling his eyes to look not at Andy but Ellis. "Get me a drink."

"There's a glass in the bathroom," Andy's faint malicious smirk. "On the sink."

Shit. But he got it, filled it half-way, came back to kneel in awkward crouch before True, long tongue lapping sloppy and water on Ellis' legs, on the floor. True blew some water out of his nose.

Now, Ellis thought. Ask him now. But True was a step ahead.

"No," showing his teeth, blunt tartary fangs. "No pictures."

"Why not?" Grim frustration, keeping his voice even, thinking I could just grab the damn box and be out of here, but the thought of actually touching it, hefting its wet weight, would it sag in the middle— " "Why not."

True and Andy, a look shared, and "I got a train to catch," ha ha, they laughed their stupid asses off at that one and all at once Andy was giving him the bum's rush, you gotta go now, my mom's going to be home. "Maybe I'll stay," firm, let's not forget who's the grown-up here. "I'd like to meet her."

Andy, smiling, cheeks still faintly sweet with babyfat. "I'll tell her you tried to touch my dick," and that was the end of that, the best he could get was a vague promise from Andy to meet him the next day, the 7–11, yeah, right. But he came, and so did Andy.

It was a ritual, irregular but not to be missed, and though Ellis was constantly disappointed, no pictures, still he could not stay away. True's voice, its rolling gravel amusement, and oh the things he said—not only tales of Ellis' humdrum days (which always came true, so much so that Ellis had begun without conscious decision to rely on them) but real prophecy, world news of a world Ellis had not even suspected, a universe so black and yet so greyly probable that he believed these stories, too, relied on them: grotesqueries and pains and distortions, people in Switzerland who drank each other's urine and cast runes from the mingled flow, a man in Pittsburgh who saved discarded surgical clamps and what he did with them, the daylight flourishing on a neighbourhood cult unique in its blue-collar sophistication and blunt brutality; True the Scheherzade of the ugly and ultimate, Andy his acolyte, and Ellis, what? The sceptic, no, nor just the listener, for at night alone these tales had begun to grow not on him but in him, wreaking changes so gradual yet so acute that, wild-eyed in the mornings, he thought it some subtle form of vengeance, a cool rot like a ticking bomb in the space between his ears. But there was no staying away, and besides True had promised to let Ellis take his picture. When, there was no saying, and Ellis would not chance a miss, so back to that strange bedroom temple, on his knees before them both.

He had never told Andy where he lived, but one night, coming back from putting out the trash, he heard above the sound of crickets a far away bark, burlesque, then a mingled laugh that froze him, hands clenched in the silence of sinister insect music and Andy, calling him, soft. He let them in, absurdly excited, was it time, should he set up or what. Andy cradled True's box, its bottom bowed and soggy, some viscous fluid dripping with majestic irregularity onto the living room carpet; Andy spoke little and True not at all, and when they left he saw the Rorschach stains, horrible trail all the way to the door.

That night he lay bedbound, staring sick and gratified, and when by dawn he did sleep woke soon after in a turmoil of arousal, behind his eyes a dream of Andy, small hairless penis and his own mouth grasping to close over it, and the fierce immediate throb of his orgasm, slick wet all over and he sat in it and wept with terror, what is happening to me. He thought of Andy's absentee mother, a vague impression from the hallway photos, blonde hair and a worried smile, a *nice* woman, yes certainly, and in his delirium he thought of holding her, spending himself in her, knowing somewhere beneath that what he really wanted was to cry on her tits about her monster son and his even more monstrous pet. He must never go back there, "Never, never, never" moaning into his cupped hands, the words as thick and warm as vomit in his mouth.

He tried, oh surely he did, was it nearly a week? True's snicker, Andy's cold smile: "Should I let him in, True?" and True considering, asking through the closed bedroom door how'd he liked his dreams lately, pretty wild, huh? Hands clenched on his neckstrap, Ellis sweating, I will *not* cry, sweating till at last Andy opened the door. "Taken any good shots?" True said, and howled, coyote scream to make his ears ring in the square hot silence of the room, banshee noise that went on and on. Finally and at once it stopped, and True, his eyes somehow a twin to Andy's: "If you want to take my picture, you have to bring me what I need. Andy can't do it any more."

"Why?"

"Because," growl, yes, like a dog, "Andy's just a kid. There are things a kid can't do, shithead, don't you know that?"

"Like what?"

At first, No, no I will not, I *will not* do these things; but he didn't get far, did he, did he, no. Because after and above all Ellis must have that picture, must hold it in his hands, not even sure any longer why he must but feeling its necessity like a disease.

So he did as he was told. Once, and twice, and by the fifth time it got if not easier—it could never, never be easy, as it could never be safe—then less ugly, or perhaps he was already so mad that another dollop of poison could do nothing but churn his madness to a finer boil. Perhaps part of him was hoping somehow to be caught, he told himself that, sitting at red lights with a torn paper bag beside him, or an object wrapped in plastic, wet plastic, a certain smell infused for ever in the atmosphere of his car; he woke at night with that smell in his nostrils, wondering if it was that he hated most, that smell, or what True made him do, sometimes, with the things he brought, or was it the things themselves, wet and smelly and inert, what was it he hated most? Finally he did not speculate, he found he no longer cared to and in fact did not care at all. It was ugly, yeah, and so was he, and so what. All that could bring meaning was to get that picture and in the meantime, why not just roll with it, get belly-deep and deeper, put your *face* in it and suck it in.—And then the mornings, weeping and gagging at the look on his own face, the smirk of the afterglow; maybe other people saw it too. What if they did?

He asked True about it, got a laugh for an answer, and he laughed too. Because it was funny, wasn't it, even True's demands, the sicker they got the funnier they were. It was like feeding a throatless mouth, no end in sight, ha ha ha, wasn't that the third time tonight he'd seen that blue Buick? Wasn't it? He shifted, nervous on the seat, and something warm, sticky-warm, sagged against his thigh, where had he gotten that? He didn't remember, didn't know for sure even what was in that bag there, look at this for me please officer, I think it might be icky. Definitely he had seen that Buick before. Slewing down a side street, tricky negotiation till he saw the Buick's tail-lights and back, fast, all the spy movie bullshit like driving without lights, he almost hit a parked car and laughed out loud. The bag broke. His ass, his legs were drenched, he stank, the car stank, he trotted stinking into the house waving the half-wrapped thing by one jaunty corner. "Hope you're hungry," wide chortling grin that sickened and died as he saw their faces, and when True at last raised his lip it was no smile he showed.

"I don't want that," bright bony sneer past Ellis to what he carried. "You're getting useless, you know that? Useless," on a growl, and Andy said, "If you can't bring True what he needs, you can't come here any more."

No sound at all, more and less than vacuum and his heart somehow gone silent too and he said, "Take me then," and no words came out and he forced them, loud, "Take me," and Andy's face wrinkled, refusing pout, but True's growl turned upwards into giggle and he said, "You finally had a good idea, asshole. Andy, pull up that shade." And the box jiggled, its tearing sides trembling as True shook his head, hard, the way a dog shakes off from water. "Take off your clothes, Ellis."

A working in him like an elixir, a pulse, rich and rapid and too strong, and like a dance he stripped, stinky jeans and smelly shirt and socks stiff and thick between the toes, stood naked at last with his hands at his sides and his vision newly narrowed; no, *focused*, and he understood, he knew and almost cried with the knowing that he was the camera, the blinkless eye, perfect observer of his own immolation and he was not going to miss a moment, not a second's worth as he went crawling to the box, the carpet worn and sorry on his knees, True suddenly panting and Andy smiling, there, behind the box, smiling like Christmas morning.

ALAN BRENNERT

Ma Qui

ALAN BRENNERT is an Emmy Award-winning scriptwriter for the hit television show *LA Law*. After writing two novels (including the fantasy *Kindred Spirits*) and a number of short science fiction stories in the mid-1970s, he moved away to pursue a career in television.

Between 1984 and 1986 he served as executive story consultant on the revived *Twilight Zone* series for CBS-TV, and admits that in the course of writing some thirteen-odd scripts for it, he "got bitten by the short story bug again". Since then he has published two collections, *Her Pilgrim Soul and Other Stories* (Tor Books) and *Ma Qui and Other Phantoms* (Pulphouse), as well as a third novel, *Time and Chance*. He has also written scripts for the TV series *China Beach* and contributed the libretto for a science fiction musical staged in New York.

Described by the author as "*Inner Sanctum* meets Vietnam", the powerful story which follows won the Science Fiction Writers of America Nebula Award.

AT NIGHT THE CHOPPERS BUZZ THE bamboo roof of the jungle, dumping from three thousand feet to little more than a hundred, circling, climbing, circling again, no LZ to land in, no casualties to pick up. Above the roar of the rotorwash come the shrieks of the damned: wails, moans, plaintive cries in Vietnamese. It's real William Castle stuff, weird sounds and screaming meemies, but even knowing it's coming from a tape recorder, even hearing the static hiss of the loudspeakers mounted on the Hueys, it still spooks the shit out of the VC. "The Wandering Soul," it's called—the sounds of dead Cong, their bodies not given a proper burial, their spirits helplessly wandering the earth. Psychological warfare. Inner Sanctum meets Vietnam. Down in the tunnels Charlie hears it, knows it's a con, tries to sleep but can't, the damn stuff goes on half the night. The wails grow louder the lower the choppers fly, then trail off, to suitably eerie effect, as they climb away. Until the next chopper comes with its cargo of souls in a box.

What horseshit.

It's not like that at all.

I watch the last of the choppers bank and veer south, and for a while, the jungle is quiet again. Around me the ground is a scorched blister, a crater forged by mortar fire, a dusty halo of burnt ground surrounding it, grasses and trees incinerated in the firefight. The crater is my bed, my bunk, my home. I sleep there—if you can call it sleep—and when I've grown tired of wandering the trails, looking for my way back to Da Nang, or Cam Ne, or Than Quit, I always wind up back here. Because this seared piece of earth is the only goddamned thing for miles that isn't Nam. It's not jungle, it's not muddy water, it's not punji sticks smeared with shit. It's ugly, and it's barren, and it looks like the surface of the fucking moon, but it was made by my people, the only signature they can write on this steaming rotten country, and I sleep in it, and I feel at home.

I was killed not far from here, in a clearing on the banks of the Song Cai River. My unit was pinned down, our back-up never arrived, we were racing for the LZ where the dust-off choppers were to pick us up. Some of us got careless. Martinez never saw the tripwire in the grass and caught a Bouncing Betty in the groin; he died before we could get him to the LZ. Dunbar hit a punji beartrap, the two spiked boards snapping up like the jaws of a wooden crocodile, chewing through his left leg. I thought Prosser and DePaul had pried him loose, but when I looked back I saw their bodies not far from the trap, cut down by sniper fire as they'd tried to rescue him. The bastards had let Dunbar live, and he was still caught in the trap, screaming for help, the blood pouring out between the two punji boards. I started back, firing my M16 indiscriminately into the treeline, hoping to give the snipers pause enough so that I could free Dunbar—

They took me out a few yards from Dunbar, half a dozen rounds that blew apart most of my chest. I fell, screaming, but I also watched myself fall; I saw the sharp blades of elephant grass slice into my face like razors as I struck the ground; I watched the blood spatter upward on impact, a red cloud that seemed to briefly cloak my body, then dissipate, spattering across the grass, giving the appearance, for a moment, of a false spring—a red dew.

Dunbar died a few minutes later. To the west, the distant thunder of choppers rolled across the treetops. I stood there, staring at the body at my feet, thinking somehow that it must be someone else's body, someone else's blood, and I turned and ran for the choppers, not noticing that my feet weren't quite touching the ground as I ran, not seeing myself pass through the tripwires like a stray wind.

Up ahead, dust-off medics dragged wounded aboard a pair of Hueys. Most of my unit made it. I watched Silverman get yanked aboard; I saw Esteban claw at a medic with a bloody stump he still believed was his hand. I ran to join them, but the big Chinooks started to climb, fast, once everyone was on. "Wait for me!" I yelled, but they couldn't seem to hear me over the whipping of the blades; "Son of a bitch, wait for *me*!"

They didn't slow. They didn't stop. They kept on rising, ignoring me, abandoning me. Goddamn them, what were they *doing*? Motherfucking bastards, come *back*, come—

It wasn't until I saw the thick, moist wind of the rotorwash fanning the grass—saw it bending the trees as the steel dragonflies ascended—that I realized I felt no wind on my face; that I had no trouble standing in the small hurricane at the center of the clearing. I turned around. Past the treeline, in the thick of the jungle, mortars were being lobbed from afar. Some hit their intended targets, in the bush; others strayed, and blasted our own position, unintentionally. I could hear the screams of VC before and after each hit; I saw Cong rushing out of the trees, some aflame, some limbless, only to be knocked off their feet by another incoming round. By now I knew the truth. I wandered, in a daze, back toward the treeline. I walked through sheets of flame without feeling so much as a sunburn. I saw the ground rock below me, but my steps never wavered, like the old joke about the drunken man during an earthquake.

At length the mortars stopped. The clearing was seared, desolate; bodies—Vietnamese, American—lay strewn and charred in all directions. I walked among them, rising smoke passing through me like dust through a cloud . . . and now I saw other wraiths, other figures standing above the remains of their own bodies; they looked thin, gaseous, the winds from the chopper passing overhead threatening their very solidity.

Prosser looked down at his shattered corpse and said, "Shit."

Dunbar agreed. "This sucks."

"Man, I *knew* this was gonna happen," Martinez insisted. "I just got laid in Da Nang. Is this fuckin' karma, or what?"

I made a mental note never to discuss metaphysics with Martinez. Not a useful overview.

"So what happens now?" I asked.

"Heaven, I guess." Dunbar shrugged.

"Or hell." Martinez. Ever the optimist.

"Yeah, but when?"

"Gotta be any time now," Prosser said, as though waiting for the 11:00 bus. He looked down at our bodies and grimaced. "I mean, we're dead, right?"

I looked at Dunbar's mangled leg. At Martinez's truncated torso. At . . .

"Hey. Collins. Where the hell are *you?*"

I should have been just a few feet away from Dunbar's body, but I wasn't. At first I thought the half dozen rounds that had dropped me had propelled my body away, but as we fanned out we saw no trace of it, not anywhere within a dozen yards. And when I came back to where Dunbar's body lay, I recognized the matted elephant grass where I had fallen—recognized too the tears of blood, now dried, coloring the tips of the grass. I squatted down, noticing for the first time that the grass was matted, in a zigzag pattern, for several feet beyond where my body fell.

"Son of a bitch," I said. "They took me."

"What?" said Martinez. "The VC?"

"They dragged me a few feet, then"—I pointed to where the matted grass ended—"two of them must've picked me up, and taken me away."

"I didn't see anyone," Dunbar said.

"Maybe you were preoccupied," I suggested.

Prosser scanned the area, his brow furrowing. "DePaul's gone, too. He went down right next to me—we were near the river, I remember hearing the sound of the water—but he's gone."

"Maybe he was just wounded," I said. At least I hoped so. DePaul had pulled me back, months before, from stepping on what had seemed like a plot of dry grass on a trail, but what revealed itself—once we'd tossed a large boulder on top of it—as a swinging man trap: kind of a see-saw with teeth. If not for DePaul, I would've been the one swinging from it, impaled on a dozen or more rusty spikes studding its surface. DePaul had bought me an extra few months of life; maybe, when I'd run forward, firing into the treeline, I'd done the same for him, distracting the snipers long enough for him to get away.

"Hey, listen," said Dunbar. "Choppers."

The mop-up crew swooped in, quick and dirty, to recover what bodies it could. The area was secured, at least for the moment, and two grunts pried loose Dunbar's mangled leg from the punji beartrap and hefted him into a bodybag. The zipper caught on his lip, and the grunt had to unsnare it. Dunbar was furious.

"Watch what you're doing, assholes!" he roared at them. He turned to me. "Do you believe these guys?"

Two other grunts gingerly disconnected an unexploded cartridge trap not far from Martinez's body, then scooped up what remained of the poor bastard—torso in one bodybag, legs in another—and zipped the bags shut. Martinez watched as they loaded them onto the chopper, then turned to me.

"Collins. You think I should— "

I turned, but by the time I was facing him he was no longer there.

"Martinez?"

Dunbar's body was hefted onto the Huey, it hit the floor like a sack of dry cement, and I could almost feel the air rushing in to fill the sudden vacuum beside me.

I whirled around. Dunbar, too, was gone.

"Dunbar!"

The Huey lifted off, the branches of surrounding trees shuddering around it, like angry lovers waving away a violent suitor, and I was alone.

Believe it or not, I enlisted. It seemed like a good idea at the time: lower-middle-class families from Detroit could barely afford to send one kid to college, let alone two, and with my older sister at Ann Arbor I figured a student deferment wasn't coming my way anytime soon. So I let myself swallow the line they feed you at the recruiter's office, about how our *real* job over here was building bridges and thatching huts and helping the Vietnamese people; they made it sound kind of like the Peace Corps, only more humid.

My dad was a construction foreman; I'd been around buildings going up all my life—liked the sound of it, the feel of it, the smell of lumber and fresh cement and the way the frame looked before you laid on the plaster-board ... I'd stand there staring at the girders and crossbeams, the wood and steel armatures that looked to my eight-year-old mind like dinosaur skeletons, and I thought: The people who'll live here will never see, never know what their house *really* looks like, underneath; but *I* know.

So the idea of building houses for homeless people and bridges for oxen to cross sounded okay. Except after eight months in Nam, most of the bridges I'd seen had been blown away by American air strikes, and the closest I'd come to thatching huts was helping repair the roof of a bar in Da Nang I happened to be trapped in during a monsoon.

All things considered, enlisting did not seem like the kind of blue-chip investment in the future it once had, just now.

For the first few days I stuck close to the crater, wandering only as far as I could travel and return in a day, searching for a way back—but the way back, I knew, was farther than could ever be measured in miles, and the road was far from clearly marked. I tried not to dwell on that. If I had, I would never have mustered the nerve to move from my little corner of hell. I wasn't sure where the nearest U.S. base was in relation to here, but I remembered a small village we'd passed the previous day, and I seemed to recall a Red Cross Jeep parked near a hut, a French doctor from Catholic Relief Services administering to the villagers. Maybe he would show up again, and I could hitch a ride back to—the question kept presenting itself—*where*? What the hell did I do, ask directions to the Hereafter? With my luck, the Army was probably running *it*, too.

(Now that was a frightening thought; frighteningly plausible. This whole thing was just fucked up enough to be an Army operation. Had I forgotten to fill out a form somewhere down the line?)

I headed back down the trail we'd followed to our deaths, but this time, along with the usual sounds of the jungle—the rustling in the bush that you hoped was *only* a bamboo viper, or a tiger—I heard the jungle's other voice. I heard the sounds the choppers, with their souls-in-a-box, only played at.

I heard weeping.

Not moaning; not wailing; none of that Roger Corman, Vincent Price shit. Just the sound of grown men weeping, uncontrollably and inconsolably—coming, it seemed, from everywhere at once. And slowly, I began to see them: VC, blood spattered over their black silk pajamas, crouched in the bush in that funny way the VN sit—squatting, not sitting, on the ground—and crying. I stopped, dumbfounded. I'd never seen a VN cry before. I'd seen them scared, hell, I'd seen them fucking terrified, but I never saw them cry. All that crap you heard about how the VN are different from us, how they don't *feel* the way we do, I knew that was bullshit. They felt; they just didn't show it the way we did. But goddamned if these guys weren't giving our guys a run for their money. Maybe, if you're a VC and you're dead, it's okay to cry. Maybe it's expected. I moved on.

And somewhere along the trail, as I followed the Song Cai in its winding path south, I began to consider that I might not, in fact, be among the dead; that I might just be alive, after all.

Maybe, I thought, the rounds that had dropped me had just wounded me; maybe the VC took my body so they could get information out of me, later. The more I thought about it, the more reasonable it sounded. They take me, nurse me back to health, so they can torture me later. (That sounded as logical as anything else in this screwy country.) And somewhere along the way, I split off from my body. Got left behind, like a shadow shaken loose from its owner. I listened to the weeping all around me—Christ, I almost wished they *were* wailing and moaning; I could've borne that a lot easier—and I decided that I wasn't, couldn't be dead.

Up ahead, the trail widened briefly into a clearing, in the middle of which stood what looked like a giant birdhouse: a bamboo hut, little more than a box really, perched on the stump of a large tree trunk. There were spirit houses like this scattered all over Nam, small homes erected for the happiness of departed relatives, or for embittered spirits who might otherwise prey on hapless villagers. The Army briefed us on the local customs and superstitions before we even arrived over here—things like, you never pat a VN on the head 'cause the head, to the Vietnamese, is the seat of the soul; and *whatever* you do, don't sit with your legs crossed so that your foot is pointing toward the other person's head, because that's the grossest kind of insult. Shit like that. Some dinks would even name their male babies after women's sexual organs to try and fool evil spirits into thinking the kid was a girl, because boys were more valuable and needed to be protected. Jesus.

So I knew about spirit houses, and when we passed this one the other day I remember thinking, hey, that's kind of neat, even better than the treehouse I built in my grandparents' yard when I was twelve, and went on walking.

Today, I stopped. Stared at it.

Today, there were people inside the birdhouse.

One was an elderly papa-san, the other a young woman, maybe twenty-eight, twenty-nine. They were burning Joss sticks, the sweet fragrance carried back on the thick wind, and around them I saw candles, tiny hand-made furniture, and a few books. I started walking again, more slowly now, and as I got within a couple of yards of the birdhouse the papa-san looked up at me, blinked once in mild surprise, then smiled and held his hand over his chest in a gassho—a traditional form of greeting and respect. His other arm,

I now noticed, was askew beneath its silk sleeve, as though it had been broken, or worse.

"Welcome, traveler," he said. He was speaking in Vietnamese, but I understood, somehow, despite it.

"Uh . . . hello," I said, not sure if this worked both ways, but apparently it did; he smiled again, gesturing to his woman companion.

"I am Phan Van Duc. My daughter, Chau."

The woman turned and glared at me. She was pretty, in the abstract, but it was hard to get past the sneer on her face. So fixed, so unwavering, it looked like it'd been tattooed on. And since I wasn't sure if her anger was directed at me or not, I decided to ignore it, turned to the old man.

"My name is William Anthony Collins," I said. I wasn't sure if having three names was requisite over here, but I figured it couldn't hurt.

"May we offer you shelter?" Phan asked cordially. His daughter glowered.

There was barely enough room in the birdhouse for two, and I had no desire to be at close quarters with Chau. I declined, but thanked him for the offer.

"Have you been dead long?" the papa-san asked suddenly. I flinched.

"I'm not dead," I said, stubbornly.

The old man looked at me as though I were crazy. His daughter laughed a brassy, mocking laugh.

I explained what had happened to me, what I *thought* had happened to me, and how I was heading for the village downriver to see if the Viet Cong had taken my body there. Phan looked at me with sad, wise eyes as I spoke, then, when I'd finished, nodded once—more out of politeness, I suspected, than out of any credence he put in my theory.

"What you say may be true," he mused, "though I have never heard of such a thing. I would imagine, however, that rather than take a prisoner to a village, where he might easily be discovered, they would take him to one of their tunnel bases."

The VC had hundreds of tunnels running beneath most of I-Corps: a spiderweb of barracks and underground command posts and subterranean hospitals so vast, so labyrinthine, that we were only just beginning to understand the full scope of them. If I had been taken prisoner in one of them, the odds of finding myself were about equal to winning bets on the Triple Crown, the World Series, and the Super Bowl, all in one year.

"In that case," I said, not really wanting to think about it, "I'll just wait for my—body—to die, and when it does, I'm gone."

Papa-san looked at me with a half-pitying, half-perplexed look, as though I had just told him the sky was green and the moon was made of rice. Hell, come to think of it, maybe the dinks *did* think the moon was made of rice.

"What about you?" I said, anxious to shift the topic. "Why are you—here?"

Phan showed no trace of pain, or grief, as he replied.

"I was mauled by a tiger and left to bleed to death," he said simply, as though that should explain everything. Then, at my blank look, he explained patiently, "Having died a violent death, I was denied entry to the next world."

I blinked. I didn't see the connection.

"Getting mauled by a tiger, that's not your fault," I said, baffled.

He looked as baffled by my words as I was by his. "What difference does fault make? What is, is." He shrugged.

I opted not to pursue the subject. Phan and Martinez would've gotten along just fine. "And your daughter?"

He looked askance at her, she threw me a nasty look, then she scrambled forward into the birdhouse, hands gripping the lip of the floor, spitting the words at me: the hard edges of the Vietnamese consonants as sharp as the bitterness in her words.

"I died childless," she snapped at me. "Is that what you wanted to hear? Are you happy? I died childless, worthless, and I am condemned because of it."

"That's crazy," I said, despite myself.

She laughed a brittle laugh. "You are the crazy one," she said, "a *ma qui*, thinking he is alive. I pity you."

"No," the papa-san said gently, "you pity no one but yourself."

She glared at him, her nostrils flaring, then laughed again, shortly. "You are right," she said. "I pity no one. I don't know why I let you keep me here. I can do anything I want. I can bring disease back to the village, kill the children of my former friends. Yes. I think I would like that." She grinned maliciously, as though taking relish in the wickedness of her thought.

"You will not," Phan warned. "I am your father, and I forbid it."

She muttered a curse under her breath and retreated to the rear of the birdhouse. The papa-san turned and looked at me sadly.

"Do not judge my daughter by what she is now," he said softly. "Death makes of us what it wishes."

Jesus Christ; these people actually believed that. And so, I guess, that's just what they got. Well, not me. No fucking way, man. Not me.

I backed away. "I have to go."

"Wait," Phan said. I halted, I'm not sure why; he leaned forward, as though to share something important with me. "If you go into the village . . . you must be careful. Do not walk in the front door of a house, because the living keep mirrors by the doorway, to reflect the image of those who enter. If a spirit sees himself in the mirror, he will be frightened off. Also, if red paper lines the entrance, stay away, for you will anger the God of the Doorway. Do you understand?"

I nodded, numbly, thanked him for his advice, and got the hell out of there, fast.

I hurried down the trail, past the weeping guerrillas in black silk, feeling a sudden, black longing for something as violent and mundane as a mortar strike; yearning for the sound of gunships, the bright spark of tracer fire, the crackling of small arms fire or the din of big Chinook choppers circling in for the kill. God *damn*. This was the dinks' Hell, not mine; I wasn't going to be a part of it, I would *not* buy into their stupid, superstitious horseshit. The weeping around me grew louder. I started running now, phantom limbs passing harmlessly through tripwires and across punji traps, even the elephant grass not so much as tickling my calves as I ran along the banks of the Song Cai—

The weeping changed. Became different: deeper. I knew instantly that it was not the cries of a Vietnamese; knew, suddenly and sickeningly, that it was an American's cries I was hearing.

I stopped; looked around. I saw no one lying wounded in the bush, but heard, now, too, a voice:

"—Jesus, Mary, and Joseph, *help me*— "

Oh, Christ, I thought.

DePaul.

I looked up. He was floating about five feet above the muddy waters of the river, like a tethered balloon, his big, six-foot frame looking almost gaseous, his black skin seeming somehow pale. His hands covered his face as he wept, prayed, swore, and wept again. At first I thought he was moving upstream, but I soon realized that it was the water flowing under him that gave the illusion of movement; he swayed back and forth slightly, but was utterly motionless, completely stationary.

It took me a moment to recover my wits. I shouted his name over the roar of the rapids.

He looked up, startled.

When he saw me—saw me looking at *him*—his face lit up with a kind of absolution. "Oh, Jesus," he said, so softly I almost couldn't hear it. "*Collins*? Are you real?"

"I sure as shit hope so."

"Are you alive?"

I dodged the question. "What the hell happened to you, man? Prosser said you went down right next to him, but your body— "

"Charlie hit me in the back." I could see the hole torn in his skin at the nape of his neck, and the matching one in front, just below his collarbone, where the bullet had exited. "I couldn't breathe. Couldn't think. Got up, somehow, ran—but in the wrong direction. Dumped into the river. Christ, Bill, it was awful. I was choking *and* drowning, and the next thing I knew— " His hand had gone, reflexively, to his throat, covering the ragged hole there. "—my body had floated downriver, then got snagged on some rock. Over there."

I followed his gaze. His body was pinned between two rocks, the waters flowing around it, flanking it in white foam. I turned back to DePaul, floating in place above the river, and I took a step forward.

"Christ, De," I said softly. "How—I mean, what— "

"*I can't get down*, man," he said, and for the first time I heard the pain in his voice; "I been here two, three days, and it *hurts*. Oh Christ, it hurts! It's not like floating, Jesus, it's like treading water, every muscle in my body aches—I'm so *tired*, man, I'm so— " He broke off into sobs; something I'd never seen him do. He looked away, let the tears come, then looked back at me, his eyes wide. "Help me, Collins," he said, softly. "*Help me.*"

"Just tell me how," I said, feeling helpless, horrified. "Why—why are you *like* this, man? You have any idea?"

"Yeah. Yeah, I know," he said, taking a ragged gulp of air. "It's—it's 'cause I died in water, see? You die in water, your spirit's tied to the water till you can find another one to— "

"*What*? Jesus Christ, De, where'd you *get* that shit from?"

"Another spook. VC, half his head blown away, wanderin' up and down the river. He told me."

"You bought *into* this crap?" I yelled at him. "These dinks believe this shit, man, *you* don't have to—you're an *American*, for Chrissake!"

"Collins— "

"You believe it, it happens. You stop believing, it stops happening. Just— "

His eyes were sunken, desperate. "Please, man. Help me?"

No matter what I thought of this shit, there was only one thing that mattered: he'd saved my life, once; and even if there was no more life in him to save, I could, at least, try to ease his pain. I *had* to try.

"All right," I said. "What can I do?"

He hesitated.

"Bring me a kid," he said, quietly.

"Why?"

He hesitated again; then, working up his nerve, he said, "To release me. A life for a life."

My eyes went wide. "*What?*"

"It's the only way," he said quickly. "You die in water, the only way to be set free is to—drown—a kid, as an offering." His eyes clouded over, his gaze became hooded and ashamed even as he said it. For a long minute the only sound was the rushing of water past the dam of DePaul's corpse, and the distant sounds of weeping carried on the wind.

Finally I said, "I can't do that, man."

"Bill— "

"Even if I believed it'd work—*especially* if I believed it'd work—I couldn't— "

"Not a healthy kid," DePaul interrupted, desperation and pleading creeping into his tone, "a sick one. One that's gonna die anyway. Shit, half the gook kids over here die before they're— "

"Are you crazy, man?" I snapped. "Gook or not, I can't— "

I stopped. Listened to what I was saying.

DePaul's face was ashen; in torment. "Collins . . . please. I hurt so bad— "

I was buying into this crap. Just like him. Someone'd filled his head with dink superstition, and now he was living—or dying—by it. That was it, wasn't it? You die, you get pretty much what you expect: Catholics, heaven or hell; atheist, maybe nothing, nonexistence, loss of consciousness; dinks—this. And we'd been over here so long, wading knee deep in their fucking country, that we were starting to believe what they believed.

But the DePaul I knew would never kill a kid. Not even to save himself. Maybe the only way to shake him loose from this bullshit was to show him that.

I waited a long minute, thinking, devising a plan, and then finally I spoke up.

"A sick kid?" I asked, carefully, as though I actually believed all this.

He looked up, hopefully. "One that's gonna die anyway. You've seen 'em, you know what they look like, you can see it in their eyes— "

"I won't bring one that's gonna live."

"No no, man, you don't have to. A sick kid. A real sick kid." God, he sounded pathetic.

I told him I didn't know how long it would take, but that I would head into the village we passed through a few days ago and see what I could do. I told him I'd be back as soon as I could.

"Hurry, man. Hurry." It was the last thing I heard before I headed back into the bush once again. He'd bought the line. Now all I had to do was show him he'd bought another—and, more important, that he could buy out of it.

The village was about two hours up the road. There was no Red Cross Jeep in sight, no Catholic Relief doctor handing out aspirin and antibiotics; just the squalid little huts, the half-naked kids running through muddy puddles probably rife with typhoid, tired-looking women doing laundry in a small stream tributary to the Song Cai. There was a huge crater at the edge of town—the mortar strike that was too late to save me and Dunbar and DePaul. Nearby roofs were scorched, at least two huts had been burned to the ground. Friendly fire. Any more friendly and half the village would be greeting me personally. I walked up the main road, peeking in windows. If I was going to make it look genuine I'd have to bring back a genuinely sickly kid; though exactly how, I still wasn't sure.

Outside one hut I heard the sound of a mother comforting a squalling baby, and decided to go in and take a look. Sure enough, just as the old Papa-san had predicted, the doorway was lined with red paper to ward off evil spirits. I stepped across the threshold. Big fucking deal. Up yours, God of the Doorway. I turned—

I screamed.

In the mirror positioned just inside, I saw a man with a foot-wide hole blasted in his chest: the torn edges of the wound charred to a crisp, the cavity within raw and red as steak tartare. A pair of lungs dangled uselessly from the slimmest of folds of flesh, swaying as I jumped back, reflexively; beside them, a heart riddled with a half dozen jagged frag wounds throbbed in a stubborn counterfeit of life.

And behind me in the mirror, a glimpse of something else: a shadow, a *red* shadow, red as the paper above the doorway . . . moving not as I moved but looming up, and quickly, behind me.

I ran.

Out of the house, down the street, away from the huts, finally collapsing on a patch of elephant grass. At first I was afraid to look down at myself, but when I did, I saw nothing—saw exactly what I'd seen up till now, the drab green camouflage fatigues stained with blood. All this time, I realized, I had seen everyone else's wounds but mine. Not till now.

I sat there, gathering my wits and my courage, trying to work up the nerve to enter another hut. I didn't think about the mirror, didn't dwell on what I'd seen. Better just to think of myself this way, the way some part of me *wanted* to see myself. When I finally got up and started round to the huts again, I steered well clear of the doors.

There was the usual assortment of sickly kids—malaria, mostly, but from the look of them, a few typhoid, influenza, and parasitic dysentery cases as well. I felt gruesome as hell, trying to choose which one to take, even knowing this was only a ruse, something to shock DePaul back to normalcy. *Just get it over with.* I looked in one window and saw what appeared to be a two-year-old girl—in a dress made of old parachute nylon, an earring dangling too large from one tiny lobe—being washed by her mother. It was only when the mother turned the child over and I saw the small brown penis that I remembered: the mother was trying to deceive the evil spirits into thinking their sickly boy-child was really a girl, and thus not worth the taking.

Jesus, I thought. Said a lot about the place of women over here. But it did mean the kid was probably seriously ill, and after I'd used her—him—to get DePaul back to normal, I could take the poor kid to the nearest Evac . . . leave it on the doorstep of the civilian ward with a note giving the name of his village.

Assuming I could *write* a note.

Assuming I could even *take* the kid in the first place.

I took a deep breath and, once the mother had left the room, walked through the wall of the hut. I didn't feel the bamboo any more than I'd felt the tripwires I'd run through. I stood over the infant, now worried that my hands would pass through him, too . . . then slowly reached down to try and pick him up.

I touched him. I didn't know how, or why, but I could touch him.

I scooped the boy up in my arms and held him to my chest. He looked up at me with old, sad eyes. All the kids here had the same kind of eyes: tired, cheerless, and somehow knowing. As though all the misery around them, all the civil wars and foreign invaders—from the French to the Japanese to the Americans—as though all that were known to them, before they'd even been born. Rocked in a cradle of war, they woke, with no surprise, to a lullaby of thunder.

I walked through the wall of the hut, the child held aloft and carried through the window. When we were clear of the building, I hefted the boy up, held him in my arms, and headed into the bush before anyone could see.

I wanted to stay off the main road, for fear that someone might see me: not me, I guess, since *I couldn't* be seen, but the kid, the boy. (What, I wondered, would someone see, if they did see? A child carried aloft on the wind? Or an infant wrapped in the arms of a shadow, a smudge on the air? I didn't know. I didn't want to find out.) Every once in a while I'd see a dead VC look up from where he was squatting, on the banks of the river or in the shade of a rubber tree, and look at me, sometimes with curiosity, sometimes resentment, sometimes fear. They never said anything. Just stared, and at length went back to their mourning, their weeping. I hurried past.

About half a mile from DePaul I caught a glimpse of a squad of still-living VC, about a dozen yards into the jungle, carrying what looked like an unconscious American GI, probably an LRRP. I immediately squatted down in the bush, hiding the kid from view as best I could, dropping a fold of blanket over his face to protect him from the prickly blades of grass. I watched as one of the VC bent down, reaching for what looked like a patch of dry dirt, his fingers finding a catch, a handle of some sort, and then the earth lifted and I saw it was actually a trapdoor in the ground itself—a piece of wood covered with a thin, but deceptive, layer of dirt. One by one the VC crawled headfirst into the tunnel, until only two were left—the two carrying the unconscious GI. I debated what to do—was there anything I *could* do?—but before I could make a decision, I saw the GI's head tilt at an unnatural angle as he was lowered into the ground . . . and I knew, then, that I'd been mistaken. He wasn't unconscious; he was dead. And, very quickly, lost from sight.

Psychological warfare. Drove Americans crazy when we couldn't recover our dead, and Charlie knew it. Just like we played on their fears with the Wandering Soul, they played on ours, in their own way. I got up and moved on.

Less than half an hour later I was back at the river. DePaul still floated helplessly above the rapids. He looked up at my approach, the torment in his face quickly replaced by astonishment and—fear?

I brought the kid to the edge of the river, looked up at DePaul, made my voice hard, resolute—all that Sergeant York shit.

"He's got malaria," I said, tonelessly. "You can tell when you pull down his lower eyelid, it's all pink; he's anemic, can't weigh more than twenty pounds. They could save him, at the 510 Evac. Or you can take him, to save yourself." I stared him straight in the eye. "Which is it, DePaul?"

I'd known DePaul since boot camp. Faced with the reality of it, I knew what he'd answer.

And as I waited, smugly, for him to say it, his gaseous, wraith-like form spun round in mid-air, rocketed downward like a guided missile, and slammed into me with vicious velocity, sending me sprawling, knocking the kid out of my arms.

Stunned, I screamed at him, but by the time I'd scrambled to my feet he had the kid in a vise grip and was holding the poor sonofabitch under the water. I ran, slammed into De with all my strength, but he shrugged me off with an elbow in my face. I toppled backward.

"I'm sorry, man," he kept saying, over and over; "I'm sorry . . ."

I lunged at him again, this time knocking him offbalance; he lost his grip on the kid, and I dove into the water after the boy. It felt weird; the water passed *through* me, I didn't feel wet, or cold, nothing at all; and the waters were so muddy I could barely see a foot in front of me. Finally, after what seemed like forever, I saw a small object in front of me and instinctively I reached out and grabbed. My fingers closed around the infant's arms. I made for the surface, the kid in my arms; I staggered out of the water, up the embankment—

I put the boy down on the ground. His face was blue, his body very still. I tried to administer mouth-to-mouth, but nothing happened; and then I laughed suddenly, a manic, rueful laugh, at the thought of me, of all people, trying to give the breath of life.

I looked up, thinking to see DePaul towering above me . . . but he was nowhere to be seen. And when I looked up at the spot above the river where he had been tethered, helplessly, for so long—

I saw the spirit-form of the little boy, floating, hovering, crying out in pain and confusion.

I screamed. I screamed for a long time.

And knew, now, why I'd been able to touch the child, when I hadn't been able to touch anything else: I was the *ma qui*, I was the evil spirit come to bear the sickly child away, and I had done my job, followed my role, without even realizing I'd been doing it. I thought of Phan, of his daughter Chau, of DePaul and of myself.

Death makes of us what it wishes.

I wept, then, for the first time, as freely and as helplessly as the VC I'd seen and heard; wept like the Wandering Soul I knew, at last, I had to be.

I must've stayed there, on the banks of the river, for at least a day, trying to find some way to atone, some way to save the soul of the child I'd led to perdition. But I couldn't. I would've traded places with him willingly, but didn't know how. And when I went back to the spirit house where Phan and his daughter dwelled, when I told him of what I'd done, he showed no horror, expressed no rage; just puzzlement that it had taken me so long to realize my place in the world.

His daughter, on the other hand, gleefully congratulated me on my deed. "*Ma qui*," she said, and this time, hearing the word, I understood it not just as ghost, but as devil, for it meant both. "Did it not feel good?"

A terrible gladness burst open, someplace inside me—a black, cold poison that felt at once horrifying and invigorating. It was relief, expiation of guilt by embracing, not renouncing, the evil I'd done. Chau, as though sensing this, laughed throatily. She leaned forward, her spiteful smile now seductive as well. "*Yêu dâu*," she said, "*yêu quái.*"

Beloved demon.

"Together we could do many things," she said, twisting a lock of long black hair in her fingers. Her eyes glittered malevolently. "Many things." She laughed again. Cruel eyes, a cold-blooded smile. I felt betrayed by my own erection. I wanted her, I didn't want her. I loathed her, and in my loathing wanted her all the more, because perverse desire was, at least, desire; I wanted my cock, dead limb that it was, inside her, to make me feel alive.

When I realized how badly I wanted it, I ran.

She only laughed all the louder.

"Beloved demon!" she called after me. "You shall be back!"

But I haven't been back. Not yet. Nor back to the crater, the place of my death, not for many months. I still search for my body, but I know that the odds of finding it, in the hundreds of miles of tunnels that honeycomb this land, are virtually nil. I search during the days, and at night I come back to my new home to sleep.

I have a birdhouse of my own, you see, just outside the village; a treehouse perched on a bamboo stump, filled with Joss sticks and candles and little toy furniture. I come back here, and I fight to remind myself who I am, what I am; I struggle against becoming the *yêu quái*, the demon Chau wishes me to be. Except, that is, when the bloodsong sings to me in my voice, and I know that I already *am* the demon—and that the only thing that stops me from acting like one is my will, my conscience, the last vestiges of the living man I once was. I don't know how long I can keep the demon at bay. I don't know how long I want to. But all I can do is keep trying, and not think of Chau, or of how wonderfully bitter her lips must taste, bitter as salt, bitter as blood.

Damn it.

Above me, the Wandering Soul cries out from its box, wailing and moaning in a ridiculous burlesque of damnation, and I think about all the things we were told about this place, and the things we weren't. Back in Da Nang, when anyone would talk about the Army's "pacification" program—about winning the "hearts and minds" of the Vietnamese—the joke used to be: Grab 'em by the balls, and their hearts and minds will follow. Except no one told us that while we were working on their hearts and minds, they were winning over our souls. The Army trained us in jungle warfare, drilled us in the local customs, told us we'd have to fight Charlie on his own terms—but never let on that we'd have to die on his terms, too. Because for all the technology, all the ordnance, all the planning that went into this war, they forgot the most important thing.

They never told us the rules of engagement.

ROBERT R. McCAMMON

The Miracle Mile

"THE MIRACLE MILE" atmospherically sets the scene for Robert McCammon's anthology *Under the Fang*, in which vampires have usurped humans as the dominant race on earth.

McCammon was only 26 years old when his first novel, *Baal*, was published in 1978. Since then he has followed it with a string of commercially successful books including *Bethany's Sin*, *The Night Boat*, *They Thirst* (more vampires), *Mystery Walk*, *Usher's Passing*, *Swan Song*, *Stinger*, *The Wolf's Hour*, and the collection *Blue World and Other Stories*.

More recently he has moved away from the horror genre with the novels *Mine* and *Boy's Life*. However, the following story proves that he has not lost the ability to take what has almost become a genre cliché and turn it into a very effective dystopian nightmare.

T HE CAR DIED OUTSIDE PERDIDO BEACH. It was a messy death, a wheeze of oil and a clatter of cylinders, a dark tide spreading across the sun-cracked pavement. When it was over, they sat there for a few minutes saying nothing, just listening to the engine tick and steam, but then the baby began to cry and it came to them that they had to get moving. Kyle got the suitcase, Allie took the bag of groceries in one arm and the baby in the other, Tommy laced up his sneakers and took the thermos of water, and they left the old dead car on the roadside and started walking south to the Gulf.

Kyle checked his watch again. It was almost three o'clock. The sun set late, in midsummer. July heat crushed them, made the sweat ooze from their pores and stick the clothes to their flesh. The road, bordered by pine woods, was deserted. This season there would be no tourists. This season there would be no lights or laughter on the Miracle Mile.

They kept walking, step after step, into the steamy haze of heat. Kyle took the baby for a while, and they stopped for a sip of water and a rest in the shade. Flies buzzed around their faces, drawn to the moisture. Then Kyle said, "I guess we'd better go on," and his wife and son got up again, the baby cradled in Kyle's arm. Around the next curve of the long road they saw a car off in a drainage ditch on the left-hand side. The car's red paint had faded, the tires were flat, and the driver's door was open. Of the car's occupants there was no sign. Allie walked a little closer to Kyle as they passed the car; their arms touched, wet flesh against wet flesh, and Kyle noted she looked straight ahead with that thousand-yard stare he'd seen on his own face as he'd shaved in the mirror this morning at dawn.

"When are we gonna get there?" Tommy asked. He was twelve years old, his patience wearing thin. It occurred to Kyle that Tommy asked that question every year, from his seat in the back of the car: *Hey, Dad, when are we gonna get there?*

"Soon," Kyle answered. "It's not far." His stock reply. They'd never walked the last few miles into Perdido Beach, not once in all the many years they'd been coming here for summer vacation. "We ought to see the water pretty soon."

"Hot," Allie said, and she wiped her forehead with the back of her arm. "Hot out here."

Over a hundred, Kyle figured. The sun reflecting off the pavement was brutal. The road shimmered ahead, between the thin pines. A black snake slid across in front of them, and up against the blue, cloudless sky hawks searched for currents. "Soon," Kyle said, and he licked his dry lips. "It's not far at all now."

It was four o'clock when the pine woods fell away and they saw the first wreckage from Hurricane Jolene. A motel with pink walls had most of its roof ripped away. A twisted sign lay in the parking lot amid abandoned cars. Curtains, cigarette butts, deck chairs, and other debris floated in the swimming pool. "Can we get out of the sun for a few minutes?" Allie asked him, and he nodded and led his family toward the pink ruins.

Some of the doors remained, but most of them had been torn from their hinges by the storm. The first unit, without a door, had a bed with a bloodstained sheet and the flies spun above it in a dark, roiling cloud. He opened the door of the next unit, number eight, and they went into a room where the heat had been trapped but the sun and the flies turned away. The room's bed had been stripped to the mattress and a lamp with flamingoes on the shade had been overturned, but it looked safe. He opened the blinds and the windows, and in his inhalation of air he thought he could smell the Gulf's salt. Allie sat down on the bed with the baby and took a squeeze tube of sun block from the grocery bag. She began to paint the infant's face with it, as the baby's pink fingers grasped at the air. Then she covered her own face and arms with the sun block. "I'm already burning," she said, as she worked the stuff into her skin. "I didn't used to burn so fast. Want some?"

"Yeah." The back of Kyle's neck was stinging. He stood over his wife and looked at the baby, as Tommy sprawled on the bed and stared at the ceiling. "She needs a name," Kyle said.

"Hope," Allie answered, and she looked up at her husband with heat-puffed eyes. "Hope would be a good name, don't you think?"

It would be a cruel name, he decided. A name not suited for these times or this world. But saying no would be just as cruel, wouldn't it? He saw how badly Allie wanted it, so he said, "I think that's fine," and as soon as he said it he felt the rage surge in him like a bitter flood tide and he had to turn away before she saw it in his face. The infant couldn't be more than six months old. Why had it fallen to him, to do this thing?

He took the thermos and went into the bathroom, where there was a sink and a shower stall and a tub with a sliding door of smoked plastic. He pulled the blind up and opened the small window in there too, and then he turned on the sink's tap and waited for the rusty water to clear before he refilled the thermos.

Something moved, there in the bathroom. Something moved with a long, slow, and agonized stretching sound.

Kyle looked at the smoked plastic door for a moment, a pulse beating in his skull, and then he reached out and slid it open.

It was lying in the tub. Like a fat cocoon, it was swaddled in bed sheets and tacky beach towels covered with busty cartoon bathing beauties and studs swigging beer. It was impossible to determine where the head and feet were, the arms bound to its sides and the hands hidden. The thing in its shroud of sheets and towels trembled, a hideous involuntary reaction of nerves and muscles, and Kyle thought, *It smells me.*

"Kill it."

He looked back at Allie, who stood in the doorway behind him with the baby in her arms. Her face was emotionless, her eyes vacant as a dreamer's. "Kill it, Kyle," she said. "Please kill it."

"Tom?" he called. He heard his voice crack. "Take your mother outside, will you?" The boy didn't respond, and when Kyle peered out from the bathroom he saw his son sitting up on the bed. Tommy was staring at him, with the same dead eyes as his mother. Tommy's mouth was halfopen, a silver thread of saliva hanging down. "Tom? Listen up!" He said it sharply, and Tommy's gaze cleared. "Go outside with your mother. Do you hear me?"

"Yes sir," Tommy said, and he did as he was told. When he was alone, Kyle opened his suitcase, reached beneath the socks and underwear and found the .38 pistol hidden there. He loaded it from a box of shells, cocked the gun, and walked back into the bathroom where the wrapped-up thing at the bottom of the tub awaited.

Kyle tried to get a grip on the towels and pull them loose, but they were held so tightly they wouldn't give. When he pulled with greater determination, the shape began thrashing back and forth with terrible strength, and Kyle let go and stepped back. The thing's thrashing ceased, and it lay still again. Kyle had once seen one that had grown a hard skin, like a roach. He had seen one with a flat, cobralike head on an elongated neck. Their forms were changing, a riot of evolution gone insane. In these times, in this world, even the fabric of nature had been ripped asunder.

He didn't have time to waste. He aimed the gun at the thing's midsection and squeezed the trigger. The noise of the shots was thunderous in the little bathroom. When he was through shooting, there were six holes in the towels and sheets but no blood.

"Chew on those," Kyle said.

There was a wet, splitting noise. Reddish black liquid soaked the towels and began to stream toward the drain. Kyle thought of a leech that had just burst open. He clenched his teeth, got out of the bathroom and closed the door behind him, and then he put the pistol back into the suitcase and snapped the suitcase shut.

His wife, son, and the baby called Hope were waiting for him, outside in the hot yellow sunshine.

Kyle checked the cars in the motel's parking lot. One had keys in the ignition, though its windshield was shattered. He got in and tried the engine; the dead battery wouldn't even give out a gasp. They started walking again, toward the south, as the sun moved into the west and the afternoon shadows began to gather.

Tommy saw them first: sand dunes rising between the palmettos. He cried out with joy and ran for the beach, where the Gulf's waves rolled up in lathery foam and gulls skimmed the blue water. He took off his sneakers and socks, threw them aside and rushed into the sea, and behind him came his father and mother, footsore and drenched with sweat. Kyle and Allie both took off their shoes and waded into the water, the baby in Allie's arms, and as the waves rolled around them onto the sand Kyle inhaled a chestful of salt air and cleansed his senses. Then he looked down the beach, its crescent curving toward the east, and the motels that stood at the edge of the Gulf.

They were alone.

Gulls darted in, screaming. Two of them fought over a crab that had been flipped onto its back. Broken shells glittered where the sand turned brown and hard. And all along the beach the motels—the blocky violet, sea green, periwinkle, and cream-colored buildings that had stood there since Kyle and Allie were teenagers—were without life, like the structures of an ancient civilization. Hurricane Jolene had done its damage; some of the motels—the Spindrift, the Sea Anchor, the Coral Reef—had been reduced to hulks, their signs battered and dangling, their windows broken out, whole walls washed away. A hundred yards down the beach, a cabin cruiser lay on its side, its hull ripped open like a fish's belly. Where Kyle recalled the sight of a hundred sunbathers tanning on their towels, there was nothing but white emptiness. The lifeguard's station was gone. There was no aroma of coconut-scented tanning butter, no blare of radios, no volleyball games, nobody tossing a Frisbee to a dog in the surf. The gulls strutted around, fat and happy in the absence of humanity.

Kyle had expected this, but the reality gnawed at his heart. He loved this place; he had been young here, had met and courted Allie here. They'd come to Perdido Beach on their honeymoon, sixteen years ago. And they'd come back, every year since. What was summer, without a vacation at the beach? Without sand in your shoes, the sun on your shoulders, the sound of young laughter, and the smell of the Gulf? What was life worth, without such as that?

A hand slid into his.

"We're here," Allie said. She was smiling, but when she kissed him he tasted a tear.

They were going to cook, out in this sun. They needed to find a room. Check in, stow the suitcase and the groceries. Think about the future.

Kyle watched the waves coming in. Tommy went underwater,

clothes and all, and rose up sputtering and yelling for the sake of it. Allie's hand squeezed Kyle's, and Kyle thought, *We're standing on the edge of what used to be, and there's nowhere left to run.*

Nowhere.

"I love you," Kyle told his wife, and he drew her tightly against him. He could feel the heat of her skin. She was going to have a bad sunburn. Hope's cheeks were red. Pick up some Solarcaine somewhere. God knows *they* don't need it.

Nowhere.

He walked out of the water. The wet sand sucked around his ankles, trying to hold him, but he broke free and trudged up across the hard sand, leaving footprints all the way to where he'd left his suitcase. Allie was following him, with the red-cheeked Hope. "Tom?" Kyle called. "Tommy, let's go!" The boy splashed and romped for a moment more, gulls spinning around his head either in curiosity or thinking he was a rather large fish, and then Tommy came out of the water and picked up his socks and sneakers.

They began to walk eastward on the beach toward the Miracle Mile. A skeleton lay half-buried in the sand just past the wrecked cabin cruiser. A child's orange pail was caught by the surf, pulled out and thrust onto shore again, the sea playing a game with the dead. The sun was getting lower, the shadows growing. The suitcase was heavy, so Kyle changed hands. The tires of a dune buggy jutted up from the waves, and farther on a body with some flesh on it was drifting in the shallow water. The gulls had been at work; it was not pretty.

Kyle watched his wife, her shadow going before her. The baby began to cry, and Allie gently shushed her. Tommy threw shells into the water, trying to get a skimmer. They had found the infant in a gas station south of Montgomery, Alabama, near nine o'clock this morning. There had been an abandoned station wagon outside at the pumps, and the child had been on the floor in the women's room. On the driver's seat of the station wagon was a great deal of dried blood. Tommy had thought the blotch looked like the state of Texas. There had been dried blood on the doorknob of the women's room too, but what had happened at that gas station was unknown. Was the mother attacked? Had she planned to come back for the baby? Had she crawled off into the woods and died? They'd searched around the gas station, but found no corpses.

Well, life was a mystery, wasn't it? Kyle had agreed to take the baby with them, on their vacation to the beach. But he cursed God for doing this to him, because he'd finally got things right in his soul.

Hope. It had to be a cosmic joke. And if God and the devil were at war over this spinning ball of black sorrows, it was terribly clear who had control of the nuclear weapons.

Biological incident.

That was the first of it. How the government tried to explain. A biological incident, at some kind of secret—up until then—testing center in North Dakota. That was six years ago. The biological incident was worse than they'd let on. They had created something from their stew of gene manipulation and bacteriological tampering that had sent their ten test subjects out into the world with a vengeance. The ten had multiplied into twenty, the twenty to forty, the forty to eighty, and on and on. They had the wrath of Hell in their blood, a contamination that made AIDS look like a common cold. The germ boys had learned how to create—by accident, yes—weapons that walked on two legs. What foreign power were we going to unleash that taint upon? No matter; it had come home to live.

Biological incident.

Kyle shifted the suitcase again. *Call them what they are,* he thought. They craved blood like addicts used to crave heroin and crack. They wrapped themselves up and hid in closets and basements and any hole they could winnow into. Their skin burst and oozed and they split apart at the seams like old suits in the sunlight. Call them what they are, damn it.

They were everywhere now. They had everything. The television networks, the corporations, the advertising agencies, the publishing houses, the banks, the law. Everything. Once in a while a pirate station broke in on the cable, human beings pleading for others not to give up hope. Hope. There it was again, the cosmic joke. Those bastards were as bad as fundamentalist preachers; their role models were Jim Bakker and Jerry Falwell, seen through a dark glass. They wanted to convert everybody on earth, make them see the "truth," and if you didn't choose to join the fold they battered you in like a weak door and chewed the faith into you.

It wasn't just America. It was everywhere: Canada, the Soviet Union, Japan, Germany, Norway, Africa, England, South America, and Spain. Everywhere. The contamination—the "faith"—knew no racial nor national boundaries. It was another cosmic joke, with a hideous twist: The world was moving toward a true brotherhood.

Kyle watched his shadow loom before him, its darkness merging with Allie's. If a man couldn't take a vacation in the sun with his family, he thought, then what the hell good was living?

"Hey, Dad!" Tommy said. "There it is!"

Kyle looked to where his son was pointing. The motel had stucco walls painted pale blue, its roof of red slate. Some of the roof had collapsed, the walls and windows broken. The motel's sign had survived the hurricane, and said THE DRIFTWOOD.

It was where Kyle and Allie had spent their honeymoon, and where they'd stayed—cabana number five, overlooking the Gulf—every summer vacation for sixteen years. "Yes," Kyle answered. "That's the place." He turned his back to the sea and walked toward the concrete steps that led up to the Driftwood, and Allie followed with Hope and the grocery bag. Tommy paused to bend down and examine a jellyfish that had washed up and been caught by the sun at low tide, and then he came on too.

The row of oceanview cabanas had been demolished. Number five was a cavern of debris, its roof caved in. "Watch the glass," Kyle cautioned them, and he continued on around the brackish swimming pool and the deck that caught the afternoon's sea breeze. He climbed another set of stairs from the pool's deck to the major portion of the Driftwood, his wife and son behind him, and he stood facing a warren of collapsed rooms and wreckage.

Summer could be a heartless thing.

For a few seconds he almost lost it. Tears burned his eyes, and he thought he was going to choke on a sob. It had been important, so vitally important, that they come to Perdido Beach again, and see this place where life had been fresh and good and all the days were ahead of them. Now, more than anything, Kyle could see that it was over. But then Allie said, in a terribly cheerful voice, "It's not so bad," and Kyle laughed instead of cried. His laughter spiralled up, was taken by the Gulf breeze and broken like the walls of the Driftwood. "We can stay right here," Allie said, and she walked past her husband into an opening where a door used to be.

The room's walls were cracked, the ceiling blotched with water stains. The furniture—bed, chest of drawers, chairs, lamps, all ticky-tacky when they were new—had been whirled around and smashed to kindling. Pipes stuck up where the sink had been in the bathroom, but the toilet remained and the shower stall—empty of intruders—was all right. Kyle tried the tap and was amazed to hear a rumbling down in the Driftwood's guts. A thin trickle of rusty water flowed from the shower head. Kyle turned the tap off and the rumbling died.

"Clear this stuff away," Allie told Tommy. "Let's get this mattress out from underneath."

"We can't stay here," Kyle said.

"Why can't we?" Her eyes were vacant again. "We can make do. We've been making do at home. We can make do on vacation too."

"No. We've got to find somewhere else."

"We've always stayed at the Driftwood." A childlike petulance rose up in her voice, and she began to rock the baby. "Always. We can stay right here, like we do every summer. Can't we, Tommy?"

"I guess so," he said, and he nudged the shattered television set with his foot.

Kyle and Allie stared at each other. The breeze came in around them through the doorway and then left again.

"We can stay here," Allie said.

She's out of it, he thought. Who could blame her? Her systems were shutting down, a little tighter day after day. "All right." He touched her hair and smoothed it away from her face. "The Driftwood it is."

Tommy went to find a shovel and broom, because there was a lot of glass on the linoleum-tiled floor. As Allie unpacked the groceries, the baby laid to rest on a pillow, Kyle checked the rooms on either side. Nothing sleeping in them, nothing folded up and waiting. He checked as many rooms as he could get into. There was something bad—neither skeleton nor fully fleshed, but bloated and dark as a slug—wearing a flower-print shirt and red shorts in a room nearer the pool, but Kyle could tell it was a dead human being and not one of them. A Gideon's Bible lay close at hand, and also the broken beer bottle with which the sunlover had slashed his wrists. On a countertop, next to the stub of a burned-out candle, was a wallet, some change, and a set of car keys. Kyle didn't look at the wallet, but he took the keys. Then he put the shower curtain over the corpse and continued his search of the Driftwood's rooms. He walked through a breezeway, past the Driftwood's office and to the front of the motel, and there he found a half-dozen cars in the parking lot. Across the street was Nick's Pancake House, its windows blown in. Next to it, the Goofy Golf place and the Go-Kart track, both deserted, their concession stands shuttered and storm ravaged. Kyle began to check the cars, as gulls cried out overhead and sailed in lazy circles.

The keys fit the ignition of a blue Toyota with a Tennessee license tag. Its engine, cranky at first, finally spat black smoke and awakened. The gas gauge's needle was almost to the E, but there were plenty of gas stations on the Strip. Kyle shut the engine off and got out, and that was when he looked toward the Miracle Mile.

It was a beautifully clear afternoon. He could see all the way to the amusement park, where the Ferris wheel and the roller coaster rose up, where the Sky Needle loomed over the Hang Out dance pavilion and the Super Water Slide stood next to the Beach Arcade.

His eyes stung. He heard ghosts on the wind, calling in young voices from the dead world. He had to look away from the Miracle Mile before his heart cracked, and he walked back the way he'd come, the keys gripped in his palm.

Tommy was at work clearing away debris. The mattress had been swept free of glass. A chair had been salvaged, and a table on which a lamp had sat. Allie had put on her swimsuit—the one with aquamarine fish on it that she'd found in a Sears store last week—and she wore sandals so her feet wouldn't be cut. The flesh of her arms and face were blushed with Florida sun. It dawned on Kyle how much weight Allie had lost. She was as skinny as she'd been their first night together, here at the Driftwood a long, long time ago.

"I'm ready for the beach," she told him. "How do I look?" She turned around for him to appreciate the swimsuit.

"Nice. Really nice."

"We shouldn't waste the sunshine, should we?"

She'd had enough sun for one day. But he smiled tightly and said, "No."

Beneath one of the yellow beach umbrellas, Kyle sat beside his wife while she fed Hope from a jar of Gerber's mixed fruit. The groceries had come from a supermarket in the same area they'd found the baby, and Allie had stocked up on items she hadn't even thought about since Tommy was an infant. Out in the Gulf, Tommy splashed and swam as the sun sparkled golden on the waves.

"Don't go too far!" Kyle cautioned, and Tommy waved his *don't worry* wave and swam out a little farther. There was a boy for you, Kyle thought. Always testing his limits. Like me, when I was his age. Kyle lay down on the sand, his hands cupped behind his head. He had been coming to Perdido Beach since he was five years old. One of his first memories was of his father and mother dancing at the pavilion, to "Stardust" or some other old tune. He recalled a day when his father had taken him on every ride on the Miracle Mile: the Ferris wheel, roller coaster, mad mouse, tiltawhirl, scrambler, and octopus. He remembered his father's square brown face and white teeth, clenched in a grin as the mad mouse shot them heavenward. They had feasted on popcorn, cotton candy, candied apples, and corn dogs. They had thrown balls at milk jugs and rings at spindles and come away empty-handed but wiser in the ways of the Miracle Mile.

It had been one of the happiest days of his life.

After Kyle's mother had died of cancer eight years ago, his father had moved out to Arizona to live near his younger brother and his wife. A little over a week past, a midnight call had come from that town in Arizona, and through the static-hissing phone line the voice of Kyle's father had said, *I'm coming to visit you, son. Coming real soon. Me and your uncle Alan and aunt Patti Ann. I feel so much better now, son. My joints don't ache anymore. Oh, it's a wonderful life, this is! I sure do look forward to seeing my sweet grandboy . . .*

They had left their house the next morning and found another house in a town ten miles away. There were still some humans left, in the little towns. But some of them were crazy with terror, and others had made fortresses out of their homes. They put bars on the windows and slept in the daylight, surrounded by guns and barbed wire.

Kyle sat up and watched his son throwing himself against the waves, the glittering water splashing high. He saw himself out there; he hadn't changed so much, but the world had. The rachet gears of God's machine had slipped, and from here on out the territory was treacherous and uncharted.

He had decided he couldn't live behind bars and barbed wire. He couldn't live without the sun, or Perdido Beach in July, or without Tommy and Allie. If those things got hold of him—if they got hold of any of his family—then what would life be? A scuttling in the dark? A moan from gore-wet lips? He couldn't think about this anymore, and he blanked his mind: a trick he'd learned, out of necessity.

He watched his wife feeding the baby. The sight of Allie cradling the child made him needful; the need was on him before he could think about it. Allie was skinny, sure, but she looked good in her new swimsuit, and her hair was light brown and pretty in the reflected sunlight and her gray eyes had the shine of life in them again, for a little while. He said, "Allie?" and when she looked at him she saw the need in his face. He touched her shoulder, and she leaned over and kissed him on the lips. The kiss lingered, grew soft and wet and his tongue found hers. She smiled at him, her eyes hazy, and she put the child down on a beach towel.

Kyle didn't care if Tommy saw. They were beyond the need for privacy. A precious moment could not be turned aside. Kyle and Allie lay together under the yellow umbrella, their bodies damp and entwined, their hearts beating hard, and out in the waves Tommy pretended not to see and went diving for sand dollars. He found ten.

The sun was sinking. It made the Gulf of Mexico turn the color of fire, and way out past the shallows dolphins played.

"It'll be getting dark soon," Kyle said at last. The moon was coming out, a slice of silver against the east's darkening blue. "I've got somebody's car keys. Want to ride up to the Miracle Mile?"

Allie said that would be fine, and she held Hope against her breasts.

The wind had picked up. It blew stinging sand against their legs as they walked across the beach. Tommy stopped to throw a shell. "I got a skimmer, Dad!" he shouted.

In the room, Allie put on a pair of white shorts over her wet suit. Tommy wore a T-shirt with the computer image of a rock band on the front, and baggy orange cutoffs. Kyle dry-shaved with his razor, then dressed in a pair of khaki trousers and a dark blue pullover shirt. As he was lacing up his sneakers, he gave Tommy the car keys. "It's a blue Toyota. Tennessee tag. Why don't you go start her up?"

"You mean it? Really?"

"Why not?"

"Allll *right*!"

"Wait a minute!" Kyle cautioned before Tommy could leave. "Allie, why don't you go with him? I'll be up in a few minutes."

She frowned, reading his mood. "What's wrong?"

"Nothing. I just want to sit here and think. I'll be there by the time you get the car ready."

Allie took the baby, and she and Tommy went around to the parking lot. In the gathering dark, Kyle sat on the mattress and stared at the cracks in the wall. This was their honeymoon motel. It had once seemed like the grandest place on earth. Maybe it still was.

When Kyle opened the Toyota's door and Tommy slid into the back seat, he was wearing his poplin windbreaker, zipped up to his chest. He got behind the wheel, and he said, "Let's go see it."

Theirs was the only car that moved on the long, straight road called the Strip. Kyle turned on the headlights, but it wasn't too dark to see the destruction on either side of them.

"We ate there last summer," Tommy said, and pointed at a heap of rubble that used to be a Pizza Hut. They drove past T-Shirt City, the Shell Shack, and the Dixie Hot Shoppe, where a cook named Pee Wee used to make the best grouper sandwiches Kyle had ever eaten. All those places were dark hulks now. He kept going at a slow, steady speed. "Cruising the Strip," he and his buddies used to call it, when they came looking for girls and good times on spring break. His first roaring drunk was in a motel called the Surf's Inn. His first poker game had been played at Perdido Beach. He'd lost his first real fight behind a bar here, and ended up with a busted nose. He'd met the first girl he'd . . . well, there had been a lot of firsts at Perdido Beach.

God, there were ghosts here.

"Sun's almost gone," Tommy said.

Kyle turned the car to a place where they could watch the sunset over a motel's ruins. It was going down fast, the Gulf streaked with dark gold, orange, and purple. Allie's hand found her husband's; it was the hand with her wedding ring on it. The baby cried a little, and Kyle knew how she felt. The sun went away in a last scarlet flash, and then it was gone toward the other side of the world and the night was closing in.

"It was pretty, wasn't it?" Allie asked. "Sunsets are always so pretty at the beach."

Kyle started driving again, taking them to the Miracle Mile. His heart was beating hard, his palms damp on the wheel. Because there it was, the paradise of his memories. He pulled the car to the side of the road and stopped.

The last of the light glinted on the rails of the roller coaster. The Ferris wheel's cars were losing their paint, and rocked in the strengthening wind. Another casualty of Jolene was the mad mouse's maze of tracks. The long red roof of the Hang Out dance pavilion, the underside of which was painted with Day-Glo stars and comets, had been stripped to the boards, but the open-air building still stood. Within the smashed windows of the Beach Arcade, the pinball machines had been overturned. Metal rods dangled down from the Sky Needle, its foundation cracked. The concession stand that used to sell foot-long hot dogs and flavored snow cones had been flattened. The water slide had survived, though, and so had a few of the other mechanical rides. The merry-go-round—a beauty of carved, leaping lions and proud horses—remained almost unscathed. Fit for the junkyard were the haunted house and hall of mirrors, but the fun house with its entrance through a huge red grin was still there.

"We met here," Allie said. She was talking to Tommy. "Right over there." She pointed toward the roller coaster. "Your father was in line behind me. I was with Carol Akins and Denise McCarthy. When it came time for us to get on, I had to sit with him. I didn't know him. I was sixteen, and he was eighteen. He was staying at the Surf's Inn. That's where all the hoods stayed."

"I wasn't a hood," Kyle said.

"You were what a hood *was* then. You drank and smoked and you were looking for trouble." She stared at the roller coaster, and Kyle watched her face. "We went around four times."

"Five."

"Five," she recalled, and nodded. "The fifth time we rode in the front car. I was so scared I almost wet my pants."

"Aw, Mom!" Tommy said.

"He wrote me a letter. It came a week after I got home. There was sand in the envelope." She smiled, a faint smile, and Kyle had to look somewhere else. "He said he hoped we could see each other again. Do you remember that, Kyle?"

"Like yesterday," he answered.

"I dreamed about the Miracle Mile, for a long time after that. I dreamed we would be together. I was a silly thing when I was sixteen."

"You're still that way," Tommy said.

"Amen," Kyle added.

They sat there for a few more minutes, staring down the darkening length of the Miracle Mile. Many lives had crossed here, many had come and gone, but this place belonged to them. They knew it, in their hearts. It was theirs, forever. Their linked initials cut into a wooden railing of the Hang Out said so. It didn't matter that there might be ten thousand more initials carved in the pavilion; they had returned here, and where were the others?

The wind made the Ferris wheel's cars creak, but otherwise silence reigned. Kyle broke it. "We ought to go to the pier. That's what we ought to do."

The long fishing pier just past the Miracle Mile, where the bait used to be cut and reeled out every hour of the day and night. He and his father used to go fishing there, while his mother stretched out on a folding chair and read the forms from the dog track up the highway.

"I'm going to need some Solarcaine," Allie said as they drove past the Miracle Mile. "My arms are stinging."

"And I'm thirsty," Tommy said. "Can we get something to drink?"

"Sure. We'll find something."

The pier—LONGEST PIER ON THE PANHANDLE, the battered metal sign said—was a half mile past the amusement park. Kyle parked in front of it, in a deserted lot. A soft drink machine stood inside the pier's admission gate, but without electricity it was useless. Tommy got his arm up inside it and grasped a can but he couldn't pull it out. Kyle turned the machine over and tried to break it open. Its lock held, a last grip on civilization.

"Damn," Tommy said, and kicked the machine.

Next door to the pier, across the lot, was the rubble of what had been a seafood restaurant. The sign remained, a swordfish riding a surfboard. "Why don't we try over there?" Kyle asked, placing his hand on his son's shoulder. "Maybe we can find some cans. Allie, we'll be right back."

"I'll go with you."

"No," he said. "You wait on the pier."

Allie stood very still. In the deepening gloom, Kyle could only see the outline of her face. "I want to talk to Tommy," Kyle told her. She didn't move; it seemed to him she was holding her breath. "Man talk," he said.

Silence.

Finally, she spoke. "Come right back. Okay?"

"Okay."

"And don't step on a nail. Be careful. Okay?"

"We will be. Watch where you walk too." He guided Tommy toward the ruins, and the wind shrilled around them.

They were almost there when Tommy asked what he wanted to talk about. "Just some stuff," Kyle answered. He glanced back. Allie was on the pier, facing away from them. Maybe she was looking at the sea, or maybe at the Miracle Mile. It was hard to tell.

"I got too much sun. My neck's burning."

"Oh," Kyle said, "you'll be all right."

The stars were coming out. It was going to be a beautiful night. He kept his hand on Tommy's shoulder, and together they walked into the wreckage beneath the surfing swordfish. They kept going, over glass and planks, until Kyle had the remnant of a cinder block wall between them and Allie.

"Dad, how're we going to find anything in here? It's so dark."

"Hold it. See that? There beside your right foot? Is that a can?"

"I can't see it."

Kyle unzipped his windbreaker. "I think it is." A lump had lodged in his throat, and he could hardly speak. "Can you see it?"

"Where?"

Kyle placed one hand against the top of his son's head. It was perhaps the most difficult movement of flesh and bone he had ever made in his life. "Right there," he said, as he drew the .38 from his waistband with his other hand. *Click.*

"What was that, Dad?"

"You're my good boy," Kyle croaked, and he put the barrel against Tommy's skull.

No. This was the most difficult movement of flesh and bone.

A spasm of his finger on the trigger. A terrible *crack* that left his eardrums ringing.

It was done.

Tommy slid down, and Kyle wiped his hand on the leg of his trousers.

Oh Jesus, he thought. A sense of panic swelled inside him. *Oh Jesus, I should've found him something to drink before I did it.*

He staggered, tripped over a pile of boards and cinder blocks and went down on his knees in the dark, the after sound of the shot still echoing. *My God, he died thirsty. Oh my God, I just killed my son.* He shivered and moaned, sickness burning in his stomach. It came to him that he might have only wounded the boy, and Tommy might be lying there in agony. "Tommy?" he said. "Can you hear me?" No, no; he'd shot the boy right in the back of the head, just as he'd planned. If Tommy wasn't dead, he was dying and he knew nothing. It had been fast and unexpected and Tommy hadn't had a chance to even think about death.

"Forgive me," Kyle whispered, tears streaking down his face. "Please forgive me."

It took him a while to find the strength to stand. He put the pistol away and zipped his windbreaker up again, and then he wiped his face and left the ruins where his son's body lay. Kyle walked toward the pier, where Allie stood with the baby in the deep purple dark.

"Kyle?" she called before he reached her.

"Yes."

"I heard a noise."

"Some glass broke. It's all right."

"Where's Tommy, Kyle?"

"He'll be here in a few minutes," Kyle said, and he stopped in front of her. He could feel the sea moving below him, amid the pier's concrete pilings. "Why don't we walk to the end?"

Allie didn't speak. Hope was sleeping, her head against Allie's shoulder.

Kyle looked up at the sky full of stars and the silver slice of moon. "We used to come out here together. Remember?"

She didn't answer.

"We used to come out and watch the fishermen at night. I asked you to marry me at the end of the pier. Do you remember?"

"Yes." A quiet voice.

"Then when you said yes I jumped off. Remember that?"

"I thought you were crazy," Allie said.

"I was. I am. Always will be."

He saw her tremble, violently. "Tommy?" she called into the night. "Tommy, come on now!"

"Walk with me. All right?"

"I can't . . . I can't . . . think, Kyle. I can't . . ."

Kyle took her hand. Her fingers were cold. "There's nothing to think about. Everything's under control. Do you understand?"

"We can . . . stay right here," she said. "Right here. It's safe here."

"There's only one place that's safe," Kyle said. "It's not here."

"*Tommy*?" she called, and her voice broke.

"Walk with me. Please." He gripped her hand tighter. She went with him.

Jolene had bitten off the last forty feet of the pier. It ended on a jagged edge, and below them the Gulf surged against the pilings. Kyle put his arm around his wife and kissed her cheek. Her skin was hot and damp. She leaned her head against his shoulder, as Hope's head was against her own. Kyle unzipped his windbreaker.

"It was a good day, wasn't it?" he asked her, and she nodded.

The wind was in their faces, coming in hard off the sea. "I love you," Kyle said.

"I love you," she answered.

68

"Are you cold?"

"Yes."

He gave her his windbreaker, and zipped it up around her shoulders and the baby. "Look at those stars!" he said. "You can't see so many stars anywhere else but the beach, can you?"

She shook her head.

Kyle kissed her temple and put a bullet into it.

Then he let her go.

Allie and the baby fell off the pier. Kyle watched her body go down and splash into the Gulf. The waves picked her up, closed over her, turned her on her stomach and made her hair float like an opening fan. Kyle looked up at the sky. He took a deep breath, cocked the pistol again and put the barrel into his mouth, pointed upward toward his brain.

God forgive me there is no Hell there is no—

He heard a low humming sound. The noise, he realized, of machinery at work.

Lights came on, a bright shock in the sky. The stars faded. Multicolored reflections scrawled across the moving waves.

Music. The sound of a distant pipe organ.

Kyle turned around, his bones freezing.

The Miracle Mile.

The Miracle Mile was coming to life.

Lights rimmed the Ferris wheel and the roller coaster's rails. Floods glared over the Super Water Slide. The merry-go-round was lit up like a birthday cake. A spotlight had been pointed upward, and combed the night above the Miracle Mile like a call to celebration.

Kyle's finger was on the trigger. He was ready.

The Ferris wheel began to turn: a slow, groaning process. He could see figures in the gondolas. The center track of the roller coaster started moving with a clanking of gears, and then the roller coaster cars were cranked up to the top of the first incline. There were people in the cars. No, not people. Not human beings. Them.

They had taken over the Miracle Mile.

Kyle heard them scream with delight as the roller coaster's cars went over the incline like a long, writhing snake.

The merry-go-round was turning. The pipe organ music, a scratchy recording, was being played from speakers at the carousel's center. Kyle watched the riders going around, and he pulled the pistol's barrel from his mouth. Light bulbs had blinked on in the Hang Out, and now the sound of rock music spilled out from a jukebox. Kyle could see them in the pavilion, a mass of them pressed together and dancing at the edge of the sea.

They had taken everything. The night, the cities, the towns, freedom, the law, the world.

And now the Miracle Mile.

Kyle grinned savagely, as tears ran down his cheeks.

The roller coaster rocketed around. The Ferris wheel was turning faster.

They had hooked up generators, of course, there in the amusement park. They'd gotten gasoline to run the generators from a gas station on the Strip.

You could make bombs out of gasoline and bottles.

Find those generators. Pull the plug on the Miracle Mile.

He had four bullets in the gun. The extras had been in case he screwed up and wounded instead of killed. Four bullets. The car keys had been in the windbreaker. *Sleep well, my darling*, he thought.

I will be joining you.

But not yet. Not yet.

Maybe he could find a way to make the roller coaster's cars jump the tracks. Maybe he could blow up the Hang Out, with all of them mashed up together inside. They would make a lovely bonfire, on this starry summer night. He gritted his teeth, his guts full of rage. They might take the world, but they would not take his family. And they would pay for taking the Miracle Mile, if he could do anything about it.

He was insane now. He knew it. But the instant of knowing was pulled away from him like Allie's body in the waves, and he gripped the pistol hard and took the first step back along the pier toward shore.

Careful. Keep to the darkness. Don't let them see you. Don't let them smell you.

Screams and laughter soared over the Miracle Mile, as a solitary figure walked back with a gun in his hand and flames in his mind.

It came to Kyle that his vacation was over.

STEVE RASNIC TEM

Taking Down the Tree

ALTHOUGH HE HAS only published one novel (*Excavation* in 1987), Steve Rasnic Tem has carved an impressive niche for himself as a prolific short story writer.

He received his Masters in Creative Writing at Colorado State University, and currently lives in Denver with his wife, the writer Melanie Tem.

Tem was the winner of the 1988 British Fantasy Award for his story "Leaks", and his recent fiction has appeared in *MetaHorror, Dark at Heart, In Dreams, Narrow Houses, The Mammoth Book of Vampires, Hottest Blood, The Dedalus Book of Femmes Fatales, The Ultimate Frankenstein, The Ultimate Dracula, The Year's Best Horror Stories* and the previous two volumes of *Best New Horror,* amongst others.

His stories have been collected in the chapbooks *Fairytales, Celestial Inventory, Absences: Charlie Goode's Ghosts* and the French volume *Ombres sur la route.*

An unusual Christmas story, "Taking Down the Tree"—like the other short shorts in this book—has quite a twist in the tale.

S EVEN DAYS AFTER CHRISTMAS AND THE great tree filling the parlor had lost its glory. Nick had stopped watering it three days before Christmas. The branches had turned a drooping grayish-green, so that ornaments were escaping the tree, dropping to the rug with a shower of needles, rolling under chairs where they'd be forgotten until spring. The ornaments themselves seemed to need nourishment during the days following Christmas: brightly colored glass balls faded, metal angels tarnished, garlands unraveled before his eyes. Christmas was over.

The week following Christmas day was the saddest part of the year. Nick knew his family shared this sentiment, but they would never say so. They were as determined as he not to spoil the holiday. His son Joseph had spent the last week lying on his stomach beside the tree, playing with the bright red train set Nick had scoured the city to find. Nick hadn't minded the trouble—the boy had behaved perfectly this year. Joseph was small for eight, which pleased Nick. Compact and easy to carry. His green pajamas matched his emerald eyes.

Carrie was a bit more substantial—plump rosy cheeks, a satisfying armful. He enjoyed holding her on his lap for the Christmas Eve reading of "The Night Before Christmas."

Carrie looked up at him now from her usual seat by the fireplace. She smiled thinly and played with the doll which looked exactly like her. Her present hadn't been difficult to find. All the dolls he'd ever seen looked like her.

"Choo! Choo choo!" Joseph looked up at Nick and laughed. "Choo choo!" he cried again. Tears were rolling down the perfect little boy's cheeks.

"I know, son, I understand," Nick said, as he knew he was supposed to say. But he didn't really understand at all. Nick had a vague impression that something was wrong, but he wasn't sure what.

"Choo choo!" Joseph cried more loudly, as if in anger. Nick wasn't sure if this was the sound of laughter or tears.

He left the parlor and went to the kitchen to find his wife. She stood by the kitchen sink, her hands like dead fish in water so soap-filled it resembled cream. She hummed softly a medley of Christmas carols, their individual pieces so brief Nick could not distinguish one from another. He lifted her hands from the water. She stared at him and smiled. Her hands were cracked, her fingers wrinkled incredibly. Nick looked around the kitchen: the turkey carcass on the counter, half-devoured and flyspecked, the stacks of yellowed dishes, the open jars of mayonnaise and salad dressing, the rock-hard platter of stuffing. "Oh, Mary," he said. "Christmas is over for another year." She nodded sadly and began humming her tunes again, so disjointed now he was sure she hummed them backwards.

Nick went into the dining room and clapped his hands loudly three times. "Christmas is over! Christmas is over!" he cried. He could hear his children wailing in the parlor. The cries of children made a very unpleasant song.

He could hear his wife sobbing to herself in the kitchen, another sad sound. But Christmas was over. There was nothing he could do. "I'm sorry!" he called. "I'm sorry! But we must put all our Christmas things away!"

Nick brought the empty boxes down from the attic. He cajoled his family into helping him remove the lights and decorations from the tree—carefully, wrapping each piece in tissue and nesting it in its proper box.

He carried the boxes up into the dark attic—an attic so large the boxes filled only one tiny corner, so large he sometimes got lost in it. When that was done he took the naked tree out to the back and shoved it into his wood-chipping machine, grinding it into a fine sawdust mulch for his rose bushes.

His family waited for him to tell them what to do.

He showed them the holiday cards that needed to be removed from the window frames, the wreaths over doorways, the special table cloth embroidered in holiday motifs that needed to be folded.

Nick was closing and taping a box when Carrie's gray kitten strode by. He reached down and lifted the cat, pulled off its head, removed its legs, and threw the mass into the top of the box. He closed the flaps and taped them.

"Bye, kitty," Carrie said softly.

They all followed him as he carried the last box to the attic. Carrie walked close, whispering to her kitten inside. Joseph marched, now and then shouting "Choo! Choo!" at the top of his lungs. Mary trailed, blank-faced, taking the steps with exaggerated care.

In the attic it was cold and empty and Nick felt as if he were about to be devoured by the dark. He wanted to hurry, to put this Christmas behind him. So he grabbed Mary more roughly than he intended, broke her into two and then into four and then into eight and filled a bright blue sack with her, her blonde hair floating to the top.

Carrie wanted to be with her cat and, after arguing about how there wasn't room, the indulgent father gave in, and bent and flattened her until she fit, but barely.

"Choo! Choo!" Joseph cried. "Choo! Choo!"

"Always the trouble maker, Joseph. You do this every year!"

"Choo! Choo!" Joseph screamed and ran.

But it was all a game. After chasing him and catching him, Nick jerked and ripped his little boy into so many pieces that Nick was quite sure Joseph would look very different come Christmas of next year.

"Choo choo," Nick said softly to the last box of Christmas, before shoving it back into the darkest corner he could find.

DOUGLAS CLEGG

Where Flies Are Born

DOUGLAS CLEGG's early career included being an underwear model, a busker in Paris in the early 1980s, a magazine features writer and a professional cowboy on the rodeo circuit. He wrote his first novel, *Goat Dance*, in 1987 and it was published two years later to excellent reviews. He has been a full-time novelist since, although, as he reveals, "I still manage to rope the dogies now and then; and I still swim daily, study yoga and shadow box."

A resident of Southern California, he has also found time to write four more books—*Breeder, Neverland, You Come When I Call You* and *The Dark of the Eye*—and his short story, "People Who Love Life", was reprinted (from *Scream Factory* magazine) in the anthology *Quick Chills II: The Best of the Small Press*.

"Where Flies Are Born" is only the author's second published short story. We await the rest of his career with what Lovecraft used to call "dread suspense".

THE TRAIN STOPPED SUDDENLY, AND ELLEN sat there and watched her son fill in the coloring book with the three crayolas left to him: aquamarine, burnt sienna, and silver. She was doing this for him: she could put up with Frank and his tirades and possessiveness, but not when he tried to hurt Joey. No. She would make sure that Joey had a better life. Ellen turned to the crossword puzzle in the back of the magazine section to pass the time. She tried not to think of what they'd left behind. She was a patient woman, and so it didn't annoy her that it was another hour before anyone told the passengers that it would be a three hour stop, or more. *Or more*, translating into six hours. Then her patience wore thin and Joey was whining. The problem with the train, it soon became apparent, was one which would require disembarking. The town, if it could be called that, was a quarter mile ahead, and so they would be put up somewhere for the night. So this was to be their Great Escape. February third in a mountain town at thirty below. Frank would find them for sure; only a day's journey from Springfield. Frank would hunt them down, as he'd done last time, and bring them back to his little castle and she would make it okay for another five years before she went crazy again and had to run. *No.* She would make sure he wouldn't hurt Joey. She would kill him first. She would, with her bare hands, stop him from ever touching their son again.

Joey said, "Can't we just stay on the train? It's cold out there."

"You'll live," she said, bringing out the overnight case and following in a line with the other passengers out of the car. They trudged along the snowy tracks to the short strip of junction, where each was directed to a different motel or private house.

"I wanted a motel," she told the conductor. She and Joey were to be overnight guests of the Neesons', a farm family. "This isn't what I paid for," she said, "it's not what I expected at all."

"You can sleep in the station, you like," the man said, but she passed on that after looking around the filthy room with its greasy benches. "Anyway, the Neesons run a bed-and-breakfast, so you'll do fine there."

The Nessons arrived shortly in a four-wheel drive, looking just past the curve of middle age, tooth-rotted, with *country* indelibly sprayed across their grins and friendly winks. Mama Neeson, in her late fifties, spoke of the snow, of their warm house "where we'll all be safe as kittens in a minute," of the soup she'd been making. Papa Neeson was older (*old enough to be my father*, Ellen thought) and balder, eyes of a rodent, face of a baby-left-too-long-in-bathwater. Mama Neeson cooed over Joey, who was already asleep. *Damn you, Joey, for abandoning me to Neeson-talk.* Papa Neeson spoke of the snowfall and the roads. Ellen said very little, other than to thank them for putting her up.

"Our pleasure," Mama Neeson said, "the little ones will love the company."

"You have children?" Ellen winced at her inflection. She didn't *mean* it to sound as if Mama Neeson was too old to have what could be called "little ones."

"Adopted, you could say," Papa Neeson grumbled, "Mama, she loves kids, can't get enough of them, you get the instinct, you see, the sniffs for babies and you got to have them whether your body gives 'em up or not."

Ellen, embarrassed for his wife, shifted uncomfortably in the seat. What a rude man. This was what Frank would be like, under the skin, talking about women and their "sniffs," their "hankerings," Poor Mama Neeson, a houseful of babies and *this man.*

"I have three little ones," she said, "all under nine. How old's yours?"

"Six."

"He's an angel. Papa, ain't he just a little angel sent down from heaven?"

Papa Neeson glanced over to Joey, curled up in a ball against Ellen's side, "don't say much, do he?"

The landscape was white and black; Ellen watched for ice patches in the road, but they went over it all smoothly. Woods rose up suddenly, parting for an empty flat stretch of land. They drove down a fenced road, snow piled all the way to the top of the fenceposts. Then, as they turned up another road, she saw the large white farmhouse, with a barn behind. *We better not be sleeping in the barn.*

Mama Neeson sighed, "hope they're in bed. Put them to bed hours ago, but you know how they romp . . ."

"They love to romp," Papa Neeson said.

The bed was large and she and Joey sank into it as soon as they had the door closed behind them. Ellen was too tired to think, and Joey was still dreaming. Sleep came quickly, and was black and white, full or snowdrifts. She awoke, thirsty, before dawn. She was half-asleep, but lifted her head towards the window: the sound of animals crunching in the snow outside. She looked out—had to open the window because of the frost on the pane. A hazy purple light brushed across the whiteness of the hills—the sun was somewhere rising beyond the treetops. A large brown bear sniffed along the porch rail. Bears should've frightened her, but this one seemed friendly and stupid, as it lumbered along in the tugging snow, nostrils wiggling. Sniffing the air; Mama Neeson would be up—four thirty—frying bacon, flipping hotcakes on the griddle, buttering toast. Country Mama.

77

The little ones would rise from their quilts and trundle beds, ready to go out and milk cows or some such farm thing, and Papa Neeson would get out his shotgun to scare off the bear that came sniffing. She remembered Papa's phrase: "the sniffs for babies," and it gave her a discomforting thought about the bear.

She lay back on the bed, stroking Joey's fine hair, with this thought in her mind of the bear sniffing for the babies, when she saw a housefly circle above her head; then, another, coming from some corner of the room, joining its mate. Three more arrived. Finally, she was restless to swat them. She got out of bed and went to her overnight bag for hairspray. This was her favorite method of disposing of houseflies. She shook the can, and then sprayed in the direction of the (count them: nine) fat black houseflies. They buzzed in curves of infinity. In a minute, they began dropping, one by one, to the rug. Ellen enjoyed taking her boots and slapping each fly into the next life.

Her dry throat and heavy bladder sent her out to the hallway. Feeling along the wall for the light switch or the door to the bathroom—whichever came first. When she found the switch, she flicked it up, and a single unadorned bulb hummed into dull light.

A little girl stood at the end of the hall, too old for the diaper she wore; her stringy hair falling wildly almost to her feet; her skin bruised in several places—particularly around her mouth, which was swollen on the upper lip. In her small pudgy fingers was a length of thread. Ellen was so shocked by this sight that she could not say a word—the girl was only seven or so, and what her appearance indicated about the Neesons . . .

Papa Neeson was like Frank. Likes to beat people. Likes to beat children. Joey and his black eyes, this girl and her bruised face. I could kill them both.

The little girl's eyes crinkled up as if she were about to cry, wrinkled her forehead and nose, parted her swollen lips.

From the black and white canyon of her mouth: a fat green fly crawled the length of her lower lip, and then flew toward the light bulb above Ellen's head.

Later, when the sun was up, and the snow outside her window was blinding, Ellen knew she must've been half-dreaming, or perhaps it was a trick that the children played—for she'd seen all of them, the two-year-old, the five-year-old, and the girl. The boys had trooped out from the shadows of the hall. All wearing the filthy diapers, all bruised from beatings or worse. The only difference with the two younger boys was they had not yet torn the thread that had been used to sew their mouths and eyes and ears and nostrils closed. Such child abuse was beyond imagining. Ellen had seen them only briefly, and afterwards wondered if perhaps she hadn't *seen* wrong. But it was a dream, a very bad one, because the little girl had flicked the light off again. When Ellen reached to turn it back on, they had retreated into the shadows and the feeling of a surreal waking state came upon her. *The Neesons could not possibly be this evil.* With the light on, and her vision readjusting from the darkness, she saw only houseflies sweeping motes of dust through the heavy air.

At breakfast, Joey devoured his scrambled eggs like he hadn't eaten in days; Ellen had to admit they tasted better than she'd had before. "You live close to the earth," Papa Neeson said, "and it gives up its treasures."

Joey said, "Eggs come from chickens."

"Chickens come from eggs," Papa Neeson laughed, "and eggs are the beginning of all life. But we all gather our life from the earth, boy. You city folks don't feel it because you're removed. Out here, well, we get it under our fingernails, birth, death, and what comes in between."

"You're something of a philosopher," Ellen said, trying to hide her uneasiness. The image of the children still in her head, like a half-remembered dream. She was eager to get on her way, because that dream was beginning to seem more real. She had spent a half-hour in the shower trying to talk herself out of having seen the children and what had been done to them: then, ten minutes drying off, positive that she had seen what she'd seen. It was Frank's legacy: he had taught her to doubt what was right before her eyes. She wondered if Papa Neeson performed darker needlework on his babies.

"I'm a realist," Papa Neeson said. His eyes were bright and kind—it shocked her to look into them and think about what he might/might not have done.

Mama Neeson, sinking the last skillet into a washtub next to the stove, turned and said, "Papa just has a talent for making things work, Missus, for putting two and two together. That's how he grows, and that's how he gathers. Why if it weren't for him, where would my children be?"

"Where are they?" Joey asked.

Ellen, after her dream slash hallucination slash mind-your-own-business, was a bit apprehensive. She would be happy not to meet Mama Neeson's brood at all. "We have to get back to the train," she said. "They said by eleven."

Papa Neeson raised his eyebrows in an aside to his wife. "I saw some flies at the windows," he said. "They been bad again."

Mama Neeson shrugged her broad shoulders. "They got to let them out at times or they'd be bursting, now, wouldn't they. Must tickle something awful." She wiped her dripping hands on the flowerprint apron, back and forth like she could never get dry enough. Ellen saw a shining in the old woman's eyes like tears and hurt.

Joey clanked his fork on his plate; Ellen felt a lump in her throat, and imaginary spiders and flies crawling up the back of her neck. Something in the atmosphere had changed, and she didn't want to spend one more minute in this house with these people.

Joey clapped a fly between his hands, catching it mid-air.

"Mama's sorry you didn't see the kids," Papa Neeson said, steering over a slick patch on the newly plowed road.

"But you're not." Ellen said. She was feeling brave. She hated this man like she hated Frank. Maybe she'd report him to some child welfare agency when she got back to the train station. She could see herself killing this man.

"No," Papa Neeson nodded. "I'm not. Mama, she don't understand about other people, but I do."

"Well, I saw them. All three. What you do to them."

Papa Neeson sighed, pulling over and parking at the side of the road. "You don't understand. Don't know if I should waste my breath."

Joey was in the backseat, bundled up in blankets. He yawned, "why we stopping?"

Ellen directed him to turn around and sit quietly. He was a good boy. "I have a husband who hits children, too."

Papa Neeson snapped, "I don't hit the kids, lady, and how dare you think I do, why you can just get out of my car right now if that's your attitude."

"I told you, I saw them," she said defiantly.

"You see the threads?"

Ellen could barely stand his smug attitude.

"You see 'em? You know *why* my kids look like that?"

Ellen reached for the door handle. She was going to get out. Fucking country people and their torture masked as discipline. Men, how she hated their power trips. Blood was boiling now; she was capable of anything, like two days ago when she took the baseball bat and slammed it against Frank's chest, hearing ribs cracking. She was not going to let a man hurt her child like that. Never again. The rage was rising up inside her the way it had only done twice in her life before, both times with Frank, both times protecting Joey.

Papa Neeson reached out and grabbed her wrist.

"*Don't hold me like that,*" she snarled.

He let go.

Papa Neeson began crying, pressing his head into the steering wheel. "She just wanted them so bad, I had to go dig 'em up. I love her so much, and I didn't want her to die from hurting, so I just dig 'em up and I figured out what to do and did it."

When he calmed, he sat back up, looking straight ahead. "We better get to the junction. Train'll be ready. You got your life moving ahead with it, don't you?"

She said, "tell me about your children. What's wrong with them?"

He looked her straight in the eyes, making her flinch because of his intensity. "Nothing, except they been dead for a good twenty to thirty years now, and my wife, she loves 'em like they're her own. I dig 'em up, see, I thought she was gonna die from grief not having none of her own, and I figured it out, you know, about the maggots and the flies, how they make things move if you put enough of 'em inside the bodies. I didn't count on 'em lasting this long, but what if they do? What if they *do*, lady? Mama, she loves those babies. We're only humans, lady, and humans need to hold babies, they need to love something other than themselves, don't they? Don't you? You got your boy, you know how much that's worth? Love beyond choosing, ain't it? Love that don't die. You know what it's like to hug a child when you never got to hug one before? So I figured and I figured some more, and I thought about what makes things live, how do we know something's alive, and I figured, when it moves it's alive, and when it don't move, it's dead. So Mama, I had her sew the flies in, but they keep laying eggs and more and more, and the kids, they got the minds of flies, and sometimes they rip out the threads, so sometimes flies get out, but it's a tiny price, ain't it, lady? When you need to love little ones, and you ain't got none, it's a tiny price, a day in hell's all, but then sunshine and children and love, lady, ain't it worth that?"

Ellen had a migraine by the time Papa Neeson dropped them off down at the junction. She barked at Joey. Apologized for it. Bought him a Pepsi from the machine by the restroom. People were boarding the train. She went to the restroom to wipe cold water across her face—made Joey promise to stand outside it and not go anywhere. The mirror in the bathroom was warped, and she thought she looked stunning: brown eyes circled with sleeplessness, the throbbing vein to the left side of her forehead, the dry, cracked lips. She thought of the threads, of the children tugging at them, popping them out to let the flies go. Ran a finger over her lips, imagining Mama Neeson taking her needle and thread, breaking the skin with tiny holes. Ears, nostrils, eyes, mouth, other openings, other places where flies could escape. Flies and life, sewn up into the bodies of dead children, buried by other grieving parents, brought back by the country folks who ran the bed-and-breakfast, and who spoke of children that no one ever saw much of.

And when they did . . .

So here was Ellen's last happy image in the mountain town she and her son were briefly stranded in:

Mama Neeson kissing the bruised cheek of her little girl, tears in her squinty eyes, tears of joy for having children to love.

Behind her, someone opened the door.

Stood there.

Waiting for her to turn around.

"Look who I found," Frank said, dragging Joey behind him into the women's room.

Two weeks later, she was on the train again, with Joey, but it was better weather—snow was melting, the sun was exhaustingly bright, and she got off at the junction because she wanted to be there. *Frank is dead.* She could think it. She could remember the feel of the knife in her hands. No jury would convict her. She had been defending herself. Defending her son. Frank had come at Joey with his own toy dump truck. She had grabbed the carving knife—as she'd been planning to do since Frank had hauled them back to Springfield. She had gone with the knowledge of what she would have to do to keep Frank out of her little boy's life forever. Then, she had just waited for his temper to flare. She kept the knife with her, and when she saw him slamming the truck against Joey's scalp, she let the boiling blood and rage take her down with them. The blade went in hard, and she thought it would break when it hit bone. But she twisted it until Frank dropped the dump truck, and then she scraped it down like she was deboning a chicken.

All for Joey.

She lifted him in her arms as she stepped off the train, careful on the concrete because there was still some ice. Joey, wrapped in a blanket, sunglasses on his face, "sleeping," she told the nice lady who had been sitting across from them; Ellen, also wearing sunglasses and too much make-up, a scarf around her head, a heavy wool sweater around her shoulders, exhausted and determined.

Joey's not dead. Not really.

It hadn't been hard to track down the Neesons. She had called them before she got on the train, and they were not surprised to hear from her. "It happens this way," Mama Neeson told her, "our calling."

Ellen was not sure what to make of that comment, but she was so tired and confused that she let it go. Later, she might think that something of the Neeson's had perhaps rubbed off on her and her son. That, perhaps, just *meeting* them might be like inviting something into life that hadn't been considered before. *Something under your fingernails.*

She carried Joey to the payphone and dropped a quarter in. Joey was not waking up. She did not have to cry anymore. She told herself that, and was comforted. Things change, people move on, but some things could stay as they were. Good things.

"Mr Neeson?"

"You're here already?" he asked. He sounded relieved.

"I took an early train."

"Mama's still asleep. She was up all night. Worries, you know. Upset for you."

"Well . . ."

"I'll be down there in a few minutes, then," he said, adding, "you're sure this is what you want?"

"Love beyond choosing," she reminded him. A spool of white thread fell out from Joey's curled hands, bouncing once, twice, on the ground, unraveling as it rolled.

ROGER JOHNSON

Love, Death and the Maiden

ROGER JOHNSON is a member of the Baker Street Irregulars, the Sherlock Holmes Society of London, and other Holmesian groups. A contributor to *The Sherlock Holmes Journal* and *Baker Street Miscellanea*, amongst others, he began contributing ghost stories ten years ago to Rosemary Pardoe's "Haunted Library" publications.

Since then his fiction has appeared in *Ghosts & Scholars*, *A Graven Image*, *Saints & Relics*, *Dark Dreams*, *Tales After Dark*, *Spectral Tales*, *Chillers for Christmas*, *Mystery for Christmas*, *Tales of Witchcraft*, two volumes of *The Mammoth Book of Ghost Stories*, and Karl Edward Wagner's *The Year's Best Horror Stories* series.

The story which follows was originally called "Mädelein"; however, after it was published, the author decided that the title it appears under here suited it perfectly, as you're about to discover . . .

I 'M GETTING OLD. IT WAS SOMETHING of a shock to realise recently that it's over fifty years since Valerie Beddoes died.

Fifty years. Just another unsolved murder case. And of course events took place shortly afterwards that rather pushed a single death to the back of the public mind. So why raise the matter now? Well, facts that I ought to have known about long ago have at last come to my notice and made some sort of sense of the affair. Some sort. If I'm right, then the whole business is even stranger than we'd thought back in 1939.

The relationship that Valerie and I shared is difficult to define. It's such a tedious cliché to say that we were "just good friends", but really that's about the truth of it. It was only after we'd said goodbye for the last time that some inkling came to me of why I'd been able to maintain a strong friendship with such a very good-looking girl without a sexual element in the relationship. We were—well, not like sister and brother, perhaps, but like close cousins.

And Valerie was an exceptionally attractive creature. Tall, shapely, blue-eyed and blonde—the Aryan fallacy taken to a perfect extreme, but one could hardly blame her for the looks she'd inherited from her Saxon forebears. And since she was intelligent and well-educated, I think that occasionally she found her beauty something of a disadvantage. Strangely, as it seemed to me then (at twenty-two I was naive in many ways, but then my generation was like that), she found it hardest to get other women to take her seriously. Margaret Pennethorne, for instance.

Playgoers under fifty are unlikely to know of Margaret Pennethorne. Even those familiar with her work may not recognise the name, since she didn't use it professionally, but she had a considerable reputation in the thirties and forties for strong historical dramas written under the pseudonym of Richard Border. *The Stone Queen* was the one that made her reputation—about Eleanor of Aquitaine—and although it hasn't been performed for years that particular play is still remembered because it also made the reputation of the young Celia Hesketh, who played Eleanor.

I was not a regular theatregoer in 1938, but I had recently seen the revival of *The Stone Queen* at the Arcadian Theatre, and when my cousin Jack Fellowes told me that he'd been invited to a party at which Richard Border was to be present I begged him to take me along. I wondered at the time why his agreement seemed to hide a sort of secret amusement. When he pointed "Richard Border" out to me the reason became clear—at least, once I'd stopped looking for a man who might perhaps have been concealed in the corner behind the two striking-looking women who were chatting so earnestly together.

Somehow I got myself introduced to the author of *The Stone*

Queen. Striking? Yes, she was, if not in any obvious way. Aged about forty, I suppose, dark-haired and with an expression of rather disconcerting amusement in her eyes. She was some inches shorter than her companion, but gave the impression of being the bigger personality. I found her then rather overwhelming. The companion, on the other hand . . .

The companion was introduced to me as "my secretary, Valerie Beddoes".

Well, you already have some idea of what Valerie looked like. After we three had chatted for a while about Queen Eleanor and her brood of kings, and my halting contributions had persuaded Miss Pennethorne that I wasn't just a celebrity-seeker, I was very pleased when Valerie took my arm and said, "Meg wants to have a word with Dolly Tappan about the design for her next play. Come along—we'll go and get another drink."

I remember trying to conceal my appraisal of her face and figure, blushing when I realised that she had caught me out. I remember joining in her delighted laughter as she said, "Like Cecily, I am very fond of being looked at. Well, by nice people, anyway. What about that drink?"

I had recently experienced a messy love affair, ending in a broken engagement. Will it surprise you to learn that I saw the lovely Valerie Beddoes not as a possible lover but as a sympathetic friend who would listen to my troubles? It seemed strange to me only in retrospect, after Jack and I had left the party, when there was only Valerie's picture in my mind. There was something about her presence that didn't allow thoughts of a sexual relationship. Odd. The very idea just didn't occur to me while we were together.

We became, as I've said, good friends. There were several interests that we shared: the music of Mozart, Thackeray's novels—other things too, including, of course, the plays of Richard Border. I visited Border's—Margaret Pennethorne's—house at Bray several times, though it was an experience that never quite pleased me because of the seemingly permanent sardonic amusement in Miss Pennethorne's eyes. She was always friendly, in a way that suggested some underlying motive, and I couldn't quite get used to the rather patronising way she would say, "I have work to do, I'm afraid. Val, why don't you two children settle down in the sitting-room and chat?"

Once she was out of the way, though, and we could hear the faint click of her typewriter through the study door, I felt more at ease. Valerie would produce cigarettes and perhaps a bottle of sherry, then she would sprawl elegantly on the couch while I took one of the big armchairs or walked restlessly about. I was young and full of serious ideas. Valerie, actually a year or two younger than I, somehow seemed more mature. She was certainly a wise conversationalist, able to listen and comment seriously on my profound political thoughts. I like to think that she was fond of me. I know that I've had no such good friends since.

We shared an interest in certain subjects, as I've indicated, but her near-obsession with the supernatural was something that quite escaped me. She had little time for ghost stories of the sort that appeared in the lurid magazines, but was fascinated (the word has lost most of its true magical force these days) by supposedly true accounts of the occult and bizarre. Perhaps it was this streak that made it inevitable that, at Margaret Pennethorne's request, Valerie should go to central Europe in search of the Bloody Countess of the Carpathians.

At that time I knew nothing of the Countess Elisabeth Bathory, though I have learned much in recent months. I was more concerned about my friend's safety in the uneasy atmosphere of a Europe that had so recently seen—how easily the word came to mind!—*Anschluss*. It was February 1939, and there was much to worry about for a sober-minded young idealist.

None of this seemed to matter to Valerie, though, nor to Margaret Pennethorne. I remember clearly how the news was broken to me when I called at the house in Bray, full of gloomy thoughts about the instability of the Munich agreement and the weakness of Neville Chamberlain. These ideas were quickly driven from me by Valerie's delighted smile and her words. "Darling! isn't it marvellous? Meg's got a new play on the boil, about a Hungarian vampire, and it's going to be even bigger than *The Stone Queen*—and I'm to do all the first-hand research for it!"

"A vampire?" I said cautiously. "Isn't that a bit outside her usual field?"

Margaret herself broke in here. The twinkle in her eyes seemed more metallic as she spoke: "Not really. I've always concentrated on the historical stuff—Eleanor, Barbarossa, Theodora—and this is really in the same vein. For heavens' sake, boy, I really believe you've never heard of Elisabeth Bathory!"

"Bathory? It—er—well, no . . ."

If there was something not quite sincere about the chuckle that greeted my reply, Valerie seemed not to notice. She took my arm and said, "I'll tell you about it. Come on. I've got coffee on the boil—and I'm sure Meg wants to be shot of us."

Still smiling, Margaret nodded and left. That smile seemed to be fixed onto her face.

(Elisabeth Bathory was a monster. Not physically, for she was held to be very beautiful, but mentally and spiritually. Her family, one of the most noble in eastern Europe, had intermarried for generations, and become marked by epilepsy, hereditary syphilis and madness. The madness erupted in this slim, dark, lovely woman.)

"I leave in two days' time," said Valerie at last. "Meg's fixed it all up. Boat-train to Dover, then Calais, Paris and across to Buda-Pesth. It'll be wonderful to get away—to be working on my own."

"Two *days*? That's a bit— "

"Oh, I'll miss you, of course, and a few other friends, but it's such an opportunity! And, you know— " (she lowered her voice a little) "—I shall be so glad just to get away from Meg for a while." She tossed a cigarette over to me, smiling at my expression. "I know it's sudden, but I think Meg's actually had the idea in mind for some time. You know how she likes to keep her work to herself until she's quite sure of it."

"Two days," I said again.

"This really will be big, you know. I told her I thought that the life of the Bloody Countess would make a stunning exercise in *Grand Guignol*. She said, 'Never mind *Grand Guignol*. This will be positively *Gross Guignol*.'"

(Elisabeth Bathory was a sadist. She is believed to have been directly responsible for the murders of over 650 young women, having them cut, slashed or burned so that their blood flowed. She would bathe in the blood of virgins in the belief that it would prolong her youth and beauty.)

"You're going alone? I suppose Margaret will provide the money, but how will you manage otherwise?"

"I'll be safe enough. Hungary may be rather unsettled, but I'm hoping also to get into Austria and Czechoslovakia. The Germans seem to have clamped down pretty firmly on crime there. Besides, my German is pretty fluent. I'll manage all right."

It was true that the private atrocities that had seemed to flourish in the uneasy Germany of the twenties had no place in Adolf Hitler's Third Reich. Peter Kürten, Karl Denke, Fritz Haarmann, Georg Grossman—they were not part of the new German Empire. It was only rumour to us that private atrocity had given way to official atrocity, on a scale that made the activities of Elisabeth Bathory seem almost petty.

(Elisabeth Bathory was a devoted wife to her noble husband, the Count Francis Nadasdy, and a devoted mother to their children. She seemed to have no difficulty in keeping her domestic life quite separate from the bloodlust and magic of her darker nature.)

"What time do you leave Victoria?"

"The train's due out at 9.25 in the morning."

"Hell! I've got to go to Birmingham tomorrow and I shan't be back till Friday evening. I can't even come to see you off. How long do you expect to be away?"

"No telling. I'm to start at the state archives in Buda-Pestah and then if I can I go on to Elisabeth's castle in eastern Czechoslovakia and to Vienna, where she had a town house. There's a special research that Meg wants me to carry out besides just gathering details of the Countess' life. She's heard from a correspondent in Austria that a torture device made for the Countess may still exist. I'm to track it down if I can and try to buy it."

(Elisabeth Bathory had special torture rooms installed in most of her several houses and castles. She would also indulge herself in private rooms when she visited friends or relatives. In the cellar of her mansion in Vienna was a spiked cage, in which her naked victim would be hauled up on a rope and pulley and prodded with hot irons until she impaled herself in her torment. The beautiful Countess, herself naked, stood beneath the cage bathing in the shower of fresh blood.)

"Good God! That's horrible."

Valerie shrugged. "Morbid, I agree, but after all, it's all in the distant past."

"You know as well as anyone that Margaret Pennethorne can make the past come alive. I suppose there's no changing your mind?"

"Not likely! I'm looking forward to this. It's a pity we shan't be able to meet again—but it isn't the end of the world, you know. I'll keep in touch, and we'll get together again as soon as I come back."

(After her eventual trial, at which in deference to her noble family she was referred to only as "a blood-thirsty, bloodsucking Godless woman, caught in the act at Csejthe Castle", Elisabeth Bathory was sentenced to lifelong imprisonment at that same castle. She was immured in a small room without doors or windows, and only a small hatch for food to be passed to her. In August 1614 she died, "suddenly and without a crucifix and without light". For three and a half years she had seen nobody and nothing.)

Two weeks later, I happened to meet Margaret Pennethorne in Hatchard's bookshop. Naturally, I asked whether she'd had word yet from Valerie. Her quizzical smile was unchanged as she shook her head.

"Aren't you worried about her at all? I mean, with Europe so volatile—?"

"Oh, no. She's a capable enough girl. She'll cope. Besides, just now I'm rather relieved to have got her off my hands. Protracted love-affairs become tedious, don't you think?"

Much later that day I understood her remark. A love affair. They had been lovers. Of course! The notion just hadn't occurred to me before (didn't I say that I was a very naïve young man?), but it explained one thing at least. In spite of her obvious and very feminine good looks, I had never been able to think of Valerie in terms of a heterosexual love. Now I knew what it was about her that had precluded such thoughts.

(Elisabeth Bathory was bisexual, and all her perversities tended toward the lesbian side of her nature. She began by mistreating the peasant girls on her estates, who were in a very real sense her own property. The Hungarian peasants' revolt of a generation before had been savagely crushed, and the peasants of Elisabeth's time had no rights—even life itself was merely a privilege. Later she became convinced that only aristocratic virgins could provide the blood she needed. Her preferred victims were under eighteen years of age, blonde and buxom, in contrast to her own dark and slender beauty.)

A day or so later, the first letter arrived from Valerie, having taken four days in the post. My own feelings towards her were changed only in that they were now quite straightforward: she was and would remain the best friend I had. I read the letter with great interest.

She had succeeded in gaining admittance to the state archives in Buda-Pesth, and had obtained (helped no doubt by her own charm and Margaret Pennethorne's money) an abridged transcript of the trial records. This was in Latin, and she intended to spend some of the time while travelling in translating as much of it as she could. Meanwhile, she was now headed for what had recently become the independent state of Slovakia, to visit that same castle of Csejthe which had been the Countess Bathory's principal residence. All was going well, and she had encountered no difficulties of any sort. Everyone she had met had been kind and helpful. I must *stop worrying*.

There was a post-script: "I quite forgot to tell you just what the object is that Meg wants me to try and find. It's an Iron Maiden."

(The Iron Maiden was not a particularly common device even in the great age of torture. The most famous example to be seen today is at Nuremberg, a bulky machine, very crudely shaped like a woman, and with a woman's face roughly depicted on the head. A section of the front is hinged like a door, and can be opened by means of a rope and pulley to reveal a hollow just large enough for a man to be placed. On the inside of the door are several long spikes, so arranged that when the door closed the upper ones would pierce the victim's eyes and the lower ones his heart and vitals.)

Unfortunately, Valerie didn't tell me where in Slovakia she would be staying, and I was unable to find Csejthe on any map available to me. Later events drove the question from my mind and it was only within the last few years that I learned that the place is now called Cachtice.

The next letter came about ten days later. Since the postmark was unreadable, I still had no clear notion of just where Valerie was; somehow I felt reluctant to approach Margaret Pennethorne again.

The castle, itself ruined, stands on a high green hill surrounded by level and fertile country. The late Sir Iain Moncreiffe of That Ilk described it as "like a land-girt St Michael's Mount"—which is more pithy and probably as accurate as Valerie's longer description. If there was any local superstition attaching to the place, Valerie doesn't mention it; she seems to have had no trouble in finding someone to act as a guide. This woman, Anna, was presumably a native Czech speaker, but she had more than a smattering of German—of a sort ... At least she was able, with little prompting, to show Valerie the very room in which the Bloody Countess had passed so many months in a living death.

(Elisabeth's family and that of her husband were Protestants— Calvinists in fact—but enjoyed the support of the Holy Roman Emperor. The estates at Csejthe were not subject to any interference from the Emperor or from the neighbouring Prince of Transylvania. Elisabeth herself was a Calvinist, a complete believer in predestination. As a noble with absolute authority, and a Christian already chosen for salvation, she had no cause to justify her acts to herself or to anyone else. Even when she turned to the devil for help—it was a sorceress who advised her that the blood of noble maidens was necessary—she remained a convinced Christian. One can only wonder whether John Calvin himself would have approved.)

Anna even told her that the Countess' house in Vienna had been situated in the Augustienerstrasse, near the Imperial Palace. As to the Iron Maiden—why, the *gnädiges Fraülein* could hardly expect a poor peasant woman to know much about that. Certainly it had existed at this castle, and she hadn't heard that it had been destroyed. Maybe it wasn't there when the authorities came at last to arrest the beautiful Countess. Maybe it had been sent away to one of her other houses. The house in Vienna, perhaps?

Fortunately, this fitted in nicely with Valerie's plans, since Margaret Pennethorne's reticent correspondent had also suggested that the torture machine might have been taken into Austria. As they said goodbye, Anna looked for a moment at Valerie and said (so Valerie thought), "You will find it, I think. You are the right sort."

(Elisabeth Bathory was given to torturing her young companions while making the long, slow journey from one house or castle to another. Later, unable to wait until she had reached her destination, she would kill the girls who travelled with her. The bodies were simply interred by the roadside, though in earlier years she had insisted upon a Christian burial for her victims.)

Even at the Austrian frontier, Valerie encountered no real difficulty. She had to be rather circumspect in writing from Vienna, but I understood that the passport officer, a true Nazi, had been most impressed by her evident Nordic beauty and fluent German. The only thing that slightly disturbed her was that more than once—at the frontier, and again a couple of times before reaching Vienna—she thought she caught a glimpse of the old peasant woman, Anna.

I never knew Vienna before the war. The only time I've spent there was in 1946 as an officer in the British occupation force. Even so, I doubt that my Vienna was any more unlike the city that Elisabeth Bathory knew. I try to put the great neo-classical and baroque structures of the Inner Stadt out of my mind but I find that there's nothing left. If I'd hoped for some sort of imaginative guidance from Valerie's letters, I was to be disappointed. A curious and disconcerting vagueness seemed to affect her—she who had always impressed me with the clarity and balance of her thoughts.

The accounts became at last almost dreamlike. I gathered that for at least a week after her arrival in the city she had more or less wandered around the Inner Stadt, admiring the Hofburg, the Opera House, the churches—and wondering, with a feeling that she couldn't quite define, whether she would meet Anna again. During these days, she must have passed many times the corner of the Augustienerstrasse and the Dorotheergasse. It didn't seem to occur to her, though, that there was anything special about the place.

(Elisabeth Bathory's mansion stood hard by the Austin Friary. As her blood-lust grew rapidly out of control, she abandoned nearly all rational precautions. The appalling screams of the tortured and dying were so loud that the good friars sometimes protested by hurling pots and pans at her windows.)

Almost every week brought a letter from Valerie—to which I couldn't reply, as, infuriatingly, she gave no address. Several times I tried to telephone Margaret Pennethorne, but there was no reply. Valerie knew that there was something particular she ought to be doing, something connected with a person she'd known in England. Or in Hungary. The letters would contain disturbing, almost surrealist, descriptive imagery of a city that was unlike any I had ever encountered. Yet, among these accounts, there were the names and descriptions of recognisable places. And then there were the people.

Soldiers, German and Austrian, goose-stepping, heel-clicking, saluting. The ominous *Heil Hitler* that seemed to have replaced the homely *Grüss Gott*. There was something in the eyes of the men that rather frightened her. All the men. The women, on the other hand . . .

It was never made clear whether she actually met Anna again but there were many references to her, brief and inconsequential, often questioning. Was her face in every crowd, or could it just be nervous imagination? Was she only one person? But there was no need to pursue that sinister line. Whatever hold Anna might have over her, she could always go to Dorothy for comfort. Dear old Dorothy, so solid and motherlike. Besides, if it hadn't been for Dorothy—

Dorothy. Dorothea. Something about the name. Something meaningful?

If it hadn't been for Dorothy, she would never have met—

She was here to find something. Someone.

—would never have met Mädelein.

There was that odd, stunted little man who often seemed to be near when she was with Dorothy. She didn't like the glances he gave her, but at least Mädelein treated him with scornful tolerance. She must do the same. Darling lovely Mädelein.

The very last letter—like the rest, it was undated, but it reached me on the 21st of June—contains one very clear statement. Valerie was in love. Irrevocably, over head and ears in love. With Mädelein. They had hardly even met—just seen each other in the street; and it was all so *proper*. Perhaps that was a part of the spell. Nothing that had happened in England (what *had* happened in England?) had been like this. How wise Dorothy had been to keep them apart at first. Not a word exchanged, but when Mädelein had smiled, showing those beautiful white, even teeth, and her eyes shining the clearest blue, then Valerie *knew*. She'd found what she was looking for.

Now, what was I to make of all this? I had been against the journey from the start. Not only was the journey itself unsafe, I thought, but the reason for it was plainly morbid and mentally unhealthy. Was I right? Something had clouded my friend's mind; I couldn't doubt that she'd become (the word repels me, but I must use it) insanely obsessed by her mad search and by the mad world in which she'd arrived. Her descriptions of Mädelein in no way eased my mind, for they were clearly descriptions of Valerie herself.

Again I tried to telephone Margaret Pennethorne. This time, at least, she answered, but it was with a brusque, "Oh, it's you. Well, you're Valerie's friend; perhaps you can tell me where the wretched kid's got to?"

"But for heaven's sake! Isn't she in Vienna?"

"You tell me. She's out somewhere spending my money, and I haven't had a word from her in weeks."

I was horrified. And somehow, I just couldn't bring myself to mention Valerie's letters to me, which were the reason why I'd called in the first place. I said something vague about passing on any news that reached me and I put the telephone down.

Fear for my friend inspired me to boldness. I wrote to the British Embassy in Vienna, explaining that I was very concerned for a young Englishwoman whom I believed to be alone in the city and possibly in some kind of trouble. If someone from the Embassy staff could find her and assure me that she was all right, I should be most grateful.

The reply came nearly two weeks later.

The body of Valerie Beddoes, identified by her passport and her belongings, had been found in her room at a small *pension* near the Rotenturmstrasse. The manageress, having been alarmed by a single dreadful scream from the room, had awoken her husband and one of the male residents and with much reluctance entered the room. When she had realised what the viscous liquid was that her bare feet were treading in, she had become hysterical and had to be sedated. The police were called at once.

Valerie Beddoes lay upon the floor of the little room, her spine broken and four ribs crushed. She was naked, so that the appalling wounds inflicted upon her could be clearly seen. Her breasts and genitals had been savagely stabbed with some sharp thick instrument like a chisel.

The police surgeon declared that he had come across nothing like it in Viennese criminal history. He could only compare it to the Whitechapel murders of 1888. Plainly it was *Lustmördern*, the work of a sexual psychopath. The coroner could only agree. Despite the landlady's stories of visitors to the young woman's room that night, whom she was unable to describe in any detail—even to being unsure of their number—it was plain that these visitors were women, and neither coroner nor police could credit that this horrible act was the work of a woman. The verdict was: murder by person or persons unknown.

It was all so sad, said the landlady; the English girl had been a little vague, perhaps, but so sweet and so very pretty.

The person or persons remained unknown. As soon as I felt able to, I sent a copy of the letter from the Embassy to Margaret Pennethorne. I expected no reply, and received none. Nor did I hear again from Vienna.

On the 3rd of September, Great Britain declared war against Germany. My time and thoughts were occupied for a long while with other matters, and when I returned at last to civilian life I deliberately put Valerie's death from my mind, preferring to remember our friendship and the good times. The wound healed, though it ached horribly at times.

And now it has opened again, all because of a suspicious voice that will not be silenced.

Over fifty years ago, I considered Valerie's pursuit of a sadistic murderess to be morbid and unhealthy. I think so still. For that reason I made no attempt to research further into the blood-soaked career of the Countess Elisabeth Bathory. Only Valerie mattered, and Valerie was dead. My only link with her had been Margaret Pennethorne, the enigmatic "Richard Border", and she was dead too, killed in the Blitz. So it was chance and not design that led me to realise that I'd made a false assumption all those years ago.

The Iron Maiden. The thing that Valerie had been looking for. Quite recently I discovered that the machine made for Elisabeth Bathory, to her own specifications (and which almost certainly was destroyed after her arrest at Csejthe), had been something rather different from the crude device preserved at Nuremberg. It was made in the form of an attractive and shapely young woman, life-sized and naked, complete with full breasts and pubic hair. The blue eyes could open and close, and the pink lips part to reveal even white teeth. The flowing blonde hair was real and so were the teeth—they had been torn from the head of one of Elisabeth's victims. When the chosen subject, who must have looked like its living image, approached this hellish doll, its arms would enfold her in an embrace, at first amusing, swiftly bone-crushing. Meanwhile, from the genitals and the nipples, sharp spikes would spring to pierce the young woman's body.

I thought then that Valerie's mind had become clouded, and that "Mädelein" was merely a narcissistic projection of her own self. I think otherwise now, since I have discovered that "Mädelein", literally translated, is a diminutive of "Mädel"—a maid.

Valerie Beddoes did find what she was looking for after all . . .

S. P. SOMTOW

Chui Chai

SOMTOW PAPINIAN SUCHARITKUL (S. P. Somtow) was born in Thailand, a grandnephew of the late Queen Indrasakdisachi of Siam and the son of celebrated international jurist and Vice-President of the International Academy of Human Rights, Sompong Sucharitkul. He grew up in Japan and Europe, was educated at Eton and Cambridge, and currently lives in California, where he recently became an American citizen.

Somtow is a highly regarded post-serialist composer; his work has been performed, broadcast and televised in four continents. He began writing fiction in the late 1970s, winning the 1981 John W. Campbell Award for Best New Writer and the Locus Award for his first novel, *Starship and Haiku*. After a number of science fiction and fantasy books such as *Mallworld*, *The Aquiliad*, *The Shattered Horse*, *Riverrun* and a pair of *V* novelisations, he has turned to horror in recent years with an acclaimed werewolf novel, *Moon Dance*, and *Valentine*, the sequel to his 1984 chiller, *Vampire Junction*.

He co-produced, wrote, directed, scored, and starred as the villainous Doctor Um-Tzec, in the 1989 horror film, *The Laughing Dead*, and is currently developing a new movie, *The Glass Pagoda*.

Given this odd meld of cultures and interests, it is perhaps not surprising to discover that "Chui Chai" is a highly individual blend of *Frankenstein* and *Re-Animator*, set in the sleazy backstreets of Bangkok.

T HE LIVING DEAD ARE NOT AS you imagine them. There are no dangling innards, no dripping slime. They carry their guts and gore inside them, as do you and I. In the right light they can be beautiful, as when they stand in a doorway caught between cross-shafts of contrasting neon. Fueled by the right fantasy, they become indistinguishable from us. Listen, I know. I've touched them.

In the 80s I used to go to Bangkok a lot. The brokerage I worked for had a lot of business there, some of it shady, some not. The flight of money from Hong Kong had begun and our company, vulture that it was, was staking out its share of the loot. Bangkok was booming like there was no tomorrow. It made Los Angeles seem like Peoria. It was wild and fast and frantic and frustrating. It had temples and buildings shaped like giant robots. Its skyline was a cross between Shangri-La and Manhattan. For a dapper yuppie executive like me there were always meetings to be taken, faxes to fax, traffic to be sat in, credit cards to burn. There was also sex.

There was Patpong.

I was addicted. Days, after hours of high-level talks and poring over papers and banquets that lasted from the close of business until midnight, I stalked the crammed alleys of Patpong. The night smelled of sewage and jasmine. The heat seeped into everything. Each step I took was colored by a different neon sign. From half-open nightclub doorways buttocks bounced to jaunty soulless synthrock. Everything was for sale; the women, the boys, the pirated software, the fake Rolexes. Everything sweated. I stalked the streets and sometimes at random took an entrance, took in a live show, women propelling ping-pong balls from their pussies, boys buttfucking on motorbikes. I was addicted. There were other entrances where I sat in waiting rooms, watched women with numbers around their necks through the one-way glass, soft, slender brown women. Picked a number. Fingered the American-made condoms in my pocket. Never buy the local ones, brother, they leak like a sieve.

I was addicted. I didn't know what I was looking for. But I knew it wasn't something you could find in Encino. I was a knight on a quest, but I didn't know that to find the holy grail is the worst thing that can possibly happen.

I first got a glimpse of the grail at Club Pagoda, which was near my hotel and which is where we often liked to take our clients. The club was on the very edge of Patpong, but it was respectable—the kind of place that serves up a plastic imitation of *The King and I*, which is, of course, a plastic imitation of life in ancient Siam . . . artifice imitating artifice, you see. Waiters crawled around in mediaeval uniforms, the guests sat on the floor, except there was a well under the table to accommodate the dangling legs of lumbering white people. The floor show was eminently sober . . . it was all classical Thai dances, women wearing those pagoda-shaped hats moving with painstaking grace and slowness to a tinkling, alien music. A good place to interview prospective grant recipients, because it tended to make them very nervous.

Dr Frances Stone wasn't at all nervous, though. She was already there when I arrived. She was preoccupied with picking the peanuts out of her *gaeng massaman* and arranging them over her rice plate in such a way that they looked like little eyes, a nose, and a mouth.

"You like to play with your food?" I said, taking my shoes off at the edge of our private booth and sliding my legs under the table across from her.

"No," she said, "I just prefer them crushed rather than whole. The peanuts, I mean. You must be Mr Leibowitz."

"Russell."

"The man I'm supposed to charm out of a few million dollars." She was doing a sort of coquettish pout, not really the sort of thing I expected from someone in medical research. Her face was ravaged, but the way she smiled kindled the memory of youthful beauty. I wondered what had happened to change her so much; according to her dossier, she was only in her mid-forties.

"Mostly we're in town to take," I said, "not to give. R&D is not one of our strengths. You might want to go to Hoechst or Berli Jucker, Frances."

"But Russell . . ." She had not touched her curry, but the peanuts on the rice were now formed into a perfect human face, with a few strands of sauce for hair. "This is not exactly R&D. This is a discovery that's been around for almost a century and a half. My great-grandfather's paper— "

"For which he was booted out of the Austrian Academy? Yes, my dossier is pretty thorough, Dr Stone; I know all about how he fled to America and changed his name."

She smiled. "And my dossier on you, Mr Leibowitz, is pretty thorough too," she said, as she began removing a number of compromising photographs from her purse.

A gong sounded to announce the next dance. It was a solo. Fog roiled across the stage, and from it a woman emerged. Her clothes glittered with crystal beadwork, but her eyes outshone the yards of cubic zirconia. She looked at me and I felt the pangs of the addiction. She smiled and her lips seemed to glisten with lubricious moisture.

"You like what you see," Frances said softly.

"I— "

"The dance is called *Chui Chai*, the dance of transformation. In every Thai classical drama, there are transformations—a woman transforming herself into a rose, a spirit transforming itself into a human. After the character's metamorphosis, he performs a *Chui Chai* dance, exulting in the completeness and beauty of his transformed self."

I wasn't interested, but for some reason she insisted on giving me the entire story behind the dance. "This particular *Chui Chai* is called *Chui Chai Benjakai* . . . the demoness Banjakai has been despatched by the demon king, Thotsakanth, to seduce the hero Rama . . . disguised as the beautiful Sita, she will float down the river toward Rama's camp, trying to convince him that his beloved has died . . . only when she is placed on a funeral pyre, woken from her deathtrance by the flames, will she take on her demonic shape once more and fly away toward the dark kingdom of Lanka. But you're not listening."

How could I listen? She was the kind of woman that existed only in dreams, in poems. Slowly she moved against the tawdry backdrop, a faded painting of a palace with pointed eaves. Her feet barely touched the floor. Her arms undulated. And always her eyes held me. As though she were looking at me alone. Thai women can do things with their eyes that no other women can do. Their eyes have a secret language.

"Why are you looking at her so much?" said Frances. "She's just a Patpong bar girl . . . she moonlights here . . . classics in the evening, pussy after midnight."

"You know her?" I said.

"I have had some . . . dealings with her."

"Just what is it that you're doing research into, Dr Stone?"

"The boundary between life and death," she said. She pointed to the photographs. Next to them was a contract, an R&D grant agreement of some kind. The print was blurry. "Oh, don't worry, it's only a couple of million dollars . . . your company won't even miss it . . . and you'll own the greatest secret of all . . . the tree of life and death . . . the apples of Eve. Besides, I know your price and I can meet it." And she looked at the dancing girl. "Her name is Keo. I don't mind procuring if it's in the name of science."

Suddenly I realized that Dr Stone and I were the only customers in the Club Pagoda. Somehow I had been set up.

The woman continued to dance, faster now, her hands sweeping through the air in mysterious gestures. She never stopped looking at me. She *was* the character she was playing, seductive and diabolical. There was darkness in every look, every hand-movement. I downed the rest of my Kloster lager and beckoned for another. An erection strained against my pants.

The dance ended and she prostrated herself before the audience of two, pressing her palms together in a graceful *wai*. Her eyes downcast, she left the stage. I had signed the grant papers without even knowing it.

Dr Stone said, "On your way to the upstairs toilet . . . take the second door on the left. She'll be waiting for you."

I drank another beer, and when I looked up she was gone. She hadn't eaten one bite. But the food on her plate had been sculpted into the face of a beautiful woman. It was so lifelike that . . . but no. It wasn't alive. It wasn't breathing.

She was still in her dancing clothes when I went in. A little girl was carefully taking out the stitches with a seamripper. There was a pile of garments on the floor. In the glare of a naked bulb, the vestments of the goddess had little glamor. "They no have buttons on classical dance clothes," she said. "They just sew us into them. Cannot go pipi!" She giggled.

The little girl scooped up the pile and slipped away.

"You're . . . very beautiful," I said. "I don't understand why . . . I mean, why you *need* to . . ."

"I have problem," she said. "Expensive problem. Dr Stone no tell you?"

"No." Her hands were coyly clasped across her bosom. Gently I pried them away.

"You want I dance for you?"

"Dance," I said. She was naked. The way she smelled was different from other women. It was like crushed flowers. Maybe a hint of decay in them. She shook her hair and it coiled across her breasts like a nest of black serpents. When I'd seen her on stage I'd been entertaining some kind of rape fantasy about her, but now I wanted to string it out for as long as I could. God, she was driving me mad.

"I see big emptiness inside you. Come to me. I fill you. We both empty people. Need filling up."

I started to protest. But I knew she had seen me for what I was. I had money coming out my ass, but I was one fucked-up yuppie. That was the root of my addiction.

Again she danced the dance of transforming, this time for me alone. Really for me alone. I mean, all the girls in Patpong have this way of making you think they love you. It's what gets you addicted. It's the only street in the world where you *can* buy love. But that's not how she was. When she touched me it was as though she reached out to me across an invisible barrier, an unbreachable gulf. Even when I entered her she was untouchable. We were from different worlds and neither of us ever left our private hells.

Not that there wasn't passion. She knew every position in the book. She knew them backwards and forwards. She kept me there all night and each act seemed as though it been freshly invented for the two of us. It was the last time I came that I felt I had glimpsed the grail. Her eyes, staring up into the naked bulb, brimmed with some remembered sadness. I loved her with all my might. Then I was seized with terror. She was a demon. Yellow-eyed, dragon-clawed. She was me, she was my insatiable hunger. I was fucking my own addiction. I think I sobbed. I accused her of lacing my drink with hallucinogens. I cried myself to sleep and then she left me.

I didn't notice the lumpy mattress or the peeling walls or the way the light bulb jiggled to the music from downstairs. I didn't notice the cockroaches.

I didn't notice until morning that I had forgotten to use my condoms.

It was a productive trip but I didn't go back to Thailand for another two years. I was promoted off the traveling circuit, moved from Encino to Beverly Hills, got myself a newer, late-model wife, packed my kids off to a Swiss boarding school. I also found a new therapist and a new support group. I smothered the addiction in new addictions. My old therapist had been a strict Freudian. He'd tried to root out the cause from some childhood trauma—molestation, potty training, Oedipal games—he'd never been able to find anything. I'm good at blocking out memories. To the best of my knowledge, I popped into being around age eight or nine. My parents were dead but I had a trust fund.

My best friends in the support group were Janine, who'd had eight husbands, and Mike, a transvestite with a spectacular fro. The clinic was in Malibu so we could do the beach in between bouts of tearing ourselves apart. One day Thailand came up.

Mike said, "I knew this woman in Thailand. I had fun in Thailand, you know? R&R. Lot of transvestites there, hon. I'm not a fag, I just like lingerie. I met this girl." He rarely stuck to the point because he was always stoned. Our therapist, Glenda, had passed out in the redwood tub. The beach was deserted. "I knew this girl in Thailand, a dancer. She would change when she danced. I mean *change*. You shoulda seen her skin. Translucent. And she smelled different. Smelled of strange drugs."

You know I started shaking when he said that because I'd tried not to think of her all this time even though she came to me in dreams. Even before I'd start to dream, when I'd just closed my eyes, I'd hear the hollow tinkle of marimbas and see her eyes floating in the darkness.

"Sounds familiar," I said.

"Nah. There was nobody like this girl, hon, nobody. She danced in a classical dance show *and* she worked the whorehouses ... had a day job too, working for a nutty professor woman ... honky woman, withered face, glasses. Some kind of doctor, I think. Sleazy office in Patpong, gave the girls free V. D. drugs."

"Dr Frances Stone." Was the company paying for a free V. D. clinic? What about the research into the secrets of the universe?

"Hey, how'd you know her name?"

"Did you have sex with her?" Suddenly I was trembling with rage. I don't know why. I mean, I knew what she did for a living.

"Did you?" Mike said. He was all nervous. He inched away from me, rolling a joint with one hand and scootching along the redwood deck with the other.

"I asked first," I shouted, thinking, Jesus, I sound like a ten-year-old kid.

"Of *course* not! She had problems, all right? Expensive problems. But she was beautiful, mm-mm, good enough to eat."

I looked wildly around. Mr Therapist was still dozing—fabulous way to earn a thousand bucks an hour—and the others had broken up into little groups. Janine was sort of listening, but she was more interested in getting her suntan lotion on evenly.

"I want to go back," I said. "I want to see Keo again."

"Totally, like, bullshit," she said, sidling up to me. "You're just, like, externalizing the interior hurt onto a fantasy-object. Like, you need to be in touch with your child, know what I mean?"

"You're getting your support groups muddled up, hon," Mike said edgily.

"Hey, Russ, instead of, like, projecting on some past-forgettable female two years back and ten thousand miles away, why don't you, like, fixate on someone a little closer to home? I mean, I've been *looking* at you. I only joined this support group cause like, support groups are the only place you can find like *sensitive* guys."

"Janine, I'm married."

"So let's have an affair."

I liked the idea. My marriage to Trisha had mostly been a joke: I'd needed a fresh ornament for cocktail parties and openings; she needed security. We hadn't had much sex; how could we? I was hooked on memory. Perhaps this woman would cure me. And I wanted to be cured so badly because Mike's story had jolted me out of the fantasy that Keo had existed only for me.

By now it was the 90s, so Janine insisted on a blood test before we did anything. I tested positive. I was scared shitless. Because the only time I'd ever been so careless as to forget to use a condom was

... that night. And we'd done everything. Plumbed every orifice. Shared every fluid.

It had been a dance of transformation all right.

I had nothing to lose. I divorced my wife and sent my kids to an even more expensive school in Connecticut. I was feeling fine. Maybe I'd never come down with anything. I read all the books and articles about it. I didn't tell anyone. I packed a couple of suits and some casual clothes and a supply of bootleg AZT. I was feeling fine. Fine, I told myself. Fine.

I took the next flight to Bangkok.

The company was surprised to see me, but I was such a big executive by now they assumed I was doing some kind of internal troubleshooting. They put me up at the Oriental. They gave me a 10,000 baht per diem. In Bangkok you can buy a lot for four hundred bucks. I told them to leave me alone. The investigation didn't concern them. They didn't know what I was investigating, so they feared the worst.

I went to Silom Road, where Club Pagoda had stood. It was gone. In its stead stood a brand new McDonalds and an airline ticket office. Perhaps Keo was already dead. Wasn't that what I had smelled on her? The odor of crushed flowers, wilting ... the smell of coming death? And the passion with which she made love. I understood it now. It was the passion of the damned. She had reached out to me from a place between life and death. She had sucked the life from me and given me the virus as a gift of love.

I strolled through Patpong. Hustlers tugged at my elbows. Fake Rolexes were flashed in my face. It was useless to ask for Keo. There are a million women named Keo. Keo means jewel. It also means glass. In Thai there are many words that are used indiscriminately for reality and artifice. I didn't have a photograph and Keo's beauty was hard to describe. And every girl in Patpong is beautiful. Every night, parading before me in the neon labyrinth, a thousand pairs of lips and eyes, sensuous and infinitely giving. The wrong lips, the wrong eyes.

There are only a few city blocks in Patpong, but to trudge up and down them in the searing heat, questioning, observing every face for a trace of the remembered grail ... it can age you. I stopped shaving and took recreational drugs. What did it matter anyway?

But I was still fine, I wasn't coming down with anything.

I was fine. Fine!

And then, one day, while paying for a Big Mac, I saw her hands. I was looking down at the counter counting out the money. I heard the computer beep of the cash register and then I saw them:

proffering the hamburger in both hands, palms up, like an offering to the gods. The fingers arched upwards, just so, with delicacy and hidden strength. God, I knew those hands. Their delicacy as they skimmed my shoulder blades, as they glided across my testicles just a hair's breadth away from touching. Their strength when she balled up her fist and shoved it into my rectum. Jesus, we'd done everything that night. I dropped my wallet on the counter, I seized those hands and gripped them, burger and all, and I felt the familiar response. Oh, God, I ached.

"Mister, you want a blowjob?"

It wasn't her voice. I looked up. It wasn't even a woman.

I looked back down at the hands. I looked up at the face. They didn't even belong together. It was a pockmarked boy and when he talked to me he stared off into space. There was no relation between the vacuity of his expression and the passion with which those hands caressed my hands.

"I don't like to do such thing," he said, "but I'm a poor college student and I needing money. So you can come back after 5 p.m. You not be disappointed."

The fingers kneaded my wrists with the familiarity of one who has touched every part of your body, who has memorized the varicose veins in your left leg and the mole on your right testicle.

It was obscene. I wrenched my own hands free. I barely remembered to retrieve my wallet before I ran out into the street.

I had been trying to find Dr Frances Stone since I arrived, looking through the files at the corporate headquarters, screaming at secretaries. Although the corporation had funded Dr Stone's project, the records seemed to have been spirited away.

At last I realized that that was the wrong way to go about it. I remembered what Mike had told me, so the day after the encounter with Keo's hands, I was back in Patpong, asking around for a good V. D. clinic. The most highly regarded one of all turned out to be at the corner of Patpong and Soi Cowboy, above a store that sold pirated software and videotapes.

I walked up a steep staircase into a tiny room without windows, with a ceiling fan moving the same sweaty air around and around. A receptionist smiled at me. Her eyes had the same vacuity that the boy at McDonalds had possessed. I sat in an unraveling rattan chair and waited, and Dr Stone summoned me into her office.

"You've done something with her," I said.

"Yes." She was shuffling a stack of papers. She had a window; she had an airconditioner blasting away in the direction of all the computers. I was still drenched with sweat.

The phone rang and she had a brief conversation in Thai that I couldn't catch. "You're angry, of course," she said, putting down the phone. "But it was better than nothing. Better than the cold emptiness of the earth. And she had nothing to lose."

"She was dying of AIDS! And now *I* have it!" It was the first time I'd allowed the word to cross my lips. "You *killed* me!"

Frances laughed. "My," she said, "aren't we being a little melodramatic? You have the virus, but you haven't actually come down with anything."

"I'm fine. Fine."

"Well, why don't you sit down. I'll order up some food. We'll talk."

She had really gone native. In Thailand it's rude to talk business without ordering up food. Sullenly I sat down while she opened a window and yelled out an order to one of the street vendors.

"To be honest, Mr Leibowitz," she said, "we really could use another grant. We had to spend *so* much of the last one on cloak-and-dagger nonsense, security, bribes, and so on; so little could be spared for research itself . . . I mean, look around you . . . I'm not exactly wasting money on luxurious office space, am I?"

"I saw her hands."

"Very effective, wasn't it?" The food arrived. It was some kind of noodle thing wrapped in banana leaves and groaning from the weight of chili peppers. She did not eat; instead, she amused herself by rearranging the peppers in the shape of . . . "The hands, I mean. Beautiful as ever. Vibrant. Sensual. My first breakthrough."

I started shaking again. I'd read about Dr Stone's great-grandfather and his graverobbing experiments. Jigsaw corpses brought to life with bolts of lightning. Not life. A simulacrum of life. Could this have happened to Keo? But she was dying. Perhaps it was better than nothing. Perhaps . . .

"Anyhow. I was hoping you'd arrive soon, Mr Leibowitz. Because we've made up another grant proposal. I have the papers here. I know that you've become so important now that your signature alone will suffice to bring us ten times the amount you authorized two years ago."

"I want to see her."

"Would you like to dance with her? Would you like to see her in the *Chui Chai* one more time?"

She led me down a different stairwell. Many flights. I was sure we were below ground level. I knew we were getting nearer to Keo because there was a hint of that rotting flower fragrance in the air. We descended. There was an unnatural chill.

And then, at last, we reached the laboratory. No shambling Igors or bubbling retorts. Just a clean, well-lit basement room. Cold, like the vault of a morgue. Walls of white tile; ceiling of stucco; fluorescent lamps; the pervasive smell of the not-quite-dead.

Perspex tanks lined the walls. They were full of fluid and body parts. Arms and legs floating past me. Torsos twirled. A woman's breast peered from between a child's thighs. In another tank, human hearts swirled, each neatly severed at the aorta. There was a tank of eyes. Another of genitalia. A necklace of tongues hung suspended in a third. A mass of intestines writhed in a fourth. Computers drew intricate charts on a bank of monitors. Oscilloscopes beeped. A pet gibbon was chained to a post topped by a human skull. There was something so outlandishly antiseptic about this spectacle that I couldn't feel the horror.

"I'm sorry about the décor, Russell, but you see, we've had to forgo the usual decoration allowance." The one attempt at dressing up the place was a frayed poster of *Young Frankenstein* tacked to the far wall. "Please don't be upset at all the body parts," she added. "It's all very macabre, but one gets inured to it in med school; if you feel like losing your lunch, there's a small restroom on your left . . . yes, between the eyes and the tongues." I did not feel sick. I was feeling . . . excited. It was the odor. I knew I was getting closer to Keo.

She unlocked another door. We stepped into an inner room.

Keo was there. A cloth was draped over her, but seeing her face after all these years made my heart almost stop beating. The eyes. The parted lips. The hair, streaming upward toward a source of blue light . . . although I felt no wind in the room. "It is an electron wind," said Dr Stone. "No more waiting for the monsoon lightning. We can get more power from a wall socket than great-grandfather Victor could ever dream of stealing from the sky."

And she laughed the laughter of mad scientists.

I saw the boy from McDonalds sitting in a chair. The hands reached out toward me. There were electrodes fastened to his temples. He was naked now, and I saw the scars where hands had been joined at the wrists to someone else's arms. I saw a woman with Keo's breasts, wired to a pillar of glass, straining, heaving while jags of blue lightning danced about her bonds. I saw her vagina stitched onto the pubis of a dwarf, who lay twitching at the foot of the pillar. Her feet were fastened to the body of a five-year-old boy, transforming their grace to ungainliness as he stomped in circles around the pillar.

"Jigsaw people!" I said.

"Of course!" said Dr Stone. "Do you think I would be so foolish as to bring back people whole? Do you not realize what the consequences would be? The legal redefinition of life and death

... wills declared void, humans made subservient to walking corpses
... I'm a scientist, not a philosopher."

"But who are they now?"

"They were nobody before. Street kids. Prostitutes. They were
dying, Mr Leibowitz, dying! They were glad to will their bodies
to me. And now they're more than human. They're many persons
in many bodies. A gestalt. I can shuffle them and put them back
together, oh, so many different ways ... and the beautiful Keo.
Oh, she wept when she came to me. When she found out she had
given you the virus. She loved you. You were the last person she
ever loved. I saved her for you. She's been sleeping here, waiting to
dance for you, since the day she died. Oh, let us not say *died*. The
day she ... she ... I am no poet, Mr Leibowitz. Just a scientist."

I didn't want to listen to her. All I could see was Keo's face. It
all came back to me. Everything we had done. I wanted to relive it.
I didn't care if she was dead or undead. I wanted to seize the grail
and clutch it in my hands and own it.

Frances threw a switch. The music started. The shrilling of the
pinai, the pounding of the *taphon*, the tinkling of marimbas and
xylophones rang in the *Chui Chai* music. Then she slipped away
unobtrusively. I heard a key turn in a lock. She had left the grant
contract lying on the floor. I was alone with all the parts of the
woman I'd loved. Slowly I walked toward the draped head. The
electron wind surged; the cold blue light intensified. Her eyes
opened. Her lips moved as though discovering speech for the first
time ...

"Rus ... sell."

On the pizzafaced boy, the hands stirred of their own accord. He
turned his head from side to side and the hands groped the air,
straining to touch my face. Keo's lips were dry. I put my arms
around the drape-shrouded body and kissed the dead mouth. I could
feel my hair stand on end.

"I see big emptiness inside you. Come to me. I fill you. We both
empty people. Need filling up."

"Yes. Jesus, yes."

I hugged her to me. What I embraced was cold and prickly. I
whisked away the drape. There was no body. Only a framework of
wires and transistors and circuit boards and tubes that fed flasks of
flaming reagents.

"I dance for you now."

I turned. The hands of the McDonald's boy twisted into graceful
patterns. The feet of the child moved in syncopation to the music,
dragging the rest of the body with them. The breasts of the chained
woman stood firm, waiting for my touch. The music welled up. A

contralto voice spun plaintive melismas over the interlocking rhythms of wood and metal. I kissed her. I kissed that severed head and lent my warmth to the cold tongue, awakened passion in her. I kissed her. I could hear chains breaking and wires slithering along the floortiles. There were hands pressed into my spine, rubbing my neck, unfastening my belt. A breast touched my left buttock and a foot trod lightly on my right. I didn't care that these parts were attached to other bodies. They were hers. She was loving me all over. The dwarf that wore her pudenda was climbing up my leg. Every part of her was in love with me. Oh, she danced. We danced together. I was the epicenter of their passion. We were empty people but now we drank our fill. Oh, God, we danced. Oh, it was a grave music, but it contented us.

And I signed everything, even the codicil.

Today I am in the AIDS ward of a Beverly Hills hospital. I don't have long to wait. Soon the codicil will come into effect, and my body will be preserved in liquid nitrogen and shipped to Patpong.

The nurses hate to look at me. They come at me with rubber gloves on so I won't contaminate them, even though they should know better. My insurance policy has disowned me. My children no longer write me letters, though I've paid for them to go to Ivy League colleges. Trisha comes by sometimes. She is happy that we rarely made love.

One day I will close my eyes and wake up in a dozen other bodies. I will be closer to her than I could ever be in life. In life we are all islands. Only in Dr Stone's laboratory can we know true intimacy, the mind of one commanding the muscles of another and causing the nerves of a third to tingle with unnamable desires. I hope I shall die soon.

The living dead are not as you imagine them. There are no dangling innards, no dripping slime. They carry their guts and gore inside them, as do you and I. In the right light they can be beautiful, as when they stand in the cold luminescence of a basement laboratory, waiting for an electron stream to lend them the illusion of life. Fueled by the right fantasy, they become indistinguishable from us.

Listen. I know. I've loved them.

KIM NEWMAN

The Snow Sculptures of Xanadu

KIM NEWMAN is the winner of the Horror Writers of America Bram Stoker Award for *Horror: 100 Best Books* (with Stephen Jones), and the British Science Fiction Association Award for his story "The Original Dr Shade". The author of such non-fiction studies as *Ghastly Beyond Belief* (with Neil Gaiman), *Nightmare Movies* and *Wild West Movies*, his novels include *The Night Mayor, Bad Dreams, Jago, Anno Dracula* and, under the "Jack Yeovil" alias, several *Warhammer* and *Dark Future* gaming adventures. His recent short fiction is collected in *The Original Dr Shade and Other Stories* and he has co-edited the anthology *In Dreams* with Paul J. McAuley.

The story that follows came about when Jonathan Carroll put an Austrian magazine who wanted an article on the 50th Anniversary of *Citizen Kane* in touch with the author. "Rather than the film-oriented think-piece they expected," explains Newman, "I produced this, which they very handsomely accepted and ran". The story was reprinted in this, slightly expanded, form in the special "non-fiction" issue of *Interzone/Million*, and was rated as one of the least popular stories published in *Interzone* that year in the annual reader's poll (along with Elizabeth Hand's "The Bacchae").

Observant readers will discover references to *The Third Man, The Haunting of Hill House, The House on Haunted Hill, Suspiria, The Shining* and *Hell House*, as well as of course Orson Welles' *Citizen Kane*, in this short but very unusual ghost story.

T here had been a private zoo here once, but now only mosquitoes thrived. In the thick, sweaty heat, they pestered Welles. During his lifetime, Charles Foster Kane had decreed Xanadu insect-free, as if the force of his unstoppable will—the power that had shaped the destinies of nations—were able to hold back the swamplands surrounding his Florida fastness. The Pleasure Dome had begun to rot while Kane still lived, as his powers ebbed and history slowly crept past him, and, with his death twenty-five years ago, the decay had begun to accelerate. The walls were breached like those of a besieged city that has finally yielded, the stinking cages of the menagerie held only dead animals, forty-foot windows were patched over with boards. Welles thought that if the place were left to nature, it would inevitably sink like the House of Usher into the giant tarn surrounding it.

A fitting set for a ghost story.

The former Boy Wonder stood outside the gates of Xanadu, the shadow of their wrought iron K motif falling upon him, and was conscious of how much he had changed since his last visit. In 1941, with an RKO contract to make a ground-breaking documentary about the Great American, he had stolen miles of footage in Xanadu as the Kane functionaries dismantled and inventoried the fortress's infestation-like collection. Statues, books, paintings, furniture, uncategorizable mementoes, jigsaw puzzles, phonograph records, vehicles, tapestries: all boxed or burned. Welles had felt that there was no waste as long as the process was caught on film. No gesture or moment was insignificant once processed by Gregg Toland's camera. Of course, he could not have foreseen that all his footage would end up like Kane's collection, listed and buried in a vault.

Up in the eaves of Xanadu, something with wings squawked, its cry like a jaguar's snarl played backwards.

Then, Welles had been slim and promising; now, he felt fat and thwarted. Charles Foster Kane Jr, a lifelong recluse crippled in the 1916 automobile accident that took his mother's life, had stirred the might of his inherited empire, and pressured RKO into abandoning *American*, just as they dissuaded *News on the March* from issuing its newsreel obituary. Junior, still nursing the hurt of his parents' divorce, acted as if he wanted the memory of Kane erased, working diligently at squashing biographies with all the zeal of an Egyptian priest wiping a dissolute pharaoh out of the history books. Now, in 1965, few people remembered whether Kane had been a real person or a made-up character. His name was sometimes good for newspaper sales—as when, in 1949, it had seemed probable that an American black marketeer found dead in a Viennese sewer was the old man's bastard son—but mainly, he was as shadowy a concept as his "Rosebud," as forgotten a heap of detritus as his Xanadu.

Down the coast, a white spurt shot up. Part of the old Kane Estate was now leased to Cape Canaveral. Junior's passion was the sky, prompted by the cripple's hope that even if he could not walk he could fly. Welles remembered Junior's involvement with Howard Hughes' "Spruce Goose" during the War, and his establishment of a Kane Aviation Company in the '50s, diversifying into jet engines and prototypical rockets. Kane components would go to the moon one day, or bear the payload of man's final war. And Kane papers and television programmes would bear the news of both events.

Welles wondered again if the summons he had received was a hoax. Xanadu seemed from the outside to be completely deserted. Sun-bleached walls crumbled invisibly, and there was no sign of habitation. He looked back at the limousine, but the driver—half his face hidden by goggle-like glasses—betrayed nothing.

As young men, Kane and Welles had been much alike, the sleek and dynamic Boy Wonders of 1894 and 1940, but they had aged differently, Kane becoming a shambling, bullet-headed mammoth, shunned by the rest of the tribe, while Welles buried himself in beard, bloat and B-movies, squandering his theatrical reputation on cameo appearances and cheap magic tricks. It all started with *American*, the dream movie, to combine fiction and documentary in unprecedented ways. The footage had never even been edited together, but still *American*, the masterpiece that never was, cast its shadow over all Welles's subsequent, tidily completed but lesser-than-expected, works: *The Ambersons, Heart of Darkness, Don Quixote, The Trial*. If *American* had been finished, things would have been different. Welles would have been greater than Ford, than Hawks, than Hitchcock. Than Eisenstein, than Murnau, than Flaherty ..

Finally, the gates were opened, and a thin, smiling man in a tropical suit led Welles to the house. The driveway was apparently unending, Xanadu growing larger with each step. Welles had heard of Dr John Montague before, had read his published account of his investigation into the notoriously haunted Hill House in Connecticut. That had ended in tragedy for one of Montague's researchers, but the scientist took care elaborately to exonerate himself in his book. Junior had commissioned the parapsychologist to look into his own family's haunted mansion. perhaps to prescribe a rite of exorcism. Welles wondered why Junior hadn't simply had Xanadu burned to the ground, and its ruins seeded with salt.

Montague chatted as they walked to Xanadu, mainly about magic and trickery. Welles was known as an expert, having once sawn Rita

Hayworth in half and capped the trick by marrying the girl. He had hoaxed the world that the Martians were coming. Montague assumed that the master magician would recognize a trick if he saw one. Welles realized there was something lacking in Montague, a failure to understand that magic was what you could not explain. That was its beauty, its trick. Probing the works, finding the concealed mirrors and strings, was the most effective method of exorcism.

The K above the door was weathered, most of its circle fallen away, leaving only a rind between the toppermost arms of the letter. It looked like an R.

"Rosebud," Welles whispered.

Rosebud had proved the most overexplored false trail in American biography. The *News on the March* team had never found an explanation for Kane's last word, and neither had the would-be makers of *American*. Joe Mankiewicz, drunk, had suggested it was the mogul's private nickname for the private parts of his second wife, the former street corner diva Susan Alexander. That had been as good a solution as any.

Welles saw Montague's team in the grounds, blending in with the overgrowth like camouflaged birds, prodding directional mikes and anemometers into various apertures. Montague talked about cold spots and ectoplasm and resonances. In the parapsychology texts, Xanadu had overtaken Borley Rectory, the Loren Home, the Frieburg Tanz Akademie, the Overlook Hotel and the Belasco Mansion as the world's most haunted house. Although Welles realized none of the rumours and reports that had filtered back to him had ever specified exactly *how* Xanadu was haunted.

Some excitement was caused among the psychic researchers by the sighting of a large bird flapping lazily out of the eaves of the West Wing. The thing Welles had heard earlier, it looked like a vast, leathery bat with a horned swordfish's head. Montague explained the creature was a living fossil, but that no-one had got close enough to one to classify it. Welles remembered recreating some shots of Xanadu in miniature at RKO, reusing some of the back projection plates from *King Kong*. He wondered how the painted pterodactyl had migrated from Hollywood to Florida.

While Xanadu was decaying, the Kane Empire had been reshaping itself—Junior taking only a capricious interest, but capable men springing up from inside the business—and preparing for a war which, ultimately, would take it from the verge of bankruptcy to corporate heights to which Kane had never even aspired. Riding the tide of national purpose, Kane papers and magazines had re-established themselves as essentials in any American living room. In the '50s, Kane interests diversified: while Junior reached for the sky, his corporation crept into television, stealing a march on the competition as the new medium took hold on American life. Organization Men in gray flannel prowled the executive suites, as the name of Kane came to mean a many-headed but single-minded beast, almost independent of Junior, infiltrating America's living rooms. Kane papers backed and then denounced Joseph McCarthy, as if the old man's ghost were still influencing editorial policies. Kane and Korea, Kane and Nixon, Kane and Kennedy, Kane and the astronauts. The old man would have loved the second half of the century more even than he had the first.

Montague listed the accomplishments of his team: trance mediums, physical mediums, psychometrists, psychotronics, psychokinetics. Ghost breakers in grey flannel, punching a time-clock and tuning in to the beyond just as his old audience had tuned in to the *Mercury Theatre of the Air*.

Even in his lightweight suit, Welles was perspiring uncomfortably. He was surprised, then, when Montague, on a doorstep as wide as an interstate highway, handed him a parka. The scientist pulled on a thick coat himself, and flipped the fur-lined hood up over his head. He looked ready to strike for the South Pole. Perplexed, Welles followed suit, wrapping the cumbersome garment around himself. He waited for the punchline, but none came.

Montague threw open the great doors of Xanadu, and stepped in, Welles followed, and was embraced by an invisible blizzard. As the doors slammed to behind them, he felt as if he had left the valley of Shangri-La and returned to Tibetan wastes. The scientist looked smug, and Welles tried to conceal his astonishment. Outside, was tropical heat. Here, within the walls of Xanadu, an arctic frost lay over everything. Welles asked if there was any scientific explanation. Montague didn't answer, but provided the information that Charles Foster Kane, born in 1864, spent his first years in a Colorado boarding house, coping with the fierce winters.

The statues and paintings were gone, but in their place were shaped blocks of ice. One of Montague's team was taking photographs of a swirling column that turned into a perfect Floradora Girl. The ice shifted and cracked as the girl performed a dance step with the grave dignity of a glacier.

The thick frost on the walls was shaped into dioramas. Welles was drawn to a screen-sized patch of sparkling ice. Street scenes turned into stage sets. The view crept up over houses and in through roofs. Welles wished he had a film crew with him. The ice pictures were the images he had dreamed of when he first conceived *American*. They melted and reformed in different configurations.

Montague stood back, and let Welles wander through the halls of Xanadu, constantly amazed, delighted and intrigued by the ice sculptures. The scientist was cool and cautious, not expressing an opinion. A lifelong measurer and tabulator, Montague was probably not even qualified to have an opinion.

Now Welles understood why the Kane people had sent for him. It was not that he could explain the ice sculptures, any more than he could explain "Rosebud." It was that he was the only one who could appreciate what was here.

The great staircase of Xanadu was thick with snow that came from nowhere and smoothed away the steps, fanning out around Welles' feet as it blanketed the parquet. The staircase was a slope suitable for skiing, for sledding. For an instant, as if a diamond bullet had pierced his brain, Welles thought he had an answer to the unanswerable. Then, like ice in the sun, it melted away.

EDWARD BRYANT

Colder Than Hell

ALMOST AS traditional as a Mediterranean story in each *Best New Horror* is a tale set during a snow storm. In this volume it's Edward Bryant's "Colder Than Hell".

Bryant first met writer Harlan Ellison, who assisted his early career, at the Clarion Writer's Workshop in 1968 and 1969, and the following year he sold his first short story, "They Come Only in Dreams", to *Adam*.

Since then his superior short fiction has appeared in a wide variety of anthologies and magazines, and the author's collections include *Among the Dead and Other Events Leading Up to the Apocalypse*, *Particle Theory*, one-third of *Night Visions 4* and *Neon Twilight*. He also collaborated with Ellison on the short novel *Phoenix Without Ashes* and has edited the original anthology, *2076: The American Tricentennial*.

Bryant is currently expanding his 1991 horror novella *Fetish* to full length and preparing a new reprint-and-original collection for Roadkill Press, entitled *Save the Last Death for Me*. His shopping mall paranoia story, "While She Was Out", was recently shown on Lifetime Cable TV and, as he explains, "I continue to irritate a variety of worthies with my book review columns in *Locus* and elsewhere."

Bryant has twice won the Nebula Award for his short fiction, and we are sure you'll find the following story a real *chiller* . . .

THE NORWEGIAN, AMUNDSEN, HAD REACHED THE South Pole on the fourteenth of December. For some reason, Logan McHenry found the lengthy newspaper account fascinating. He had reread it many times since purchasing the latest issue of the Laramie *Daily Boomerang* when Opal and he had picked up supplies in Medicine Bow. The date on the paper was now nearly three months out of currency. The crease along the edges of the folded newsprint had begun to split.

"Damned Scandehoovians," said Logan. "They know cold up there, but they don't know *real* cold," he added vehemently.

He got up from the straight-back chair by the fire and walked stiffly over to the small kitchen window. With his thumbnail he scraped a silver cartwheel-sized patch free of ice. Logan could see nothing. Just the endless, blinding white of wind-whipped snow. "Don't look like it's gonna let up," he said.

"Hasn't looked like it was going to let up for six days now," his wife commented. She slowly and expertly carved the peel away from a fist-sized potato. Opal was thin, whip-tough, taller than her husband. He had never much liked that.

Logan continued staring out at the unvarying blizzard. "Maybe I better lay in some more wood." He gestured vaguely at the pile of quarter-splits piled against the wall to her side. "We got maybe enough to last until night."

"Mighty cold out there," said his wife.

"Ain't gonna get no warmer."

"How cold do you figure?"

Logan shrugged. "Last time I checked, it was somethin' like eighteen below. And then the wind cuts it pretty fierce."

"Want to take that out when you go?" Opal gestured at the full bucket of peels, scraps, and trash.

"No, I don't want." He wasn't sure why he said it. *Just to be contrary.* "All right," he contradicted himself. "I'll set it out. Wind'll blow it clean to Nebraska."

She stared at him a moment. "Thank you kindly," she said.

Logan pulled on his heavy cloth coat. He tugged the worn old Stetson down tight over his ears and wrapped the long woolen muffler over the crown, down under his chin, and then looped back around his neck. He slipped on the sheepskin-lined work gloves. "I'm ready," he said. "Help me with the door?"

Something tickled the inside of one nostril. He couldn't help himself—Logan emitted an enormous sneeze. He winced. It was painful. The dry skin at the bottom of his nose was cracking.

"Company's coming," said Opal automatically. It was how she always answered when he sneezed. Logan's usual response to a sneeze—when he said anything at all—was the standard "Gesundheit." Opal's "Company's coming" was, she said, something her family had said for as long as she could remember.

It was strange—whenever Logan heard the phrase, he usually thought also of *his* mother's saying that one of those unexplainable, wracking shivers was because "Someone's walking over your grave." Different thing entirely, he knew, but somehow the situations seemed the same, at least on the surface. *Walking over your grave.*

He picked up the handle of the trash bucket. Logan could already feel the knives of the Wyoming wind jamming into his joints; piercing and then twisting with icy blades. But it was worse when he opened the door.

The cold sucked at him, tried to pull him bodily out of the house. Logan braced himself, his free hand locked on the jamb. Opal had the strong fingers of both slender hands wound around the doorknob. "Be back in five minutes," he shouted. He knew his wife could not hear him in the blizzard din.

Logan let loose of the jamb and let the wind pull him forward to the edge of the porch. Behind him he felt the heat vanish as Opal tugged the back door shut. He was alone with the wind and the snow. And the cold.

He staggered forward and wrapped his free arm around the corner post. Then he ran his hand down to waist level. Three ropes were tied to the post. The one angling off to the left led a hundred yards to the barn. The other end of the center rope was nailed to the door of the outhouse. The right-hand rope stretched tautly between porch and the root cellar, perhaps ten yards distant.

The man couldn't see any of the three destinations. In every case, the ropes fuzzed indistinctly and vanished a few feet into the snow. That same snow sawed past him like sand, moving nearly horizontally. He knew the drifts on the other side of the house must be right up to the eaves.

First things first. Logan shook out the contents of the bucket. They vanished instantly into the blizzard's maw. He would use the bucket to carry wood back from the barn. He'd need one hand to hold the rope.

Without the rope's guidance, he'd be confused in a foot, lost in a yard. Probably dead in the length of his own body. Maybe not immediately, but in short order. He was under no illusion how long he could last in this storm.

Before starting for the wood, he squinted at the thermometer nailed to the corner post. Getting colder. Thirty below. The gauge only went to forty. Logan shook his head.

According to his daddy's old railroad watch—he'd checked it before abandoning the shelter of the kitchen—it was high noon.

The snow.

It felt like thousands of tiny mouths, lined with needle teeth, all sucking the heat from his skin. He had to admit to himself that it was frightening, once he was away from the porch, to be surrounded completely by the blizzard. With the handle of the bucket still clutched firmly, he moved hand over hand toward the barn. For perhaps the hundredth time, he chewed himself out for not hauling in nearly enough wood when the first flakes of the storm had drifted down.

But who knew? Wyoming blizzards, even in the dead of winter in the middle of the Shirley Basin, usually blew themselves out in a day, two at the most. Logan had never seen anything like this storm. He'd heard stories of the big one in 1899—the tellers never tired of listing the stock that had died, and there had been plenty—but Opal and he had still been in Pennsylvania then.

The dark plank wall of the barn loomed out of the storm like a cliff. Logan staggered into the lee side and luxuriated for a moment at being given a respite from the wind. Then the wind's direction changed and the icy nails raked at his face.

Logan took hold of the peg that lifted the latching bar and opened the door. It was dark inside. That didn't matter; he knew exactly where the wood was stacked.

He heard a hoof stamping and an anxious whicker.

"You need some more hay?"

The horse whinnied.

"All right, boy. Hold your— " He laughed at himself and did not finish the line. Logan set down the pail, then picked up a few bats of powdery alfalfa and dropped them over the side of the stall. The big bay, Indian, brushed Logan's arm with his muzzle, then leaned down toward the hay. The man turned, bent, and broke off a chunk of crusted snow from the drift that extended from the door into the barn. Double-handed, he dropped it into Indian's water pan.

"Better than nothing, boy."

Logan found the wood in the dark, wedged as many splits as he could into the bucket, set another three pieces under his left arm, and shoved open the door against the wind. He slid his right hand along the rope to the house.

Three times, the wind almost broke his grip. Each time he recoiled against the blast, then hunched over the rope and kept pushing his way toward the porch. One of the sticks of firewood slipped out from beneath his free arm. He did not try to retrieve it. The wood disappeared into the snow as though it had never existed at all.

In this storm, Logan thought, *anything* could as easily vanish—a horse, a cow, a human being. A wife. Why had he thought that? he wondered.

And then he wondered that he wondered.

They had married when she was sixteen and he was twenty. That had been in the year this god-forsaken territory of Wyoming became the forty-fourth state of the Union. Neither of them had even dreamed they would find themselves here two decades later.

1890—a year of unbounded promise for all. Almost all, he amended the thought. There had been the killing of the hundreds of Sioux redmen at Wounded Knee. There had been stories of massacre in Dahomey, a faroff African kingdom. Other accounts in the newspapers of death in Madagascar, Angola, other distant places.

Logan had always been fond of reading the papers, although he wasn't all that enamored of regular books. When Opal and he had married, her mother had given them a copy of *Hedda Gabler*, a play by another of those Scandehoovians. It was brand spanking new, but he had never read it. He didn't even know where it was now.

The farmstead in Pennsylvania had failed and the bank had assumed control. At the end, the McHenrys had been given a generous three days to vacate. They had gone west.

Wyoming—and the Shirley Basin—had welcomed them in the spring. Summer had been moderate, the autumn bounty generous. Then winter had come.

Somehow they had stayed on for eight years. Both of them were stubborn.

They lived by themselves.

At first, it was not by choice. Logan blamed himself for their marriage being barren of progeny. He knew Opal blamed herself equally. So many days they stared at each other silently, accusations against self unvoiced. So many nights they lay silently in their narrow bed. Sometimes Logan would turn on his side and look at Opal. In the dim moonlight he would see her staring at the low ceiling. Opal would sense his look, then meet his eyes. At least he thought she was looking at him. With her deep-set eyes lying in shadow, it was difficult to tell.

The wind blew hard and constantly, and the cold lay upon the land. The springs seemed all too short, the summers increasingly parching. The autumns became as arid as their marriage bed.

The winters savaged them.

Of course I love her. Logan stared at the outside of the kitchen door until the wind nearly rocked him off balance. He clutched at the firewood and cradled it close to the warmth of his body. *Of course.*

He reached out with a stick of pine and tapped on the door, knocked harder, finally beat on the slab fiercely until the dark door became an oblong of light and heat. Opal stood in the doorway staring at him for what seemed a long time. Then she stepped back and beckoned him enter.

Logan could not feel his fingers or toes.

"Doesn't look good," said Opal.

Logan protested.

His wife sat him down in the ladder-back chair by the kitchen stove. She shoved two of the sticks he'd brought in with him into the stove, then put on a pan of water to heat. "Get them off, and right now," she mumbled, grabbing the boots in question, one at a time, and wrestling them off his feet. "How do they feel?" she said, peeling the socks loose. They stank.

"Can't rightly feel nothing at all."

"Fingers too?"

"Same thing," Logan said.

"Give them here." Opal took his right hand between her own two hands and rubbed. At first there was no sensation. Then Logan saw the gray flesh begin to grow pink, then glow a flushed red. Opal rubbed his left hand with the same result. Steam was beginning to rise from the pan on the stove. The woman set it down on the floor and put Logan's feet in the water. Sensation was slow in coming, but eventually it did arrive.

Finally, Opal stood from her ministrations and said, "You wait right here."

"Wasn't going nowhere." Logan didn't crack a smile. Needles of pain lanced through his fingers and toes.

His wife put on his coat, slipped on her own gloves. "Won't be gone but a few minutes," she said. She slipped out the kitchen door, seemingly opening it so narrowly that only a small amount of snow sheeted in. Opal was a skinny woman.

She told the truth. She was not gone long. When she returned, Opal dropped the large armload of cut wood on the floor by the stove, took a few deep breaths of warm air, then turned and headed out the door again. She brought back two more loads of firewood.

"That ought to be enough," said Logan after the third trip. "It will get us through tonight. You'd better stop, or pretty soon I'll be out looking for your frozen carcass in the blizzard."

Opal surveyed the pile of pine splits. Snow and ice had melted in a shallow puddle around the wood. "Reckon you're right." She turned toward him. "Ready for some coffee?"

Logan nodded. Opal slipped another piece of wood into the stove and slid the coffee pot over the hottest iron lid. It was still the breakfast brew. What she finally poured into her husband's cup was black as coal and smelled vile. Logan hunched over the coffee until it was cool enough to sip.

Opal scraped a patch of frost off the kitchen window-glass and stared out at the constant snow. "You know something," she said, "you lose your fingers or your feet, and you'll have the makings of a mighty poor dryland farmer."

"Rancher," he corrected automatically. "We're ranchers now."

"Rancher," she said. "No matter. We'd do poorly."

"So?"

"Maybe," Opal continued slowly, "it's time we thought about moving on to the Wasatch Valley over there in Utah, or maybe even go clear on out to California." She paused. It was a long speech for her.

Howling, the wind whipped around the eaves of the small house.

"So you think we should go?" said Logan. "And save my hands, my toes?"

She stared back at him mutely.

"Or perhaps you feel if I lose those limbs, we'll *have* to leave the Shirley Basin."

"That's not what I said." Opal's eyes seemed for a moment to gleam the milky white of their namesake. Then they were blue again. The wind's howl rose in pitch and volume.

Logan felt suddenly obstinate. "If we don't live here," he said, "we will die here."

The wind screamed.

Logan didn't know from where the idea had come to him, or, indeed, *when* it had come. Maybe it had always been there. He listened as the wind keened wildly and the snow rattled against the walls, the shake roof, the frost-blinded windowpanes.

He had picked up a cold from his sojourn out to the barn and back. His nose ran continually now; the rag he used as a handkerchief had grown sodden. The wracking sneezes were the worst, though.

And every time, Opal smiled thinly, sympathetically, and said, "Company's coming."

If company was indeed coming, it would not be for a while yet. The storm had continued through the afternoon and into the evening. In the lantern light, his father's watch said that the time was past midnight. The wind did not abate. The shrieking was like the red-hot prickles he had felt earlier when his fingers and toes defrosted. The sound entered his head and stayed there, even when the wind varied its pitch.

He could not sleep.

Logan watched his wife slumber. Opal's gentle snores indicated she was able to ignore the blizzard and sleep.

Unless—The thought came to him and lodged in his head like a straw driven by a tornado. Unless she was pretending.

Why would Opal pretend such a thing?

Logan puzzled over that a long time, almost until his concentration on the problem had brought him close to uneasy sleep. But he was brought up short by the realization: Opal could not possibly be sleeping. The storm forbade that. She must be pretending in order to fool him, and she was fooling Logan so that he would not know what she truly felt and thought.

He watched her for the remainder of the long night. He stared at Opal, waiting for his wife to make the slightest mistake. He knew she would trip herself up sooner or later. All he had to do was to be patient.

His patience was inexhaustible as the hours ticked away and some distant dawn approached invisibly.

One mistake and he would have her.

The wind screamed triumphantly.

It happened after breakfast.

Opal had fixed a platter of flapjacks, with a plate of salted beef on the side. She had also brewed a fresh pot of coffee that tasted slightly better than yesterday's preparation.

The taste of the food almost allayed Logan's suspicions.

The knife-edges of wind in his head kept him from hearing most of Opal's slender pronouncements as the morning wore on with no apparent respite from the storm. This portion of Wyoming still reeled.

After breakfast, Logan pushed back from the table and said, "I'll be getting some wood now."

Opal nodded, fixed him for a moment with her alien and intense look, and said, "Will you take that out?" She gestured toward the bucket of scraps and trash.

Logan remembered the previous day when he had had to manage both the empty bucket and the wood. He recalled what had happened to fingers and toes. He could walk today, and he could touch things.

He knew suddenly that what Opal really wanted was for him no longer to be able to do those things. With no fingers or toes, perhaps even without feet or hands, then they would have to move on. They would be obliged to move to a more temperate place, some foolish golden paradise as California was reputed to be, a heaven on earth where oranges and other fruit would be free for the plucking from the tree.

But at what cost to his soul?

The wind—

"All right," said Logan. "I will take it out."

And he did. He did it carefully and quietly and without argument, so that she would suspect nothing.

And then he brought back three loads of wood from the barn, one after another, the painful product of following the rope back and forth as ice crystals flayed the exposed flesh of his face.

"That's enough for now."

Opal smiled agreement. "I will get some more food stocks from the cellar." She put on her cold-weather clothing.

The wind—

Logan got the door for his wife. He braced his legs and held the back door open for her. A wind gust exposed the length of her to his sight; then the snow closed in and she was gone.

Her husband glanced at the thermometer. There was no mercury in the gauge. The bulb had shattered. It could never be colder than now.

Logan didn't even think about what he was doing. He looked down at the three ropes fastened to the porch. It was far too cold to fiddle with the ice-encrusted knots. He took the clasp knife from his pocket and unfolded the blade. Then he sawed at the right-hand rope. He didn't hesitate when the final strands began to ravel. He sliced across them with the knife. Tension whipped the free end of the rope into the storm.

It was gone.

The man chopped at the center rope, the one that led to the outhouse. He could make do for the duration of the storm. It was what the bucket really was for. Cut through, this rope also vanished in the snow.

Logan hesitated, then sawed at the remaining rope that could guide him to the barn. The wood was there, and so was Indian, but the storm surely could not last another full day and night. He would not need the barn.

The third rope parted, strand by strand, and was abruptly gone.

The wind laughed as Logan retreated into the kitchen and shut the door. He paused a moment, then slid home the bolt that locked it.

Logan spent much of the day reading old issues of the Laramie

Daily Boomerang. He discovered himself always returning to the issue detailing Roald Amundsen's arduous conquest of the Southern Pole. The entire account fascinated him.

But he was equally intrigued by the subsidiary story detailing other polar expeditions. Logan had long been fascinated by the Englishman, Robert Falcon Scott, who had led a successful scouting expedition to the ice pack in 1900, twelve years before. There had been speculation that Scott might become the first man to trek to the South Pole. The Norwegian had apparently beaten him to that goal.

"At least Scott is a white man," muttered Logan. But then, it occurred to him, so was Amundsen.

Logan wondered how Scott might feel, finding out that he had been beaten out by a longtime rival. Would it be like death?

The light had begun to fail. Logan looked around him.

Was twilight falling, the storm abating? He turned up the wick of the lamp, but the dark continued to encroach.

Maybe he was just out of kerosene.

Logan shook his head. He had felt himself begin to drift, nodding, perhaps beginning to catch up to the sleep that had eluded him for so long.

Someone knocked at the back door.

Logan jerked awake.

He heard another knock. It was a solid rapping sound, discernible above the wind.

Logan got up from the chair and tentatively started to cross the kitchen. He didn't have to unbolt the door, after all. If that was Opal still out there . . . But it couldn't be. He had cut the ropes hours before.

He didn't have to unlock the door.

The door opened anyway.

Logan saw the hand appear through the snow blowing into the opening between the door and jamb. The fingers were slender and gray, curving around the door's edge. The wrist extended into the kitchen, the lower arm—

The man hit the door with his shoulder, slamming it shut with all the hysterical strength he could muster.

Shut.

Sheared off below the elbow, the wrist and hand tumbled to the plank floor. The fingers shattered with the sound of tinkling crystal. Bright shards of icy flesh scattered across the floor like broken glass.

Still hunched against the door, Logan stared down at the floor. The lamplight still flickered, but he could see ruby fragments melting.

The ice-jewels became drops of blood.

The light on the bits of flesh and bone and blood transfixed him, he didn't know for how long.

And when Logan came back to himself, still wedged against the door, there was no blood on the floor. There was nothing.

And the door was still locked.

From outside, the wind said everything. But the wind was inside now too.

Dear Lord, he wanted to sleep.

Logan thought it was morning. He was not sure because the watch had stopped during the night. *At the time the door had been flung open and the hand thrust inside* . . . No, because he had forgotten to wind it.

He levered himself upright. He had been sitting on the floor beside the door. His muscles were cramped, his limbs stiff and sore.

The man realized the fire in the kitchen stove had gone out. He clumsily stuffed wood into the grate, picked up some of the shavings used for tinder, tried to light them with the sulfur match that lay on the table. The match went out without passing on its flame.

Logan couldn't find another match. There must another one somewhere. There must be an entire box.

After a while he gave up looking and hauled a comforter from the bed across the room. He draped it around his shoulders and sat down in the ladder-back chair. He needed to think for a moment. The wind didn't allow him to do that.

Logan realized that the kerosene lamp was out, yet he could still see. A gray light filtered dimly through the window.

Was the blizzard over?

He didn't feel any warmer with the realization. He didn't feel much of anything at all. His arms and legs felt much as they had upon completing that trip from the barn days before when he had gotten his frostbite. Had it been days?

Logan wasn't sure.

But he was increasingly certain that the storm was abating.

The wind still shrilled, but the sound of snow raking the side of the house was no longer there. Yes, the blizzard had dwindled.

That meant he was no longer trapped. That meant people could come to the house.

That meant—

Company's coming.

His nose tickled.
Logan tried to get up from the chair, could not, sank resignedly.
"Opal— " he said. He could say no more.
He began to sneeze uncontrollably.

NANCY A. COLLINS

Raymond

NANCY COLLINS won the Horror Writers of America Bram Stoker
Award for her first novel, *Sunglasses After Dark* (1988) and the
British Fantasy Society's Icarus Award for Best Newcomer.

Born in rural Arkansas, she moved to New Orleans in 1982 and
currently lives in New York City with underground film-maker/
musician Joe Christ. Her subsequent novels include *Tempter* and
In the Blood, and her short fiction has appeared in a wide variety
of magazines and anthologies, such as *Cemetery Dance*, *Pulphouse*,
Midnight Graffiti, *There Won't Be War* and *The Year's Best Fantasy
and Horror: Fourth Annual Collection*. She is also the current writer
for DC Comics' *Swamp Thing* series.

Like much of Collins' fiction, "Raymond" takes a familiar horror
icon—in this case the werewolf—and stands it on its head.

I REMEMBER THE FIRST TIME I saw Raymond Fleuris.
It was during Mrs Harper's seventh-grade homeroom; I was staring out the window at the parking lot that fronted the school. There wasn't anything happening in the parking lot, but it seemed a hell of a lot more interesting than Old Lady Harper rattling on about long division. That's when I saw the truck.

Beat-up old trucks are not what you'd call unusual in Choctaw County, but this had to be *the* shittiest excuse for a motor vehicle ever to roll the streets of Seven Devils, Arkansas. The bed overflowed with pieces of junk lumber, paint cans, and rolls of rusty chicken wire. The chassis was scabby with rust. It rode close to the ground, bouncing vigorously with every pothole. The front bumper was connected to the fender by a length of baling wire, spit, and a prayer.

I watched as the truck pulled up next to the principal's sedan and the driver crawled out from behind the wheel.

My first impression was that of a mountain wearing overalls. He was massive. Fat jiggled on every part of his body. Thick rolls of it pooled around his waist, straining his shirt to the breaking point. The heavy jowls framing his face made him look like a foul-tempered bulldog. He was big and fat, but it was mean fat; no one in their right mind would have ever mistaken him for jolly.

The driver lumbered around the front of the truck, pausing to pull a dirty bandanna out of his back pocket and mop his forehead. He motioned irritably to someone seated on the passenger's side, then jerked the door open. I was surprised it didn't come off in his hand. His face was turning red as he yelled at whoever was in the passenger's seat.

After a long minute, a boy climbed out of the truck and stood next to the ruddy-faced mountain of meat.

Normally I wouldn't have spared the Fleurises a second look. Except that Raymond's head was swaddled in a turban of sterile gauze and surgical tape and his hands were covered by a pair of old canvas gloves, secured at the wrists with string.

Now *that* was interesting.

Raymond was small and severely underweight. His eyes had grayish-yellow smears under them that made it look like he was perpetually recovering from a pair of shiners. His skin was pale and reminded me of the waxed paper my mama wrapped my sandwiches in.

Someone, probably his mama, had made an effort to clean and press his bib overalls and what was probably his only shirt. No doubt she'd hoped Raymond would make a good impression on his first day at school. No such luck. His clothes looked like socks on a rooster.

By the time the lunch bell rang, everybody knew about the new kid. Gossip runs fast in junior high, and by the end of recess, there were a half-dozen accounts of Raymond Fleuris's origins floating about.

Some said he'd been in a car wreck and thrown through the windshield. Others said the doctors up at the State Hospital did some kind of surgery to cure him of violent fits. Chucky Donothan speculated that he'd had some kind of craziness-tumor cut out. Whatever the reason for the head bandages and the gloves, it made Raymond Fleuris, at least for the space of a few days, exotic and different. And that means nothing but trouble when you're in junior high.

Raymond ended up being assigned to my homeroom. Normally, Mrs Harper had us sit alphabetically; but in Raymond's case, she assigned him a desk in the back of the room. Not that it made any difference to Raymond. He never handed in homework and was excused from taking tests. All he did was sit and scribble in his notebook with one of those big kindergarten pencils.

Raymond carried his lunch to school in an old paper bag that, judging from the grease stains, had seen a lot of use. Once I accidentally stumbled across Raymond eating his lunch behind the Science Building. His food consisted of a single sandwich made from cheap store-bought white bread and a slice of olive loaf. After he finished his meal, Raymond carefully flattened the paper bag, folded it, and tucked it in the back pocket of his overalls.

I felt funny, standing there watching Raymond perform his little after-lunch ritual. I knew my folks weren't rich, but at least we could afford paper bags. Maybe that's why I did what I did when I saw Chucky Donothan picking on Raymond the next day.

It was recess and I was hanging with my best friend, Rafe Mercer. We were talking about the county fair coming to town next month. It was nowhere near as big or as fancy as the State Fair up in Little Rock; but when you're stuck in a backwater like Seven Devils, you take what you can get.

"Darryl, you reckon they'll have the kootchie show again?" Rafe must have asked me that question a hundred times already. I didn't mind, though, because I was wondering the same thing. Last year Rafe's older brother, Calvin, got in on the strength of some whiskers and his football-boy physique. Not to mention a dollar.

"I don't see why not. It's been there every year, ain't it?"

"Yeah, you're right." Rafe was afraid he would graduate high school without once getting the chance to see a woman in her bra and panties. He looked at the pictures in his mama's wish books, but that wasn't the same as seeing a *real live* half-naked lady. I could understand his concern.

Just about then Kitty Killigrew ran past. Both me and Rafe were sweet on Kitty, not that we'd admit it to her—or ourselves—this side of physical torture. She was a pretty girl, with long coppery-red hair that hung to her waist and eyes the color of cornflowers. Rafe went on to marry her, six years later. That fucker.

"Hey, Kitty! What's going on?" Rafe yelled after her.

Kitty paused long enough to gasp out one word. "Fight!"

That was all the explanation we needed. Schoolyard fights attract students like shit draws flies. Rafe and I hurried after her. As we rounded the corner of the building, I could see a knot of kids near the science building.

I pushed my way through my schoolmates in time to see Chucky Donothan kick Raymond Fleuris's feet out from under him.

Raymond flopped onto his back in the dirt and laid there. It was evident that the fight—if you could call it that—was pretty one-sided. I couldn't imagine what Raymond might have done to piss off the bigger boy; but knowing Chucky, the fact Raymond had weight and occupied space was probably insult enough.

"Stand up and fight, retard!" Chucky bellowed.

Raymond got to his feet, his eyes filled with pain and confusion. His bandage-turban was smeared with dirt. With his oversized canvas gloves and shit-kicker brogans, Raymond looked like a pathetic caricature of Mickey Mouse. Everyone started laughing.

"What's with the gloves, retard?" Chucky sneered. "What's the matter? You jerk off so much you got hair on your palms?"

Some of the girls giggled at that witticism, so Chucky continued pressing his attack. "Is that your big secret, Fleuris? You a jag-off? Huh? Huh? Is that it? Why don't you take 'em off so we can see, huh?"

Raymond shook his head. "Paw sez I can't take 'em off. Paw sez I gotta keep 'em on all time." It was one of the few times I ever heard Raymond speak out loud. His voice was thin and reedy, like a clarinet.

The crowd fell silent as Chucky's naturally ruddy complexion grew even redder.

"You tellin' me *no*, retard?"

Raymond blinked. It was obvious he didn't understand what was going on. It dawned on me that Raymond would stand there and let Chucky beat him flatter than his lunch bag without lifting a finger to protect himself. Suddenly, I didn't want to watch what was going on anymore.

"Chuck, leave him be, can't you see he's *simple*?"

"Butt out, Sweetman! Less'n you want me to kick *your* ass, too!"

I cut my eyes at Rafe. He shook his head. "Hell, Darryl, I ain't about to get the shit knocked outta me on account of Raymond Fleuris!"

I looked away.

Satisfied he'd quelled all opposition, Chucky grabbed Raymond's left arm, jerking on the loosely fitted glove. "If you ain't gonna show us, I guess I'll *make* you!"

And that's when the shit hit the fan.

One second Raymond was your basic slack-jawed moron, the next he was shrieking and clawing at Chucky like the Tasmanian Devil in those old Bugs Bunny cartoons. His face seemed to *flex*, like the muscles were being jerked every-which-way. I know it sounds stupid, but that's the only way I can describe it.

Raymond was on the bully like white on rice, knocking him to the ground. We all stood there and gaped in disbelief, our mouths hanging open, as they wrestled in the dirt. Suddenly Chucky started making these high-pitched screams and that's when I saw the blood.

Chucky managed to throw Raymond off of him just as Coach Jenkins hustled across the playground, paddle in hand. Chucky was rolling around, crying like a little kid. Blood ran from a ragged wound in the fleshy part of his upper arm. Raymond sat in the dirt, staring at the other boy like he was from Mars. There was blood on Raymond's mouth, but it wasn't his. The bandage had come unravelled in the brawl, giving everyone a good look at the three-inch scar that climbed his right temple.

"What—the—blazes—is going on here!" Coach Jenkins always had trouble refraining from swearing in front of the students, and it looked like he was close to reaching critical mass. "Donothan! Get on your feet, boy!"

"He *bit* me!" Chucky wailed, his face filthy with snot and tears.

Coach Jenkins shot a surprised look at Raymond, still sitting in the dirt. "Is that true, Fleuris? Did you bite Donothan?"

Raymond stared up at Coach Jenkins and blinked.

Coach Jenkins' neck pulsed and he looked at the ring of now-guilty faces. "Okay, who started it?"

"Donothan did, sir." I was surprised to hear the words coming from my mouth. "He was picking on Raymond."

Coach Jenkins pushed the bill of his baseball cap back and tried to keep the vein in his neck from pulsing even harder. "Did anyone try to stop it?"

Silence.

"Right. Come on, Donothan. Get up. You, too, Fleuris. We're going to the principal's office."

"I'm *bleeding!*"

"We'll have the nurse take a look at it, but you're *still* going to the office!" Jenkins grabbed Chucky by his uninjured arm and jerked him to his feet. "You should be ashamed of yourself, Donothan!" He hissed under his breath. "Pickin' on a cripple!"

I stepped forward to help Raymond. It was then that I noticed one of his gloves had come off in the fight.

"Here, you lost this."

Raymond snatched his glove back, quickly stuffing his bare hand into it. But not before I had time to notice that his ring finger was longer than the others.

When I was a kid, Choctaw County was pretty much like it was when my daddy was growing up. If not worse. Sure, we had stuff like television and a public library by then, but by the time I was twelve the old Malco Theatre went belly-up: another victim of the railroad dying off.

One of the biggest thrills of the year was going to the county fair. For five days in late October the aluminium outbuildings dotting what had once been Old Man Ferguson's cow pasture became a gaudy wonderland of neon lights.

If you went to the fair every night, you'd eventually see the entire population of Choctaw County put in an appearance. It was one of the few times the various ethnic groups and religious sects congregated at the same place, although I'd hardly call it "mingling." The blacks stayed with the blacks while the whites stayed with the whites. There was also little in the way of cross-over between the Baptists, Methodists, and Pentecostal. Families came by the truckload, dressed in their Sunday-go-to-meeting clothes. I never knew there were so many people in the county.

Rafe and I were wandering the booths lining the midway, looking for the kootchie show. Rafe hadn't shaved in three weeks, hoping he could build up enough beard to pass for sixteen.

We bumped into Kitty, who was chewing on a wad of cotton candy and contemplating a banner that showed a dwarf supporting a bucket of sand from a skewer piercing his tongue.

"Hey, Kitty. When'd you get here?" I asked, trying to sound casual.

"Hey, Darryl. Hey, Rafe. I rode over with Veronica about a half-hour ago. You just get here?" There was a strand of pink candy floss stuck at the corner of her perfect mouth. I watched in silent fascination as she tried to dislodge it with the tip of her tongue.

Rafe shrugged. "Kind of."

"Seen the World's Smallest Horse yet?"

"No."

"Don't bother. It's a rip-off; just some dumb old Shetland Pony at the bottom of a hole dug in the ground." She poked her half-eaten cotton candy in my face. "You want the rest of this, Darryl? I can't finish it. You know what they say: sweets to the sweet."

"Uh, no thanks, Kitty." People keep saying that to me on account of my last name, Sweetman. I hate it, but short of strangling everybody on the face of the earth, there's no way I can avoid it. And no one believes me when I tell them I can't stand sugar.

"I'll take it, Kitty." Rafe was a smoothy, even then. Did I mention he ended up marrying her after high school? Did I mention I haven't talked to him since?

Kitty frowned and pointed over my shoulder. "Isn't that Raymond Fleuris?"

Rafe and I turned around and looked where she was pointing. Sure enough, Raymond Fleuris was standing in front of the "Tub-O-Ducks" game, watching the brightly colored plastic ducks bobbing along in their miniature millrace. Although his hands were still gloved, he no longer wore his bandage on his head, and his dark hair bristled like the quills of a porcupine.

Rafe shrugged. "I saw his daddy shovelling out the livestock barn; the carnival lets the temporary workers' families ride for free."

Kitty was still looking at Raymond. "You know, yesterday during recess I asked him why he had brain surgery."

I found my voice first. "You *actually* asked him that?"

"Sure did."

"Well, what did he say?"

Kitty frowned. "I dunno. When I asked him, he looked like he was trying *real hard* to remember something. Then he got this goofy grin on his face and said 'chickens'."

"*Chickens?*"

"Don't look at me like *I'm* nuts, Rafe Mercer! I'm just tellin' you want he said! But what was *really* weird was how he said it! Like he was remembering going to Disneyland or something!"

"So Raymond Fleuris is weird. Big deal. C'mon, I wanna check out the guy who cuts a girl in half with a chainsaw. Wanna go with us, Kitty?" Rafe mimed pulling a cord and went *rup-rup-ruppppp!*, waving the wad of cotton candy like a deadly weapon.

Kitty giggled behind her hand. "You're *silly!*"

That was all I could take. If I had to stay with them another five minutes I'd either puke or pop Rafe in the nose. "I'll catch up with you later, Rafe. Okay? Rafe?"

135

"Huh?" Rafe managed to tear his eyes away from Kitty long enough to give me a quick, distracted nod. "Oh, yeah. Sure. Later, man."

Muttering under my breath, I stalked off, my fists stuffed in my pockets. Suddenly the fair didn't seem as much fun as it'd been ten minutes ago. Even the festive aroma of hot popcorn, cotton candy, and corndogs failed to revive my previous good mood.

I found myself staring at a faded canvas banner that said, in vigorous Barnum script: **Col. Reynard's Pocket Jungle**. Below the headline a stiffly rendered red-headed young man dressed like Frank Buck wrestled a spotted leopard.

Lounging behind the ticket booth in front of the tent stood a tall man dressed in a sweat-stained short-sleeved khaki shirt and jodhpurs. His hair was no longer bright red and his face looked older, but there was no doubt that he was Colonel Reynard: Great White Hunter. As I watched, he produced a World War Two surplus microphone and began his spiel. His voice crackled out of a public address system, adding to the noise and clamor of the midway.

"Hur-ree! Hur-ree! Hur-ree! See the most ex-zotic and danger-rus ani-mals this side of Aff-Rika! See! The noble tim-bur wolf! King of the Ark-Tik Forest! See! The wild jag-war! Ruthless Lord of the Am-A-Zon Jungle! See! The hairy orang-utang! Borny-Oh's oh-riginal Wild Man of the Woods! See! The fur-rocious Grizzlee Bear! Mon-Arch of the Fro-zen North! See these wonders and more! Hur-ree! Hur-ree! Hur-ree!"

A handful of people stopped and turned their attention toward the Colonel. One of them happened to be Raymond Fleuris. A couple came forward with their money. Raymond just stood there at the foot of the ticket podium, staring at the red-headed man. I expected the Colonel to make like W. C. Fields, but instead he waved Raymond inside the tent.

What the hell?

I didn't really want to see a bunch of half-starved animals stuck in cages. But there was something in the way Colonel Reynard had looked at Raymond, like he'd recognized him, that struck me as curious. First I thought he might be queer for boys, but The Great White Hunter didn't look at me twice when I paid for my ticket and joined the others inside the tent.

The "Pocket Jungle" reeked of sawdust and piss. There were raised platforms scattered about the tent, canvas drop-cloths covering the cages. Colonel Reynard finally joined us and went into his pitch, going on about how he'd risked life and limb collecting the specimens we were about to see. As he spoke, he went from cage to cage, throwing back the drop-cloths so we could see the animals trapped inside.

I hadn't been expecting anything, and I wasn't disappointed. The "jaguar" was a slat-thin ocelot; the "timber wolf" was a yellow-eyed coyote that paced the confines of its cage like a madman; the "grizzly" was a plain old black bear, its muzzle so white it looked like it'd been sprinkled with powdered sugar. The only thing that really was what it was supposed to be was the orangutan.

The ape was big, its wrinkled old-man's features nearly lost in its vast face. It sat in a cage only slightly larger than itself, its hand-like feet folded in front of its mammoth belly. With its dropping teats and huge girth, it resembled a shaggy Buddha.

Just as the Colonel was wrapping up his act, Raymond pushed his way from the back of the crowd and stood, motionless, gaping at the "timber wolf."

The coyote halted its ceaseless pacing and bared its fangs. A low, frightened growl came from the animal as it raised its hackles. The Colonel halted in mid-sentence and stared first at the coyote, then at Raymond.

As if on cue, the ocelot started to hiss and spit, flattening its ears against its sleek skull. The bear emitted a series of low grunts, while the orangutan covered its face and turned its back to the audience.

Raymond stepped back, shaking his head like he had a mite in his ear. The muscles in his face were jerking again, and I imagined I could smell blood and dust and hear Chucky Donothan squealing like a girl. Raymond staggered back, covering his eyes with his gloves. I heard someone in the crowd laugh; what it sounded like was a short, sharp, ugly bark.

Colonel Reynard snapped his fingers once and said in a strong voice, "Hush!" The animals grew silent immediately. He then stepped toward Raymond. "Son . . ."

Raymond made a noise that was somewhere between a sob and a shout and ran from the tent and into the crowds and noise of the midway. Colonel Reynard followed after him, and I followed the Colonel.

Raymond made for the cluster of aluminum outbuildings that served as exhibition halls. The Colonel didn't see Raymond dodge between the Crafts Barn and the Tractor Exhibit, but I did. I hurried after him, leaving the light and activity of the fairground behind me. I could dimly make out Raymond a few dozen yards ahead.

I froze as a tall, thin shadow stepped directly into Raymond's path, knocking him to the ground. I pressed against the aluminum shell of the Crafts Barn, praying no one noticed me lurking in the darkened "alley."

"You all right, son?" I recognized Colonel Reynard's voice, although I could not see his face.

Raymond shuddered as he tried to catch his breath and stop crying at the same time.

The carny helped Raymond to his feet. "Now, now, son . . . There's nothing to be ashamed of." His voice was as gentle and soothing as a man talking to a skittish horse. "I'm not going to hurt you, boy. Far from it."

Raymond stood there as Colonel Reynard wiped his face clean of tears, dirt and snot with a handkerchief.

"Let me see your hands, son."

Raymond shrank away from the stranger, crossing his gloved hands over his heart. "Paw sez if I take 'em off he'll whup me good. I ain't ever supposed to take 'em off ever again."

"Well, I say it's okay for you to take them off. And if your daddy don't like it, he'll have to whup on me first." The carny quickly untied both gloves and let them drop. Raymond's hands looked dazzlingly white, compared to his grimy face and forearms. Colonel Reynard squatted on his haunches and took Raymond's hands into his own, studying the fingers with interest. Then he tilted Raymond's head to one side. I could tell he was looking at the scar.

"What have they done?" The Colonel's voice sounded both angry and sad. "You poor child . . . What did they do to you?"

"Here now! What you doin' messin' with my boy?"

It was Mr Fleuris. He passed within inches of me, but if he noticed my presence it didn't register on his face. I wondered if this was how the first mammals felt, watching the dinosaurs lumber by their hiding place in the underbrush. The big man reeked of manure and fresh straw.

Raymond cringed as his father bore down on him.

"Raymond—Where the hell's yore gloves, boy? You know what I told you bout them gloves!" Mr Fleuris lifted a meaty arm, his sausage-sized fingers closing into a fist.

Raymond whimpered in anticipation of the blow that was certain to land on his upturned face.

Before Horace Fleuris had a chance to strike his son, Colonel Reynard grabbed the big man's wrist. In the dim light it looked as if the Colonel's third finger was longer than the others. I heard Mr Fleuris grunt in surprise and saw his upraised fist tremble.

"You will not touch this child, understand?"

"Dammit, leggo!" Fleuris' voice was pinched, as if he was both in pain and afraid.

"I *said* 'understand?'"

"I heared you the first time, damn you!"

The Colonel let Fleuris' arm drop. "You are the child's father?"

Fleuris nodded sullenly, massaging his wrist.

"I should kill you for what you've done."

"Here, now! Don't go blamin' me for it!" Fleuris blustered. "It was them doctors up at the State Hospital! They said it'd cure him! I tried to tell 'em what the boy's problem was, but you can't tell them big-city doctors squat, far as they're concerned! But what could I do? We was gettin' tired of movin' ever time the boy got into th' neighbor's chicken coop . . ."

"Now he'll *never* learn how to control it!" Reynard stroked Raymond's forehead. "He's stuck in-between the natures, incapable of fitting into your world . . . or ours. He is an abomination in the eyes of Nature. Even animals can see he has no place in the Scheme!"

"You like the boy, don't you?" There was something about how Fleuris asked the question that made my stomach knot. "I'm a reasonable man. When it comes to business."

I couldn't believe what I was hearing. Mr Fleuris was standing there, talking about *selling* his son to a complete stranger like he was a prize coon dog!

"Get out of here."

"Now hold on just a second! I ain't askin' for nothin' that ain't rightfully mine, and you know it! I'm the boy's pa and I reckon that calls for some kind of restitution, seeing how's he's my only male kin . . ."

"*Now!*" Colonel Reynard's voice sounded like a growl.

Horace Fleuris turned and fled, his fleshy face slack with fear. I never dreamed a man his size could move that fast.

I glanced at where Reynard stood, one hand resting on Raymond's shoulder. Colonel Reynard's face was no longer human, his mouth fixed in a deceptive smile. He fixed me with his murder-green eyes and wrinkled his snout. "That goes for you too, man-cub."

To this day I wonder why he let me go unharmed. I guess it's because he knew that no one was going to listen to any crazy stories about fox-headed men told by a pissant kid. No one wanted to believe crap like that. Not even the pissant kid.

Needless to say, I ran like a rabbit with a hound on my tail. Later I was plagued by recurring nightmares of a fox-headed animal-tamer dressed in jodhpurs that went around sticking his head in human mouths, and of a huge orangutan in overalls that looked like Mr Fleuris.

By the time Christmas break came around everyone had lost interest in Raymond's disappearance. The Fleuris family had moved sometime during the last night of October to parts unknown. No one missed them. It was like Raymond Fleuris had never existed.

I spent a lot of time trying not to think about what I'd seen and heard that night. I had other things to fret about. Like Kitty Killigrew going steady with Rafe.

Several years passed before I returned to the Choctaw County Fair. By then I was a freshman at the University of Arkansas at Monticello, over in Drew County. I'd landed a scholarship and spent my week-days studying in a bare-ass dorm room while coming home on weekends to help my daddy with the farm. I had long since talked myself into believing what I'd seen that night was a particularly vivid nightmare brought on by a bad corndog. Nothing more.

The midway didn't have a kootchie show that year, but I'd heard rumors that they had something even better. Or worse, depending on how you look at it.

According to the grapevine, the carnival had a glommin' geek. Since geek shows are technically illegal and roundly condemned as immoral, degrading, and sinful, naturally it played to capacity crowds.

The barker packed as many people as he could into a cramped, foul-smelling tent situated behind the freak show. There was a canvas pit in the middle of the tent, and at its bottom crouched the geek.

He was on the scrawny side and furry as a monkey. The hair on his head was long and coarse, hanging past his waist, as did a scraggly beard. His long forearms and bowed legs were equally shaggy, coated with dark fur that resembled the pelt of a wild goat. It was hard to tell, but I'm certain he was buck naked. There was something wrong with the geek's fingers, though that might have been on account of his four-inch long nails.

As the barker did his spiel about the geek being the last survivor of a race of wild men from the jungles of Borneo, I continued to stare at the snarling, capering creature. I couldn't shake the feeling that there was something *familiar* about the geek.

The barker finished his bit and produced a live chicken from a gunny sack. The geek lifted his head and sniffed the air, his nostrils flaring as he caught the scent of the bird. An idiot's grin split his hairy face and a long thread of drool dripped from his open jaws. His teeth were surprisingly white and strong.

The barker tossed the chicken into the pit. It fluttered downward, squawking as it frantically beat the air with its wings. The geek giggled like a delighted child and pounced on the hapless bird. His movements were as graceful and sure as those of a champion mouser dispatching a rat. The geek bit the struggling chicken's head off, obviously relishing every minute of it.

As the crowd moaned in disgust and turned their faces away from what was happening in the pit, I continued to watch, even though it made my stomach churn.

Why? Because I had glimpsed the pale finger of scar tissue traversing the geek's right temple.

I stood and stared down at Raymond Fleuris crouched at the bottom of the geek pit, his grinning face wreathed in blood and feathers.

Happy at last.

CHARLES L. GRANT

One Life, in an Hourglass

CHARLES L. GRANT is the undisputed master of "quiet" horror. He made his fiction debut in 1968 with the story "The House of Evil" in *The Magazine of Fantasy and Science Fiction* and, after producing a number of science fiction novels, he began to develop his unique brand of dark fantasy in such books as *The Hour of the Oxrun Dead*, *The Nestling*, *The Pet*, *For Fear of the Night*, *In a Dark Dream*, *Dialing the Wind*, *Stunts*, *Fire Mask* and *Something Stirs*.

His short fiction has been collected in *Tales from the Nightside*, *A Glow of Candles* and *Nightmare Seasons*, and he was the editor of the acclaimed *Shadows* (twelve volumes), *Midnight* and *Greystone Bay* anthologies.

Grant also publishes a number of fantasy adventures and spoofs under the pseudonyms "Geoffrey Marsh" and "Lionel Fenn", however he is best known for his series of stories set in Oxrun Station, a fictional western Connecticut town where all manner of strange things happen.

Not unlike Ray Bradbury's Green Town, Illinois—the setting for "One Life, in an Hourglass". It was visited late one October night many years ago by Cooger and Dark's Pandemonium Shadow Show (as told in Bradbury's classic novel *Something Wicked This Way Comes*). Now Grant takes us back to Green Town, where childhood fears still hold sway, and the influence of the evil Mr Dark is not forgotten . . .

D EMONS WALKED THE HALLS IN THE long hour past sunset, and gargoyles leered through the bedroom windows, moving with the branches of the deep maple outside. The carpet had been woven from human hair, still growing at the edges. The mirror over the dresser had been forged from cold flame that continued to escape from a crack in the lower corner. Dust turned grey along the baseboards. Water dripped in the kitchen. In the closet, behind the clothes, eyes that were slanted, swaying, each a different color, all of them staring.

In the milk-glass scalloped cover of the ceiling light, the dark shadows of corpses. Spiders, moths, a horse-fly, gnats; cleaned out once a month and there once again by the end of the week.

The lingering stench of dried blood.

Cora put the book down beside her on the mattress, adjusted the two pillows behind her back, and rubbed her eyes until the pain forced her to stop. When her vision cleared, sparks and flares faded, everything was gone but the dead insects; when her vision cleared, she was alone.

A small, second-floor apartment in a large house on Parleroad Lane. Front room, kitchen, bedroom, bathroom. Old wallpaper, old furniture, old sounds when the floorboards were trod upon in the silence.

She stretched her legs out, making them rigid, relaxing them, wiggling her toes. Not bad legs, she decided, examining them by the light of the dime store lamp on the nightstand. A little fleshy around the thighs, not as taut as she'd like, but not bad legs for a woman a zillion years older than she wanted to be. The rest of her wasn't all that bad, either. Her arms, when she lifted them, had no discernible flab; her breasts, when she peered down at them, were too small to develop much sag; her tummy had just the slightest bulge in spite of the garbage she usually ate for dinner. What the hell. All in all, not at all bad.

It just wasn't great.

Her palm itched; she scratched it lightly so it wouldn't tickle.

Then she scratched hard along her scalp, hair once in a while snagging on a nail, finished by clasping her hands behind her head, blowing out a breath as warm as the air around her, lifting her knees and looking between them to the dresser, the mirror, the flowers she had taped around the thin wood frame. Most of them were dead. A few brittle petals scattered among the bottles of perfume and nail polish, the tray that held bobby pins and paper clips and a single-garnet necklace and whatever else she couldn't be bothered to put away.

A slip hung halfway out of a half open drawer.

She couldn't see it, but she knew that the pleated skirt she had worn that day lay on the floor, huddled where it had been dropped.

Pigsty, she thought without a moment's concern.

It didn't matter; she wouldn't be here that long.

She swung her legs over the side of the bed and sat up, stared at her feet, sniffed, stared at the wall, and listened to the hushed voice of the street creeping in through the open window—the trees whispering to each other, someone walking a dog and talking to it loudly, music from down the block, cars up on Main Street.

She listened.

She reached up under her t-shirt and scratched at her ribs.

For crying out loud, Cora, make up your mind.

Something in her throat, then—a sob, maybe, or a laugh. Whatever it was, it marked her indecision. Her apprehension. Her belief that this was the year it would happen. All the waiting was over. All her nightmares turned to dreams. Never before, not since the first time she had returned to Green Town, in autumn, in October, had she felt this way. The other times were only wishes; this time, she was certain.

It frightened her.

What if . . .? she wondered, and wouldn't let herself wonder anymore.

Hello, child, he had said
I'm not a child, I'm sixteen.

She stood and stretched her arms toward the ceiling, spread her fingers, and waited until she felt the muscles edge toward the lip of a cramp. A sigh when she heard whispering in the front room. She stood with a shake of her head and walked into the front room, dropped onto the overstuffed couch, crossed her legs.

"Okay," she said. "What do you think?"

An overstuffed armchair to the left of the couch, both facing a console television Keith had given her as a surprise. A copper-and-glass coffee table cluttered with magazines, opened mail, old catalogues, several cut-glass tumblers with hardened milk on the bottom. The table had been Johnny's gift—to force, he had said with a sailor's rolling laugh, this crazy room back into the twentieth century. It hadn't. The standing lamps were fringed, the walls papered with twining daisies and stalwart ivy, the sideboard by the window Victorian ornate. The seashell ashtray on the table next to the couch had been carried back from Maine by the ever-anxious Rex. He had thought it cute; she had never used it.

"Well?"

On the wall beside the television, the fireplace. Pure ornament now, because it had been plugged up by the landlord before she'd returned the third or fourth time, she couldn't really remember. On the mantel were several framed pictures—Johnny and her, Keith and her, Rex and her, Drake and her, and one of her alone, down in the back garden the day she'd turned sixteen.

And on the mantel as well, four hourglasses. Faceted crystal. Round walnut top, square walnut base. The first three were full of grey at the bottom, their tops long since empty; the last one had nearly run out, running slowly.

So very slowly.

Well, Miss Sixteen, he had said, I would say you're about the most beautiful creature I have ever seen in my life.

Liar, she had answered with a giggle.

He smiled.

She shivered, out there in the meadow, Mother's shawl around her shoulders. Shivered again when he brushed a tender thumb across her cheek.

Miss Sixteen, he had whispered.

Cora, she had answered, half closing her eyes, lips opening just a little. Cora Fallman.

Ah, he said, and you can call me Mr Dark.

Her foot tapped the air impatiently. "Well?"

Pewter everywhere—mugs and bowls and vases and trays and small pitchers and a creamer she had discovered in a Quebec shop last summer.

No one spoke.

Her foot stilled.

"Helpless," she muttered, slapping the cushions, pushing herself to her feet. "What good are you?"

Not much, she answered for them, the ghosts and memories of her past, and returned to the bedroom where she posed in front of the dresser mirror, pouting, pursing her lips, a sideways coy glance, chin tucked against her shoulder, chest out and elbows back, finally standing back and ordering someone, for God's sake, to make up their mind before she lost hers.

It isn't mind, it's nerve, something said into her ear.

She nodded.

Nerve is right, but nervous is better.

Yet, if she didn't leave now, didn't go out there as she'd done a hundred times in thirty years, he might leave without her.

Quickly, before she could change her mind, she pulled herself into a sweater, a fresh pair of jeans, low boots, and a down jacket. A check to be sure all the windows were locked, a furtive glance at the last hourglass and a faint shudder of fear, and she hurried down two flights of stairs, paused in the vestibule to check her pockets for the house key, then out to the sidewalk, into the night.

She didn't run, but the streets passed her by; she didn't look around, but she knew the houses just the same—the big ones, the old ones, the here and there new ones that somehow instantly fit, as if Green Town wouldn't permit even a single shingle to clash. Pumpkins on the porches. Ears of maize tied to the doors. Witches and black cats in cardboard in the windows.

It had always been that way. Always. It was what she liked about the place—the world went to the moon, the world went to Mars, the world sometimes went to war, but Green Town never changed. It had found what it needed and threw out all the rest; it found what it liked and somehow made it adapt.

Sometimes, though, it was disconcerting.

Once, she had arrived from New York City, and the change nearly terrified her; once, she had driven in from Dallas and had nearly driven right back out again.

But she had stayed nonetheless.

Each time, she had stayed.

Until Halloween was over, and she was still alone, and had to go.

Come with me, Cora Fallman.
I will. God, yes, I will.

Rolfe's moon meadow was empty.

She stood there, the town far behind her, and watched the sky for a while. Too soon, of course. She knew that. Yet she couldn't take a chance that he might come early, look around, not like what he saw, and leave again on the wind. So she waited, stamping her feet, rubbing her hands, cursing herself for forgetting her gloves. She walked a little to get the blood going, wandered over to the railroad tracks and knelt beside the northbound rail. A palm on cold iron. No vibration. Nothing there.

"Okay," she said to the black tree-wall on the other side. "No big deal, I'll come back tomorrow."

No big deal, she thought as she trudged across the crumbling furrows, kicking at stunted stalks of corn long since gone to harvest; the hell it isn't.

Sleep came with dreams.

The hourglass ran.

When she woke up, the dreams were still there, scuttling away into the corners as she rubbed her eyes and realized her lips were pulled back in a grin.

Tonight.

She knew it.

Good Lord, it was tonight.

She laughed in the shower, swallowing water and sputtering laughter. She laughed downstairs at breakfast, for the first time in ages not angry that her home had been turned into a boarding-house by a family she didn't know, the only rule of sale being that they save her an apartment in the attic. She dressed as gaily as possible for a walk downtown, intending to say goodbye at last and not at all feeling sorry.

Tonight. Good Lord, tonight.

But when she reached Main Street, her mood was tempered by dark clouds creeping around the edge of town. No, not rain. Not today. It wouldn't dare. By contrast, the circle of blue above the shops, the bars, the First National Bank, was almost too bright to look at, the air like thin ice, the breeze that teased her around each corner a chilly caress she didn't mind.

"Hey, Cora!"

Amazingly, perhaps miraculously, the United Cigar Store was still there. The wooden Cherokee Indian, however, had been taken inside; protection against vandals who had painted it orange five Halloweens before.

Not everything remained the same; not everything could be saved.

"Cora, hey!"

At the corner she turned and smiled as a young man, lank and blond and red-cheeked and running, waved at her to stop, hang on, hold up a minute. He had to grab a lamppost to keep from skidding into the street, and she grabbed his hand to steady him while he exaggerated gasping, his other hand clamped dramatically to his chest.

"I've been calling you for ages," he said. "Where were you, dreamland?"

She shrugged. "Looking around, that's all. Memories. You know."

They had met when she'd stepped off the bus in front of the barbershop three days ago. A collision, actually. He'd been carrying a crate of fruit to the greengrocer down the block, and she'd been trying to make sure she wouldn't trip over her own well-traveled suitcase. Fruit and underwear, then, all over the pavement. Anger to laughter. Hands helping her to her feet, chasing after a nightgown that had decided to ride the wind to Indiana.

Dinner that night.

Lunch the next day.

She felt no guilt at all since she hadn't known, not then, that she'd be leaving him so soon. And even if she had known, there would have only been relief—Parker Arnold wouldn't end up like Keith and Rex and all the rest.

A finger tapped her forehead lightly. "Hey, in there."

She giggled. "Sorry."

She took his arm and let him lead her across the street, accepting an invitation to a late lunch at one of the new places a few blocks on. Why not? she thought. A free meal, a few laughs, and when I'm gone, he'll find someone else he thinks he loves.

You are not going, young lady, and that's final.
Mother!
Stop your caterwauling! You sound like a spoiled child!
Mother, you're not going to stop me. He loves me.
You're only sixteen, don't be foolish.
I am not being foolish.
And you are not going.

They sat at a table near the window, in the Ploughman's Lunch, and watched the pedestrians dodge the traffic, each other, and hold the line against the increasing wind. She couldn't see the clouds, but even inside she could feel the storm coming.

Him, she prayed. Please let it be him.

"Too bad," Parker said, using his fork to point at the weather outside.

"It won't last."

"I mean, the rain. Sure looks like it."

A slight pressure against her knee. She almost frowned.

He sighed. "It would have been great."

Sometimes, even in the short time that she'd known him, Parker could exasperate her with his enigmatic speech. She figured he read too many plays from the 1940s—lots of meaningful pauses and symbols and such. He was a teacher, after all; it was probably in his blood.

She poked him with a spoon. "Would you mind explaining just what the hell you're talking about?"

He winced.

She stuck out her tongue playfully. He didn't like swearing; it almost made him cute.

"The carnival thing."

The pressure against her knee increased just enough for her to realize it was no accident.

She ignored it. "What carnival thing?"

He fumbled in his back pocket, nearly knocking over his water glass, pulled out a folded sheet of paper, and dropped it next to her plate.

She gaped at it.

"It won't bite, you know," he said with a laugh.

Yes, it will. Lord, yes, it will.

Carefully, as if it were a cursed Egyptian scroll, she smoothed it out on the tablecloth. Closed her eyes. Felt her breath catch and hitch in her lungs. Felt her heart try to claw its way free.

COOGER AND DARK'S PANDEMONIUM SHADOW SHOW

She didn't have to read any more.

A woman walked past their table, turned, and looked over Parker's shoulder. "Excuse me," she said. "I don't mean to be forward, but . . . don't I know you?"

Cora blinked shadowtears from her eyes and looked up.

The woman, in a topcoat and veiled hat, the veil pinned up, was too heavily made up for her age to be ignored. Fifty-five, sixty, and obviously not what she saw in the mirror. She smiled when Parker twisted around to look up at her, smiled at Cora expectantly.

"I don't think so," Cora answered politely.

The woman's smile trembled, a white-gloved hand pointing to her own breast. "Eileen Islin. Thirty years ago. We worked in the bank?" The smile vanished, snapped off. The woman stepped away. "Oh, of course not, forgive me." She held her black purse tight against her side. "Forgive me," she said to Parker. "I didn't mean . . ." Another look. "I'm sorry, but you look so *much* like her, I thought . . . I'm sorry."

And she was gone.

Cora let her eyes close.

"Now that," said Parker, "was one weird lady."

No, she thought. Just one with a memory too close for comfort.

It was bound to happen sooner or later, this time. She should have stayed in her rooms the way she usually did. But Parker had drawn her out, let her see the town again, and she hadn't been able to resist. Again. As she hadn't resisted with Keith and Rex and Johnny and Drake.

Suddenly she yanked her napkin from her lap and dropped it over her plate. Stood. Made a false hasty check of her watch. "Oh Lord, I just remembered something," she explained as Parker began a protest. "I'll call you later, all right?" A sweet smile, a kiss to his cheek. A whisper in his ear: "I'll call you, don't worry."

The clouds were closer, heavier, the circle of blue shrinking as the wind raced through her hair.

She tried not to cry out, to dance, to wave her arms, to kiss every man she passed as she raced home. She tried not to smell every autumn blossom in every garden, not to return every Halloween pumpkin's grin. She tried not to weep when she burst into the living room and stood before the mantel.

The last hourglass was nearly empty.

"Soon," she whispered to it. "Soon."

But not soon enough.

She paced through each room, willing the sun to make its move, willing the moon to begin its climb.

She paced and laughed and clapped her hands and felt the joy; paced and laughed and clapped her hands and felt the cold.

Mother, let me out!
You will stay in there, child, until you come to your senses.
Mother, please! He's waiting!
Go to bed, Cora. There's nothing more you can do.

She didn't know how to dress and so didn't bother to change. It didn't matter. He would take her no matter what. Gloves this time, however, and a muffler to keep the wind from sluicing down her neck.

She hurried without running.

She listened for the sound of the calliope and train.

The storm flicked lightning over the western horizon.

Impatience grabbed her at last, and she ran across the deserted meadow, leaves flying like startled bats around her head, glaring up at the sky, glaring at the empty tracks, pressing her fists to her temples to stop the pounding there.

When exhaustion finally stopped her, dropped her to her knees, she ordered herself to be patient. It was the only way. She had waited this long, she could wait a few minutes longer.

The cold of the ground seeped through her jeans. The wind finally slowed, though the lightning moved closer. She watched the flaring white warily, having seen it before, knowing what it could do, and what it had done. It shouldn't be here. Not this year. He was coming, not the fire.

"I'll be waiting, Miss Sixteen."
"Yes."
"But if you fail— "

151

"No, don't say that!"

"I'll be waiting nevertheless. Sometime, but always here."

"But— "

And he had laughed and he had kissed her and he had pressed into her hands an exquisitely wrought hourglass of crystal and wood: and he had whispered that Time would be hers always so long as she knew how to fill it and protect it with the fire of their love.

"Corny," she whispered and grinned to the ground, to the approaching storm, to the dark. "God, that was so corny."

The fire of their love.

How sweet sixteen that was.

How agonizingly true.

"So where are you?" she demanded of the dark and Mr Dark. "Where the hell are you?"

A glow, white and bobbing at the meadow's far edge.

Holding back a cry, she leapt to her feet and pushed at her hair and dusted the weeds and dirt from her knees and watched the light bounce toward her, flaring at the belly of the storm overhead, blinding her for a moment, cutting a silver path across the meadow. She wanted to run toward it, but commanded herself to remain calm. He mustn't see her as too anxious; he mustn't know his power.

"Cora?"

She almost screamed.

The light grew, and grew brighter.

"Cora?"

It wasn't him.

Damn, it wasn't him!

Before she could duck, veer away, somehow find a hole in the night to cover her, the flashlight swept over her face, away and abruptly back. Parker's footsteps on the ground sounded like the dirge of hollow drums.

"Hey, there you are!"

Cora felt the tears and didn't bother to hide them.

"Cora," Parker said, wrapping an arm around her waist. "God, I'm glad I found you. You ran away so fast this afternoon, I didn't get a chance to tell you where the exhibit was. I waited at the library for over an hour before— "

"Exhibit?" She pushed him away, but gently, listening to her voice grow too suddenly old. "What exhibit?"

"The flyer I showed you," he said, as if she should have known. "You know, that carnival exhibit. Didn't you read it?"

No, she thought. Lord, no, not all.

He chuckled. "I didn't think so." He hugged her again around the waist, and this time she didn't, couldn't remove his hand. "So I went to your rooms, and the landlady let me in because we were so worried when you didn't answer. As soon as I saw you weren't there, I had a thought. I don't know why, but I did." His face grinned, in a burst of lightning, as he passed the beam over the meadow. "Pretty smart, huh?"

Not here, she thought: he won't be here, not this year.

A finger nestled under her chin. "Hey, don't cry. I didn't mean to scare you. Honest."

Not here.

He put something into her hands, turning her so that the wind was at his back, so that he sheltered her. "This came for you after you'd left."

Weary; so weary as her fingers, no longer young, no longer nimble, tore the gaily wrapped package open and held its contents to her chest.

"Hey," he said, putting the beam on her prize. "Hey, you've got some of those on the mantel, right?" The beam shifted, and she averted her face, covered it with a free hand. "Sorry again. But it's beautiful, you know. The hourglass, I mean. That wasn't sand in the others, though, was it? It didn't look like it."

"No," she said quietly, to hide the years that sped toward her on the lightning.

He laughed. "Looked like ashes, actually. My aunt has my uncle on the mantel. Morbid, I'll tell you."

"Yes," she whispered.

He leaned closer, the beam tightening, brightening. "Damn, this one's empty. I think you got gypped."

For the first time that night, there was thunder.

She almost laughed at the melodramatics of it, and the storm.

His grip on her waist strengthened, the smell of him now and of his autumn-cold clothes. "Cora." Hoarsely.

She inhaled slowly, deeply, and felt the warmth, felt the heat; she lowered herself and him to the ground where she fumbled off the top of the hourglass *he* had sent her. He had. So he still loved her. And this just wasn't the time, this just wasn't the year.

"What . . . what are you going to put in it?" Parker wanted to know, lightly kissing her brow.

The hourglass between them.

The heat of her as she kissed him back.

"It's dumb," he said breathlessly, pulling away for a second. "It's really dumb, but I really think I love you."

"And I do love you," she answered, bringing him back. "For a time."

Embracing him, and kissing him.

"For a time."

Letting him know the fire of her love.

GRANT MORRISON

The Braille Encyclopedia

GRANT MORRISON lives and works in Glasgow, Scotland, and is the writer of numerous successful and critically acclaimed graphic novels, including the "controversial" *St Swithin's Day* and *The New Adventures of Hitler*, *Bible John*, *Dare*, and the revisionist Batman book, *Arkham Asylum*.

His plays *Red King Rising* (examining Victorian morality through the eyes of Lewis Carroll's Alice) and *Depravity* (about the life of Aleister Crowley) were performed to full houses during their respective runs at the 1989 and 1990 Edinburgh Fringe Festival. *Red King Rising* won both the Fringe First and Independent awards, while *Depravity* was recipient of the Evening News Award.

Morrison has also won the Speakeasy, UK Comic Art, Eagle and Inkpot Awards for Best Writer and Best Graphic Novel of 1990 (*Arkham Asylum*). He is currently working on *Sebastian O* (a graphic novel inspired by the *fin de siecle* Decadent writers); *Table and Chairs*, a new play, and *Mystery City*, a novel. He continues to write the monthly *Doom Patrol* for DC Comics, plays and sings with the band Super 9, and is the author of various short stories and articles.

"The Braille Encyclopedia" is perhaps somewhat reminiscent of Clive Barker's *Books of Blood* and, like those ground-breaking stories, has the power to both shock and awe the reader at the same time.

B LIND IN THE CITY OF LIGHT, Patricia walked carefully back through the Cimitière Père-Lachaise.

"Are you all right?" Mrs Becque said again. "Now be careful here, the steps are a little slippery . . ."

Patricia nodded and placed her foot tentatively on the first step. Through the soles of her shoes she could feel the edge of a slick patch of moss.

"Are you all right?" Mrs Becque said again.

"I'll be fine," Patricia said. "Really."

All around, she could feel the shapes of sepulchers and headstones. The echoes they returned, the space they displaced, the subtle patterns of cold air they radiated; all these things gave the funeral monuments of Père-Lachaise a weight and solidity that lay beyond sight. From the locked and chambered earth, a fragrance arose. The elaborate alchemy of decay released a damp perfume which combined with the scent of spoiled wreaths and hung like a mist around the stones. Rain drummed on the stretched skin of Patricia's umbrella.

"So what did you think?" said Mrs Becque. "Of Wilde's monument, that is? Did you like it?"

"Lovely," Patricia said.

"Of course, the vandals have made a terrible mess, writing all over the statue, but it's still very impressive, don't you think?"

Mrs Becque's voice receded into a rainy drone. Patricia could hardly mention how amused she'd been when she'd run her hands over Epstein's stone angel, only to discover that the balls of the statue had been chopped off by some zealous souvenir fiend. Mrs Becque would most certainly disapprove of so ironic a defacement, but Patricia felt sure that Oscar Wilde would have found the whole thing thoroughly entertaining. Mrs Becque, in fact, seemed to disapprove of almost everything and Patricia was growing desperately tired of the woman's constant presence.

"We must get in out of this awful rain," Mrs Becque was saying. They crossed the street, found a café and sat down.

"What would you like, dear?" asked Mrs Becque. "Coffee?"

"Yes," Patricia said. "Espresso. And a croissant. Thanks."

Mrs Becque ordered, then eased herself up out of her seat and set off in search of a telephone. Patricia took her book from her bag and began to read with her fingertips. She found no comfort there. More and more often these days, books did nothing but increase her own sense of isolation and disaffection. They taunted and teased with their promise of a better world but in the end they had nothing to offer but empty words and closed covers. She had grown tired of experiencing life at second hand. She wanted something that she had never been able to put into words.

A waiter brought the coffee.

"Something else for you, sir?" he said.

Patricia started up from her book. Someone was sitting at her table, directly opposite. A man.

"I'm fine with this," the man said. His voice was rich and resonant, classically trained. Every syllable seemed to melt in the air.

"I hope you don't mind," the man said. He was talking to Patricia now, using English. "I saw you sitting all alone."

"No. Actually, I'm with someone," Patricia said. She stumbled over the words, as she might stumble over the furniture in some unfamiliar room. "She's over there. Over there." She gestured vaguely.

"I don't think you're with anyone at all," the man said. "You seem to me to be alone. It's not right that a pretty girl should be alone in Paris."

"I'm not," Patricia said flatly. The man was beginning to disturb and irritate her.

"Believe me," the man said. "I know what you want. It's written all over your face. I *know* what you want."

"What are you talking about?" Patricia said. "You don't know me. You don't know anything about me."

"I can read you like a book," he said. "I'll be here at the same time tomorrow, if you wish to hear more about the Braille Encyclopedia."

"I beg your pardon?" Patricia's face flushed. "I really don't . . ."

"Everything all right, dear?"

Patricia turned her head. The voice belonged to Mrs Becque. Foreign coins chinked into a cheap purse.

"It's just this man . . ." Patricia began.

Mrs Becque sat down. "What man?" she said. "The waiter?"

"No. That man. There." Patricia pointed across the table.

"There's no one there, Patricia," Mrs Becque said, using the voice she reserved for babies and dogs. "Drink up your coffee. Michel said he'd pick us up here in twenty minutes."

Patricia lifted her cup in numbed fingers. Somewhere the espresso machine sputtered and choked. Rain fell on the silent dead of Père-Lachaise, on the streets and the houses of Paris, covering the whole city like a veil, like a winding sheet . . .

Patricia raised her head. "What time is it?" she said.

In her room, in the tall and narrow hotel on the Boulevard St Germain, Patricia sat listening to traffic. Outside, wheels sluiced through rain.

Rain sieving down through darkness. Rain spattering on the balcony. Rain dripping, slow and melancholy, from the wrought-iron railing.

She sat on the edge of the bed, in the dark. Always in the dark. No need for light. The money she saved on electricity bills! She sat in the dark of the afternoon, ate another slab of chocolate and tried to read. It was hopeless; her fingers skated across the braille dots, making no sense of their complex arrangements. Unable to concentrate, she set her book down and paced to the window again. Soon it would be evening. Outside, in the dark and the rain, Paris would put on its suit of lights. Students would gather to argue over black coffee, lovers would fall into one another's arms. Out there, in the breathless dark and the flashing neon, people would live and be alive; and here, in this room, Patricia would sit and Patricia would read.

She sat down heavily and, unutterably miserable, slotted a cassette into her Walkman. Then she lay back on the bed, staring wide-eyed into her private darkness.

Debussy's "La Mer" began to play—the first wash of strings and woodwind conjured a vast and empty shore. White sand, desolate under a big sky. White waves smashed on the rocks. Patricia was writing something on the sand. Lines drawn on a great blank page of sand. She could not read what she was writing but she knew it was important.

Patricia licked dry lips, tasting chocolate.

What did he look like? The man in the café. The man with the voice. What would he look like if she could see him?

She unzipped her skirt and eased her hand down between her legs. The bed began to creak faintly, synchronizing itself with Patricia's harsh, chopped breathing . . .

She was stretched out on watered silk in a scented room of flowers and old wine and he was there with his voice and his breath on her body his breath circulating in the grottoes of her ear and in her mouth and his skin and the mesh of muscles as he went into her

. . .Debussy's surf broke against the walls of her skull. White wave noise drowning out the traffic and the rain, turning the darkness into incendiary light.

The music had come to an end. The room was too hot. An airless box. Patricia was suffocating in the dark. She rose, unsteadily, and faced the mirror's cold eye. She knew how she must look: a fat, plain girl, playing with herself on a hotel bed.

"Stop it or you'll go blind," she said quietly. She felt suddenly sick and stupid. She would never meet anyone, never do or be anything. It all came down to this stifling room. No matter where she went, she found herself in this room. Reading. Always reading. Nothing would ever happen.

The dark closed in.

"I knew you'd be here," the man said. "I knew it."

"I don't see how you could just know," said Patricia and felt stupid. She was saying all the wrong things.

"Oh, I know," he said. "I'm trained to recognize certain things in people. Certain possibilities. Certain . . . inclinations." His hand alighted on hers and she jumped. "I can tell we're going to be friends, Patricia."

"I don't even know your name," she said. She was becoming frightened now. She felt somehow that she was being *circled*. His voice was drawing a line around her. Sweat gathered between her breasts.

"My name?" He smiled. She could hear him smile. "Just call me L'Index."

"Sorry?" Patricia felt sure she must have misheard him. She tried not to be afraid. Being afraid was what had made her lonely.

"L'Index," the man repeated. "Like a book. L'Index."

"I can't call you that," Patricia said.

"You can. You must." He reached out and took her hand. It was like a soft trap, fastening around her wrist. "Dear Patricia. You must. You will. I will show you such things . . ." The fear was almost unbearable. She wanted to run. She wanted to go back. Back to that room, that book, like the coward she was. The man was holding open a door. Beyond lay darkness, it was true, but then again, Patricia was no stranger to the dark.

"L'Index," she said.

When Mrs Becque returned to the café to collect Patricia, Patricia had gone. One of the waiters had seen her leave with someone but found it impossible to describe the man. No one could describe the man. He had come and he had gone: a gray man in the rain. Invisible. The police were alerted. Half-heartedly they scoured the city, then gave up. Patricia's parents mounted their own futile search. The newspapers printed photographs of a rather plump, blind girl, smiling at a camera she could not see. Her eyes were pale blue, their color diluted to invisibility. Eyes full of rain, like puddles in a face. Very soon the papers and the public lost interest. Patricia's room lay untenanted. A stopped clock. The girl was never found and the police file stayed open, like a door leading nowhere.

The Chateau might have seemed like a prison were it not for the fact that it appeared to perpetually renew its own architecture. No door ever led twice to the same room, no corridor could ever be followed to the same conclusion, no stair could be made to repeat its steps.

Additionally, the variety of experiences offered by life in the Chateau was of such diversity that life outside could only be timid and pale by comparison. Here, there was no sin which could not be indulged to exhaustion. Here, the search for fresh sensation had long ago led to the practice of continually more refined atrocities. Here, finally, there were no laws, no boundaries, no limits, no judgment.

And the motto above the door read simply "Hell is more beautiful than Heaven."

Tonight was to be a special night. In the red room, in the room of the Sign of Seven, whose walls beat like a heart, Patricia lay in a tumble of silk cushions. She found a vein in her thigh and slowly inserted the needle. After the first rush, her head seemed to unlock and divide like a puzzle box. Her nervous system suffered a series of delicious shocks and smoke spilled into her brain. She licked red lips and began to shake. The tiny bells pinned to her skin reacted to her shudders. Her body became a tambourine. She drew a long breath. The room was hot and sweat ran on her oiled skin, trickling from the tongues of the lewd tattoos which now adorned her belly.

Above the pulse of the room, Patricia could hear the boy spitting, still spitting. L'Index had allowed her to touch the boy—to run her nails through his soft hair, to pluck feathers from the clipped and ragged wings he wore on his back and to finger the scars of his castration.

"What's he doing?" she said dreamily. "Why is he spitting?"

L'Index had come back into the room. He closed the door and waited for the boy to finish.

"He's been spitting into this glass," L'Index said. "Here."

Patricia took from him a beautiful crystal wineglass. L'Index knelt down beside her. Heat radiated off his body and he smelled faintly of blood and spiced sweat.

"The boy is an angel," L'Index said. "We summoned him here from Heaven and then we crippled and debauched him."

Patricia giggled.

"Our own little soiled angel," L'Index continued. "Come here, angel."

The boy shuffled across the room, slow as a sleepwalker. His wings rustled like dry paper.

"What shall I do with this?" Patricia asked, weighing the glass in her hand.

"I want you to drink it," L'Index said. "Drink."

Patricia dipped her tongue into the warm froth of saliva.

"He has AIDS, of course," L'Index said casually. "The poor creature has been the plaything of god knows how many filthy old whores and catamites. As you might expect, his spit is a reservoir of disease." He paused, smiling his almost-audible smile. "Nevertheless, I do insist that you drink it."

Patricia heard the boy whimpering as he was forced onto his hands and knees. She swirled the liquid round in the glass.

"Drink it *slowly*."

She heard the chink and creak of a leather harness. A match was struck. Was there no limit to what he would ask of her?

"All right," she said, nosing the glass like a connoisseur. It smelled of nothing. "I told you. I'll do anything."

And she drank, slowly, savoring the bland, flat taste of the boy's saliva. The whole glass, to the dregs. As she drank, she could hear the boy gasp—sodomized. Patricia licked the rim of her glass.

"You were lying," she said. "AIDS. I knew you were lying."

The boy cried out, with the voice of a bird. L'Index had done something new to him. Patricia waited for L'Index to undo the harness and sit down beside her.

"I knew I was right about you, when I saw you all those months ago," L'Index said. He tugged on the ring that was threaded through her nipple, pulling her toward him. Automatically, she opened her mouth and allowed him to place an unclean treat on her tongue.

"I knew you were worthy of admission."

"Admission?" said Patricia. "Admission into what?" The sound of her own voice seemed to recede and return. She was beginning to feel strange.

"Do you remember when I mentioned to you the Braille Encyclopedia?" L'Index asked.

"Yes." Fragments of music flared in Patricia's head. Choral detonations. She felt that she was falling through some terrible space. "The Braille Encyclopedia. Yes. What is it?"

"Not a thing," L'Index said. "A society. Here. On your knees. Touch me."

He took her hand.

"But you've never let me . . ." she began, growing excited. White noise blasted through her, like a stereo pan, from ear to ear.

"I'm letting you now," he said. "You've shown a rare appetite for all the sweet and rotting fruits of corruption. Sometimes, I'm almost frightened by your dedication. Now, I think it's time you were allowed to taste the most exquisite delicacy." He set her hand to his bare chest. Her fingers brushed his skin and she started.

"What is it?" Patricia lightly traced her fingertips across tiny raised scars. Alarm returned as she realized that his entire body, from neck to feet, was similarly disfigured. She ran along a row of dots, suddenly unable to catch a breath.

"It's braille," she said. "Oh, God, it's braille . . . I feel so strange . . ." He filled her mouth and stopped her speech. Like a nursing child, she sucked and swallowed and allowed her hands to crawl across his skin.

"You drank angel spit," L'Index said. His voice was full of echoes and ambiguous reverberations. "You drank the rarest of narcotics. Now it's time to read me, Patricia. Read me!"

She read.

Entry 103   THE DEFORMATION OF BABY SOULS
Entry 45   THE HORN OF DECAY
Entry 217   THE MIRACLE OF THE SEVERED FACE
Entry 14   THE ATROCIOUS BRIDE
Entry 191   THE REGIMENTAL SIN
Entry 204   BLEEDING WINDO . . .

Patricia snatched back her hand and pulled away, terrified. L'Index came into her face, spattering her useless eyes.

"What are you?" she whispered. She blinked and sperm tears ran down her cheeks. Somewhere, the fallen angel whimpered in the darkness.

"There are several hundred of us," L'Index explained. "And together we form the most comprehensive collection of impure knowledge that has ever been assembled. Monstrous books, long thought destroyed, have survived as marks on our flesh. Through us, an unholy tradition is preserved."

"And what about me," Patricia said.

"One of our number died recently," L'Index said. "It happens, of course, in the due process of time. Usually, we initiate a relative, often a child. My grandfather, for instance, was the Index before me. In this case, however, that was not possible. Part of my job is to find a suitable successor . . ."

Gripped by an extraordinary fear, Patricia dropped to the floor.

"Don't be afraid, Patricia," L'Index said. "Not you."

As she lay there, he pissed on her hair. She lifted her face into the hot stream, grateful for an act of degradation she could still understand. It helped her to know he still cared.

"Will you abandon your last claim to self? Will you embrace the final release, Patricia? That is what I'm asking of you. Will you step over the threshold into a new world?"

"You sound like an evangelist," she said. His urine steamed in her hair. Patricia breathed deeply, inhaling a mineral fragrance. Slowly her heart rate came to match the pulsing of the room.

She thought of what she had been and of what he had helped her become.

She held her breath for a moment. Counted to ten.

"Yes," she said hoarsely. "Yes."

They came singly, they came in twos and in groups: the Braille Encyclopedia. Some were driven in black limousines with mirrored windows and no registration plates. Others walked, haltingly. Men, women, hollow-eyed children. They came from all directions, traveling on roads known only to a few mad or debased souls. They came and the doors of the Chateau opened to receive them. There was an almost electrical excitement in the air. The current ran through enchanted flesh, conjuring static in the darkness. Blue sparks played on fingertips as the Braille Encyclopedia made its way into the Chateau. They were, each of them, blind, even the youngest. Silent and blind, blue ghosts, they entered the darkness. And the doors closed behind them.

Patricia did not hear them enter, nor did she hear L'Index welcome his guests. She sat in her chamber, listening to the fall of surf on an interior beach. On the bedside cabinets were vibrators, clamps, unguents, suction devices, whips: all the ludicrous paraphernalia of arousal. She was familiar with each and every item and she had endured or perpetrated every possible permutation of indecency that the body could endure.

Or so she had thought.

She touched her own smooth skin. She had removed the bells and the rings and toweled the oil away. Her skin was blank, like a parchment upon which L'Index wished to write unspeakable things. The music of Debussy crashed through her confusion.

We are all of us, she thought, written upon by time. Our skin is pitted and eroded by the passage of years. No one escapes. Why not then defy time by becoming part of something eternal? Why not give up all claims to individual identity and become little more than a page in a book which renews itself endlessly? It was, as L'Index had said, the final surrender.

Patricia removed her headphones and made her way downstairs.

L'Index was waiting for her and he introduced her to the members of the Braille Encyclopedia. Blind hands stroked her naked body and, finding it unmarred, lost interest. She trembled as, one by one, they approached and examined her with a shocking frankness. Shameless fingers probed and penetrated her: the dry-twig scrapings of old men and women, the thin furtive strokes of wicked children. By the end of their examination, Patricia teetered on the brink of delirium. Her darkness filled with inarticulate flashes and fireworks displays of grotesque color and grossly ambiguous forms.

"They don't speak," she said. It seemed terribly important.

"No," said L'Index simply.

She felt them crowd around her in a circle, felt the pressure and the heat of unclothed flesh. No sound. They made no sound.

"Are you ready?" L'Index asked, touching Patricia's shoulder gently. She nodded and let him lead her into a tiny room at the back of the Chateau. Soundproofed walls. A single unshaded bulb, radiating a light she could not see. L'Index kissed her neck and instructed her not to move under any circumstances. She wanted to say something, but she was too afraid to speak. The words jammed at the back of her throat.

And then the door opened. Someone she did not know came into the room. Patricia suddenly wanted to run. The light was switched off and candles were lit, filling the room with a sickly sweet narcotic scent.

Patricia heard then a thin metallic ring. A sharp-edged sound. The brief conversation of scalpels and needles and blue-edged razors.

"L'Index?" she said nervously. "L'Index, are you there? I'm afraid . . ."

No one answered. Patricia rocked on the balls of her feet. The air was too hot, the candlesmoke too bitter. She gulped lungfuls of oily, shifting smoke.

Someone came toward her, breathing harshly, sometimes mewing.

"L'Index?" she whispered again, so quietly that it was no more than the ghost of a name. In her head, the noise and the colors mounted toward an intensity she felt she could not possibly bear.

The first cut caused her to spontaneously orgasm. Her brain lit up like a pinball machine. She swayed and she cried out but she did not fall as hooks and needles were teased beneath her skin.

Moaning, coming again and again, Patricia was delicately scarred and cicatriced. Alone on a private beach, she realized what word it was that she had scrawled in the sand. And in that moment of understanding, the surf surged in and obliterated every trace of what she had written. Her identity was finally erased in the white glare of a pain so perfect and so pure that it could only be ecstasy. Fat, awkward Patricia was at last, at last, written out of existence by articulate needles.

She came to her senses and found that she was still standing. Thin spills of blood streamed down her body, pooling on the floor. She touched her stomach. The raw wounds stung but she could not help but run her fingertip along the lines of braille. She read one sentence and could hardly believe that such abomination could possibly exist let alone be described. Her whole body was a record of atrocities so rare and so refined that the mind revolted from the truth of them. How could things like this be permitted to exist in the world? She felt dizzy and could read no more.

"I'm still alive. I'm still alive," was all she could say. At last, she fell but L'Index was there to catch her.

"Welcome to the Encyclopedia," he said, salting her wounds so that they burned exquisitely. "Now you are Entry 207—The Meat Chamber."

She nodded, recognizing herself, and he led her out of the room and down an unfamiliar corridor. She could feel herself losing consciousness. There was something she had to ask him. That was all she could remember.

"The Chateau," she said, slurring her words. "Who owns the Chateau?"

"Can't you guess?" L'Index said.

He brought her into the ballroom, where they were all waiting for her. Hundreds of people were waiting for her. She smiled weakly and said, "What now? Can I please sit down?"

"These gatherings happen only rarely," L'Index said. "The entire Encyclopedia is not often assembled together in one place and so our lives take on true meaning only at these moments. I can assure you that what is about to follow will transcend all your previous experiences of physical gratification. For you, this will be the ultimate, most beautiful defilement. I promise."

He sat her down in a heavy wooden chair.

"I envy you so much," he said. "I'm only the Index, you see. The mysteries and abominations of the flesh are denied to me."

He pulled a strap across her arms, tugged it tight and buckled it.

"What are you doing?" she said. "Is this the Punishment Chair? It's not, is it?" She began to panic now as he clamped her ankles to the legs of the chair. The Encyclopedia was arranging itself into a circle again. Footsteps sounded down the corridor.

"This is the Chair of Final Submission," L'Index said. "Goodbye, my love."

And he clamped her head back.

"Oh no," she said. "Wait. Don't . . ."

A clumsy bolt and bit arrangement was thrust into her mouth, chipping a tooth and reducing her words to infantile sobs and gobblings.

The footsteps advanced and the Encyclopedia parted to make a passage. Shiny steel chinked slyly in a leather bag. L'Index leaned over and whispered in her ear.

"Remember, you may always consult me . . ."

She bucked and slammed in the chair but it was fixed to the floor by heavy bolts.

"Oh my sweet," L'Index said. "Don't lose heart now. Remember what you were: alone, lonely and discontented. You will never be lonely again." His breath stank of peppermint and sperm. "Now you can pass into a new world where nothing is forbidden but virtue."

A bag snapped open. A needle was withdrawn. It rang faintly, eight inches long.

"Give yourself up now to the world of the Braille Encyclopedia! Knowledge shared only by these few, never communicated. Knowledge gained by sense of touch alone."

And she finally understood then, just before the needles punctured her eardrums. Her bladder and her bowels let go and the odors of her own chemical wastes were the last things she smelled before they destroyed that sense also. Finally her tongue was amputated and given to the angel to play with.

"Now go," L'Index said, unheard. There was sadness in his voice. His tragedy was to be forever excluded from the Empire of the Senseless. "Join the Encyclopedia."

Released from the chair, The Meat Chamber stumbled into the arms of her fellow entries in the Braille Encyclopedia. Bodies fell together. Blind hands stroked sensitized skin. They embraced her and licked her wounds and made her welcome.

She screamed for a very long time but only one person there heard her. Finally she stopped, exhausted.

And then she began to read.

And read.

And read.

ELIZABETH HAND

The Bacchae

"I THINK I have seldom encountered a story as repulsive as 'The Bacchae'", wrote a disgruntled reader of *Interzone*, who continued: "It was a vile parade of anti-male hatred, an exhibition of baroque man-killing justified, so it seems, by the crimes of discarded beer cans and a dying fish." He (of course it was a he) concluded, ". . . I hope that you'll never again subject the magazine's readers to similar chuckling depictions of agony (male or female)".

The test of all good horror fiction is for it to have some kind of impact on the reader, and the author of the above letter was obviously greatly disturbed by Elizabeth Hand's story, which is as it should be. She knows what she's doing, as her story "On the Town Route" in *Best New Horror 2* proved.

The author of the novels *Winterlong*, *Aestival Tide*, *The Eve of Saint Nynex* and *Waking the Moon*, her short fiction has appeared in numerous magazines and anthologies, including several "Year's Best" collections. Her literary criticism and articles appear regularly in the *Washington Post Book World*, *Detroit Times* and *Penthouse*, among other publications, and she is a contributing editor to *Reflex* magazine and *Science Fiction Eye*.

As to whether "The Bacchae" is, as our letter writer complained, "nothing more than a snuff movie in prose, heaped with feathers, jewels and furs", we'll leave you to decide . . .

S HE GOT INTO THE ELEVATOR WITH him, the young woman from down the hall, the one he'd last seen at the annual Coop Meeting a week before. Around her shoulders hung something soft that brushed his cheek as Gordon moved aside to let her in: a fur cape, or pelt, or no, something else. The flayed skin of an animal, an animal that when she shouldered past him to the corner of the elevator proved to be her Rottweiler, Leopold. He could smell it now: the honeyed stench of uncured flesh, a pink and scarlet veil still clinging to the pelt's ragged fringe of coarse black hair. It had left a crimson streak down the back of her skirt, and stippled her legs with pink rosettes.

Gordon got off at the next floor and ran all the way down the hall. When he got into his own apartment he locked and chained the door behind him. For several minutes he stood there panting, squinting out the peephole until he saw her turn the corner and head for her door. It still clung to her shoulders, stiff front legs jouncing against the breast of her boiled-wool suit jacket. After the door closed behind her Gordon walked into the kitchen, poured himself a shot of Jameson's, and stood there until the trembling stopped.

Later, after he had changed and poured himself several more glasses of whisky, he saw on the news that the notorious Debbie DeLucia had been found not guilty of the murder of the young man she claimed had assaulted her in a parking garage one evening that summer. The young man had been beaten severely about the face and chest with one of Ms. DeLucia's high-heeled shoes. When he was found by the parking lot attendant most of his hair was missing. Gordon switched off the television when it displayed photographs of these unpleasantries followed by shots of a throng of cheering women outside the courthouse. That evening he had difficulty falling asleep.

He woke in the middle of the night. Moonlight flooded the room, so brilliant it showed up the tiny pointed feathers poking through his down comforter. Rubbing his eyes Gordon sat up, tugged the comforter around his shoulders against the room's chill. He peered out at a full moon, not silver nor even the sallow gold he had seen on summer nights but a colour he had never glimpsed in the sky before, a fiery bronze tinged with red.

"Jeez," Gordon said to himself, awed. He wondered if this had something to do with the solar shields tearing, the immense satellite-borne sails of mylar and solex that had been set adrift in the atmosphere to protect the cities and farmlands from ultraviolet radiation. But you weren't supposed to be able to see the shields. Certainly Gordon had never noticed any difference in the sky, although his friend Olivia claimed she could tell they were there.

Women were more sensitive to these things than men, she had told him with an accusing look. There was a luminous quality to city light that had formerly been sooty and grey at best, and the air now had a russet tinge. Wonderful for outdoor setups—Olivia was a noted food photographer—or would be save for the odd bleeding of colours that appeared during developing, winesap apples touched with violet, a glass of Semillon shot with sparks of emerald, the parchment crust of an aged camembert taking on an unappetizing salmon glow.

It would be the same change in the light that made the moon bleed, Gordon decided. And now he had noticed it, even though he wasn't supposed to be sensitive to these things. What did that he mean, he wondered? Maybe it was better not to notice, or to pretend he had seen nothing, no sanguine moon, no spectral colours in a photograph of a basket of eggs. Strange and sometimes awful things happened to men these days. Gordon had heard of some of these on television, but other tales came from friends, male friends. Near escapes recounted in low voices at the gym or club, random acts of violence spurred by innocent offers of help in carrying groceries, the act of holding a door open suddenly seen as threatening. Women friends, even relatives, sisters and daughters refusing to accompany family on trips to the city. An exodus of wives and children to the suburbs, from the suburbs to the shrinking belts of countryside ringing the megalopolis. And then, husbands and fathers disappearing during weekend visits with the family in exile. Impassive accounts by the next of kin of mislaid directions, trees where there had never been trees before. Evidence of wild animals, wildcats or coyotes perhaps, where nothing larger than a squirrel had been sighted in fifty years.

Gordon laughed at these tales at first. Until now. He pulled a feather from the bed-ticking and stroked his chin thoughtfully before tossing it away. It floated down, a breath of tawny mist. Gordon determinedly pulled the covers over his head and went back to sleep.

He was reading the paper in the kitchen next morning, a detailed account of Ms. DeLucia's trial and a new atrocity. Three women returning late from a nightclub had been harassed by a group of teenage boys, some of them very young. It was one of the young ones the women had killed, turning on the boys with a ferocity the newspaper described as "demonic." Gordon turned to the section that promised full photographic coverage and shuddered. Hastily he put aside the paper and crossed the room to get a second cup of coffee. How could a woman, even three women, be strong enough to do that? He recalled his neighbour down the hall. Christ. He'd take the fire stairs from now on, rather than risk seeing her again.

He let his breath out in a low whistle and stirred another spoonful of white powder into his cup.

As he turned to go back to the table he noticed the MESSAGE light blinking on his answering machine. Odd. He hadn't heard the phone ring during the night. He sipped his coffee and played back the tape.

At first he thought there was nothing there. Dead silence, a wrong number. Then he heard faint sounds, a shrill creaking that he recognized as crickets, a katydid's resolute twang, and then the piercing, distant wail of a whippoorwill. It went on for several minutes, all the way to the end of the message tape. Nothing but night sounds, insects and a whippoorwill, once a sharp yapping that, faint as it was, Gordon knew was not a dog but a fox. Then abrupt silence as the tape ended. Gordon started, spilling coffee on his cuff, and swearing rewound the tape while he went to change shirts.

Afterward he played it back. He could hear wind in the trees, leaves pattering as though struck by a soft rain. Had Olivia spent the night in the country? No: they had plans for tonight, and there was no country within a day's drive in any direction from here. She wouldn't have left town on a major shoot without letting him know. He puzzled over it for a long while, playing back the gentle pavane of wind and tiny chiming voices, trying to discern something else there, breathing or muted laughter or a screen door banging shut, anything that might hint at a caller. But there was nothing, nothing but crickets and whippoorwills and a solitary vixen barking at the moon. Finally he left for work.

It was the sort of radiant autumn day when even financial analysts wax rapturous over the colour of the sky—in this case a startling electric blue, so deep and glowing Gordon fancied it might leave his fingers damp if he reached to touch it, like wet canvas. He skipped his lunchtime heave at the gym. Instead he walked down to Lafayette Park, filling his pockets with the polished fruit of horsechestnuts and wondering why it was the leaves no longer turned colours in the fall, only darkened to sear crisps and then clogged the sewers when they fell, a dirty brown porridge.

In the park he sat on a bench. There he ate a stale ersatz croissant and shied chestnuts at the fearless squirrels. A young woman with two small children stood in the middle of a circle of duncoloured grass, sowing crusts of bread among a throng of bobbing pigeons. One of the children pensively chewed a white crescent. She squealed when a dappled white bird flew up at her face, dropped the bread as her mother laughed and took the children's hands, leading them back to the bench across from Gordon's. He smiled, conspiratorially tossed the remains of his lunch onto the grass and watched it disappear beneath a mass of iridescent feathers.

A shadow sped across the ground. For an instant it blotted out the sun and Gordon looked up, startled. He had an impression of something immense, immense and dark and moving very quickly through the bright clear air. He recalled his night-time thoughts, had a delirious flash of insight: it was one of the shields torn loose, a ragged gonfalon of Science's floundering army. The little girl shrieked, not in fear but pure excitement. Gordon stood, ready to run for help; saw the woman, the children's mother, standing opposite him pointing at the grass and shouting something. Beside her the two children watched motionless, the little girl clutching a heel of bread.

In the midst of the feeding pigeons a great bird had landed, mahogany wings beating the air as its brazen feathers flashed and it stabbed, snakelike, at the smaller fowl. Its head was perfectly white, the beak curved and as long as Gordon's hand. Again and again that beak gleamed as it struck ferociously, sending up a cloud of feathers grey and pink and brown as the other birds scattered, wings beating feebly as they tried to escape. As Gordon watched blood pied the snowy feathers of the eagle's neck and breast until it was dappled white and red, then a deeper russet. Finally it glowed deep crimson. Still it would not stop its killing. And it seemed the pigeons could not flee, only fill the air with more urgent twittering and, gradually, silence. No matter how their wings flailed it was as though they were stuck in bird-lime, or one of those fine nets used to protect winter shrubs.

Suddenly the eagle halted, raised its wings protectively over the limp and thrashing forms about its feet. Gordon felt his throat constrict. He had jammed his hands in his pockets and now closed them about the chestnuts there, as though to use them as weapons. Across the grass the woman stood very still. The wind lifted her hair across her face like a banner. She did not brush it away, only stared through it to where the eagle waited, not eating, not moving, its baleful golden eye gazing down at the fluttering ruin of feather and bone.

As her mother stared the little girl broke away, ran to the edge of the ruddy circle where the eagle stood. It had lifted one clawed foot, thick with feathers, and shook it. The girl stopped and gazed at the sanguine bird. Carelessly she tossed away her heel of bread, wiped her hand and bent to pluck a bloodied feather from the ground. She stared at it, marvelling, then pensively touched it to her face and hand. It left a rosy smear across one cheek and wrist and she laughed in delight. She glanced around, first at her mother and brother, then at Gordon.

The eyes she turned to him were ice-blue, wondering but fearless; and absolutely, ruthlessly indifferent.

He told Olivia about it that evening.

"I don't see what's so weird," she said, annoyed. It was intermission of the play they had come to see: Euripides' "The Bacchae" in a new translation. Gordon was unpleasantly conscious of how few men there were at the performance, the audience mostly composed of women in couples or small groups, even a few mothers with children, boys and girls who surely were much too young for this sort of thing. He and Olivia stood outside on the theatre balcony overlooking the river. "Eagles kill things, that's what they're made for."

"But here? In the middle of the city? I mean, where did it come from? I thought they were extinct."

All about them people strolled beneath the sulfurous crimelights, smoking cigarettes, pulling coats tight against the wind, exclaiming at the full moon. Olivia leaned against the railing and stared up at the sky, smiling slightly. She wore ostrich cowboy boots with steel toes and tapped them rhythmically against the cement balcony. "I think you just don't like it when things don't go as you expect them to. Even if it's the way things really are supposed to be. Like an eagle killing pigeons."

He snorted but said nothing. Beside him Olivia tossed her hair back. Thick and lustrous darkbrown hair, like a caracal's pelt, hair that for years had been unfashionably long. Though lately it seemed that more women wore it the way she did, loose and long and artlessly tangled. As she pulled a lock away from her throat he saw something there, a mark upon her shoulder like a bruise or scrape.

"What's that?" he wondered, moving the collar of her jacket so he could see better.

She smiled, arching her neck. "Do you like it?"

He touched her shoulder, wincing. "Jesus, what the hell did you do? Doesn't it hurt?"

"A little." She shrugged, turned so that the jaundiced spotlight struck her shoulder and he could see better. A pattern of small incisions had been sliced into her skin, forming the shape of a crescent, or perhaps a grin. Blood still oozed from a few of the cuts. In the others ink or coloured powder had been rubbed so that the little moon, if that's what it was, took on the livid shading of a bruise or orchid: violet, verdigris, citron yellow. From each crescent tip hung a gold ring smaller than a teardrop.

"But why?" He suddenly wanted to tear off her jacket and blouse, search the rest of her to see what other scarifications might be hiding there. "Why?"

Olivia smiled, stared out at the river moving in slow streaks of black and orange beneath the sullen moon. "A melted tiger," she said softly.

"What?" The electronic ping of bells signalled the end of intermission. Gordon grasped her elbow, overwhelmed by an abrupt and unfathomable fear. He recalled the moon last night, not crescent but swollen and blood-tinged as the scar on her shoulder. "What did you say?"

A woman passing them turned to stare in disapproval at his shrill voice. Olivia slipped from him as though he were a stranger crowding a subway door. "Come on," she said gently, brushing her hair from her face. She flashed him a smile as she adjusted her blouse to hide the scar. "We'll miss the second act." He followed her without another word.

After the show they walked down by the river. Gordon couldn't shake a burgeoning uneasiness, a feeling he might have called terror were it not that the word seemed one he couldn't apply to his own life, this measured round of clocks and stocks and evenings on the town. But he didn't want to say anything to Olivia, didn't want to upset her; more than anything he didn't want to upset her.

She was flushed with excitement, smoking cigarette after cigarette and tossing each little brand into the moonlit water snaking sluggishly beside them.

"Wonderful, just wonderful! The Post really did it justice, for a change." She stooped to pluck something from the mucky shadows and grimaced in distaste. "Christ. Their fucking beer cans— "

She glared at Gordon as though he had tossed it there. Smiling wanly he took it from her hand and carried it in apology. "I don't know," he began, and stopped. They had almost reached the Memorial Bridge. A path curved up through the tangled grasses toward the roadway, a path choked with dying goldenrod and stunted asters and Queen Anne's Lace that he suspected should not be such a luminous white, almost greenish in the moonlight. Shreds of something silver clung to the stunted limbs of lowgrowing shrubs. The way they fluttered in the cold wind made him think again of the atmospheric shields giving way, leaving the embarrened earth beneath them vulnerable and soft as the inner skin of some smooth green fruit. He squinted, trying to see exactly what it was that trembled from the branches. His companion sighed loudly and pointedly where she waited on the path ahead of him. Gordon turned from the shrubs and walked more quickly to join her.

"We should probably get up on the street," he said a little defensively.

Olivia made a small sound showing annoyance. "I'm tired of goddam streets. It's so peaceful here . . ."

He nodded and walked on beside her. A little ways ahead of them the bridge reared overhead, the ancient iron fretwork shedding green and russet flakes like old bark. Its crumbling concrete piers were lost in the blackness beneath the great struts and supports. The river disappeared and then materialized on the other side, black and gold and crimson, the moon's reflection a shimmering arrow across its surface. Gordon shivered a little. It reminded him of the stage set they had just left, all stark blacks and browns and greens. Following a new fashion for realism in the theatre there had been a great deal of stage blood that had fairly swallowed the monolithic pillars and bound the proscenium with bright ribbons.

"I thought it was sort of gruesome," he said at last. He walked slowly now, reluctant to reach the bridge. In his hand the beer can felt gritty and cold, and he thought of tossing it away. "I mean the way the king's own mother killed him. Ugh." The scene had been very explicit. Even though warned by the *Post* critic Gordon had been taken aback. He had to close his eyes once. And then he couldn't block out their voices, the sound of knife ripping flesh (and how had they done that so convincingly?), the women chanting *Evohe*! *evohe*!, which afterwards Olivia explained as roughly meaning "O ecstasy" or words to that effect. When he asked her how she knew that she gave him a cross look and lit another cigarette.

No wonder the play was so seldom revived. "Don't you think we should go back? I mean, it's not very safe here at night."

"Huh." Olivia had stopped a few feet back. He turned and saw that she didn't seem to have heard him. She squatted at the river's edge, staring intently at something in the water.

"What is it?" He stood behind her, trying to see. The water smelled rank, not the brackish reek of rotting weeds and rich mud but a chemical smell that made his nostrils burn. The ruddy light glinted off Olivia's hair, touched her steel boot-tips with bronze. In the water in front of her a fish swam lethargically on its side, sides striped with scales of brown and yellow. Its mouth gaped open and closed and its gills showed an alarming colour, bright pink like the inside of a wound.

"Ah," Olivia was murmuring. She put her hand into the water and lifted the fish upon it. It curled delicately within her palm, its fins stretching open like a butterfly warming to the sun as the water dripped heavily from her fingers. It took him a moment to realize it had no eyes.

"Poor thing," he said; then added, "I don't think you should touch it, Olivia. I mean, there's something wrong with it— "

"Of course there's something wrong with it!" Olivia spat, so vehemently that he stepped backward. The mud smelled of ammonia where his heels slipped through it. "It's dying, poisoned, everything's been poisoned— "

"Well then for Christ's sake drop it, Olivia, what's the sense in *playing* with it— "

Hissing angrily she slid her hand back through the water. The fish vanished beneath the surface and floated up again a foot away, fins fluttering pathetically. Olivia wiped her hand on her trousers, heedless of the dark stain left upon the silk.

"I wasn't playing with it," she announced coldly, shaking her head so that her jacket slipped to one side and he glimpsed the gold rings glinting from her shoulder. "You don't care, do you, you don't even notice anymore what's happened. There'd be nothing left at all if it was up to people like you— "

He swore in aggravation as she stormed off in the direction of the bridge, then hurried after her. Muck covered his shoes and he stumbled upon another cache of beer cans. When he looked up again he saw Olivia standing at the edge of the bridge's shadow, hands clenched at her sides as she confronted two tall figures.

"Oh fuck," Gordon breathed. He felt sick with apprehension but hurried on, finally ran to stand beside her. "Hey!" he said loudly, pulling at Olivia's arm.

She stood motionless. One of the men held something small and dark at his side, a gun, the other wore a tan trenchcoat and looked calmly back and forth, as though preparing to cross a busy street. Before Gordon could take another breath the second man was shoving at his chest. Gordon shouted and struck at him, his hand flailing harmlessly against the man's coat. His other hand tightened around the beer can and he felt a sudden warm rush of pain as the metal sliced through his palm. He glanced down at his hand, saw blood streaming down his wrist and staining the white cuffs of his shirt. He stared in disbelief, heard a thudding sound and then a moan. Then running, stones rattling down the grassy slope.

The man in the trenchcoat was gone. The other, the man with the gun, lay on the ground at river's edge. Olivia was kicking him in the head, over and over, her boots scraping through the mud and gravel when they missed him and sending up a spume of gritty water. The gun was nowhere to be seen. Olivia paused for an instant. Gordon could hear her breathing heavily, saw her wipe her hands upon her trousers as she had when she freed the dying perch. "Olivia," he whispered. She grunted to herself, not hearing him, not looking; and suddenly he was terrified that she *would* look and see him there watching her. He stepped backwards, and as he did so she glanced up. For an instant she was silhouetted against the glimmering water, her white face spattered with mud, hair a coppery nimbus about her shoulders. Behind her the moon shone brilliantly, and on the opposite shore he could see the glittering lights of the distant airfield. It did not seem that she saw him at all. After a moment she looked down and began to kick again, more powerfully, and this time she would bring her heel back down across the man's back until Gordon could hear a crackling sound. He looked on paralyzed, his good hand squeezing tighter and tighter about the wrist of his bleeding hand as she went on and on and on. One of her steel boot-tips tore through his shoulder and the man screamed. Gordon could see one side of his face caved in like a broken gourd, dark and shining as though water pooled in its ragged hollows. Olivia bent and lifted something dark and heavy from the shallow water. Gordon made a whining noise in his throat and ran away, up the hill to where the crimelights cast wavering shadows through the weeds. Behind him he heard a dull crash and then silence.

A crowd had gathered in front of his apartment building when he finally got there. He shoved a bill at the cab driver and stumbled from the car. "Oh no," he said out loud as the cab drove off, certain the crowd had something to do with Olivia and the man by the river: policemen, reporters, ambulances.

But it didn't have anything to do with that after all. There was music, cheerful music pouring from a player set inside one of the ground floor windows. Suddenly Gordon remembered talk of this at the Coop meeting last week: a party, an opportunity for the tenants to get to know one another. It had been his neighbour's idea, the one with the dog. Someone had strung Christmas lights from another window, and several people had set up barbecues on the gray front lawn. Flames leaped from the grills, making the shadows dance so it was impossible to determine how many people were actually milling about. Quite a few, Gordon thought. He smelled roasting meat, bitter woodsmoke with the unpleasant reek of paint in it—were they burning *furniture*?—and a strange sweetish scent, herbs or perhaps marijuana. The pain in his hand had dulled to a steady throbbing. When he looked down he closed his eyes for a few seconds and grit his teeth. There was so much blood.

"Hi!" a voice cried. He opened his eyes to see the woman from down the hall. She was no longer wearing her Rottweiler, nor the expensively tailored suits she usually favoured. Instead she wore faded jeans and the kind of extravagantly beaded and embroidered tunic Gordon associated with his parents' youth. These and the many jingling chains and jewels that hung from her ears and about her wrists and ankles (she was barefoot, in spite of the cool evening) gave her a gypsy air. In the firelight he could see that her face *sans* makeup was childishly freckled. She looked very young and very happy.

"Mm, hi," Gordon mumbled, moving his bloodsoaked arm from her sight. "A block party." He tried to keep his tone polite but uninterested as he pushed through the crowd of laughing people, but the young woman followed him, grinning.

"Isn't it great? You should come down, bring something to throw on the grill or something to drink, we're running out of hooch— "

She laughed, raising a heavy crystal wineglass and gulping from it something that was a deep purplish colour and slightly viscous, certainly not wine. When she lowered the goblet he saw there was a small crack along its rim. This had cut the girl's upper lip which spun a slender filament of blood down across her chin. She didn't notice and threw her arm around his shoulders. "Promise you'll come back, mmm? We need more guys so we can *dance* and stuff, there's just never enough guys anymore— "

She whirled away drunkenly, swinging her arms out like a giddy spinning child. Whether purposely or not the goblet flew from her hand and shattered on the broken concrete sidewalk. A cheer went up from the crowd. Someone turned the music up louder. A number of people by the glowing braziers seemed to be dancing as the girl was, drunkenly, merrily, arms outstretched and hair flying. Gordon heard the tinkling report of another glass breaking, then another; then the sharper crash of what might have been a window. He put his face down and fairly ran through the swarm to the front door, which had been propped open with an old stump overgrown with curling ivy. The neatly lettered sign warning against strangers and open doors had been yanked from the doorframe and lay in a twisted mass on the steps inside. Gordon kicked it aside and fled down the hall to the firestairs.

There were people in the stairwell, sitting or lying on the steps in drunken twos and threes. One couple had shed their clothes and stood grunting and heaving in the darkened corner near the fire extinguisher. Gordon averted his eyes, stepping carefully among the others. A small pile of twigs had been ignited on the floor and sweet-smelling smoke trailed upward through the dimness. And other things were scattered upon the steps: branches of fir-trees scenting the air with balsam, sheaves of goldenrod, empty wine bottles. One of these clattered underfoot, nearly tripping him. Gordon looked over his shoulder to see it roll downstairs, bumping the head of a woman passed out near the bottom and then spinning across the floor, finally coming to rest beside the couple in the corner. No one noticed it; no one noticed Gordon as he flung open the door to the fifth floor and ran to his apartment.

He walked numbly through the kitchen. The answering machine blinked. Mechanically he reset it as he passed, paused between the kitchen and living room as the tape began. A sound of wind filled the room, wind and the rustle of many feet in dead leaves. Gordon swallowed, pressed his shaking hands together as the tape played on behind him. The wind grew louder, then softer, swelled and whispered. And all the while he heard beneath the faint staticky recording the ceaseless passage of many feet, and sometimes voices, murmurous and laughing, eerie and wild as the wind itself. The tape ended. The apartment was silent save for the dull insistent clicking of the answering machine begging to be switched off, that and the muffled sound of laughter from outside.

Gordon stepped warily into the next room. He had forgotten to leave a light on. But it was not dark: moonlight flooded the space, glimmering across the dark wooden floor, making the shadowed bulk of armchairs and sofa and electronic equipment seem black and strange and ominous. On the sill of the picture window that covered an entire wall the moonlight gleamed upon one of his treasures, a fish of handblown Venetian glass, hundreds of years old. Its mauve and violet swirls glowed in the milky light, its gaping mouth and crystalline eyes reminding him of the perch he had seen earlier, eyeless, dying. He stepped across the living room and stood there at the window staring down at the glass fish. And suddenly his head hurt, his chest felt heavy and cold. Looking at the glass fish he was filled with a dull puzzling ache, as though he were trying to remember a dream. He pondered how he had come to have such a thing, why it was that this marvel of spun glass and pastel colouring had ever meant more to him than a blind perch struggling through the poisonous river. His hand traced the delicate filigree of its spines. They felt cold, burning cold in the cloudy light spilling through the window.

There was a knock at the door. Gordon started, as though he had been asleep, then crossed the darkened room. Through the peephole he saw Olivia, her hair atangle, a streak of black across one cheek. Her expression was oddly calm and untroubled in the carmine glare of the EXIT light. He tightened his hand about the doorknob, biting his lip against the pain that shot up through his arm as he did so. He wondered dully how she had gotten into the building, then remembered the chaos outside. Anyone could come in; even a woman who had seemingly just kicked a man to death by the polluted river. Perhaps it was like this all across the city, perhaps doors that had been locked since the riots had this evening suddenly sprung open.

"Gordon," Olivia commanded, her voice muffled by the heavy door that separated them. He was not surprised to feel the knob twist beneath his throbbing palm, or see the door swing inward to bump against his toe. Olivia slipped in, and with her a breath of incense-smelling smoke, the muted clamour of voices and laughter and pulsing music.

"Where'd you go?" she asked, smiling. He noticed that behind her the door had not quite closed. He reached to pull it shut but before he could grasp it she took him by the hand, the one that hurt. Grunting softly with pain he turned from the door to follow her into the living room.

"What's happening?" he whispered. "Olivia, what is it?" Without speaking she pulled him to the floor beside her, still smiling. She pulled his jacket from him, then his shoes and trousers and finally his bloodstained shirt. He reached to remove her blouse but Olivia pushed him away ungently, so that he cried out. As she moved above him his hand began to bleed again, leaving dark petals across her blouse and arms. The pain was so intense that he moaned, tried in vain to slow her but she only tightened her grip about his upper arm, tossing her hair back so that it formed a dark haze against the window's milky light. The blouse slipped from her shoulder and he could see the scars there, the little golden rings against her skin, drops of blood like rain flashing across her throat. Behind her the moon shone, bloated and sanguine. He could hear voices chanting counterpoint to the blood thudding in his temples. It took him a long time to catch his breath afterward. Olivia had bitten him on the shoulder, hard enough to bruise him. The pain coupled with that from his cut hand had suddenly made everything very intense, made him cry out loudly and then fall back hard against the cold floor as Olivia slipped from him. Now only the pain was left. He rubbed his shoulder ruefully. "Olivia? Are you angry?" he asked. She stood impassively in front of the window. The torn blouse had slipped from her shoulder. She had kicked her silk trousers beneath the sofa but pulled her boots back on, and moonlight glinted off the two wicked metal points. She seemed not to have heard him, so he repeated her name softly.

"Mmmm?" she said, distracted. She stared up at the sky, then leaned forward and opened the casement. Cold air flooded the room, and a brighter, colder light as well, as though the glass had ceased to filter out the lunar brilliance. Gordon shivered and groped for his shirt.

"Look at them," whispered Olivia. He got unsteadily to his feet and stood beside her, staring down at the sidewalk. Small figures capered across the broken tarmac, forms made threatening by the lurid glow of myriad bonfires that had sprung up across the dead grey lawn. He heard music too, not music from the radio or stereo but a crude raw sound, thrumming and beating as of metal drums, voices howling and forming words he could not quite make out, an unknown name or phrase—

"*Evohe*," whispered Olivia. The face she turned to him was white and merciless, her eyes inflamed. "*Evohe*."

"What?" said Gordon. He stepped backwards and stumbled on one of his shoes. When he righted himself and looked up he saw that there were other people in the room, other women, three four six of them, even more it seemed, slipping silently through the door that Olivia had left open behind her. They filled the small apartment with a cloying smell of smoke and burning hair, some of them carrying smoking sticks, others leather pocketbooks or scorched briefcases. He recognized many of them: though their hair was matted and wild, their clothes torn: dresses or suits ripped so that their breasts were exposed and he could see where the flesh had been raked by their own fingernails, leaving long wavering scars like signatures scratched in blood. Two of them were quite young and naked and caressed each other laughing, turning to watch him with sly feral eyes. Several of the older women had golden rings piercing their breasts or the frail web of flesh between their fingers. One traced a cut that ran down her thigh, then lifted her bloodied finger to her lips as though imploring Gordon to keep a secret. He saw another grey-haired woman whom he had greeted often at the newstand where they both purchased the *Wall Street Journal*. She seemingly wore only a furtrimmed camel's-hair coat. Beneath its soft folds Gordon glimpsed an undulating pattern of green and gray and gold. As she approached him she let the coat fall away and he saw a snake encircling her throat, writhing free to slide down between her breasts and then to the floor at Gordon's feet. He shouted and turned to flee.

Olivia was there, Olivia caught him and held him so tightly that for a moment he imagined she was embracing him, imagined the word she repeated was his name, spoken more and more loudly as she held him until he felt the breath being crushed from within his chest. But it was not his name, it was another name, a word like a sigh, like the whisper of a thought coming louder and louder as the others took it up and they were chanting now:

"*Evohe, evohe . . .*"

As he struggled with Olivia they fell upon him, the woman from the newstand, the girl from down the hall now naked and laughing in a sort of grunting chuckle, the two young girls encircling him with their slender cool arms and giggling as they kissed his cheeks and nipped his ears. Fighting wildly he thrashed until his head was free and he could see beyond them, see the open window behind the writhing web of hair and arms and breasts, the moon blazing now like a mad watchful eye above the burning canyons. He could see shreds of darkness falling from the sky, clouds or rain or wings, and he heard faintly beneath the shrieks and moans and panting voices the wail of sirens all across the city. Then he fell back once more beneath them.

There was a tinkling crash. He had a fleeting glimpse of something mauve and lavender skidding across the floor, then cried out as he rolled to one side and felt the glass shatter beneath him, the slivers of breath-spun fins and gills and tail slicing through his side. He saw Olivia, her face serene, her liquid eyes full of ardour as she turned to the girl beside her and took from her something that gleamed like silver in the moonlight, like pure and icy water, like a spar of broken glass. Gordon started to scream when she knelt between his thighs. Before he fainted he saw against the sky the bloodied fingers of eagle's wings, blotting out the face of a vast triumphant moon.

DAVID J. SCHOW

Busted in Buttown

DAVID J. SCHOW is another regular in *Best New Horror*, although the short short story which follows marks something of a departure from his usual contributions.

The author of the novels *The Kill Riff* and *The Shaft* (the latter still published only in Britain), and the collections *Seeing Red* and *Lost Angels*, Schow has also co-written the nonfiction study *The Outer Limits: The Official Companion* and edited the horror movie anthology *Silver Scream*.

Recent projects include a mini-collection of eight non-supernatural stories, *Look Out He's Got a Knife*, introduced by Robert Bloch, and a third book-length collection, *Headshots*. On the movie front, he wrote *Critters 3* and *4*, both released directly to video, and has completed a script for *The Crow*, based on the cult comic book. He is also thinking about writing a "sci-fi comedy remake" of *It Conquered the World*, which would be "wetter and funnier".

R OOK WAS IN AND OUT IN three flat.
His ethics were few, but rigid. Nonapparent, but ironclad, like dementia, rules visible only to himself. Rook jazzed on ripping off pawnshops. An educated person might suggest the act appealed to Rook's sense of symmetry, but Rook was not educated. Born an angry Mex, he sensed he would die an angry Mex, and so he devoted himself to the immediate goal of riding the razor and getting his. Whoever got in his way, in this bad old world, deserved to eat pain.

Symmetry. Rook crowbarred the rusty iron bars off the bathroom window one by one. He knew the silver racingstripe pattern of the alarm tape was just for show, and seconds later the McKnight Small Loan Company had a midnight visitor. Rook enjoyed stealing items he had previously thieved from other establishments, then rehocking them at different pawnshops. Symmetry.

His heart galloped with the suspense of it all: if there was one thing Rook had, it was heart. The scars on his face and arms throbbed with the beat of his own blood. He ignored his distinguishing marks until times such as these—action time, crisis time, payoff time. His heartbeat reminded him of the old wounds, like ritual incisions that had failed in their magical purpose and left his soul open for barter. His hands sought out the scars and rubbed them, seeking appeasement and prompting a fast-forward playback of memories: flights, Juvie, County, the gang strafings. That one time the hubby had wanted to grapple for his billfold; that other time when Rook himself had been mugged minutes after relieving some white cunt of her purse at knifepoint. She'd only had 50 bucks and two credit cards. Shit. Not worth the crescent ridge on the back of his skull: the ghosts that had laid him flat had used a tire iron for persuasion.

He eased through McKnight's bathroom window. Skinny had its advantages. Rook was lanky and buttless, thin arms bound by still jailtime sinew, narrow waist, legs too short for the pro hoops, and the gnarliest feet on the entire West Coast. He hid them inside fat Nikes, purchased with pawnshop profits. He grimaced when he heard one of his treasured fliers slam-dunk itself into McKnight's toilet. He was in.

Not inside the high-value prison of McKnight's cage, no, but in to pick and choose from the front shelves. Free to pilfer the fruits of the failures and strangers and junkies who kept Noddy the Queen in business. His prefigured grab was a videotape deck or two, plus pocket goodies, whatever was lying loose. Penetrating steel mesh and confounding the mechanics of Noddy's half-ton safe were beyond Rook's mean capabilities. Rook would not dream, but he would lend the cage a passing glance of avarice for the things he had convinced himself he would never have. Society was to blame.

184

At least Noddy had not taken the paranoid route of bike locking goods to the shelves. In the past year, Rook had hit Noddy twice and sold his own swag back to him once. Some citizens just never learned. Or maybe Noddy was scamming the insurance buckos.

Life went on, in its way.

Three flat, and Rook was out the window. Two DiscMans and a dictation recorder in a nylon backpack. One of those techie tape decks that could play videos from Europe; something about scanning a different bias, more lines to the screen. Rook appreciated adaptability. He had also appropriated a silver cigarette case (though he did not smoke), a tray of quarters (a whopping seven bucks there, easy), a cheap metalzoid batwing ring with a fake eyeball in the center, and two sticks of gum Noddy had left on the counter.

Rook chewed one and saved the other for later.

At least, the cigarette case *looked* like silver.

The alley was silent, dark and quiet as a PG cinema. Rook looked both ways before crossing. In, then out. He was innocent again.

Until the spotlight nailed his buttless backside. A metallic loud-speaker voice told him not to move. This was not in Rook's nature. Keep haulin' keep changin' . . .

He was supposed to *stay right where he was.*

. . . keep your ass out of the cinderblock Hilton. Rook was sprinting before the echo died.

The LAPD cruiser was slewed across the mouth of the alley, giving Rook a half-block lead. To pull in, the cops would first have to back up. Not a hell of a lot they could hit at the distance. Moving target, bad light, handguns.

Rook lit out for where he knew the fence to be.

The usual protests were shouted from behind, fading as he made yardage. No gunshots. He could hear his big Nikes slapping puddles, his breath wheezing, in and out, loud to him. His brain saw it all slo-mo and grainy, a film noir cliché. He'd die at the fence, nine-millimeter slugholes perforating him. He'd rasp out a little speech, blaming society, then tilt his head, close his eyes, and get ready to rip off God, or the Devil.

Nobody was shooting movies here.

He smashed the fence fullspeed and leapt, tearing loose a slat and falling rearward with a palmful of splinters. The trashcan he'd used to launch his running jump spun out, topheavy, and in one grand, awkward flail he was headed for the pavement.

He skinned his forearm on impact—a fresh scar in the making—and grabbed wildly to recover the backpack. He'd stolen that, too. It had been right in front of him, begging to be taken.

Already, running footsteps. They'd stop at 10 paces, drawn down, dead bang, and if he blinked at them the music would be over. It was called *making a threatening motion.*

He hooked the fence, scrambling with cockroach speed through the egress he'd just made. Breaking. Entering. First out, now in. Panic and adrenalin helped him ignore the blunt nail head that skewered the heel of his hand. He felt an abrupt, rude blurt of blood. He did not see it. It was what he paid to win darkness, for hiding.

Hey! The cops pounded up to their 10-foot limit. The drama point. Rook hated cop shows.

Rook blew through in total dark, overturning another garbage can, blind from the lack of light in somebody-or-other's backyard. He got his Nikes under him again and hugged the first turn in the fence he could feel. His abraded and punctured arm tried to betray him. He clamped.

Police baton flashlights, now, there at the broken slat. Police voices, mere yards away, making police decisions.

"Christ, don't stick your *head* in there, Jimbo!"

"Fuggit, I wanna nail the little prick!"

"He might have a gun, come on, man. From the shop, if not on him before. Hold up."

A hiss of disgust. "Fuck. He's gone, Duke."

Rook did not let his breath free. Drama time had passed him by in a flash. Beat. Beat. Nobody moved.

Then: "Hell with it. He didn't have no gun."

"Jimbo, who *cares?*"

"He *didn't have a gun,* Duke, you buttwad! He was so jumped he woulda started shootin'. I coulda plucked the sumbitch!"

"Yeah, so? Then what?"

"We got plenty of fuckin' guns in the *car,* Duke. We coulda stuck one in his hand. Shitfire."

"Oh, now we're Mister Gung-Ho tonight. S'matter with you? Domestics getting too dangerous for you? We don't bag him today, we'll bag him tomorrow. Problem with you, Jimbo, is too goddamn many donuts. All that sugar is spiking your killer instincts."

Pause. "Bite me where I pee, Duke."

Steamvalve hiatus, from Duke. "Fag."

Rook was starting to suffocate, his brain hammering him with the need to draw new air, his lungs cement. This was not the first time he'd had to outlast cop macho.

"Come on. Before somebody steals the car."

Later, Rook could brag about besting LA's finest. Too swift. Too bad there was no home video to prove how he'd outclassed them.

It might have been half an hour, or a week, that Rook played frozen cat in the dark, trying crazily to concentrate on sugar and cop metabolism. When he finally budged, his muscles cracked audibly across his joints. The alley and yard were as silent as the pillow in a buried casket.

Rook still had the stolen knapsack, still full of stolen freedom. No bullet holes. An ounce of flesh, a drop of blood had bought him options for one more day. In a curious flash of felon superstition, he felt not only protected, but invulnerable, as though he'd passed some cosmic test. Now he could walk home untouched.

Who'd want to steal from a thief who didn't boast?

Not that the good feeling in his heart would permit him to ignore the white van curbing itself behind him, not for a second, no way. It parked smoothly. Crisp sound. New tires. Good suspension. A panel job with no rear windows. A mystery van loaded with spies, perhaps.

Or a hit.

Paranoid bullshit. Any pro running a mobile attack play wouldn't bother popping Rook. His senses tingled to the rear anyway. Dat ole debbil magic, keeping an eye on his poor felonious ass.

Rook kept pace and didn't gawk back. Never panic.

Never let them know you see them . . . till it's fight or flight.

He made distance efficiently. Another half block and he could forget the van. False alarm.

The feathered dart took him high in the neck, *whap*, missing his jugular vein by an inch.

Rook had turned his head back to look. And given them a clean shot at his strike zone. Something hot as slag overran his vascular pipework, and put him out better than the best orgasm of his life.

He heard the voices again. Distantly, as before. Not Duke and Jimbo. Two new contestants. They talked about him. He could not see them.

Perhaps he was still in the alley.

"Blood types as AB positive. See?"

"This machine comes up wrong if you do it too fast."

"I say we got a winner."

"I say wait for the tissue workup."

Maybe it *was* Jimbo and Duke. They'd run off to the donut shop and gotten better educations.

"Hand me the phone. King Seven-oh Baker, this is mobile unit Four. We have a prelim match for Tucson, available now."

A new voice, not human. "*That's a copy, Mobile Four. Ice him down and bring him on home.*"

"Clean out that puncture and spike him."

Rook was stretchered. He cracked his eyes and saw a guy wearing a white surgical breathing filter. A lot of LED pinpoints. Lurching city lights as the van rolled.

"Where the hell is that fucking . . . oh here."

Rook was strapped down.

"Whoa, whoa, Artie, he's awake!"

"So do it! Just—!"

A needle invaded the crook of his arm. Another puncture. More warmth. Rook fogged. As smooth as he'd slid into Noddy's pawnshop, the drugs invaded him.

"Go back to sleep, pal." The voice was muffled by the mask.

"Check," said the driver. "And mate. Guy's got stamina."

"We needed a guy with heart."

Artie chuckled, upfront. "You check out those DiscMans and shit? You need one?"

"Why not. Nobody's gonna inventory this citizen. Not for what he stole, anyway."

Rook felt coldpacks nestle into his armpits and crotch. Distantly, so distantly. Sleepybye time. It was first class dope. He'd never get to that second stick of gum. He blamed society, but nobody could hear him.

He'd never feel the knives, either, when they slid in to steal what was his. In and out.

If there was one thing Rook had, it was heart. But not for very much longer.

RUSSELL FLINN

Subway Story

RUSSELL FLINN is a new writer whose fiction, interviews and articles have so far appeared in such small press publications as *Dark Dreams* (UK), *Phenix* (Belgium), *New Blood* (USA) and the 1991 British Fantasy Society collection *Stirring Within*. He cites his influences as Ramsey Campbell ("of course"), Robert Bloch, Ian McEwan and Alan Bennett.

However, disenchanted with his career as an author, Flinn had all but given up writing when we approached him about reprinting the story which follows. "In curious synchronicity with the acceptance of my story for *Best New Horror 3*," he reveals, "I discovered my notes for all the stories so rashly truncated, and which I now feel compelled to complete. The first will be one of unease, self-discovery/denial and tainted sexuality—certainly worthy of researching if not writing!"

After reading "Subway Story", we think you'll agree that Flinn has a talent that shouldn't be allowed to go to waste.

"To Scarlet"

EMERGING FROM BEHIND THE brewery, Whittle saw the same four women loitering by the subway. To his right, the Careers Centre, and a man chasing amongst the roosting pigeons. The women, he consigned to his eyecorners, prodding passage with his briefcase. Today, he was too angry with Daniel to notice them as he usually would. The one similarity was that they both got in Whittle's way. Each day that week, the boy had pushed him as far as he dare, silent impertinence. Whittle no longer enjoyed his work in the bookshop, thanks to the young assistant. My God, the runt had even learned the formalities and regulations assiduously, as if to make the comparison more overt!

The boy had sensed Whittle's militant mood, too, for he had been at Terry's heels all day. Well, friend or partner, Terry would hear of his dissatisfaction. The boy did nothing that did not harden Whittle to his purpose. He stamped up out of the grey hood of the subway, slamming his doors behind him and eating in the company of a bottle of wine. Perhaps writing would improve his mood. He scribbled the letter to the newspaper while he still felt fierce, and posted it the next morning.

A daunting morning, and not just through the realism of his dream of the four tramp women and their subway tomb. Perhaps that would teach him not to ignore them in future! But even more, Terry was evidently learning tardiness from the boy. A glance at the wallclock only made them both smile, shrug. Peevishly, he directed troublesome customers on to the two of them. Mightn't the boy bear up best under pressure: less time to scheme. He glared at the crewcut and embryonic moustache, the tattoo and t-shirt. How adult childish people yearned to be. Whittle himself, was too confident, too competent, to concern himself with how he looked to others.

Still, some effort was being made somewhere, for the ensuing week was almost bearable. Only the exteriors of the shop seemed temperamental. Rain lashed, then began to pour in quicksilver strands, shoring the paving slabs up to the sky. Subsequently, the shoppers seemed damp and grey days afterwards, and the subway, on such evenings, sounded alive with clocks. He had to skip bleary pools and bent-double beer cans.

The Monday following, his mind was already trained on the four women before he had arrived at their lair. Why was that? Not because of his alarm that they remained, even in the downpours; they had been there as long as he had been using the subway, though he recalled there being less of them. He was usually tempted to speak, but of what? Instead, he rushed past, around the clock hands of the streetlamp and its shadow. If only he had not dreamt of them! Better still, if he had not forgotten the details of it, but they had run together in his mind as if the rain had reached them. He should worry. Weren't his dreams populated by strangers these days, in varying degrees.

When the dull duo had arrived that morning, it was in time for him to hear the epilogue of some argument. "I don't care," Terry repeated. "It isn't what I expect from you. Or what I pay you for." Whittle was momentarily jubilant. Enough to let it pass that he saw to the salaries. The sense of promise diminished: they became amiable as the day wore on. Whittle was not above suspecting that the tiny scene had been staged for his benefit.

There was a more pleasing surprise still to come. His letter was in the evening paper. Disconcertingly close to the bottom of the page, but what did that matter? His views held it aloft from the rest. Terry said nothing next day, which convinced Whittle he had seen it. Unemployment was one of Terry's pet subjects—hence his willingness to employ all too hastily, a most unsuitable assistant for the bookshop.

"You won't forget the Trivial Pursuit evening Sal and I arranged, will you?" Terry asked as Whittle was locking the door. He cursed, now he was reminded. Before Whittle could ask if the boy was invited, Terry had rushed away.

He strolled gradually, wondering if the offer were an oblique apology. The precinct, empty but for litter and youths of no fixed direction. Expletive minstrels hefting stereos like hods. Display dummies eyed him blindly, asexually erotic with beckoning hands. Darker nights had dared him to see them move.

The mouth of the subway had snared some shadows and was drawing them in. Only three women this time. Maybe there was a fifth he was yet to see, for their patiently furtive manner did not differ from when they were four. Nearing them, the patchy raincoats and fronds of print dress, he grew clammy. He saw how dirt defined their fingernails. Their hair, drawn tightly back, resembled unhealthy grey skin. What else had paralysed his smirk, while he was about it? Their clinging together, or the quivering trunks of bare, unshaven legs that passed within inches of his face as he descended? What had they once been? A chorus line act for whom old habits died hard? He smiled until he imagined them lifting their dresses for kicks. He had once seen one of them menstruating onto a flattened newspaper.

Later, he walked into a room filled with people he did not know. Thankfully, one of them was not the boy. "And this is Darren," Terry announced rather ambiguously, handing refilled glasses to the second couple.

"Terry's told us about you. You both keep that shop running well.

Not difficult, is it?" one asked, stoking cold embers of conversation. Why ask, if they thought they knew! So, Terry was not above lying to them. Or did he believe it himself, the way he beamed down at them. Then the board gathered them round.

He laughed only occasionally, but it was a strained sound. On his walk over, the subway had again slicked him with its chilly misery. He had been meaning to ask that Daniel be sacked, accumulating nerve. He had to convince himself that his mental rehearsals for their tete à tete hadn't simply made Terry an irascible ventriloquist's foil, and he hadn't quite made sense of what he could make out from the far side of the tunnel. Four raincoats draped upon a shopping trolley, except that it was just the same four, stooping unnervingly low over it. Closer, aiming his face from them, he had seen it was a pram, and the crumpled pillow they prodded and patted had been a baby. It was struggling to stay in the light, beyond the shadows filling its pram. He should have said something, but was more doubtful of what that comment might have been. Only that babies were less discerning in their choice of company. Besides, hadn't he been glad to get by them unnoticed?

Terry's living room was almost as dim, and as cramped as if he were squinting. No wonder he was away before the lifts home were allocated, his footsteps like striking matches as he crossed the car park. The subway now looked ironically less threatening than he had made it. The women's absence helped. He searched for traces of the pram, making amends now he was braver, but it could have been anywhere. A sickening premonition was only a froth of cement, not the calcified brain it resembled. Whose child could it have been?

Theirs, you fool. He was making too much of it all. It could only have been theirs, no matter how that notion disgusted him. He walked the rest of the way home, clucking disapprovingly. Even next morning's sunlight proved all his fears wrong.

During the lunchbreak, he had to scour Terry's book-keeping, but it was as scrawled as the subway's graffiti, as meaningless. It had probably taken Terry until then to recall the suggested trip to Portmeirion. The conversation was as sketchy as his details. "Don't you want to go?" he asked, just as Whittle's disinterest had begun to labour.

"I never said I wanted to. We don't have to go everywhere we mention. Some things are just meant for idle talk." How pompous that last had made him sound! Terry's eyes were flinching away.

"That's not the impression I got first time." Then a customer upstaged him. Whittle heard the boy asking Terry where Portmeirion was.

‚Perhaps it was too soon for replies, he thought as he left the newsagents, disillusioned with his paper. He would not be happy if agreement meant apathy. The car park and subway were both dogged with litter. Once more, the baby crawled to mind. Some children had commandeered a battered pram, hemmed with frays. The canvas was darkly damp. Too much damage to have been that of the night before, surely. A florid woman broke out of her car and chased the children off. When she saw the pram, she deflated; had it been worth the effort? He tried to pass without glancing. The litter applauded underfoot, slow and sarcastic. There was no harm in pushing the pram to the back of his mind. In his street, his home was dull with streetlighting, a block of rusty limestone. He ate in silence, as his mother might have made him.

He took time in answering when the phone rang, in case it was Terry.

At first, he had thought it must be an indecent call, but there were words amid the breathing. Emotion had made them incomprehensible. Poorly restrained violence, if the language was any indication. My God, it *was* indecent! He could only be grateful he had not been provoked into speaking. If the caller were random, he must give no clue to his identity. But what on Earth had possessed the man?

The following day was better, possibly because his anxiety had been directed elsewhere. His nightmares had tried to convince him he had heard not one voice, but four, and that he had answered the call with his number. But the unclear line might have masked the digits—what point was there in arguing with a dream? He could always change the number. In fact, the call had made him glad of work. His whole house had begun to feel like that dim hallway. The shuffling at his door had been vindictive litter, and lurking sets of shadows only the trees in roving headlights. Terry hurried to remind him that Whittle would be alone with the boy for the next two days.

"Take care of him, won't you?" What Terry had intended as a joke, was sour in his absence. Forgetting the days previous, Daniel behaved as though he had interpreted the comment as a trigger for insolence and tension. The moment the door caught in his wake, it was the setting of a trap. A weight of potential confrontation in the air. The boy spent the first day marking the attendance of the shelves (Jack Vance was late, Orwell unaccountably absent). Whittle chased up deliveries, which might have been best saved for when he could no longer avoid addressing the boy. In the afternoon, the phone was unavoidable, however. Requests for books about dyslexia that sounded like a tasteless joke gone on too long. An elderly man who would know the cover if he saw it, but refused to come to the shop to look. Whittle realised how closely he was listening to their voices, recognised none as that from the call.

That night, he had heard something being killed in the subway.

The relic of a pram was gone, though the women felt close. He was just looking for things to trouble him, far beyond his concern for the baby. He seemed to have forgotten how much he disliked children. Margins of shadow hid the subway walls. Echoes pursued him with his own footsteps, made papery and thin. He was thinking of Terry when he found he had left his paper at the shop, that perhaps it was because they had spoken so little in childhood that they had mistaken each other for friends. A depressing thought. He turned back. Local children had gathered an arsenal of stones on the grass verge beside the entrance. The cry had come from below, waiting until he was within earshot.

Was it a warning or a plea? He daren't investigate until he knew. A train passed, and for a helpless moment, he feared something had become trapped on the line. But it was the subway, as the echo proved. Sudden recollections of the baby appalled him, until he heard it begin to yelp and whine. A dog hit by traffic, dragging itself from sight to die. Shuffling told him how badly it was injured, the image too graphically real. Could youths be kicking it to death, though the rising cries suggested it was going to breech the corner so that he could see for himself. What could he do then, but hurry away. Whenever the noises in the road waned, the cries continued, like a can being scraped clean in his skull.

A pity about the paper. There had been two replies to his letter, both furious with him. Possibly the caller on the phone had been provoked in just such a way. Reasonable, but unsettling. Were it true, then his name and address beneath the letter had betrayed him.

He nursed himself during the night, as a wife should have. How passionately could someone feel about unemployment? Being entitled to freedom of speech should not be reason enough to place one in danger. There he went again! What danger was this? Only that evidenced in his neurotic rechecking of every lock in the house, and didn't that only confine him with the phone? Yes, he argued, but things were so much different in the real world. You could have an irrational fear of a subway, for instance. Caution might be a better word, if less honest. Too late, the thought had darkened his room immeasurably.

He left for work early, before dawn. The subway was empty, but for a faint shuffling. Litter whispered. Lit windows, strung together by a train, rollercoasted overhead. If there had been blood, or a corpse, he had not seen any. The Council, no doubt.

That afternoon, the shop seemed full of customers, as he had never seen it. Outside, was the reason. Crowds of football fans had been misdirected into the precinct, pushing over the wire baskets of litter and glaring into the shop windows. "Where are the police when this happens, eh?" one old man was calling, too loudly.

He kept the shop door open—mightn't visibly locking them incite the gang in some way. Meanwhile, the gathering in the shop tried to incite him, if only to fear. "I can't stand them. Nothing good ever comes of gangs. Get a few people together and you see all their worst aspects. They get you cornered. Brings out the monster in them, all this ganging up. They get you cornered." Good God, they had all begun to sound like his letter. Trying to control his thoughts was like fighting a blanket in the wind.

"Groups trouble me," was his only offering, and even that he could read two ways. When at last the gangs drained away, lubricated by the arrival of some police vans, the shop began to empty. That was when Whittle noticed how Daniel had been unmoved during the whole episode. Well, he wasn't a stone's throw from the kind of people out there, was he? Too stupidly macho to know when to be afraid. When a uniformed officer came to see if any damage had been done, Whittle refused to let the boy speak.

He watched the papers. One businessman, who claimed to patronise training schemes, called him "bloody-minded" to suggest that crime was not simply a by-product of unemployment, but an easy alternative to applying for work. Of course, if the man had to stoop to insults—why, what could he know of the idler's state of mind? Even Whittle could recall stealing from his mother's purse when money was scarce. "Aren't big city take-overs just muggings in pinstripe, brought on by the lassitude of deprived goals?" he wrote, but declined to continue. The reply had been orchestrated to provoke, with no thought beyond that. Terry rang, but it was not his voice that Whittle sought. Neither mentioned the boy, which was as well.

It was twilight or dawn in the dream, for taut sunlight had yet to illuminate the subway's midsection. Litter poised and sprang in the breeze, glass gleamed faintly. It was bothering him more than he realised; the baby too, for the images highlighted baby-snatching. His mind had taken it literally, ropes of dull graffiti dropping down between the grid of mortar, plunging into the shrieking pram. When he looked again, the pram had gone. The pools where it had stood must have been water darkened by rusty wheels. The walls and ceiling looked ready to drip on him, darkly. He ran, but was permitted no escape. Even in the streets, with their endless walls and corridors, and at home in his blackened hallway, he still wasn't sure he had thrown it off. There was a group of figures at the top of his stairs, but not when he woke.

Daniel did not arrive for work the next day. "Saturday's a kid's favourite day," Whittle called from the stockroom. "He may just be feeling off it." They both knew he should have rung in, but neither seemed to want to say so. "Maybe he lives off his parents."

"You mean, with them," Terry said. God, he was naive. Besides, if they rang, he would first have to tell Terry what had happened the night before, after he had locked up. Not that it was relevant, except in that it was so childish.

Since the precinct had been practically deserted, it had not taken him long to realise that he was being followed. He had hesitated by the department store, where four of the dummies had been leant head-to-head, as if the frame for a wigwam. A trick of the light made them sway greyly, and then he saw that it was the boy skulking after him. There was no crime in that, but even so, he was impelled to move on. Slyly, the boy duplicated. Whittle had tried to keep sight of him only in the glass, but it confused him. At times, there seemed more than one figure, each somehow different. He might have been wrestling with his nerves to approach his employer.

Churlishly, Whittle had kept going, even when finally he heard the boy calling to him. Panic had run him to ground at the subway, and it was there that he saw the chance to scheme. He had waited until the boy was in view, before plunging down the gradient. The flagstones had snapped at his feet with his own belated echoes. Something caught his shoulder, and he had heard the women stirring from some dark spot. Good, for they would be in the halflight in time for the boy to arrive. Imagine his horror! Seeing what Whittle had meant by leading him there would make him think twice before hounding him again.

Perhaps he had not been tempted to enter. He did not emerge, nor had he heard him enter. He waited, refusing to call out in the thickening silence. He'd not have his joke turned upon him. Let the boy sulk elsewhere or stay hidden. Whittle could hear the women shuffling back and forth.

No harm could have come to the child, for God's sake. The women were harmless, even to the fainthearted like himself. The boy's absence was just an extended version of his silence in the subway. That was all. He should enjoy the respite, the opportunity to speak unhindered to Terry.

He avoided the subway all weekend, superstitiously, though every bus route he used took him past it. Worse, it looked so meaningless, the women so small. They were squabbling over scraps of paper, or rags. He tried to smile at how he had once seen the boy, a still life by the till titled VACANT by his folded newspaper. Then there had been the window cleaner, the sight of whom outside had made him think of a portrait tending to its own frame. But then he had to look at the other things in his mind. Where the sun strained whitely down, gleaming ghosts of shoppers were trapped in streets behind the panes. Whenever he turned, he wasn't sure why. Wherever he looked, the four women were masquerading as different people, or ducking. They were even in the bookshop as he sidled past, long as shadows. Perhaps that was all they were, since they were gone as soon as he recognised them.

Sunday found him wishing for the patience to sketch or write, willing for any medium to express his thoughts. He strolled to the seafront, looking aimless as the tourists, with every detail of the picture he could make of the subway evolving. Clenching teeth of reddish railings (rusty with blood?), oesophagus of brick, tongues of tarmac and ribs of mortar. How pretentious it made him feel. Only the sight of blank paper would make it all futile.

He arrived home to find a neighbour posed artificially by her rose tree, not pruning. The sight of him broke the spell. "Your phone was ringing while you were out." Something had made him slam the door on her. True, her voice had suggested, unreasonably, that she knew the substance of the calls. Had she read his letter, and shared the caller's sympathies?

There was a note from Terry to join him at his local, but the phone was engaged for as long as Whittle wanted to decline. Why spoil his own weekend because of that damned boy! Whittle was still young enough to enjoy himself. They didn't have the monopoly, these youths, for all their tattoos and aftershave. Dinner over, he resolved to walk back via the subway, as a test of mettle. The drinks would help.

Terry was trying not to loiter in the shady doorway. He dimly remembered the pub from one of the Quiz League forays, all polished nubs of brass and coarse oak. It resembled a beached ship to Whittle, who had given up on the similes his mind kept floating. They writhed to the tables, through columns of couples like a dance floor between numbers. When he spoke, it was almost a shout. Terry listened too intently for comfort; Whittle's eyes ached with holding his gaze. Beside him, a drunk rocked. A dummy on a careless ventriloquist's knee.

"Saw your letter the other day. Sal pointed it out. Didn't know you felt so strongly about it."

"About lots of things." The boy.

Terry didn't seem to think beyond the letter. "Sure. Some things need saying." The boy, tell him!

"They certainly do." But Terry had turned away. Girls entered, gaudy as parrots. The boys who had tired of being rifled for drinks moved to the bar. "What's become of Daniel, I wonder," Terry said. Like smoke shifting between the standing room, Whittle saw grey faces and hair, fastening his tongue to the roof of his mouth. It was glossy, tablelegs, not unshaven skin, that shifted through the others. Maybe they truly were nothing but smoke he was fashioning himself.

"I can't imagine," he lied. He drank so as not to speak further, but he needn't worry. Terry had simply been timing his moment.

"I've heard from him already, Darren, don't worry. I just want to know what you were thinking of."

Whittle's face felt sprinkled with embers. The jukebox began to sing. Pop music, he thought. The kind that sounds so much like the needle has stuck. "I don't understand. He's called you?"

"He said you led him to that subway in East Marsh Street. You used to get spooked over it even as a kid, didn't you? It was lucky that he knew what to expect in it. I don't suppose it even occurred to you he might have fallen."

Whittle let himself become angry, now that he knew the boy was safe. "I did no such thing. He just followed me, being abusive, if you must know. If he's telling tales already, I'm not surprised. I told you what to expect from him. He wants to pry us apart."

Terry gaped, but it was enough time to tell him about the phone call he'd had, and how it was occurring to Whittle who it had been. "A random, anonymous attack would be a child's style. He's lucky I never involved the police, Terry."

But after that, Terry had walked out, leaving Whittle to wonder if the boy had yet won. He must make Terry listen, no matter how traumatic it was for them both. Yet once outside, with all the smoke he had breathed in blowing out as steam, the streets were empty. Singing louts cascaded into him in the doorway. Then he had only to go home.

This time it took longer to determine exactly who it was behind him. Deserted roads amplified and multiplied his footsteps, which made him feel oddly lonelier. Alleys repeated his noises for a while after each passing, until it was clear he wasn't just being followed. They had succeeded in unnerving him too, with each flinch and angry turn. It was either light clinging to misty windows, or a cautious drunk, but nothing he was expecting. A gathering of bin-liners by a restaurant door quivered lazily in the glow. They had looked nothing like the raincoats that came to mind.

Was this the way Terry had taken? Yes, he thought he saw him slink jaggedly around the far corner as Whittle entered. Not again! Phone calls, pursuits, petty squabbles: he was in danger of being overwhelmed by the childish! Did he hope to haunt Whittle by repeating the Daniel episode; if so, then he would be disappointed. He'd not be cowed twice.

He would feel less nervous within sight of Terry again, but couldn't easily manage it until they were in sight of the subway. Whittle ducked into the darkest alley he dared, and let Terry pass. That made him infinitely relieved, particularly when his partner looked so anxious. Presumably, he hoped to catch Whittle to apologise, or something less civilized.

He saw him go down into the subway. He heard the structure turning down Terry's sounds. He tried to pick out a path bare of gravel. Even so, nearer the rectangular mouth, he felt less able to disguise his trepidation. Was he so desperate to scare himself!

He leant over the railings without touching them, until his face felt pinched with blood. Snatched himself back when he was dizzy enough to reel. In the silence, he hadn't heard Terry's footsteps emerge from over the railtracks. But neither did he answer Whittle's calls. Had he drunk so much beforehand that he had slipped in the litter, too drowsy to reply? He had walked right enough, but a sober man could just as easily fall. Of course, Whittle must strive to help, then Terry would be obliged to speak.

It took five minutes that seemed considerably longer to find his way around to the other exit. There had been something unlucky in the prospect of descending the way his friend had: possibly in that he too may slip. Past the cottage on stilts that passed for a signal-box, into East Marsh Street. If he hurried, he may still see Terry turning off at the junction, and so abandon the search. He was disappointed. Robinson Street was bare; litter settled down for the night in bins.

He shouldn't try to gather nerve, for fear of second thoughts. He could feel how the slope tried to pitch him forward into the shadows. The lamp filament glowed, suffocated by dust. Even the walls it lit looked as uncertain as packed dirt. All but the brightest graffiti had sunk back into the recess. Turning onto the main tunnel saved him a journey. It was empty, except where it was cut short by shadows. So Terry had gone on, if Terry it had been. He preferred to doubt that, but was swivelling softly to flee when he kicked the thing out of the darkness. Not a rat, he flinched. No, a shoe. And lying just within his recovering sight, the raincoat Terry had been wearing, collars curled like leaves—no, hold on! In the vague light he shouldn't be so sure. How could he hope to stop surmise now—any of the darker stains on the walls could be more than paint. Beneath the huddled coat, which he half-expected to turn over and curse him drunkenly, there was a smaller rag, like a sock. He picked out the arms of the baby-jacket and gagged his thoughts with a gasp. It felt chewed damp. Though armed with suspicions, he still did not know how to account for it, except that it must have been enough of a reason to leave.

Standing so sharply had him teetering: which way had he come? Why should it matter, echoes tracked him along both routes, water pattering. It struck him from where, when the central pool was long dry. The sewers? They pattered like feet too large to scamper. He had to go back for the coat and shoe. Some tramp might steal them, if they weren't already his.

When he knew that what he heard was growing near, he was already frozen by the sight of it. More than one pair of feet, that was what had escaped him, and moving the clothes had been very like vibrating a spider-web. He turned to the sounds.

The shadow was worse, a draped and spidery hand. It was coupled up with a crowd of bodies, a sluggish scrum. He could see no separate head. Smell rather than sight told him they were soiled and naked, and how quickly they moved for all their clumsy linking. The women? He saw that the fifth and sixth were male, even down to the one's tattoo. Good God, were they all drunk?

Incensed, he shoved out at their collective body with his hands and fell. He mustn't! Plastic flew up at his sides, greased his elbows and heels from under him. Something fell on him—no, it was their shadow, and then themselves. He had to move, not touch them, not panic. Screaming he could not stop, seeing the ring of dusty eyes and single, sinking mouth: a circuit of teeth.

THOMAS LIGOTTI

The Medusa

"THE MOST STARTLING and unexpected discovery since Clive Barker"
is how *The Washington Post* described the fiction of Thomas Ligotti.
A regular toiler in the small presses for many years, he has recently
been turning up in such anthologies as *The Best Horror from Fantasy
Tales*, *Prime Evil*, *Fine Frights*, *A Whisper of Blood*, *The Year's Best
Fantasy and Horror* and the previous two volumes of *Best New
Horror*.

He has been a featured author in *Weird Tales*, and his recent
short fiction has been collected in *Songs of a Dead Dreamer* and
Grimscribe: His Lives and Works. "The Medusa" is yet another
example of Ligotti's oblique and haunting prose . . .

I

BEFORE LEAVING HIS ROOM FOR THE first time in nobody knows how long, Lucian Dregler transcribed a few stray thoughts into his notebook.

The sinister, the terrible never deceive: the state in which they leave us is always one of enlightenment. And only this condition of vicious insight enables us a full grasp of the world, *all* things considered, just as a frigid melancholy grants us full possession of ourselves.

We may hide from horror only in the heart of horror.

Could I be so unique among dreamers, having courted the Medusa—my first and oldest companion—to the exclusion of all others? Would I have her respond to this sweet talk?

Relieved to have these fragments safely on the page rather than in some precarious mental notebook, where they were likely to become smudged or completely effaced, Dregler slipped into a relatively old overcoat, locked the door of his room behind him, and exited down innumerable staircases at the back of his apartment building. A winding series of seldomly travelled streets was his established route to a certain place he now and then frequented, though for time's sake—in order to *waste* it, that is—he chose even more uncommon and chaotic avenues. He was meeting an acquaintance he had not seen in quite a while.

The place was very dark, though no more than in past memory, and much more populated than it first appeared to Dregler's eyes. He paused at the doorway, slowly but unsystematically removing his gloves, while his vision, still exceptional, worked with the faint halos of illumination offered by lamps of tarnished metal, which were spaced so widely along the walls that the light of one lamp seemed barely to link up and propagate that of its neighbour. Gradually, then, the darkness sifted away, revealing the shapes beneath it: a beaming forehead with the glitter of wire-rimmed eyeglasses below, cigarette-holding and beringed fingers lying asleep on a table, shoes of shining leather which ticked lightly against Dregler's own as he now passed cautiously through the room. At the back stood a column of stairs coiling up to another level, which was more an appended platform, a little brow of balcony or a puny pulpit, than what one might call a sub-section of the establishment proper. This level was caged in at its brink with a railing constructed of the same rather wiry and fragile material as the stairway, giving this area the appearance of a makeshift scaffolding. Rather slowly, Dregler ascended the stairs.

"Good evening, Joseph," Dregler said to the man seated at the table beside an unusually tall and narrow window. Joseph Gleer stared for a moment at the old gloves Dregler had tossed onto the table.

"You still have those same old gloves," he replied to the greeting, then lifted his gaze, grinning: "And that overcoat!"

Gleer stood up and the two men shook hands. Then they both sat down and Gleer, indicating the empty glass between them on the table, asked Dregler if he still drank brandy. Dregler nodded, and Gleer said "Coming up" before leaning over the rail a little way and holding out two fingers in view of someone in the shadows below.

"Is this just a sentimental symposium, Joseph?" inquired the now uncoated Dregler.

"In part. Wait until we've got our drinks, so you can properly congratulate me." Dregler nodded again, scanning Gleer's face without any observable upsurge in curiosity. A former colleague from Dregler's teaching days, Gleer had always possessed an open zest for minor intrigues, academic or otherwise, and an addiction to the details of ritual and protocol, anything preformulated and with precedent. He also had a liking for petty secrets, as long as he was among those privy to them. For instance, in discussions—no matter if the subject was philosophy or old films—Gleer took an obvious delight in revealing, usually at some advanced stage of the dispute, that he had quite knowingly supported some treacherously absurd school of thought. His perversity confessed, he would then assist, and even surpass, his opponent in demolishing what was left of his old position, supposedly for the greater glory of disinterested intellects everywhere. But at the same time, Dregler saw perfectly well what Gleer was up to. And though it was not always easy to play into Gleer's hands, it was this secret counter-knowledge that provided Dregler's sole amusement in these mental contests, for

> Nothing that asks for your arguments is worth arguing, just as nothing that solicits your belief is worth believing. The real and the unreal lovingly cohabit *in our terror*, the only "sphere" that matters.

Perhaps secretiveness, then, was the basis of the two men's relationship, a flawed secretiveness in Gleer's case, a consummate one in Dregler's.

Now here he was, Gleer, keeping Dregler in so-called suspense. His eyes, Dregler's, were aimed at the tall narrow window, beyond which were the bare upper branches of an elm that twisted with spectral movements under one of the floodlights fixed high upon the outside walls. But every few moments Dregler glanced at Gleer, whose babylike features were so remarkably unchanged: the cupid's bow lips, the cookie-dough cheeks, the tiny grey eyes now almost buried within the flesh of a face too often screwed up with laughter.

A woman with two glasses on a cork-bottomed tray was standing over the table. While Gleer paid for the drinks, Dregler lifted his and held it in the position of a lazy salute. The woman who had brought the drinks looked briefly and without expression at toastmaster Dregler. Then she went away and Dregler, with false ignorance, said: "To your upcoming or recently passed event, whatever it may be or have been."

"I hope it will be for life this time, thank you, Lucian."

"What is this, *quintus*?"

"*Quartus*, if you don't mind."

"Of course, my memory is as bad as my powers of observation. Actually I was looking for something shining on your finger, when I should have seen the shine of your eyes. No ring, though, from the bride?"

Gleer reached into his open shirt and pulled out a length of neck-chain, dangling at the end of which was a tiny rose-coloured diamond in a plain silver setting.

"Modern innovations," he said neutrally, replacing the chain and stone. "The moderns must have them, I suppose, but marriage is still marriage."

"Here's to the Middle Ages," Dregler said with unashamed weariness.

"And the middle-aged," refrained Gleer.

The men sat in silence for some moments. Dregler's eyes moved once more around that shadowy loft, where a few tables shared the light of a single lamp. Most of its dim glow backfired onto the wall, revealing the concentric coils of the wood's knotty surface. Taking a calm sip of his drink, Dregler waited.

"Lucian," Gleer finally began in a voice so quiet that it was nearly inaudible.

"I'm listening," Dregler assured him.

"I didn't ask you here just to commemorate my marriage. It's been almost a year, you know. Not that that would make any difference to you."

Dregler said nothing, encouraging Gleer with receptive silence.

"Since that time," Gleer continued, "my wife and I have both taken leaves from the university and have been traveling, mostly in

Europe and the Mediterranean. We've just returned a few days ago.
Would you like another drink? You went through that one rather
quickly."

"No, thank you. Please go on," Dregler requested very politely.

After drinking the last of his brandy, Gleer continued. "Lucian, I've
never understood your fascination with what you call the Medusa. I'm
not sure I care to, though I've never told you that. But through no
deliberate efforts of my own, let me emphasize, I think I can further
your, I guess you could say, pursuit. You are still interested in the
matter, aren't you?"

"Yes, but I'm too poor to affort Peloponnesian jaunts like the one
you and your wife have just returned from. Was that what you had
in mind?"

"Not at all. You needn't even leave town, which is the strange
part, the real beauty of it. It's very complicated how I know what
I know. Wait a second. Here, take this."

Gleer now produced an object he had earlier stowed away somewhere in the darkness, laying it on the table. Dregler stared at the
book. It was bound in a rust-coloured cloth and the gold lettering
across its spine was flaking away. From what Dregler could make
out of the remaining fragments of the letters, the title of the book
seemed to be: *Electro-Dynamics for the Beginner*.

"What is this supposed to be?" he asked Gleer.

"Only a kind of passport, meaningless in itself. This is going to
sound ridiculous—how I know it!—but you want to bring the book
to this establishment," said Gleer, placing a business card upon the
book's front cover, "and ask the owner how much he'll give you
for it. I know you go to these shops all the time. Are you familiar
with it?"

"Only vaguely," replied Dregler.

The establishment in question, as the business card read, was
*Brother's Books: Dealers in Rare and Antiquarian Books, Libraries
and Collections Purchased, Large Stock of Esoteric Sciences and
Civil War, No Appointment Needed, Member of Manhattan Soci-
ety of Philosophical Bookdealers, Benjamin Brothers, Founder and
Owner.*

"I'm told that the proprietor of this place knows you by your
writings," said Gleer, adding in an ambiguous monotone: "He thinks
you're a real philosopher."

Dregler gazed at length at Gleer, his long fingers abstractedly
fiddling with the little card. "Are you telling me that the Medusa
is supposed to be a book?" he said.

Gleer stared down at the table-top and then looked up. "I'm not
telling you anything I do not know for certain, which is not a great

deal. As far as I know, it could still be anything you can imagine, and perhaps already have. Of course you can take this imperfect information however you like, as I'm sure you will. If you want to know more than I do, then pay a visit to this bookstore."

"Who told you to tell me this?" Dregler calmly asked.

"You can't ask that, Lucian. Everything falls apart if you do."

"Very well," said Dregler, pulling out his wallet and inserting the business card into it. He stood up and began putting on his coat. "Is that all, then? I don't mean to be rude but— "

"Why should you be any different from the usual? But one more thing I should tell you. Please sit down. Now listen to me. We've known each other a long time, Lucian. And I know how much this means to you. So whatever happens, or doesn't happen, I don't want you to hold me responsible. I've only done what I thought you yourself would want me to do. Well, tell me if I was right."

Dregler stood up again and tucked the book under his arm. "Yes, I suppose. But I'm sure we'll be seeing each other. Good night, Joseph."

"One more drink," offered Gleer.

"No, good night," answered Dregler.

As he started away from the table, Dregler, to his embarrassment, nearly rapped his head against a massive wooden beam which hung hazardously low in the darkness. He glanced back to see if Gleer had noticed this clumsy mishap. And after merely a single drink! But Gleer was looking the other way, gazing out the window at the tangled tendrils of the elm and the livid complexion cast upon it by the floodlights fixed high upon the outside wall.

For some time Dregler thoughtlessly observed the wind-blown trees outside before turning away to stretch out on his bed, which was a few steps from the window of his room. Beside him now was a copy of his first book, *Meditations on the Medusa*. He picked it up and read piecemeal from its pages.

> The worshipants of the Medusa, including those who clog pages with "insights" and interpretations such as these, are the most hideous citizens of this earth—and the most numerous. But how many of them *know* themselves as such? Conceivably there may be an inner cult of the Medusa, but then again: who could dwell on the existence of such beings for the length of time necessary to round them up for execution?
>
> It is possible that only the dead are not in league with the Medusa. We, on the other hand, are her allies—but always against ourselves. How does one become her *companion* . . . and live?

We are never in danger of beholding the Medusa. For that to happen she needs our consent. But a far greater disaster awaits those who know the Medusa to be gazing at them and long to reciprocate in kind. What better definition of a marked man: one who "has eyes" for the Medusa, whose eyes have a will and a fate of their own.

Ah, to be a thing without eyes. What a break to be *born* a stone!

Dregler closed the book and then replaced it on one of the shelves across the room. On that overcrowded shelf, leather and cloth pressing against cloth and leather, was a fat notebook stuffed with loose pages. Dregler brought this back to the bed with him and began rummaging through it. Over the years the folder had grown enormously, beginning as a few random memoranda—clippings, photographs, miscellaneous references which Dregler copied out by hand—and expanding into a storehouse of infernal serendipity, a testament of terrible coincidence. And the subject of every entry, major and minor, of this inadvertent encyclopedia was the Medusa herself.

Some of the documents fell into a section marked "Facetious," including a comic book (which Dregler picked off a drugstore rack) that featured the Medusa as a benevolent superheroine who used her hideous powers only on equally hideous foes in a world without beauty. Others belonged under the heading of "Irrelevant," where was placed a three-inch strip from a decades-old sports page lauding the winning season of "Mr (*sic*) Medusa". There was also a meager division of the notebook which had no official designation, but which Dregler could not help regarding as items of "True Horror." Prominent among these was a feature article from a British scandal sheet: a photoless chronicle of a man's year-long suspicion that his wife was periodically possessed by the serpent-headed demon, a senseless little guignol which terminated with the wife's decapitation while she lay sleeping one night and the subsequent incarceration of a madman.

One of the least creditable subclasses of the notebook consisted of pseudo-data taken from the less legitimate propogators of mankind's knowledge: renegade "scientific" journals, occult-anthropology newsletters, and publications of various Centers of sundry "mythic" studies. Contributions to the notebook from periodicals such as *The Excentaur*, a back issue of which Dregler stumbled across in none other than Brother's Books, were collectively categorized as "Medusa and Medusans: Sightings and Material Explanations." An early number of this publication included an article which attributed the birth of the Medusa, and of all life on Earth, to one of many extraterrestrial visitors, for whom this planet has been a sort of truckstop or comfort station en route to other locales in other galactic systems.

All such enlightening finds Dregler relished with a surly joy, especially those proclamations from the high priests of the human mind and soul, who invariably relegated the Medusa to a psychic underworld where she serves as the image par excellence of romantic panic. But unique among the curiosities he cherished was an outburst of prose whose author seemed to follow in Dregler's own footsteps: a man *after his own heart*. "Can we be delivered," this writer rhetorically queried, "from the 'life force' as symbolized by Medusa? Can this energy, if such a thing exists, be put to death, crushed? Can we, in the arena of our being, come stomping out—gladiator-like—net and trident in hand, and, poking and swooping, pricking and swishing, *torment* this soulless and hideous demon into an excruciating madness, and, finally, annihilate it to the thumbs-down delight of our nerves and to our soul's deafening applause?" Unfortunately, however, these words were written in the meanest spirit of sarcasm by a critic who parodically reviewed Dregler's own *Meditations on the Medusa* when it first appeared twenty years earlier.

But Dregler never sought out reviews of his books, and the curious thing, the amazing thing, was that this item, like all the other bulletins and ponderings on the Medusa, had merely fallen into his hands unbidden. (In a dentist's office, of all places.) Though he had read widely in the lore of and commentary on the Medusa, none of the material in his rather haphazard notebook was attained through the normal channels of research. None of it was gained in an official manner, none of it foreseen. In the fewest words, it was all a gift of unforeseen circumstances, strictly unofficial matter.

But what did this prove, exactly, that he continued to be offered these pieces to his puzzle? It proved nothing, exactly or otherwise, and was merely a side-effect of his preoccupation with a single subject. Naturally he would be alert to its intermittent cameos on the stage of daily routine. This was normal. But although these "finds" proved nothing, rationally, they always did suggest more to Dregler's imagination than to his reason, especially when he pored over the collective contents of these archives devoted to his oldest companion.

It was, in fact, a reference to this kind of imagination for which he was now searching as he lay on his bed. And there it was, a paragraph he had once copied in the library from a little yellow book entitled *Things Near and Far*. "There is nothing in the nature of things," the quotation ran, "to prevent a man from seeing a dragon or a griffin, a gorgon or a unicorn. Nobody as a matter of fact has seen a woman whose hair consisted of snakes, nor a horse from whose forehead a horn projected; though very early man probably did see dragons—known to science as pterodactyls—and monsters more improbable than griffins. At any rate, none of these zoological fancies violates the fundamental laws of the intellect; the monsters of heraldry and mythology do not exist, but there is no reason in the nature of things nor in the laws of the mind why they should not exist."

It was therefore in line with the nature of things that Dregler suspended all judgements until he could pay a visit to a certain bookstore.

II

And it was late the following afternoon, emerging from daylong doubts and procrastinations, that Dregler entered a little slot-like shop squeezed between a grey building and a brown one. Nearly within arm's reach of each other, the opposing walls of the shop were solid with books. The higher shelves were all but unreachable except by means of a very tall ladder, and the highest shelves were apparently not intended for access. Back numbers of old magazines—*Blackwoods*, *The Spectator*, the *London* and *American Mercurys*—were stacked in plump, orderless piles by the front window, their pulpy covers dying in the sunlight. Missing pages from forgotten novels were stuck forever to a patch of floor or curled up in corners. Dregler noted page two hundred and two of *The Second Staircase* at his feet, and he couldn't help feeling a sardonic sympathy for the anonymous pair of eyes confronting an unexpected dead end in the narrative of that old mystery. Then again, he wondered, how many thousands of these volumes had already been browsed for the last time. This included, of course, the one he held in his own hand and for which he now succumbed to a brief and absurd sense of protectiveness. Dregler blamed his friend Gleer for this subtle aspect of what he suspected was a farce of far larger and cruder design.

Sitting behind a low counter in the telescopic distance of the rear of the store, a small and flabby man with wire-rimmed glasses was watching him. When Dregler approached the counter and lay the book upon it, the man—Benjamin Brothers—hopped alertly to his feet.

"Help you?" he asked. The bright tone of his voice was the formal and familiar greeting of an old servant.

Dregler nodded, vaguely recognizing the little man from a previous visit to his store some years ago. He adjusted the book on the counter, simply to draw attention to it, and said: "I don't suppose it was worth my trouble to bring this sort of thing here."

The man smiled politely. "You're correct in that, sir. Old texts like that, worth practically nothing to no one. Now down there in my basement," he said, gesturing toward a narrow doorway, "I've got literally thousands of things like that. Other things too, you know. The *Bookseller's Trade* called it 'Benny's Treasurehouse'. But maybe you're just interested in selling books today."

"Well, it seems that as long as I'm here . . ."

"Help yourself, Dr Dregler," the man said warmly as Dregler started toward the stairway. Hearing his name, Dregler paused and nodded back at the bookdealer; then he proceeded down the stairs.

Dregler now recalled the basement of this store, along with the three lengthy flights of stairs needed to reach its unusual depths. The narrow street-level above was no more than a messy little closet in comparison to the expansive disorder down below: a cavern of clutter, all heaps and mounds, with bulging tiers of bookshelves laid out according to no easily observable scheme. It was a universe constructed solely of the softly jagged brickwork of books. But if the Medusa was a book, how would he ever find it in this chaos? And if it was not, what other definite form could he expect to encounter of a phenomenon which he had avoided precisely defining all these years, one whose most nearly exact emblem was a hideous woman with a head of serpents?

For some time he merely wandered around the crooked aisles and deep niches of the basement. Every so often he took down some book whose appearance caught his interest, unwedging it from an indistinct mass of battered spines and rescuing it before years rooted to the same spot caused its words to mingle with others among the ceaseless volumes of "Benny's Treasurehouse", fusing them all into a bonded babble of senseless, unseen pages. Opening the book, he leaned a threadbare shoulder against the towering, filthy stacks. And after spending very little time in the cloistered desolation of that basement, Dregler found himself yawning openly and scratching himself unconsciously, as if he were secluded in some personal sanctum.

But suddenly he became aware of this assumption of privacy which had instilled itself in him, and the feeling instantly perished, perhaps because he suspected its deception. Now his sense of a secure isolation was replaced, at all levels of creaturely response, by its opposite. For hadn't he written that "personal well-being serves solely to excavate within your soul a chasm which waits to be filled by a landslide of dread, an empty mould whose peculiar dimensions will one day manufacture the shapes of your *unique* terror."

Whether or not it was the case, Dregler felt that he was no longer, or perhaps never had been, alone in the chaotic treasurehouse. But he continued acting as if he were, omitting only the yawns and the scratchings. Long ago he had discovered that a mild flush of panic was a condition capable, in certain strange and unknown ways, of *seasoning* one's more tedious moments. So he did not immediately attempt to discourage this probably delusory sensation. However, like any state dependent upon the play of delicate and unfathomable forces, Dregler's mood or intuition was subject to unexpected metamorphoses.

And when Dregler's mood or intuition passed into a new phase, his surroundings followed close behind: both he and the treasurehouse simultaneously crossed the boundary which divides playful panics from those of a more lethal nature. But this is not to say that one kind of apprehension was more excusable than the other; they were equally opposed to the likings of logic. ("Regarding dread, intensity in itself is no assurance of validity.") So it meant nothing, necessarily, that the twisting aisles of books appeared to be tightening around the suspicious bibliophile, that the shelves now looked more conspicuously over-swollen with their soft and musty stock, that faint shufflings and shadows seemed to be frolicking like a fugue through the dust and dimness of the underground treasurehouse. Could he, as he turned the next corner, be led to see that which should not be seen?

The next corner, as it happened, was the kind one enters rather than turns—a cul-de-sac of bookshelves forming three walls which nearly reached the rafters of the ceiling. Dregler found himself facing the rear wall like a bad schoolboy in punishment. He gazed up and down its height as if contemplating whether or not it was real, pondering if one could simply pass through it once one had conquered the illusion of its solidity. Just as he was about to turn and abandon this nook, something lightly brushed against his left shoulder. With involuntary suddenness he pivoted in this direction, only to feel the same airy caress now squarely across his back. Continuing counterclockwise, he executed one full revolution until he was standing and staring at someone who was standing and staring, back at him from the exact spot where he, a mere moment before, had been standing.

The woman's high-heeled boots put her face at the same level as his, while her turban-like hat made her appear somewhat taller. It was fastened on the right side, Dregler's left, with a metal clasp studded with watery pink stones. From beneath her hat a few strands of straw-coloured hair sprouted onto a triangle of unwrinkled forehead.

Then a pair of tinted eyeglasses, then a pair of unlipsticked lips, and finally a high-collared coat which descended as a dark, elegant cylinder down to her boots. She calmly withdrew a pad of paper from one of her pockets, tore off the top page, and presented it to Dregler.

"Sorry if I startled you," it said.

After reading the note, Dregler looked up at the woman and saw that she was gently chopping her hand against her neck, but only a few times and merely to indicate some vocal disability. Laryngitis? wondered Dregler, or something chronic. He examined the note once again and observed the name, address, and telephone number of a company that serviced furnaces and air-conditioners. This, of course, told him nothing.

The woman then tore off a second pre-written message from the pad and pressed it into Dregler's already paper-filled palm smiling at him very deliberately as she did so. (How he wanted to see what her eyes were doing!) She shook his hand a little before taking away hers and making a silent, scentless exit. So what was that reek Dregler detected in the air when he stared down at the note, which simply read: "Regarding M."

And below this word-and-a-half message was an address, and below that was a specified time on the following day. The handwriting was nicely formed, the most attractive Dregler had ever seen.

In light of the past few days, Dregler almost expected to find still another note waiting for him when he returned home. It was folded in half and stuffed underneath the door to his apartment. "Dear Lucian," it began, "just when you think things have reached their limit of ridiculousness, they become more ridiculous still. In brief—we've been had! Both of us. And by my wife, no less, along with a friend of hers. (A blond-haired anthropology prof whom I think you may know, or know of; at any rate she knows you, or at least your writings, maybe both.) I'll explain the whole thing when we meet, which I'm afraid won't be until my wife and I get back from another jaunt. (Eyeing some more islands, this time in the Pacific.)

"I was hoping that you would be skeptical enough not to go to the bookstore, but after finding you not at home I feared the worst. Hope you didn't have your hopes up, which I don't think has ever happened to you anyway. No harm done, in any case. The girls explained to me that it was a quasi-scientific hoax they were perpetrating, a recondite practical joke. If you think you were taken in, you can't imagine how I was. You can't believe how real and serious they made the whole ruse seem to me. But if you got as far as the bookstore, you know by now that the punch line to the joke was a pretty weak one. The whole point, as I was told, was merely to stir your interest just enough to get you to perform some mildly ridiculous act. I'm curious to know how Mr B. Bros. reacted when the distinguished author of *Meditations on the Medusa* and other ruminative volumes presented him with a hopelessly worthless old textbook.

"Seriously, I hope it caused you no embarrassment, and both of us, all *three* of us, apologize for wasting your time. See you soon, tanned and pacified by a South Sea Eden. And we have plans for making the whole thing up to you, that's a promise."

The note was signed, of course, by Joseph Gleer.

But Gleer's confession, though it was evident to Dregler that he himself believed it, was no more convincing than his "lead" on a Bookstore Medusa. Because this lead, which Dregler had not credited for a moment, led further than Gleer, who no longer credited it, had knowledge of. So it seemed that while his friend had now been placated by a false illumination, Dregler was left to suffer alone the effects of a true state of unknowing. And whoever was behind this hoax, be it a true one or a false, knew the minds of both men very well.

Dregler took all the notes he had received that day, paper-clipped them together, and put them into a new section of his massive scrapbook. He tentatively labelled this section: "Personal Confrontations with the Medusa, Either Real or Apparent."

III

The address given to Dregler the day before was not too far for him to walk, restive peripatetic that he was. But for some reason he felt rather fatigued that morning; so he hired a taxi to speed him across a drizzle-darkened city. Settling into the spacious dilapidation of the taxi's back seat, he took note of a few things. Why, he wondered, were the driver's glasses, which every so often filled the rear-view mirror, even darker than the day? Did she make a practice of thus "admiring" all her passengers? And was this back-seat debris—the "L"-shaped cigarette butt on the door's armrest, the black apple core on the floor—supposed to serve as objects of *their* admiration? Dregler questioned a dozen other things about this routine ride, this drenched day, and the city outside where umbrellas multiplied like mushrooms in the greyness; and he was now satisfied with his lack of a sense of well-being. Earlier he was concerned that his flow of responses that day would not be those of a man who was possibly about to confront the Medusa. He was apprehensive that he might look on this ride and its destination with lively excitement or as an adventure of some kind; in brief, he feared that his attitude would prove, to a certain extent, to be one of insanity. To be sane, he held, was either to be sedated by melancholy or activated by hysteria, two responses which are "always and equally warranted for those of *sound* insight." All others were irrational, merely symptoms of imaginations left idle, of memories out of work. And above these mundane responses, the only elevation allowable, the only valid transcendence, was a sardonic one: a bliss that annihilated the visible universe with jeers of dark joy, a *mindful* ecstasy. Anything else in the way of "mysticism" was a sign of deviation or distraction, and a heresy to the obvious.

The taxi turned onto a block of wetted brownstones, stopping before a tiny streetside lawn overhung by the skeletal branches of two baby birch trees. Dregler paid the driver, who expressed no gratitude whatever for the tip, and walked quickly through the drizzle toward a golden-bricked building with black numbers—two-o-two—above a black door with a brass knob and knocker. Reviewing the information on the crumpled piece of paper he took from his pocket, Dregler pressed the glowing bell-button. There was no one else in sight along the street, its trees and pavement fragrantly damp.

The door opened and Dregler stepped swiftly inside. A shabbily dressed man of indefinite age closed the door behind him, then asked in a cordially nondescript voice: "Dregler?" He nodded in reply. After a few reactionless moments the man moved past Dregler, waving once for him to follow down the ground-floor hallway. They stopped at a door that was directly beneath the main stairway leading to the upper floors. "In here," said the man, placing his hand upon the doorknob. Dregler noticed the ring, its rosewater stone and silver band, and the disjunction between the man's otherwise dour appearance and this comparatively striking piece of jewelry. The man pushed open the door and, without entering the room, flipped a light-switch on the inside wall.

To all appearances it was an ordinary storeroom cluttered with a variety of objects. "Make yourself comfortable," the man said as he indicated to Dregler the way into the room. "Leave whenever you like, just close the door behind you."

Dregler gave a quick look around the room. "Isn't there anything else," he asked meekly, as if he were the stupidest student of the class. "This is it, then?" he persisted in a quieter, more dignified voice.

"This is it," the man echoed softly. Then he slowly closed the door, and from inside Dregler could hear the footsteps walking back down the hallway and up the staircase above the room.

The room was an average understairs niche, and its ceiling tapered downward into a smooth slant where angular steps ascended upward on the other side. Elsewhere its outline was obscure, confused by huge bedsheets shaped like lamps or tables or small horses; heaps of rocking chairs and baby-chairs and other items of broken furniture; bandaged hoses that drooped like dead pythons from hooks on the walls; animal cages whose doors hung open on a single hinge; old paint cans and pale tarps speckled like an egg; and a dusty light fixture that cast a grey haze over everything.

Somehow there was not a variety of smells imperfectly mingled in the room, each telling the tale of its origin, but only a single smell pieced like a puzzle out of many: its complete image was dark as the shadows in a cave and writhing in a dozen directions over curving walls. Dregler gazed around the room, picked up some small object and immediately set it down again because his hands were trembling. He found himself a solid carton of something to sit on, kept his eyes open, and waited.

Afterward he couldn't remember how long he had stayed in the room, though he did manage to store up every nuance of the eventless vigil for later use in his voluntary and involuntary dreams. (They were compiled into that increasingly useful section marked "Personal Confrontations with the Medusa", a section that was fleshing itself out as a zone swirling with red shapes and a hundred hissing voices.) Dregler recalled vividly, however, that he left the room in a state of panic after catching a glimpse of himself in an old mirror that had a hair-line fracture slithering up its center. On his way out he lost his breath when he felt himself being pulled back into the room. But it was only a loose thread from his overcoat that had gotten caught in the door. It finally snapped cleanly off and he was free to go, his heart livened with dread.

And he never let on to his friends what a success that afternoon had been for him, not that he could have explained it to them in any practical way even if he desired to. As promised, they did make up for any inconvenience or embarrassment Dregler might have suffered as a result of, in Gleer's words, the "bookstore incident". The three of them held a party in Dregler's honor, and he finally met Gleer's new wife and her accomplice in the "hoax". (It became apparent to Dregler that no one, least of all himself, would admit it had gone further than that.) Dregler was left alone with this woman for only a brief time, and in the corner of a crowded room. While each of them knew of the other's work, this seemed to be the first time they had personally met. Nonetheless, they both confessed to a feeling of their prior acquaintance without being able, or willing, to substantiate its origins. And although plenty of mutually known parties were established, they failed to find any direct link between the two of them.

"Maybe you were a student of mine," Dregler suggested.

She smiled and said: "Thank you, Lucian, but I'm not as young as you seem to think."

Then she was jostled from behind ("Whoops," said a tipsy academic), and something she had been fiddling with in her hand ended up in Dregler's drink. It turned the clear bubbling beverage into a glassful of liquid rose-light.

"I'm so sorry. Let me get you another," she said, and then disappeared into the crowd.

Dregler fished the earring out of the glass and stole away with it before she had a chance to return with a fresh drink. Later in his room he placed it in a small box, which he labelled: "Treasures of the Medusa."

But there was nothing he could prove and he knew it.

IV

It was not many years later that Dregler was out on one of his now famous walks around the city. Since the bookstore incident, he had added several new titles to his works, and these had somehow gained him the faithful and fascinated audience of readers that had previously eluded him. Prior to his "discovery" he had been accorded only a distant interest in critical and popular circles alike, but now every little habit of his, not the least of all his daily meanderings, had been turned by commentators into "typifying traits" and "defining quirks". "Dregler's walks," stated one article, "are a constitutional of the modern mind, urban journeys by a tortured Ulysses *sans* Ithaca." Another article offered this back-cover superlative: "the most baroque inheritor of Existentialism's obsessions."

But whatever fatuosities they may have inspired, his recent books—*A Bouquet of Worms*, *Banquet for Spiders*, and *New Meditations on the Medusa*—had enabled him to "grip the minds of a dying generation and pass on to them his pain". These words were written, rather uncharacteristically, by Joseph Gleer in a highly favourable review of *New Meditations* for a philosophical quarterly. He probably thought they might revive his friendship with his old colleague, but Dregler never acknowledged Gleer's effort, nor the repeated invitations to join his wife and him for some get-together or other. What else could

Dregler do? Whether Gleer knew it or not, he was now one of them. And so was Dregler, though his saving virtue was an awareness of this disturbing fact. And this was part of his pain.

"We can only live by leaving our 'soul' in the hands of the Medusa," Dregler wrote in *New Meditations*. "Whether she is an angel or a gargoyle is not the point. Each merely allows us a gruesome diversion from some ultimate catastrophe which would turn us to stone; each is a mask hiding the *worst* visage, a medicine that numbs the mind. And the Medusa will see to it that we are protected, sealing our eyelids closed with the gluey spittle of her snakes, while their bodies elongate and slither past our lips to devour us *from the inside*. This is what we must never witness, except in the imagination, where it is a charming sight. And in the word, no less than in the mind, the Medusa fascinates much more than she appalls, and haunts us just *this side* of petrification. On the other side is the unthinkable, the unheard-of, that-which-should-not-be: hence, the Real. This is what throttles our souls with a hundred fingers—somewhere, perhaps in that dim room which caused us to forget ourselves, that place where we left ourselves behind amid shadows and strange sounds—while our minds and words toy, like playful, stupid pets, with *diversions* of an immeasurable disaster. The tragedy is that we must steer so close in order to avoid this hazard. *We may hide from horror only in the heart of horror.*"

Now Dregler had reached the outermost point of his daily walk, the point at which he usually turned and made his way back to his apartment, that *other* room. He gazed at the black door with the brass knob and knocker, glancing away to the street's porchlights and lofty bay windows which were glowing like mad in the late dusk. From bluish streetlights hung downward domes: inverted halos or open eyes. Then, for the first time in the history of these excursions, a light rain began to sprinkle down, nothing very troublesome. But in the next moment Dregler had already sought shelter in the welcoming brownstone.

He soon came to stand before the door of the room, keeping his hands deep in the pockets of his overcoat and away from temptation. Nothing had changed, he noticed, nothing at all. The door had not been opened by anyone since he had last closed it behind him on that hectic day years ago. And there was the proof, as he knew, somehow, it would be: that long thread from his coat still dangled from where it had been caught between door and frame. Now there was no question about what he would do.

It was to be a quick peek through a hand-wide crack, but enough to risk disillusionment and the dispersal of all the charming traumas he had articulated in his brain and books, scattering them like those peculiar shadows he supposed lingered in that room. And the voices, would he hear that hissing which heralded her presence as much as the flitting red shapes? He kept his eyes fixed upon his hand on the doorknob as it nudged open the door. So the first thing he saw was the way it, his hand, took on a rosy dawn-like glow, then a deeper twilight crimson as it was bathed more directly by the odd illumination within the room.

There was no need to reach in and flick the lightswitch just inside. He could see quite enough as his vision, still exceptional, was further aided by the way a certain cracked mirror was positioned, giving his eyes a reflected entrance into the dim depths of the room. And in the depths of the mirror? A split-image, something fractured by a thread-like chasm that oozed up a viscous red glow. There was a man in the mirror; no, not a man but a mannikin, or a frozen figure of some kind. It was naked and rigid, leaning against a wall of clutter, its arms outstretching and reaching behind, as if trying to break a backwards fall. Its head was also thrown back, almost broken-necked; its eyes were pressed shut into a pair of well-sealed creases, two ocular wrinkles which had taken the place of the sockets themselves. And its mouth gaped so widely with a soundless scream that all wrinkles had been smoothed away from that part of the old face.

He barely recognized this face, this naked and paralyzed form which he had all but forgotten, except as a lurid figure of speech he once used to describe the uncanny condition of his soul. But it was no longer a charming image of the imagination. Reflection had given it charm, made it acceptable to sanity, just as reflection had made those snakes, and the one who wore them, picturesque and not petrifying. But no amount of reflection could have conceived seeing the thing itself, nor the state of being stone.

The serpents were moving now, coiling themselves about the ankles and wrists, the neck; stealthily entering the screaming man's mouth and prying at his eyes. Deep in the mirror opened another pair of eyes the color of wine-mixed water, and through a dark tangled mass they glared. The eyes met his, but not in a mirror. And the mouth was screaming, but made no sound. Finally, he was reunited, in the worst possible way, with the thing within the room.

Stiff inside of stone now, he heard himself think. *Where is the world, my words?* No longer any world, any words, there would only be that narrow room and himself and the oldest companion of his soul. Nothing other than that would exist for him, could exist, nor, in fact, had ever existed. In its own rose-tinted heart, his horror had at last found him.

JOEL LANE

Power Cut

JOEL LANE is the author of a number of disturbing short stories published in *Ambit*, *Darklands*, *Skeleton Crew*, *Dark Dreams*, *Winter Chills*, *Exuberance*, *Fantasy Tales* and *The Year's Best Horror Stories*, amongst others.

He works in educational publishing in Birmingham, and besides writing fiction, poems and critical articles (including a minute analysis of Ramsey Campbell's early novels in *Foundation*), his interests include social theory, rock/folk music, ghost stories and the urban environment.

The last two are certainly reflected in "Power Cut" which, like Kim Newman's "The Original Dr Shade" in *Best New Horror 2*, paints a bleak and disturbing picture of contemporary Britain. The author points out that it was written in 1990, just after the Prime Minister's resignation . . .

THE PROCESSION STARTED IN CHAMBERLAIN SQUARE and moved along New Street, thinning out as the roadway narrowed. There were several hundred people, wearing overcoats against the iron wind; it was early December. Each of the marchers carried a lit candle in a glass jar or paper shield. Every so often, one of them would stop to relight a flame that had blown out. Above their heads, premature Christmas lights hung from wires strung across the roadway.

At this time in the evening, there wouldn't be much traffic for the procession to interrupt. As usual Lake felt he'd been singled out. He waited in a side road, watching the passing figures from his car. Candlelight gave their hands and parts of their faces a peculiar glow. Lake wished he could drive through them. Who were they trying to impress? There was nobody around to pay attention. Minutes passed, and the number of marchers began to unnerve him.

His flat had been empty since the previous weekend. It was colder than he expected. There were only a few letters for him; but then, most of his correspondence went through his office in London. Not many people knew his private address. Lake put a take-away meal into the oven to warm up, and lit the gas fire in the living room. He was just in time for the local news round-up on Central TV. Sure enough, there was a mention of the candlelit procession; and similar events in other cities. The week before, they'd quoted Lake as saying that to spend public money on a local hospice for AIDS victims would be to betray the local community.

The hold that the welfare state lobby seemed to have over the media didn't impress Lake at all. Why should ordinary people have to shoulder the responsibility for AIDS? Besides, there were deeper issues at stake. To modernise the health service was an essential step towards the new society. The Midlands had to be dragged out of the mire of 1950s welfare state apathy, and brought to life the same way as was happening in the South. So many people just didn't seem capable of understanding. Even his own party didn't have the clarity of purpose it had had a few years back. Things weren't making sense; the leadership had crumbled. But Lake refused to panic. He felt strangely calm, sitting in the silent flat and still cold, in spite of the gas fire; it was as though the blue flames were only for display.

He tried calling Alan, but heard only a disembodied voice telling him to leave his name and number. Lake felt suddenly at a loss for words. Just before the machine cut out, he managed to speak. "It's Matthew. Ring me." They hadn't seen each other in weeks, but Lake knew he could depend on Alan. The thought was a flicker of symbolic warmth.

The next morning, he wondered if something had been wrong with the take-away; perhaps he shouldn't have reheated it. But he

222

didn't have the normal symptoms of food poisoning—gut pains, nausea, diarrhoea. It felt more as though something inside him were coated with frost. He rubbed the mist from the bedroom window, then breathed it back in place. The room was chilly, but well above zero. Outside, the day was unexpectedly bright.

After breakfast, which he couldn't taste, Lake phoned his doctor. The receptionist took a message, but wouldn't make him an appointment. "Dr Wilson will contact you as soon as possible, I'm sure." Well, he'd intended to have a quiet weekend; he needed a break from work. It would be Christmas soon, and there were people he had to get in touch with—friends and family. He'd been head-butting the brick walls in Westminster for too long; he was lonely. Realising that made him feel paralysed. What if nobody was there?

It was noon when he phoned Alan. This time there was an answer. "Hello? Who's that?"

"Alan, it's me." There was no response. "It's Matthew. How are you?"

"Oh, I'm fine. No problems." There was a silence. Lake felt it stretch across twelve miles of telephone cable, like a thread leading him into a maze of blind tunnels. He took a deep breath; still silence.

"Alan. Are you there?"

"Yes. What can I do for you?" The voice was deliberately empty of anything recognisable. Why was Alan pretending to be a stranger?

"Can I see you?"

"Yes. If your X-ray telescopic vision is in working order. We're on opposite sides of the city, after all. Then there's the curvature of the earth to consider. And you're probably facing in the wrong direction anyway." More silence. "Where were you when I needed you, Matthew? Where would you be now if I still did? Where would *I* be if I still did? Tell me something."

"What? . . . Go on, what is it?"

"Do you know what flowers grow in winter?" Lake wasn't sure he'd heard that correctly; but the next sound was the click of the receiver. He went on listening to the dead line for minutes, like a child pressing a shell to his ear to hear the sea.

Lunch tasted of less than breakfast. Midway through the afternoon, Lake switched on the TV and watched an hour of soap opera. The rage and torment of the characters stuttered in his mind. He blinked away tears and felt them trickle to the corners of his mouth, where he tasted their fresh salt. Feeling somewhat better, he phoned his doctor and got the receptionist again. "Dr Wilson is not available. There's no space in his appointment schedule. I'm sorry." Lake stared at the receiver as if it had bitten his ear.

Well, he'd have to hire another doctor. He didn't have to wait for help.

It was dark by four o'clock, and far colder than the morning had been. Lake typed out a series of letters to constituents on the solid Underwood typewriter he kept at home. His sense of perspective restored, he went out for a short walk. As far as the off-license and back again. Harborne's streets were reassuringly empty. Rain shattered the windscreens of parked cars. Through a few uncurtained bay windows, he saw glass flowers, bookcases, paintings hung on dark-panelled walls. Lake felt a shock of loss and didn't understand why. He'd always fought his own battles. It didn't seem to matter that he had no friends. He'd been a grammar-school pupil; there was no old-boy public school network to support him. He believed in power and the respect that power earned. You could trust authority; you couldn't trust people.

The way back took him under a railway bridge that crossed the main road. A car came up the hill towards him, and in the same moment, a train flickered past overhead. Lake felt as though his heart had stopped. He stood quite still. To one side, the streetlamp lit up points of rain on the dark thorns of a shrub. He reached out and touched them. They pricked his hand, without breaking the skin. He drew his hand back and pressed it against the flat bottle in his coat pocket. What was wrong with him?

Lake ate alone, at home. This seemed to have been the most isolated and purposeless day of his life. Something had to change. He phoned Alan, but put down the receiver before it could ring at the other end. Alan had sounded disturbed; he was evidently having problems. It wasn't Lake's business to help. Things like that were beyond him. How was he going to make this weekend a success? By eight o'clock, the whisky was at least a technical fire in his stomach and mind. He'd have to hit town tonight. But he'd better not drive in this condition. And which town? He didn't want to risk being recognised. Secrecy, he thought, was not only necessary but correct.

The train to Wolverhampton took him through Dudley and Tipton, past empty and poorly-lit streets whose terraced houses were more than a century old. Security lights flooded the ground floors of the factories. Whenever the carriage window looked onto darkness, Lake saw his own face flicker across the view. He was shivering, like his reflection. A copy of the *Express and Star* was spread face down on the seat opposite; he picked it up and tried to read better news into its headlines. The sports pages at the back were easier to follow, because they meant nothing to him.

He caught a taxi from the station to the club, though he could have walked there in a few minutes. The centre of Wolverhampton was surprisingly quiet for a Saturday night. The sky was cloudy; mist made the upper air a canvas for the town's light. A car park jumped in perspective, becoming a cobbled yard. Everything bright seemed closer than it was; and warmer, too. Lake felt himself sobering up. He'd have to reverse that.

Two hours later, he was walking back along the same route. His companion was a tall youth in a grey leather jacket and black jeans; his name was Gary. He lived in a rented room on the other side of town. It was too late to go back to Birmingham, and Lake wouldn't have wanted that anyway. This arrangement suited him; he understood business better than he understood people. Why was he doing this? It wasn't recklessness, he knew that. With Alan it might have been, if he hadn't tried to hedge his bets. Now it was more like giving himself up. The cold shifted inside him, touching him as he breathed. In the club, nobody had spoken to him or given him a second glance. He'd have to pay to get what he wanted. Which proved he'd been right all along.

Gary's room was in a terraced house opposite a paper yard, where flaking white blocks were piled up as if to thaw them out. There was a long series of bell-buttons next to the front door. The unlit hall smelt of fresh cat urine. Moving quietly, Gary led his client up the uncarpeted staircase. Three flights, each with a time-switch to restore darkness. Lake imagined he could follow Gary by sensing his body heat, even at a distance. Suddenly, he felt an absolute need for physical contact—a strange feeling which seemed to have no connection with what was going on. A wall opened into a small but high-ceilinged bedroom, decorated with faded newspaper cuttings and photographs. The floor was littered with envelopes, notebooks and old newspapers, the pages merged by damp. It was more like a press office than a bedroom. If Gary was going to bring people back here, he really should keep the place tidy. Was he a student? Gary sat down on the bed and lit a cigarette. Lake sat beside him, feeling too cold to unbutton his coat.

"Can you put the fire on?" Gary shrugged in reply, as if to say *What fire?* His cigarette brightened as he inhaled, which made the wall behind him seem darker. Lake stretched his arms, biting back a yawn. Why were there so many newspaper cuttings on the walls? He couldn't read any of the headlines. Shadows were falling on every exposed surface, like dust. But there was no lampshade. Lake stared at the naked light-bulb, hanging from a cord in the centre of the whitewashed ceiling. Its light was slowly weakening. No, it was still as bright as before. But the darkness was pressing in around it. Lake shook his head and stood up. "God, I'm pissed." Gary watched him without making a comment. Something on the wall caught Lake's attention: a news item that looked familiar. He stood close to it. His own breath stung his lips.

The plaster of the wall was almost covered with cuttings from local and national newspapers. Every mention in print of anything that Lake had said or done—even where his name appeared in election results or candidate lists—was here. Several of the cuttings displayed his face, a blur of dots on yellowed paper. His appearance hadn't changed much in ten years. Lake turned round. "What the fuck is this?" Gary was still lying on the bed, propped up on one elbow and almost smiling, like a picture in a magazine. He blew a smoke-ring.

Lake pulled at one of the sheets of newsprint. It was glued to the wall, but most of it came away. He tore down another cutting; then several at once. Underneath, the plaster was surprisingly clean and whole. He felt a streak of cold along the side of his hand, and saw the head of a rusty nail protruding from the wall. Blood immediately began to spread on the cuff of his right sleeve, like a flower petal, or an oil flame. "Oh, Jesus." He turned back to the bed. "I've cut my hand." Gary looked and nodded, but didn't move. Lake sat down beside him. Blood splashed onto the pale blue duvet. It dulled at once, becoming a shadow. Lake tried to pull his sleeve up over the cut. "Help me. I could get blood poisoning." He stared at the boy. "Help me. Please!" Quite calmly, Gary reached out, took Lake's hand, and stubbed out his cigarette on it. There was no cruelty in the action. It was exactly as though the hand were an ash-tray. Lake felt the cold stiffen inside him, blind and enclosed, like a fist. He couldn't open his mouth. Slowly, trying to balance himself, he stood up, then walked out into the unlit hall. A few seconds later, the bedroom door closed behind him.

Outside, the street was empty; Lake tried to remember the way back into town. He could see the distant lights of tower blocks around the station. It seemed to get colder the further he walked. The wind felt like having crystals of frost rubbed into your skin. He thrust his hands into his coat pockets, careless of the bloodstains. But when his right hand stuck to the coat lining, he had to pull it free. In the metallic light of the streetlamp, he saw white threads of snow glittering at the edges of the wound. His legs were shaking too much for him to walk. Was there nobody to help him? Ahead of him, he could see people crossing the road, on their way down another street. He tried to catch up with them. As he neared the corner, he saw that each of them was carrying a light.

The street was lined with dark, unrecognisable office buildings; there were very few doorways. People were walking along the roadway and the pavements, with lit candles in their hands. Lake couldn't see how many people there were; but white petals of wax were already scattered across the tarmac. He stepped forward. "Help me." Silent figures walked past him on both sides. They didn't seem to notice Lake, or even to notice each other. Lake stood directly in front of one of them, daring the marcher to walk through him. But the man stopped, looking at Lake with candles in his eyes. Others stopped too, until Lake was surrounded in the middle of the road. There were a dozen or more of them. The rest of the procession moved on. In the circle of lights, Lake could see that the marchers' faces were covered with wax.

A gap appeared in the circle. One of the candles had gone out. Lake felt the ache in his hand disappear, as though the wound had closed. Another gap. He couldn't feel the cold in his chest now. He touched his own face, and felt nothing. Three more candles went out. The taste of the air had gone, and the smell of burning wax. Lake turned around; a ripple of dark shivered in the air. There were only four candles left. He cried out: *Help me, don't leave me. Please.* But he couldn't hear his own voice. He carried on begging silently, making gestures. Drops of wax fell and froze around him like snow. The holder of the last candle was standing close by. If only Lake could reach his face to pull off the wax mask, he would have made contact. He was lifting a hand when the stranger bent his head to blow out the flame and with it, the streetlamps.

NICHOLAS ROYLE

Moving Out

SINCE GRADUATING from London University, Nicholas Royle has worked as a waiter, English teacher in Paris, actor, information officer, festival organiser and magazine sub-editor. He is currently chief sub-editor on a national weekly magazine and plays football—as goalkeeper—for two other magazines he has worked for in the past.

Recent short stories can be found in *Interzone, Dark Horizons, Chills, Terror Australis 3, Exuberance 7* (a Nicholas Royle special), *Final Shadows, In Dreams, Narrow Houses, Dark Voices 4: The Pan Book of Horror*, several volumes of *The Year's Best Horror Stories* and both previous editions of *Best New Horror*.

He has edited the original anthologies of psychological horror, *Darklands* and *Darklands 2*, and his first novel, *Counterparts*, is published by Paper Drum.

Royle specialises in powerful stories about urban paranoia, as "Moving Out" so ably demonstrates . . .

I DON'T KNOW WHAT SHE TOLD her friends about her reasons for moving out, but I wasn't convinced it was just because of the new job. It was based on the east coast, seventy miles away. She could hardly commute, could she? her look seemed to say.

But did she really have to shift *all* her stuff and *buy* a flat rather than rent somewhere?

I thought we'd got on OK in my flat; it seemed to work fine. There was no indication that she tired of my frequent games and traps, which were never anything more than elaborate jokes.

Sometimes, for fun, I used to try and frighten her; tense my muscles and affix an expression to my face, then move slowly towards her. She'd return the stare as long as she could, then fear crept suddenly into her eyes and I had to laugh to break the spell. "Did I really frighten you?" "Yes," she said, hurt. "I'm sorry." I showed concern and concealed my pleasure. It was only a game.

She took everything. Her collection of masks left a very empty wall in the bedroom, stubbled with nails. The bathroom shelf was suddenly made bare; forgotten tubs of moisturising cream and rolled-up flattened tubes of toothpaste, even these things were taken. I saw her cast a mournful eye over my tailor's dummy.

"When I get my own place," she had once said, "will you give me this?"

She often asked. I didn't know why it was so important to her; she could have picked one up in any junk shop. I saw her from the kitchen one day, when she hadn't heard me come in from outside. She was kneeling at the mannequin's castors and clinging to its waist. Crying her eyes out.

I still didn't understand its significance.

She moved on a Saturday. I went along to help. Her new job came with a car, an estate, which was good because she would never have squeezed everything into my Mini.

I was ignored when I offered to drive. I knew what she'd say if she bothered to answer: I wasn't insured because we weren't married.

She didn't even give me a chance to climb in next to her, before moving swiftly away from the kerb, spinning her wheels through gutterfuls of litter.

I looked at the features of the Mini as I approached it. The radiator grille—the car's mouth—had been buckled for a couple of weeks, and one of the eyes had a smashed lens. I had to wrench the door open. The engine wheezed into life and I moved off. The front offside wheel scraped against the wheel arch, but a bald tyre was a small sacrifice. I'd said I'd help her move, and help her I would, with or without her cooperation.

I had my work cut out keeping up with her. She darted and surged, switching lanes in her haste like there was no one else on the road. I had to rely on steady progress, the weight of the boxes in the back of her car and the re-tuning I'd had done two months earlier.

Her block of flats had a lift. If there hadn't been so many heavy boxes and bags to carry, she would have climbed the stairs, despite her flat being on the sixth floor. She had always hated lifts.

It wasn't just the discomfort of being crammed into what was basically a large tin, with a number of strangers; nor was it the embarrassment of awkward silences and accidentally crossed stares. Lifts terrified her.

Which offered me endless opportunities whenever we went anywhere and had to use a lift.

I only had to stand there, glaze my eyes over and turn slowly towards her, and she would panic.

"No, Nick! No!"

She once bolted out of a lift in a multi-storey carpark and ran straight into an old Vauxhall. She might have got away with a few bruises, had the car been stationary.

Some months later, one afternoon when she had gone out for a walk to help build up her strength, I rigged up a dummy out of some of my clothes, which I found in the wardrobe, and had it hanging in a noose from the kitchen doorway by the time she got back.

The relapse set her back about three months.

I regretted doing it but as I explained, it was only a joke.

It always puzzled me why she liked masks when she was so easily frightened by faces.

"A mask is only a mask," she said. "It's not ambiguous. There's nothing behind it." But in order to frighten her, I always had to start off by masking my features.

"There's nothing but wall behind my masks," she'd explained.

"Why do you like them so much?" I demanded.

"People used to believe that traumatic events that had not yet taken place could send back echoes from the future," she explained. "These echoes would sometimes register in masks."

"Like a satellite dish?" I quipped.

She gave me a black look.

"Why don't they show up in faces?" I asked.

"Because we block them. A mask can't. That's why you scare me when you fix your face like a mask. Sometimes the echoes are like the real thing."

I stared at her now from the corner of the lift in her new home, but she looked no more distressed than she had when I'd snatched glances in her mirror during the drive up. Now it was her turn to wear a mask, the mask of tragedy. Yes, it would hurt, but she had to make the break. That kind of thing. Stony-faced resolve, with just the occasional glimpse of what looked like terror animating her glass eyes. She only had to say, if she didn't want me there.

But not a word was uttered. In fact, I couldn't recall the last time she had addressed me at all. I was blurring reality and imagination, not sure afterwards if she had said something or if I had imagined it from the look on her face.

The flat was on two floors. Not bad for the price and with a sweeping view of the sea front and port. At night the lights on the promenade would be pretty.

The staircase leading to the upper rooms was situated in the middle of the flat between the kitchen and the living room. You could walk right around the enclosed staircase, through the kitchen, the hallway and the living room. Actually under the stairs there was a cupboard, at its tallest about as tall as me.

I was able to follow her around from room to room and remain unseen. I tailed her just close enough to let her know I was there. She stopped and looked round, eyes flashing with anger and fear, but I was always just out of sight.

Later, after a light meal, I tried to talk to her. As if *I'd* done anything to upset *her*. "What's wrong?" I asked her.

She didn't feel like talking.

She slumped in a chair in front of the French windows. The curtains were closed, which meant she couldn't see the view. I pulled them back for her. It was dark now. The lights *were* pretty.

But with a snort she'd jumped up and quit the room as soon as I opened the curtain.

Anyone can take a hint, but it's somehow nicer to sit down and talk things out.

She clung to the edge of the sink, her face white as enamel. "I'll make a drink," I suggested.

Thrusting out an arm she opened the fridge door and bent down to get the milk out. She started when she saw the car keys next to the butter. I'd put them there just after we'd arrived.

"What's the matter?" I pleaded.

I'd often hidden her things in the fridge at my flat, as a joke; her reaction never more than a laugh or a groan.

She slammed the fridge door, ignoring me, and ran upstairs where she shut herself in her bedroom.

I took the keys out of the fridge and put them quietly down on the table, then sat down and thought about what might happen next. The simplest would be for me just to go. Would that be seen as giving in or a dignified withdrawal? Two of her Malaysian leather masks gazed unresponsively down at me from the wall above the portable television.

I became aware of a murmur of conversation through the ceiling. I stood up and craned my neck. Although the actual words were indistinguishable, I could tell it was her voice, and unanswered.

I walked quietly down the hall to the telephone extension. Hoping she wouldn't hear the click, I lifted the receiver to my ear.

". . . Mini was his."

I frowned. What were they talking about?

". . . but the things that are happening here, I'm terrified. I feel like I'm going mad or something. I keep hearing this terrible squealing."

I dropped the phone and rubbed my forehead, which was prickling with perspiration.

I couldn't decide what was the best thing to do, given her state of mind. But since my presence was obviously not helping, I decided to call it a day.

Closing the front door quietly behind me, I stepped into early morning darkness and thick fog. The car was some minutes' walk away. The plastic-covered seat was cold and sweating, the windscreen obscured inside and out. I proceeded, hunched over the wheel, the choke full out, wiping the condensation away with tissues and the fog with protesting wipers. The headlamps pushed into the fog, illuminating nothing but clouds of billowing moisture. The full beam was less help.

More by chance than navigation I found the dual carriageway and caught up with a set of red lights, which, when I narrowed the gap to eighteen inches, I could see belonged to a large container lorry.

In order to continue to enjoy the false security of the lorry's slipstream, I was obliged to accelerate to sixty miles per hour. I could scarcely credit the drivers who from time to time overtook me in the outside lane. My own knees had liquefied in the fear that I would fail to register the lorry's brake lights, should they come on.

Because of the unshrinking blanket of fog, I never saw the sign warning of roads merging and so remained ignorant of the danger until six lanes of traffic suddenly tried to squeeze into three.

Given the appalling visibility and the speed the influx of traffic was travelling at (coming from the west, where the fog would be thinner), there were bound to be some casualties.

A USAF jeep shunted me into the lorry I'd been sheltering behind, and an Audi overtaking on the outside caught my wing.

Then, dimly, I began to understand what she had meant about the echoes. Sometimes, she had said, the echoes are like the real thing.

I only stayed long enough to pick up the tailor's dummy.

It would function as a present and as a surprise. Hopefully, she would have calmed down overnight and was probably already indulging herself in contrition.

Driving back up with the dummy lying silently on the back seat, I saw its bulk whenever I checked the rear-view mirror. Was it not too silent and bland? It needed a mask.

Also in the mirror I saw the mask I would give it.

The car coughed and clanked, but somehow made it.

She was out, at work, as I'd anticipated.

I went to the cupboard under the stairs. Three boxes sat in a corner and a couple of coats hung on hooks. The dummy, with its mask, was the same height as me.

Patiently I awaited the end of the working day.

I heard the key in the front door, the shuffle of letters, the tap of an executive briefcase on kitchen linoleum.

Footsteps. A yawn. More steps.

She pulled open the door.

A tremor went through her body; she stepped back; her mouth fell open but any sound was choked in her throat.

All apologies, I slid forward towards her, castors squealing.

"No, Nick! No!" she managed to scream.

NORMAN PARTRIDGE

Guignoir

IN HIS *Locus* column, Ed Bryant described Norman Partridge as
"One of the most astonishing new writers to make a splash in 1991
... His imagination is fresh; his versatility is amazing. Best of all, he
knows how to violate reader expectations and get away with it."

Partridge's stories have been making a splash in such magazines
as *Cemetery Dance*, the British Fantasy Society's *Chills*, *Amazing
Stories* and the anthologies *Final Shadows*, *Copper Star*, *Chilled to
the Bone*, *Dark at Heart*, *Dark Voices 4: The Pan Book of Horror*,
Shivers and *New Crimes 3*, amongst others.

"'Guignoir' is one of several stories set in Fiddler, California,"
explains the author. "Strange things happen there. Sometimes supernatural, sometimes not. Haunted cars have been known to prowl the
roads, jukeboxes play '50s songs about dead teenagers, and everybody
thinks that they know everybody else's business."

The following story was inspired by a photograph of a carnival peep
show displaying the car of mass-murderer Ed Gein ("*Look! See The
Car That Hauled The Dead from Their Graves!*"). Gein's exploits
were also the inspiration for Robert Bloch's seminal slasher novel,
Psycho, and Tobe Hooper's film *The Texas Chainsaw Massacre*, but
the story which follows owes nothing to either.

"DON'T WORRY, ELLIE," THE KID SAID, sparking his cigarette lighter. "He's afraid of fire."

Blue flame singed my cheek. I reached for the kid, my manacled arms straining against steel chains anchored in the mildewed floor. I pawed the cobwebbed air just inches short of his face, the manacles chafing my wrists, my hands wild wriggling things, like hungry green tarantulas.

I growled.

The kid's girlfriend jumped away. The back of her head struck the greystone wall making a hollow sound, like a cartoon echo.

The kid laughed. "Get a grip, Ellie. He really is afrai— "

I caught a handful of leather jacket. The kid leaped backward, but I held on until the chains whipped taut and the manacles pinched me to the bone. Green scars peeled off my wrists. Lines of blood welled up underneath.

The kid smirked at me, just out of reach.

"You little bastard," I whispered.

He backhanded me and my forehead caved in. "You ain't doin' it right," he said, flatly. "Frankenstein can't talk."

"That's right," his girlfriend pouted.

Again the kid backhanded me, and the monster mask slipped across my face. I couldn't see through the eye holes, but I could smell the sharp odor of melting rubber mixed with the animal scent of the kid's leather jacket.

The girl laughed, then shouted, "Perry, watch out!"

Another cartoon echo. I tore off the melted remains of my mask. Perry slumped against the plywood wall. His eyes bulged: the Wolfman's fingers were clamped around his thick neck.

The girl jumped at the Wolfman, scratching for all she was worth. His furry mask came away in her hand and she squealed when she saw his face. Unbelieving, she looked at him, then looked at me. "Perry, they've got the same face!"

"Yeah," Perry said, glaring at my twin brother Larry. "And both of 'em are uglier than Frankenstein. But they don't scare me none."

That wasn't true. Neither part of it.

Larry's fingers dug in, thumb squeezing hard, but the kid didn't squirm. "Tough boy," Larry said. "You ain't afraid of nothin', huh?" He eyed the girl. "Your boyfriend is awfully brave. How about you? Maybe the four of us can get together tonight and do something really scary. We'll go for a ride in the Death Car, just like old Hank Caul used to. How about that?"

Tears welled in the girl's eyes. Larry had struck a nerve. I unlocked the manacles and moved toward her, remembering her laughter.

"You pricks," Perry croaked. "Hank Caul got her sister, almost got her— "

Larry's werewolf fingers squeezed, cutting off Perry's words. My brother grinned at me then, and I grinned back.

I stroked the girl's blond hair and she turned away, sobbing. "Larry, I'd like you to meet Ellie," I said, and Larry nodded. I took Ellie by the shoulders and wiped away her tears, knowing that I'd terrified her simply by remembering her name.

Warm tears. I rubbed them between my thumb and forefinger. I couldn't help asking. I had to know. "Ellie, did Hank Caul get your sister's skin? Is that why you're so shook up?"

She stared at me, speechless. Then she ran, her long hair spilling over her shoulders, blond hair flecked with blood from my wounded wrists.

I let her go.

Perry tried to break free. Larry wrenched something shiny out of the kid's hand, then marched him down the hall, past Count Dracula and the Phantom of the Opera. I followed, my heavy boots thudding over plywood floor that had been painted to look like mildewed stone. Though I was perfectly willing to share grins with Larry, I knew that Pa would hold both of us responsible for whatever happened to the kid, and I hoped my twin wasn't going too far.

Larry slammed Perry against the Mummy's coffin. The midway lights angled through the doorway, slashing across the kid's face. Pasty, terrified. His lower lip quivered when Larry whispered in his ear, and then Larry shoved him down the stairs and into the crowd.

The kid hit the ground hard. Dust puffed up around him. His greasy D.A. was a mess. The gawkers gathered round as if a new attraction had been announced. Come one, come all. See the amazing crow-eating boy . . .

Larry's arm shot out, his fingers flexing stiff, and a bone-handled hunting knife jabbed the dirt between the kid's legs.

"That wasn't very smart," Larry said.

I saw Ellie elbowing into the crowd. Trying to hide. Larry saw her too.

"Girl, you come here."

God knows why, but she did.

Larry slipped two tickets into her hand and grinned. "You and your boyfriend come see the Death Car. On me."

"I don't want to hear any excuses." Pa locked the battered suitcase and slapped the lid for emphasis. "Like I told you boys a million times: what one does, both do. It's up to you two to watch out for each other."

I wanted to tell Pa that was exactly what we'd been doing, but his good eye cut me down before I could get my mouth working.

"No excuses," he repeated. "We've got to be careful in this town. Hank Caul did his dirty work right here, and a lot of these folks don't see the entertainment value of our little tent show. Some of 'em had friends or relations who went for their last ride in the Death Car, and they sure don't like the idea of us makin' six bits from every gawker who wants to see it."

Again, Pa slapped the suitcase. Larry and I called it Fort Knox, and I wondered for the millionth time how much money was squirreled away inside. Maybe a lot, maybe nothing worth dreaming about. The Death Car wasn't the attraction it had been five years ago when Caul's stab'n'skin murder spree was still big news, and I felt sure that Pa had come back to the little town of Fiddler to stir up the pot, maybe get some national press about local outrage. It was worth a try. Lately Pa had tightened the purse strings, and I was getting pretty tired of working in the Castle of Horrors just to keep some change in my pocket.

"Pa, the kid pushed us," Larry began.

"Yeah, and you gave him free tickets," I chided.

"Not another word. You two let me do the thinkin'." Pa stared us down and made sure we had that straight. "The Ezell boys are gonna take the rest of your shift at the Castle, so you two can make yourselves useful around here. I'm expectin' company, and I want the Death Car lookin' pretty as a hunnert-dollar whore."

As usual, Larry couldn't keep his mouth shut. "It must be damned important company for you to close the show early," he said. "Is Ed Sullivan comin' to visit? He finally gonna put us on TV?"

"It ain't for you to worry about," Pa said humorlessly. "I got some phone calls to make. I'll be back in an hour. No funny stuff. Remember: what one does, both do."

Pa opened the trunk of the Death Car and placed the battered suitcase inside. "Safer than Fort Knox," he said.

Larry smiled. "Yep, no one wants to mess with the bogeyman's wheels."

"Yeah," I said, "ain't superstition a wonderful thing?"

The Death Car was a 1950 Nash Ambassador—hardly the stuff of legend. On the highway it didn't warrant a second glance, but inside the carnival tent, surrounded by poster-sized morgue photos and ringed above and below with a network of blood-red baby spots that had cost Pa a small fortune, the Nash became Hank Caul's Death Car, *an abattoir on wheels, ladies and gentlemen, serviced by the devil himself.*

The gawkers believed all that, of course. Some of them even believed that the Death Car ate flesh and drank blood, but I knew the truth: the Nash was indeed a monster, but a monster of a different kind—a giant leech that sucked Windex, paste wax and free time. My free time.

Larry misted the rear window and set to work with a squeegee. "I told the old bastard we should've skipped this town," he said. "Jesus, Hank Caul's stompin' grounds. It'll be a miracle if we get outta here alive."

I nodded. "Pa's up to something. That's why we came back to California. He wants to get the gawkers interested in Caul's car again." I worked a chamois over the trunk, admiring the dark cherry gleam. "Maybe we should hang around tonight, just to make sure the old man isn't in over his head. That kid we rousted might show up with some friends. If Pa has a deal going, the kid could sour it real easy if he did something to the car."

"Frank, you know Pa won't go for it. Christ, he won't even let us count the daily receipts, let alone elbow in on one of his deals." Larry's voice dropped a gravelly octave in perfect imitation of the old man. "I'm the brain and you boys are the muscle, and muscle don't talk business."

We both laughed.

"Besides, we're busy tonight." Larry grinned lecherously. "On the way over here I met a young filly who thinks that twins are real interesting, especially twins who can kick ass."

I grinned, matching Larry's. Even though we were twins, I certainly couldn't call *the grin* mine. Larry was adventurous and outgoing; but he was also content with the seamy pleasures of the carny circuit. I was not. I longed for something better, bigger; something that went beyond rubber masks and stone walls made of plywood. The other stuff, the *grinny* stuff, made me feel like I wasn't much better than a gawker.

Still, I grinned. Larry's grin. "What one does . . .," I began in the old man's gravelly rasp.

". . . both do," Larry finished.

Her hair was stringy. My fingers passed through it and away, into the soft, perfumed fur that rimmed her neck.

Larry brushed her mink coat away from her leg, his left hand playing itsy-bitsy-spider as it traveled the length of her thigh.

"That's good," she whispered. "When I heard what you boys did to Perry Martin, I just knew you'd be good. Not many folks around here will stand up to that little rooster, him being the sheriff's son and all."

Larry's hand froze mid-thigh. We exchanged worried looks. If Pa found out that we'd fucked with the local law, there would be hell to pay.

She giggled and encouraged the itsy-bitsy-spider to continue on its way.

We were fifty-five feet above the midway, atop the Ezell boys' pride and joy: a revved-up Ferris Wheel that the carny folks had named The Hammer in honor of Bud Ezell's wild method of operation. When Bud wasn't spinning the gawkers silly, he contented himself by trying to bounce them out of their seats. For this reason, the open cabs installed by the manufacturer in Jacksonville had been replaced by enclosed cabs that, coincidentally, provided a great deal of privacy. Bud took full advantage of this—he wasn't above accepting bribes from gawkers eager to be "trapped" above the midway with their ladyfriends while The Hammer experienced sudden mechanical difficulties. And he was always willing to raise Larry and me up to the heavens in the company of a young lady as long as we promised to share all the details over coffee the next morning.

The cab rocked. She clutched at the hem of her coat, her fists crossing. Black fur closed over her thighs and Larry's hand disappeared underneath. Her wet lips covered mine and I tasted cherry lipstick. My fingers slipped under the fur collar—soft silk lining, small breasts.

Already I'd forgotten her name.

She moaned; her body stiffened. Then she pushed our hands away and opened her coat. Moonlight washed over her sweaty breasts. Nipples the color of olive meat, dappled with safety-cage shadow.

"Sweet Sunday," she said. "I've never done it on a Ferris Wheel before."

"Yeah?" Larry chuckled. "Well, I've never done it with a lady in mink."

She smiled dreamily. "Nice, isn't it? I got it in New York City. Daddy and I flew out last year for a morticians' convention." She paused a beat to gauge our reaction, and after deciding that we'd been suitably impressed, she added, "I'm the only girl in Fiddler who has one."

Far below, lights blinked out along the midway. Threading her fingers through the safety cage, she leaned forward. The cab tilted, giving us a better view of the carnival grounds.

"Guess travelling doesn't impress you boys. You've probably been most everywhere. It must be exciting, seeing so many different places."

"Not really," Larry said. "The midway looks the same everywhere."

I agreed. "We get tired of the carnival just like you get tired of Fiddler. To us, the Castle of Horrors is that church you're sick of going to every Sunday, and the Death Car is that old clunker you're tired of driving."

"You boys drive the Death Car?" She gasped, missing my point entirely.

Larry clapped his hands. "Do we drive the D.C.? Honey, we've turned that baby's odometer. When our daddy dies we'll be the sole owners of that miserable Nash."

Suddenly she was as interested as the most persistent gawker. "But isn't it haunted? Aren't the seat covers made of human skin, and isn't it painted with blood, and— "

The cab rocked with Larry's laughter.

She straightened indignantly. "Well, that's what people say." Her voice sounded small and wounded.

I explained that the wild stories about Hank Caul's car increased our business. I told her what a boring bucket of bolts the Nash had been when Pa bought it at public auction, how we'd added the sand-colored upholstery and painted the body red, and how we'd started the stories about the car being haunted, and somehow *alive*. "Really, Hank Caul was just a sick little guy who had a thing about hunting knives," I said. "His car was just as boring as he was. Nobody's going to pay six bits to hear that, though, so we had to help things along. Luckily, Pa and I are born storytellers."

"Well, I'm sorry," she began, "but you just don't know what you're talking about. It's pure *fact* that Hank Caul skinned his daddy's corpse. And it's a *fact* that his mama was a witch, and slept with her own son, *and* made Hank wear his daddy's skin when they did it. That's why he killed all those people. Even my daddy says it's true."

Larry smirked. "The undertaker believes in witches?"

"And a lot more than that," she said. "Daddy says that people still see Hank Caul's ghost out on the back roads looking for his skin."

"His what?"

"His skin!" She sighed. "Don't you two know anything? Hank Caul skinned himself alive before cuttin' his own throat! It's a well-known *fact*! Why just the other day I heard my daddy talking about it!"

Larry tickled her belly. "I'm glad Hank didn't get your pretty skin."

Color rose in her cheeks. Her fingers drifted over Larry's chest. She'd heard enough, said enough. She wasn't here for any of that.

We got back to what she was here for.

We rocked back and forth, listening to the rusty complaints of the cab. I noticed tiny scratches on her legs. Red skin. Razor burn. She'd been nervous or overeager about a big night out on the town. She wasn't beautiful and she wasn't young. I wondered how long she'd been waiting. In a place like Fiddler, she'd have to be very careful. She couldn't do it with just anyone, not if she wanted to keep her daddy happy.

I expect that I'd nearly ruined things for her. She didn't want to know about the carnival—the gawkers never do. No, she wanted to believe the lies, wanted to lay two tough roustabouts who'd fucked with the local big shots.

Larry nuzzled her furry shoulder, making love to a coat, not even realizing what he was doing. The way he was going at it, I figured the least he could do was pay her six bits. Disgust churned in my belly, and then she was kissing me. She put a finger to my lips and promised that good things come to those who wait.

I stared through the safety cage, up at the stars, promising myself that I wouldn't think anymore. I'd be like her, like Larry. Like all the others who believed in stories. I'd believe too, and then she'd be a lady in mink, an angel out of nowhere . . .

After awhile she undid my belt. Her lips closed around me. Then I heard Pa laugh. I looked through the mesh of the safety cage and saw him exchange handshakes with two men in front of the Death Car tent. One of the men—a skinny guy wearing a black suit—held Fort Knox. Pa held a black suitcase crisscrossed with white leather straps.

Then the cab rocked, and the stars came into full view, and I closed my eyes and squeezed a handful of mink.

The trailer door banged open. Pa came down the narrow hallway, the black suitcase in his hand bumping against the pine wallboard. I pulled a blanket over my head and pretended to snore.

Pa pulled back the blanket. "Hey, Sleepin' Beauties, I got somethin' to show— "

I squinted up at him. His good eye darted toward the empty bathroom, then back to me.

"Where's your brother?"

A chill ran over me, and not because I was missing the blanket. The other half of the bed was indeed empty. I thought back to The Hammer and the woman, half remembering Bud Ezell getting us down long after the night air had turned cold. Then an argument—Larry volunteering to take the mink lady for a ride in the Death Car, me saying she could get home on her own. Had he whispered something about wanting more? I couldn't recall.

"Hey, I asked you a question," Pa said.

"I don't know. He could be just about anywhere, I guess."

For once, Pa didn't seem to mind a less-than-straightforward answer. "We'll just have to celebrate twice, then," he said, setting the suitcase on the bed. "I got somethin' here that'll sure enough put us back in business."

I stretched. "Unless you've got Hank Caul's bones in there, I don't think— "

Pa's laughter cut me off. "Better'n that. Last night I bought the motherfucker's *skin*."

A self-satisfied grin spread across the old man's face. I'm not exaggerating when I say that Pa's grin, more than the thought of the contents of the suitcase, made my skin crawl.

Pa unfastened the scuffed leather straps that criss-crossed the suitcase, keyed the lock, and opened it. I saw a hand, fleshy-brown and twisted like an old leather work-glove, and then a foot. A face, sagging and empty, scarred. A neck dotted with a silver bolt.

Pa gasped. "*Goddamn!* This ain't what they showed me last night. I swear it ain't!"

I slipped the Frankenstein mask over my fingers and let it rest there. I remembered the mink lady's lips, Pa and the men standing below The Hammer. I remembered closing my eyes.

"Pa, how much did you pay them? Where's Fort Knox?"

Tears welled in the old man's eyes. "They got the whole damn stake!"

The trailer door banged open again. A werewolf shouldered down the hallway.

"Larry, where the hell have you been?" Pa asked.

The werewolf pulled off his mask. Bud Ezell stood before us, sweaty and panting. "It's only me, Mr McSwain. I ran all the way over here . . ."

"What is it, boy? Spit it out!"

"The Death Car," he said. "It's gone!"

I drove into Fiddler behind the wheel of Bud's piece-of-shit truck, just another farmhand passing through. Not that anyone would have noticed me even if I'd been driving the Death Car and wearing Hank Caul's skin—the valley fog that swam in the streets was that thick.

I passed the mortuary, a brick building cloaked in fog, then turned down a narrow access road that led to a ranch-style house hidden behind it. A black Cadillac was parked in a driveway lined with freshly planted bare-root roses, now little more than naked stems jutting from the dark soil like so many tiny bones. There was no sign of the Death Car.

Damn. This wasn't going to be easy. Larry wasn't inside sleeping it off, and I was sure that I'd have seen him if he'd been heading back to the carnival. Even in the fog, I wouldn't have missed the Death Car.

Leave it to Larry to put what remained of our business in danger. I didn't know which I should look for first, my brother or the Death Car.

Bud's truck coughed and complained as I down-shifted and pulled to the shoulder. *Family first*, I told myself, repeating another of Pa's favourite sayings. First Larry, then the car. And then we'd figure out what to do about Fort Knox.

I climbed out, stretched, and took a quick look around. No neighboring houses, and no one out for a morning stroll. I sauntered up the driveway, pausing only to touch the Caddy's hood. It was cold, still beaded with moisture. The Caddy hadn't been moved today.

No one answered my knock. A spade was planted nearby in the flower bed—apparently the house's owner hadn't considered the black chuckles such an obvious symbol might elicit from people who knew his profession. Hiding in the porch shadows, I tromped the flimsy blade flat. Then I angled the tool against the front door molding and set to work.

The house was empty. No people, not much stuff. The first bedroom I came across belonged to a man who favored black suits and white shirts. A yellow notebook lay open on his mahogany desk, page after page filled with scribbles analyzing the wholesale prices of silk and velvet, charts that recorded seasonal flower prices, and notes about the best way to close a sale—the usual things you might expect a businessman to fret over.

The second bedroom—the master bedroom—belonged to a woman.

No one had slept in the mink lady's bed. I opened her closet. Satin dresses, lacy nightgowns, but no mink coat.

Silk blouses tickled my hand as I reached deeper, and then my fingers brushed something rough and heavy—a green coat with red leather sleeves. A Greek soldier, sword in hand, sneered at me from the back of the coat. Above him, large furry letters spelled FIDDLER SPARTANS.

I slipped the coat off its hanger. A name was stitched over the breast.

PERRY.

I stared down at the corpse. A farm woman, her skin wrinkled, her hands soft with powder, as if she'd been making biscuits when she keeled over and no one had bothered to dust the flour off her hard, plump fingers.

He approached me quietly, but not so quietly that I didn't hear his expensive Italian shoes whispering over the wool carpet. He stopped at arms length, just outside my field of vision, no doubt trying to decide why a mourner had appeared in work clothes and muddy boots.

I turned quickly and caught him shaking his head over the soiled carpet. His jaw dropped a bit in surprise—mine did too, in recognition—but he caught himself and smiled benignly, the way undertakers do.

"It's a shame," I said, remembering The Hammer and the skinny, black-suited man I'd seen holding Fort Knox.

"Yes," he agreed. "She was a fine woman."

He wiped away a tear.

God, I stared at that tear like a gawker with a hardon for the Death Car. The power to do that on cue. Amazing. Unnatural. Like slicing a monster mask and getting blood. Suddenly, a jolt of fear shot through my legs.

Maybe he knew. Of course he did. He'd have to know. After all, funerals were designed for gawkers, and to be in the funeral business you'd have to understand how their minds worked. You'd almost have to know, or else you couldn't make them happy.

The undertaker smeared the tear across his cheek. He blinked, and a drop of milky discharge oozed at the corner of his left eye. The bottom lid hung loose, away from the eyeball, and looking down at him I saw the rosy-pink rim of his inner flesh. I trembled with excitement, staring at tiny veins rimmed with old, rubbery flesh; but then he daubed his swollen eyelid with a soiled handkerchief and disappointment washed over me.

"Just an infection," he said. "Nothing to worry about . . . nothing contagious." And then, "Did you know Mrs Fleming? Are you a relative?"

"Where is your daughter?"

"Why, she's . . . I mean, she's not here. Do you know . . . my daughter?"

I grinned Larry's grin; it was as if the old bastard couldn't remember her name either. I grabbed his tie and pulled him close, staring into his red, basset-hound eye. "I fucked your daughter last night. At the carnival. Up on the Ferris Wheel. And I saw some things going on down below."

A look of recognition bloomed on the undertaker's face as he detected something of Pa in mine. "It wasn't my idea. Willie—Sheriff

Martin—he has the money. He said it was money made from Fiddler's grief, from us . . ."

I didn't want him to get started on excuses. I shook him and asked, "Where's Hank Caul's skin?"

"There isn't any such thing. I mean, of course there is but it's buried, it's on his corpse up in Fiddler cemetery in an unmarked grave. The business about his skin has been blown out of proportion over the years, just like all the other stories about Hank. It's an old wives' tale, like the stories about bloody footprints and hitchhiking ghosts." He wiped at his infected eye. "And Willie said that if we could get your father to believe a story like that . . . Look, if you don't hurt me I'll pay you what I can. I'm quite well-fixed for cash."

I pictured Pa salivating over a shadowy heap of rubber, Pa exhaling like a stunned gawker . . .

I slapped the undertaker, hard.

A tear spilled from his healthy eye. "God, you don't have my daughter, do you? I mean, you haven't hurt her, have you?"

I wiped his tear away, rubbed it into my thumb. I couldn't help asking. I had to know. "Did you know that your daughter fucks little boys?"

"Wait, now, there's no call— "

I slapped him again; his bad eye oozed. "Did you know that your daughter fucks Perry Martin?"

Whatever steel was left in the old man boiled up. "You lying sonofabitch. My daughter wouldn't touch that little bastard."

He'd gone all white. He wasn't lying. He knew nothing about his daughter and Perry Martin. And he knew nothing about his daughter's whereabouts. That, along with the simple fact that he hadn't recognized me immediately, meant that he knew nothing about my twin brother, either.

"Your daughter is a very careful girl," I said. "I expect that there's a lot you don't know about her. But I'm not lying when I tell you that she's Perry Martin's tool." I grinned. "You should understand that. I believe you have the same relationship with Perry's father."

His head dropped. He didn't even squirm.

I took hold of the undertaker's drooping eyelid. It felt slick, like oily rubber, the way a monster mask feels when it's brand-spanking-new.

"Old man," I said, "you've disappointed me."

And then I pulled.

I found the mink lady's address book in her bedroom, right next to a cute little princess phone. Both the phone and the address book were pink. There wasn't a listing for an Ellie, but there was an Ellen Baker. I dialed her number, knowing that she was the weakest link.

She answered on the fifth ring, laughing a laugh that I remembered. "This better be good," she said. "I'm washing my hair."

I wanted to ask her if she was getting the blood out, but I resisted the temptation. "Ellie, are you alone?"

"Of course I am, Perry. You know that Mom and Dad are— "

"Look out at the fog, Ellie. What do you see in the fog?"

"Hey, you're not Perry— "

"Hank Caul's out in the fog, Ellie."

Silence.

"Hank is looking for you. He wants your skin."

A pause. She was fighting the gawker inside her. "You're the guy from the carnival, aren't you?"

"Don't say that. Don't even remember that you were at the carnival. That's my advice, Ellie."

The telephone hummed. The gawker was taking hold.

"Ellie, I think that I can stop Hank. Keep him away from you. See, he's inside me. I guess I spent too much time driving his car. God, it's so hard to explain . . ."

I paused. Now *that* was a good story, and it had come bubbling out of nowhere. I let it sink in.

"That damned car," she whispered, giving in so easily.

"I don't want to hurt you, Ellie, but Hank does. Maybe if you help me I can make him leave you alone."

"I don't want to be hurt! Don't let him— "

"I can't promise anything, Ellie . . . but I'll try. I really will."

"They're up at Hank Caul's place. That's what you want to know, isn't it? They're going to bury your brother in Caul's old orange grove. After what your brother did to him Perry got so crazy. And then when he told *her* about it . . . Mister, believe me, I didn't have anything to do with it. I didn't even want to watch. But Perry made me, and Mel— "

I hung up before she could finish saying the mink lady's name.

Melody. Melissa. Melinda. Melanie.

Nothing special there.

The Mink Lady.

That was a name the gawkers would appreciate.

I threw the address book into the closet, suddenly afraid that I'd see the Mink Lady's real name written inside.

There was no need to ruin a good story.

The suit was too tight in the shoulders, and the Caddy made nothing but wide turns. Those were my only real complaints.

Lights off, I edged the black car against the side of the weather-beaten farmhouse. I got out and circled the property, telling myself that if just one house on earth was haunted, this would be the one. But I saw no sign of Hank Caul's ghost, heard no spectral whispers in the fog. And the only smell was the thick odor of moss and rot.

All I saw was an abandoned house. I couldn't make the gawker's leap of faith. I was incapable of such an act. The Death Car had taught me too much about mythology, not the kind you find in books, but the kind that's worth six bits. Hank Caul's house only brought Pa-thoughts surging through my brain—buy this place real cheap . . . fix it up . . . one hell of a tourist trap.

Ghosts weren't real. Neither was fear. The cold truth was that they were things to be sold. Commodities. Only the gawkers believed otherwise.

I kicked in the back door and explored the house. It hadn't changed much in the five years since we'd bought the Death Car at public auction. Even then, the gawkers had been frightened by ghost stories. How else could you explain the fact that no one bid on the house that day, even though the hillside location of the Caul property offered one of the best views in the county?

The view couldn't be appreciated today, not even from the attic window. Fog pooled above the valley floor, suspended from the hills like a sagging spider-web. God, but it was a perfect place for stories. Maybe Pa had been thinking too small when he bought the Nash. Maybe we *should* have bid on the house.

The idea gnawed at me. For the second time in so many hours, I felt disappointment in someone I'd admired.

A car door slammed in the distance. I came across the sagging porch and spotted a glowing fire in the east orchard, a speck of orange nestled in a foggy blanket.

A spider lurked among the fruit trees. I was sure of it. A big red spider with an engine of bone and seats of human flesh, or so the stories told. And somewhere near the spider, two little flies who believed.

I reached into my pocket, my fingers closing on five-o'clock-shadow stubble and bristly eyebrows. Starting down the muddy path that descended to the east orchard, I slipped the undertaker's face over my own.

No fruit hung from the gnarled branches. It was the wrong season. The oranges had fallen unpicked, and I had to watch my step, weaving a path through clumps of shriveled black fruit that reminded me of the rubber shrunken heads that hung in the Castle of Horrors.

I moved fast, noisily, waiting to be noticed.

The Mink Lady stood on the other side of the fire, daintily prodding Larry's clothes into the flames with a long stick. The Death Car was parked behind her; there was no sign of Perry Martin. A steamy sizzle rose from the blaze. Maybe the wood was green. Or maybe it was Larry's blood burning.

She tossed Larry's boots into the flames. Oily smoke curled from the rubber soles; her eyes followed it up and she noticed me. "What are you doing here?" she asked, blinking as the smoke turned and wafted into her face.

I stopped short, safe in the fog. "Where's the suitcase?" I asked.

Her answer came fast. "What suitcase? What are you talking about?"

Beneath her father's face, I smiled. They were two of a kind, this pair; she knew nothing more of his activities than he'd known of hers.

Perry Martin came around the Death Car, a shovel gripped in his right hand. "What's going on?" he asked. "Who are you talking to?"

"Perry, it's my daddy."

They stared at me, cringing like guilty children. Daddy wasn't supposed to know about his little girl and Perry-the-stud, let alone these goings on.

I waited for them to make a move. The fire crackled and hissed. Rubber dripped from Larry's boots; the laces burned like fuses. I daubed my left eye with a handkerchief. For now, I would stay in character.

She was the first to speak. "We have to tell him, Perry."

"No!"

"But he can help us, and I promise he won't tell."

I nodded.

A sheepish smile spread across Perry's face. He dropped the shovel and came through the smoke, stories pouring from his mouth. "It was a fair fight," he lied. "The guy was asking for it. He jumped me at the carnival— "

Fair. Yes. Larry was drunk. That made it fair.

"—really thought that he was hot shit— "

Fair. Fair to use your little whore to lure him into town.

"It was kind of an honor thing. I wanted to show him that— "

Fair to kill him in his own car, with his pants down around his ankles.

"—and strangers just can't walk into Fiddler and act like they own the place. We live here. We own it."

I sucked a deep, clean breath through the undertaker's lips. My picture of Larry's death wasn't exaggeration. It wasn't imagination. It was the way it must have happened.

249

It was the death of a gawker.

Perry stopped short. He looked at my face, closely.

"Jesus," he whispered. "You're a fuckin' dead man."

I stared at his terrified expression, realizing that revenge was a grinny thing. A gawker's itch. It couldn't be bothered with.

All the hate spilled out of me then. The shoulder seams of the undertaker's suit popped as my open palms hit Perry's chest; he *whuffed* a sharp exhalation and tripped into the fire.

The Mink Lady screamed. "Daddy! You're crazy!"

"I'm dead," I corrected.

Perry rolled away from the flames. I jumped over him and grabbed the shovel. Swinging hard, I belted him between his shoulderblades. He cried out and tried to rise, but my second blow landed lower, in a soft place, and Perry dropped, screaming something about his kidneys.

The Mink Lady slapped me and I pulled her close. I let her see my mask, and then I took it off and showed her who I was. She tried a half-hearted lie but gave it up the first time I shook my head. When I opened the trunk, I didn't have to tell her to climb inside.

Perry wasn't in a chatting mood, but his words were heartfelt. Between the *fuck you*'s and the *screw you*'s he told me a lot about the Martin family. Unfortunately, he didn't have much respect for his father, let alone any involvement in the family business, and he certainly didn't know anything about Fort Knox.

Soon it dawned on Perry that I was interested in his old man. His eyes glimmered with hope. I guess he figured that he might get out of this alive.

Perry Martin was that stupid.

I hit him in the face until he was unconscious. He came to in the hole he'd been digging, face to face with Larry's naked corpse. He begged me to let him out, but a wave of the shovel told him that I wasn't having any of it. He still had his hunting knife, but he had no ideas about using it on me. I had to beg him to unsheathe it, and even then he thought I was trying to trick him.

He was right, of course. I made up a story about voodoo rites, rattling on about zombies in New Orleans. Then I told him the truth about his father and Fort Knox, playing up the money angle. I explained that we were going to be partners, at least for a while.

"Man, you're crazy," he said, but he did as he was told, and, truthfully, I believe he enjoyed the assignment I gave him.

I warmed my hands over the fire while Perry worked, wishing that I had his letterman's jacket. But it was up the hill, neatly folded on the Caddy's front seat, an expressionless Frankenstein mask in its pocket. Then I thought about Larry's dead face, lips so straight,

ungrinning, looking like me, or at least the part of me that worried
and scraped by, knowing that there was something better to be had
from life. I wondered if his wearing that expression meant that Larry
finally understood me. I hoped so. I hoped that in death my brother
had lost the grinny madness that always held him back.

Held *us* back.

When the fire died down, I climbed into the Death Car and turned
on the heater. Down in the hole, Perry was about half finished with
the task I'd given him. In the trunk, the Mink Lady shifted, trying
to get comfortable.

I found a fifth of bourbon in the glove compartment. There was
a box of fishhooks, too; and a Mickey Spillane novel that Larry had
been reading.

The book was called *I, the Jury*. I took a drink and turned to
page one.

Three hours later, I cut through Caul's orange grove and worked my
way back to the highway. If anything, the fog was thicker now, and
I sniffed gas fumes long before I spotted the service station. Fact is,
I nearly bumped into the attendant, a bent little man who smelled
of Pennzoil.

"Got a pay phone?" I asked.

He pointed. I didn't like the way he looked at me. I didn't like
his eyes.

"Where's yer car?"

"I don't need gas. I need some change . . . I've only got a five."

He grunted; you'd think I'd asked him for the moon. Then he
disappeared into the fog and returned with a greasy handful of bills
and coins. "S'pose you want me to dial yer number for ya, too,"
he said.

I turned away, cringing as if I'd been slapped.

"Willie Martin," the voice said.

"It's me, Willie. It's Hank Caul."

A barking laugh. "Oh, sure. Hank Caul. You just dig yourself out
of the grave, Hank? You gonna move into town, or are you gonna
spruce up the old homestead?"

"I've got Perry. I've got your son, sheriff."

"Now wait one damn min— "

"I'm done waiting, sheriff. I guess I don't have to tell you
what you did the other night made me pretty mad. Pretending
to sell my skin and all, I mean. Unless you bring me the money
you stole, I'm going to carve your little Perry like a Halloween
pumpkin."

"Listen to me, asshole. This *is* one of you carny assholes, isn't it? If you hurt my boy you're as good as dead."

"This is Hank Caul. I'm already dead, sheriff. And I *do* have your boy."

Silence.

"Okay, then, where do we stand?"

"Jed's Gas out on 198. Be there at midnight, alone, with the money. Wait for a sign."

"No soap. Let's do this thing right now."

"Midnight, Willie. One minute early and it's pumpkin-carving time. I won't be strong enough until midnight. I need the moonlight."

I looked into the fog, waiting for an answer. Pure bullshit, that moonlight stuff, but I could feel the gawker in him puzzling over it.

"Okay. Midnight."

He was lying. I could almost see him reaching for his car keys.

"You'd better be smart, sheriff. You'd better know that I mean what I say."

"Sure."

"Don't lie, Willie. We've had enough of that between us, you and me. If you really want to do something right now, visit your local undertaker. You'll see just how serious I am."

A deep breath. Then, "You killed him?"

"I taught him what happens to people who fuck with my legend," I said, and hung up before Willie Martin could reply.

The attendant overheard the whole conversation. I palmed Perry's knife and shouldered out of the booth. Before the old man knew what hit him, the blade slipped between his jawbone and the flesh of his left cheek.

He didn't scream. He grunted. And then he pulled away, one eye dancing.

"You crazy sonofabitch," he said.

His eyes. The right one staring at me. The left one dead, bloody. My legs went to jelly. Pa's eyes, shining with loathing.

He held his slashed mask together with his right hand; blood coursed from the meaty wound beneath. I was about to apologize when a knife appeared in his left hand. "C'mon," he said. "If you got any balls, that is. No one robs Jed Davis."

So that was the way he planned it—a sucker play, and he expected me to fall for it like a gawker in the Castle of Horrors. Pathetic.

I shook my head. "You should have trusted me, Pa. I could have handled it." I pulled the undertaker's face out of my pocket and threw it on the ground. "You've got no secrets from me, so you can forget the act. It's small potatoes, just the kind of thing that's been holding us back all these years."

He stared at the face on the oily pavement and didn't say a word.

"It's the money, isn't it, Pa? That's all you want, only you don't want to share it with your own flesh-and-blood anymore."

"No," the old man said, waving his knife. "You're crazy. You ain't my son. Any money around here is *mine*."

"Wrong, Pa. Larry lost the car, but you lost the money. But what's worse is you lied. All that what-one-does-both-do stuff. Pure crap. Larry and I were different, Pa. We really were." I inched forward. "Larry was always a gawker. That was his great weakness, and he died for it." I tossed the knife from right hand to left. "Now you're a gawker, too." My hand tightened around the bone hilt. "That's the truth, Pa. Any way you slice it."

"I don't know what you're talkin' about," he said, backing into a tire rack. "You're nuts!"

"Maybe, but at least I never bought a suitcase full of rubber. I'm not a gawker, Pa. I never will be. I'm thinking big now. Big time. Big stories. I'm thinking we should have bought Hank Caul's house."

He nearly deflated. For just a moment he looked like a six-bit-a-head carny operator who'd just seen a profit sheet from Disneyland. I came at him then, almost sorry because he might have been something once. If he hadn't believed the stories, he might have made us rich. But he'd let a small-town sheriff take him for a ride, and he'd blown our stake.

And he'd kept me down for a damn long time.

I kicked the knife out of his hand.

His good eye danced, electric with fear.

"Take anything you want. There's money in the register."

I kept my head. I didn't want to get grinny. "Six bits is what I charge," I said, my voice strong and even. "Six bits a ticket. You know that, Pa."

"You gotta understand that I ain't your— "

Blood geysered into the air as I worked the knife through the old man's mask and face, slicing so fast that I couldn't tell where one ended and the other began.

At midnight I torched the Caddy. A great plume of orange fire roared into the sky, and I could only imagine the look on Willie Martin's face as he watched from Jed's Gas down in the valley.

As I climbed the stairs I heard Perry screaming about the abuse he was taking as my partner, but his protest had all the half-hearted enthusiasm of a cranky child fighting bedtime. When he finally stopped whining, I opened the closet door. He'd finished off the bourbon just like I'd hoped—I'd left one of his hands untied and the fifth in his pocket—and then he'd been too drunk to try to escape. He hadn't even thought to break the bottle and cut the ropes.

The ropes were tangled and the closet was dark, so to speed things up I broke apart the clothes rods and slipped the wood through the loops, ordering Perry to twist this way and that. When he was free, I fastened the manacles around his wrists and steered him out of the closet. Even drunk, he noticed the Frankenstein mask lying on the floor; light from the Caddy fire spilled through the moth-eaten drapes and swirled around it, orange light given physical presence by dust motes we'd kicked alive.

"Boy, Frankie's face looks so *real*," Perry said. "I bet it'd scare fucking Boris Karloff!"

I agreed. "Do you think it will scare your old man?"

Perry nodded vigorously, rattling his chains like the ghost of Christmas Past. I reminded him of the money we were going to make and made him repeat the plan that I had no intention of following. Then I lit a candle and burned a lock of Larry's hair, mumbling a phony voodoo chant for effect.

Perry swayed back and forth, buying the whole routine.

I slid the mask over his head.

Jerked the rubber bolts from side to side.

Two dozen fishhooks bit home.

I could barely hear him over Perry's screams, but I recognized the shouting voice as the one I'd heard over the telephone at Jed's Gas. "Frank McSwain!" he yelled. "That *is* your name, isn't it? This is Willie Martin. It's time to deal."

Perry writhed on the dusty floor. I stepped over him and broke the windowpane with my elbow, the leather sleeve of Perry's jacket protecting my arm.

I peered through the torn drapes. Willie Martin stood below in the light of the Caddy fire—Perry with twenty pounds and twenty years. An old man stood next to him. I got a brief look at his face, and then both men disappeared behind a cloud of smoke.

"I've got your father down here, McSwain. Maybe we can work out a trade."

I leaned into the shadows, biting back laughter. So Willie Martin wasn't a gawker after all. No, he was a showman, but his little drama was wasted on me—I'd left Pa dead and faceless in an orchard of rubber shrunken heads, and this old geezer didn't even have a good mask.

"Frank?" the old guy called. "Larry, are you up there too? Listen, boys, they got us dead to rights, but they'll let us live if you turn over the kid."

I had to hand it to the sheriff. The old guy's voice was good. I pulled Perry to his feet, shoved him to the window, then yanked him away.

"Jesus, boys," the old guy in the mask growled. "This ain't the spook show. Use your brains. C'mon down or I'm a goner."

I flicked Perry's cigarette lighter and touched the flame to the drape.

The rest happened too fast. Fire crawled up the drape and skittered across dry wallpaper, reaching for the ceiling. I grabbed the steel chain and pulled Perry to his feet. Shouts rang out below. The front door banged open as I came down the stairs, dragging Perry behind me. A flashlight beam zigzagged across the sheet-shrouded furniture and froze on me, a tight circle illumimating the scowling Spartan on my jacket. I yanked the steel chain, spinning Perry into the light.

The cold beam haloed his blood-drenched mask.

A gun barrel sparked.

The mask sank away, into the dark.

Perry hit the floor.

Everything stopped.

The flashlight beam lingered on Perry for a moment, then cut to me.

I grinned at the man who'd turned my Pa into a gawker.

"No," Willie Martin whispered. "Jesus, no."

His gun came up but Perry's knife had already left my hand. It caught the sheriff just under the right collarbone; he staggered backward. I wrestled the gun out of his hand, pushing him toward his son's corpse.

Then I left him there, alone and staring.

The deputies were slow, and that was good, because Willie Martin's gun was almost empty. I shot three of them. If there were others, they disappeared into the fog.

The old man with the Pa mask couldn't run. He was shot up pretty bad, but he wasn't dead yet. Still, he wouldn't tell me where Fort Knox was, and he kept to his Pa act the whole time. I kind of admired him for that—somehow it made up for the things I'd lost, including Fort Knox. I helped him into the back of Willie Martin's patrol car and left him there with the heater running.

I filled up the Nash at Jed's Gas, free of charge. I imagine a lot of other drivers did the same that night. I didn't want to waste money on the pay phone, so I went inside to make one last call.

She didn't answer for a long time, and when she did I could barely hear her voice.

"It's me," I said.

Silence.

"I just wanted to let you know that Hank won't be coming for you."

Silence.

"I think it's over. Maybe he's gone. The people he made me kill . . . well, I can't believe what he made me do to them, but I think they might have deserved it." I paused. "Anyway, I think his spirit will rest in peace now."

"God, I hope so," she whispered.

I hung up, wondering who Ellie would call first. I wondered how many gawkers lived in Fiddler. How long would it take them to learn of Hank Caul's ghostly rampage? And once they'd found out, how soon would they forget that a carny roustabout had anything to do with it?

I drove south.

The fog cleared around Earlimart. I flipped on the radio and found a late night station out of Fresno. Between bursts of static, Bo Diddley asked the musical question, "Who do you love?"

I looked into the rearview mirror. Not a headlight in sight.

Bo Diddley sang about a house made of rattlesnake hide.

I liked that.

I don't know what kind of story I'll make up. I'll have to ditch the Death Car, of course, but I'm tired of that story anyway. It'll be nice to make a change.

It's funny. I started off wanting revenge, and for a while I wanted money. Somewhere in there I even wanted Hank Caul's house. Now I only want a good story. That's all a guy like me really needs. Something new. Fresh. Something that will nail the gawkers to the wall.

I close my eyes, just for a second, and say goodbye to the Death Car story. Suddenly I hear screaming . . . *an engine made of bone* . . . but then I realize that it's only the woman in the trunk.

I hope that she's warm enough.

I open my eyes. Moonlight washes over the cherry-red hood.

She can wear her mink coat. She can wear Larry's skin.

The gawkers will like that.

The Mink Lady story.

I press the gas pedal to the floor and the Nash roars forward.

The Mink Lady screams.

I remember her lips. They tasted of cherries.
I imagine a house made of rattlesnake hide.
A dynasty of fear.
I'm thinking big.

WILLIAM F. NOLAN

Blood Sky

WILLIAM F. NOLAN has operated a miniature railroad for children, raced sports cars, acted in motion pictures, painted outdoor murals, served as a book reviewer for the *Los Angeles Times*, taught creative writing, and plotted Mickey Mouse adventures for Walt Disney.

However, he is better known for his work as a novelist, editor, biographer, essayist, screenwriter and as the author of more than 120 short stories. His *Logan's Run* was made into an MGM movie and a CBS-TV series, and along with the two sequels has been collected in *Logan: A Trilogy*, with illustrations by the author.

He is currently adapting Peter Straub's novel *Floating Dragon* for MGM/NBC-TV as a two-part miniseries, and Clive Barker's "The Inhuman Condition" as the second half of an ABC-TV Movie of the Week, *Devil's Night*. Meanwhile, David Cronenberg is adapting Nolan's book *Yankee Champion* for Warner Bros, as a vehicle for Mel Gibson, which Cronenberg will also direct.

His ninth novel, *Helltracks*, was recently published and he is currently working on *ten* more books. Amongst his many honours, the author has twice won the Edgar Allan Poe Special Award for contributions to the mystery genre.

"Blood Sky" is a terrifying glimpse into the mind of a serial killer, made all the more disturbing by the author's matter-of-fact treatment of the subject.

S OMETIMES, SLEEPING HERE ALONE IN THESE strange Montana motel rooms, I have some weird dreams, so I figured I'd put some of them down in my notebook to give insight into them.

Like the carnival dream. I'm a kid in the dream, maybe ten or eleven, and my Grandpa (on my Mom's side of the family) takes me to this carnival. It's one of the cheap road shows, run-down and seedy, with holes in the tents, and with most of the rides in bad shape, and with the Ferris Wheel all rusted and unsafe looking. The clowns look sad and the hoochy-kooch girls have sagging bellies and dead-fish eyes and wear lipstick like slashes of blood across their lips. They try to look sexy, but they're just pathetic. They make you sick.

Gramps says let's try some of the games and he buys two tickets for us to try the shooting gallery. I miss most of the painted ducks but Gramps hits every one, knocks them all down, and the guy in the booth, real fat and mean in a dirty white shirt all stained under the armpits, hands Gramps his prize. It's a live chicken. (In dreams, I guess you can win prizes like that.) Gramps takes the bird under his arm and we go into this water ride called the Tunnel of Terror. You get in this creaky dark green boat and it takes you around corners in the dark where things jump out at you, and horns blare and you hear people screaming. (I hate being confined in dark places.)

Suddenly, in the middle of the ride, the boat stops dead still in the water and we're sitting there alone, just me and Gramps. It's real quiet. Just the water lapping at the sides of the boat and the two of us breathing there in the dark. Gramps takes the chicken and holds it out in front of him. Then he starts to chuckle and next thing in the dream he's got his hands around the bird's neck and he strangles it. Then he hands me the dead chicken, with the head lolling loose. The chicken is wet and mushy, and I tell Gramps I don't want to hold it. Worms are coming out of it.

I throw the dead chicken into the water and when I turn back to Gramps his face is all lit in red, the Devil's face, and he has fur on his tongue and his eye sockets are empty, like the sockets in a skull. He puts his hands around my neck and begins to squeeze.

Good boy, he says, my good, good boy.

And I wake up.

Now what does a dream like this really mean?

A week later . . .

Another bad dream. Really bad. In fact, I'm writing this entry at 6 a.m. in the morning (there's a blood sky outside my motel window) because the nightmare woke me up and I can't get back to sleep, thinking about it. So I might as well write it down.

It started real ordinary. The scary ones all seem to start that way, easy and natural, and they gradually slip into the awful parts, taking you along into a dark area you don't want to get into, that you get terrified of, and would never go to if you weren't dreaming.

This one began in warm yellow sunlight, with me walking along a road that cut through this piney wood. (There were other kinds of trees there, too, but I don't know much about different trees so I can't say what they were.) Anyway, there were plenty of trees, with a mass of pine needles under my feet, and with thick green foliage everywhere.

There was the crisp smell of sunlight and the church smell of the pines and the cheeping of birds. All straight out of a kid's picture book, and that's what I think inspired this part of the dream, because I remember when I was seven, that Gramps bought me this picture book of forests around the world, and I just got totally lost in that book, trying to imagine what it would be like to walk through those magical-looking forests, with the tall trees all around me.

And that's how it was in this dream—just me alone at age seven, in this pine forest, enjoying the peace and quiet. But then it started getting dark. Fast. A lot faster than in real life. All the birds stopped singing and the sun dropped out of the sky like a falling stone. The path I was on narrowed, and the trees seemed to be pressing in closer. And it got cold. A wind had come swirling up, with voices in it, crying Run, Eddie! Something bad is coming, Eddie! Better run, boy! Catch you if you don't run fast. Run!

And I took off like a wet cat. Started booting it along that path with tree branches whipping at me, slashing at my face and cutting my shirt like swords. I was crying by then, and really scared, because the whole forest seemed to come alive and the trees all had mouths full of sharp teeth, like daggers, and now they were leaning over to bite at my flesh. I felt pain, and blood was running into my eyes, blinding me.

Then I saw a cabin. Just ahead, with the path going right up to the door. It was open. I ran inside, slamming the door behind me and leaning against it, sobbing and shaking all over.

Suddenly I wasn't a seven-year-old kid anymore. I was me, now, at my age, and I was buck naked. My flesh (no cuts or blood!) was puckered with the cold as the night wind sliced through the cracks in the cabin's roof and walls.

Then I realized (the way you do in dreams) that a big deeply-upholstered chair (we had one back in Kansas) was directly in front of the fireplace and I hunched down in that chair, pressing against the cushions for warmth, shivering, with my arms crossed over my chest. There was no warmth from the fireplace—only dead black ashes.

That's when I heard the sound of something coming out of the forest toward the cabin. Clump, clump, clump. Heavy footsteps. Heading for me. Coming for me. Something awful.

And getting closer every second.

I was sweating. As cold as it was, I was in a sweat of fear. My eyes searched for escape. There was no back door to the place, no windows. What could I do? Where could I go?

Then the door bulged. Like it was under a terrible pressure. Something was bending it inward. A deep voice, old and raspy, cried out. Let me in, Eddie! Open the door!

I jumped from the chair and ran to the far wall, pressing my back against the rough wood, my eyes bugging as the door just *exploded* open.

And Gramps was there. Just like in the carnival dream. Only instead of carrying a chicken he had a long dark green coat over his arm. He was smiling at me.

Nothing to be afraid of, boy. It's just me an' your mom.

And that's when I saw that it wasn't a coat over his arm. It was my mother's body, loose like a sack and dark green with grave mold. Dark green and rotting.

Your mama's hungry, boy. I brought her here for a feed. She needs to eat.

And he walked over and grabbed me by the neck and kind of draped my mother's body around me, with her rotted arms hanging over my shoulders and her moldy legs pressing against my naked skin. The stink that came off her was the stink of the grave, of deep earth and things long dead.

I was helpless. Then, slowly, her head raised itself and her dead face was right in front of *my* face, maybe an inch away, and she was smiling a broken-toothed idiot's smile and her eyes were filmed with red, wormy veins, and I could see her tongue moving like a fat dark snake inside the rotted cavern of her mouth.

Eddie . . . my little boy. Didn't I always take care of you, sweetie? Now it's your turn to take care of your Mommy . . .

And she buried her teeth in my neck, ripping out a huge gobbet of my flesh and starting to chew . . .

Which is when I woke up here in the motel, covered with cold slimy sweat. My muscles were twitching and I could hardly breathe.

It was one of the worst nightmares I've ever had.

Now, why would I ever have a dream about being devoured by my mother's corpse? She's not even dead, for one thing. Why should I dream of her being dead? There's no reason on earth I should have a dream like this. No reason.

The science people tell us that if we don't dream every night we go crazy. That our minds need to let off steam, as it were, and that dreaming is natural for everybody. Maybe. But I hate having dreams I can't control and being a victim to them. Having dreams is supposed to keep you from going nuts, but what if they *make* you nuts? I mean, if I had dreams as bad as this every night I'd go insane. And I very much want to retain my sanity.

I had the dream about my mother two days ago and I think I've figured it out. For one thing, I consider myself on the level of a professional shrink (which is why I'd never go to one). I've always been able to study people and what makes them tick, and I am quite good at reading beneath the surface of a person.

So I analyzed my dream in relation to my inner self. I think there must be a deep-buried part of me that thinks my mother was kind of smothering me, that she fed off me emotionally after my father began treating her so bad, beating her up and everything. Not that she was the huggy-kissy type. Not at all. I've mentioned in this notebook before how she didn't like any open affection, no outward displays. But, inside, I think she turned to me as a kind of replacement for my father. It was subtle, but it was there, and I sensed it somehow, even as a kid.

For example, she didn't like sharing me with anybody. When Gramps would come over (even Mom called him that) and he'd want to take me home with him for the weekend, take me to the park for ice cream and a ride on the merry-go-round they had there, she always said no, I couldn't go with him to his house because I had to do chores over the weekend. Once every summer she did let me go out to a cabin Gramps had rented near a lake in the woods (the cabin in my dream looked a lot like it) and I had some great times swimming out there and eating the fresh peach ice cream that Gramps made himself.

I have one bad memory connected with the lake. It was what I did to a litter of pups, six of them. I put them all in a cardboard box and then took them to the edge of the wooden dock and then pushed them under the water. When the bubbles didn't come up anymore I knew they were dead. I can't remember exactly why I did that except for the power feeling it gave me, that charge I get as I'm taking a life, that's still with me, even today. When I strangle someone, when I drive my thumbs deep into their neck, when I feel them kick and struggle and then go limp like a loose sack in my hands, it's a very satisfying kind of thing. Fulfilling, really. It's not a sexual thing, not like the wet dreams I used to have as a kid, and it doesn't give me a hardon. It's more like what I've heard from people who take drugs—a sudden high, a rush of pure pleasure. You kind of tingle all over.

Killing has always given me that. Which is one reason it's so hard to quit.

But getting back to the dream ... I suppose it came from my subconscious, based on that deep-down feeling that Mom used me as a kind of emotional *food* when I was a kid. The dream makes some sense on that basis.

I feel better now, having figured it out. It was still terrible, having it, and I hope I don't have any more like it, but at least I've got it analyzed.

And I'm proud of myself for that.

There's a feeling in Montana that you're back in the Old West. Lots of the men wear cowboy hats and walk around in fancy cowhide boots. Every town you go to is full of Western artifacts and every area has its Western ghost town. It's kind of like the Civil War is in the South. You go there and it seems the Civil War just ended about a month ago. People still talk about it and there are souvenirs and Confederate flags and banners. In Montana, it's the Old West which is very much alive. Real John Wayne country. Including a lot of rodeos.

There was one going on here in Conrad, just a mile or two beyond the main part of town, and I decided it might be fun to go see it. Get my mind off what the papers were saying. I'd never been to a rodeo. Had read about them and seen movies. In fact, I remember one with Steve McQueen in it. He played a guy named Junior somebody and I enjoyed watching that one.

I found out that a rodeo was a lot like going to a circus. Everything is noisy, with bucking horses and cowgirls in flashy spangled outfits and bright-painted clowns for the bulls to chase and big grandstands full of people eating popcorn and drinking Cokes. (Is there anywhere on this whole planet where people don't drink Coca-Cola? I've seen photos of Coke signs in the deserts of Arabia and the jungles of Africa—and you can bet that when they build a city on Mars the first thing they'll be shipping in is truckloads of Coca-Cola. Me, I'd like to have just a tiny percentage of the profits from these zillions of Cokes they sell all over the world every day. I'd be a rich man for sure.)

I got a pretty good aisle seat in the main grandstand and nibbled on some roasted peanuts and watched these whooping cowboys get tossed off these fierce-looking bulls. They'd roll their eyes, these big bulls would, with white froth looping from their mouths, and just shake off the riders like water off a dog's back. The second a cowboy hit the dirt a clown would jump out to lure the bull away from the fallen rider—and when the bull went after the clown he'd jump into a barrel and the bull's horns would bang into the wood while the cowboy got up and limped back to the chutes. Not all of them limped, but most did. I couldn't figure why anybody would want to try riding a bull or a wild, crazy-eyed bucking horse. Even when you won, the prizes weren't anything to write home about. There are plenty of broken bones and skull fractures in a rodeo. Dumb way to make a living.

I read somewhere that they use a real tight strap around the balls of the bull to make him jump harder and higher. And they do other things just as bad. This article I read told all about it. I like getting the inside scoop, because there's always more to everything than you see on the surface. (There's sure a lot more to Yours Truly than most people ever guess at!)

The calf-roping was fun to watch—and these boys could ride and rope like the rest of us breathe air. It was something to see the way they competed against the clock, making every move count. Makes you realize how much time we waste in our lives. What I need in my life right now is a goal to work toward. Not just getting control of the compulsion, I mean having a solid future in mind. But when I try to think of the future it's all blank, like a sheet of white paper. Like getting a fortune cookie in a Chinese cafe and breaking it open to read your fortune and finding out there's no little slip of paper inside. Just an empty cookie. That's how my whole life seems these days. Like that cookie.

I was thinking such thoughts when I felt a hand touch my left shoulder.

Hi, pardner, you look a mite thirsty. How 'bout a beer?

I looked up at this attractive cowgirl in a short, fringed skirt, white boots decorated with silver stars, a spangled blouse and red bandanna, topped by a wide-brim Western sombrero. A beer tray was balanced from a strap on her shoulder. I don't like beer, I told her.

That's okay. I've sold enough today. Mind if I sit? I'm kind of tuckered.

I don't mind, I said.

And I moved over on the wooden slat seat to give her some room. She sat down, slipping the tray from her shoulder and letting it rest against her booted leg. The skin between her skirt and her white boot tops was very tan. A real outdoor Montana type.

You got a cigarette?

I've given up smoking, I told her. Cigarettes can kill you.

Lotta things can kill you, she said. I also drink Scotch whiskey and that can kill me. When I visit my sister in California I could get killed by an earthquake. Or a dog with rabies could bite me. Hell, I could even meet up with the Big Sky Strangler—but right now, I just want a cigarette.

Her remark about meeting the Big Sky Strangler seemed almost surreal. The last thing this woman figured was that she was talking to him right this minute. Strange. Life can be strange.

It wasn't easy for me to quit cigarettes, I told her. It's something I really had to work at.

What do you want from me? she asked sharply, a Boy Scout merit badge?

You can make fun of it if you want to, I said, but I'm proud of what I've done.

She patted my shoulder. You're right, I was just being a bitch. Didn't mean to put you down, darlin', but I get a little testy about this time of day. This is no sweet job, lugging heavy cans of beer up and down these lousy grandstands, and getting my fanny pinched by drunken cowboys who think I can't wait to climb into the saddle with 'em. Lotta creeps in this world.

I can see how it's a rough job, I told her.

She took off her big white hat and pushed at her hair. It was the same color hair as the one that I killed in Butte, a kind of sandy brown.

I'm gonna take off early, call it a day, she said. Do you like fish?

I blinked. Oh, I guess they're all right. I neither like nor dislike them, I said. I never had one as a pet.

She let out a hoot and slapped her hat against one knee.

No, no. What I meant is, do you like *eating* them?

I had to laugh at myself on that one. I'd taken her question in a literal sense. Her personality was throwing me off. I'm never much good with direct women.

My boyfriend, bastard that he is, just rode off into the sunset, leaving me with a fridge full of trout and no one to feed 'em to. So what do you say to a free fish dinner?

I say great, I told her. In fact, I appreciate the offer.

Good. You may be straight arrow, but I think you're cute. She shook my hand and her grip was firm.

I'm Lorry Haines, she said.

Ed Timmons, I said back to her.

I didn't want to eat alone tonight, she said. Now I won't have to.

Lorry Haines drove me to a small cream-colored frame house trimmed in blue with a neat little fenced yard.

I met Bobby at a rodeo in Billings, she told me as she started dinner. He was a bronc rider, top of his class. Tall and hunky with muscle in all the right places. We hit it off and he asked me to leave town and tour the circuit with him.

266

Is Billings your home town? I asked.

Yeah. I grew up there. When I met Bobby, I was working in a clothing store. Went to the rodeo that weekend with a girl friend and there was ole Bobby, tall in the saddle, with a glint in his eye. Before the weekend was over I'd agreed to quit my job and follow him around the circuit.

That's when you started selling beer, eh?

Yeah. They always need people in the stands. It was easy to get work.

What happened between you and Bobby?

Oh, it was great for awhile. He was Bobby Superstud, knew just about everything there is to know about giving a girl a good time in the sack.

Uh huh, I said, beginning to feel a little uncomfortable.

But we fought like a couple of bobcats. Over all kinds of stuff. Then, last night, I came home here to this house and found a note from the bastard. A kiss-off note. He just up and took off. Probably with some bimbo he met in town.

Then this place isn't yours?

Nope. I never owned me a house. This belongs to a friend of Bobby's, a retired rodeo rider. He's out of town this weekend, so we got it. I'll be leaving tomorrow.

Where will you go?

Who knows? I'm just a rolling stone these days.

Funny, I told her. That's what a lot of people have called me.

Yeah? And she smiled. Just a couple of rolling stones, you and me.

She'd been fixing dinner as we talked, bustling around the kitchen while I sat at a small Formica table in the dining nook. She asked me to help her fix the salad, so I started cutting up the lettuce she'd washed.

You could always go back to Billings, I said. Aren't your folks still there?

Sure, but we never got along. We're not on what you might call the best of terms. Mom's a real bitch, if you want to know the truth. And Dad's no bargain, either.

So what *are* you going to do?

She turned from the trout, which were browning in the pan, and grinned at me. I dunno, she said. Maybe I'll join a convent.

I grinned back at that. Yeah. I can see you as the praying cowgirl nun!

I know one damn thing, she said. After tomorrow, I'm finished with rodeos.

The food was ready and she laid it out on the table. We sat down

267

and began eating. The trout was great—covered in cornmeal, all brown and crusty, just the way I like it—and I told her so.

Thanks, pardner! she said.

We ate in silence for awhile, then she canted her head and gave me a little cat-grin.

Anybody ever tell you how cute you are?

I knew it was coming, but it still shook me. This direct sexual approach. Like the older woman in Butte. I didn't know how to handle it. I never have.

You're the cute one, I said. Bet a lot of guys have been after you since you grew up.

She bit into a dinner roll. Then she took a swallow of coffee. Then she looked at me again.

You like oral sex? she asked.

I woke up the next morning alone in the bed. Lorry was already dressed and packed.

You better get your butt in gear, darlin', because ole Jeeter, who owns this place, is due back today. And that man can be mean as a snake in a sock. We'd best be gone.

She was right. It would be hard to explain just who I was if this Jeeter guy showed, so I took a quick shower, got dressed, gobbled down the breakfast Lorry fixed for me (great little cook!) and got out of there.

We'd talked in bed after we had sex. About the future. About us pairing up on the road. Just two rolling stones. It sounded good to me at the time, since the sex with Lorry had been real fine and I needed somebody like her to help me straighten out. Naturally I didn't tell her about the compulsion, or that I'd ever killed anybody.

The thing is, and I know whoever reads this will get a big laugh out of it, but the thing is I was in love. For the first time in my whole life. Truly in love. They say that love can strike like lightning, that one minute you're not in love and the next minute you are. And that's how it happened with me and Lorry. There was something about her that just ignited my blood. I don't mean just the great sex we had, I mean her whole *being*. She gave off a kind of wondrous aura. I don't expect you to understand because I don't myself. But it happened, and a fact is a fact.

Lorry owned an orange VW—a Volkswagen bug. I'd never driven one before and I was not impressed with its performance. It had so little power that it was almost impossible to pass other cars on the Interstate.

A bug's not supposed to be fast, she told me with a grin. This is no sports car. VWs were made to *last*. This one's twenty-five years old.

She told me she'd had it for the last three years and it had never given her any mechanical trouble.

I don't like it, I said. Ted Bundy drove a Volkswagen.

Who?

The guy that killed all those coeds, I told her. Cut their heads off, on a lot of them. He drove a gold VW.

So he drove a bug, she said. So what? It's not going to turn you into a mass murderer.

I blinked at that. Talking to her about Bundy was stupid. I had to avoid that kind of talk.

I want you to sell it, I said.

Sell it! Her voice jumped up a couple octaves. You gotta be nuts. I'm not selling my bug.

I didn't look at her, just kept driving. I'd made her angry. Our first day together and already we were fighting.

When we get into Great Falls, I said, I want you to find a dealer and get rid of this car.

You're *serious*, aren't you?

Yes.

But Eddie, we need wheels. If we're gonna travel around together we need a car.

Fine. Buy another. Just so it isn't a VW.

A silence. Then she said, hard-toned: And what if I say no?

Then we split, I said.

Over a *car*! Her brows were lifted in astonishment.

I took the next off ramp from I-15 and pulled to a stop on an access road under a big tree. Then I turned off the engine and reached for her. She came into my arms smooth as butter. I kissed away the frown between her eyes. She kissed me back. Things were a lot better.

I'm really not trying to give you a bad time, I said. It's just that whenever I'm in this car I'll be thinking of Ted Bundy and what he did to those coeds—and I don't want to do that.

She nestled her head against my shoulder.

Okay, she said, if it bothers you so much, I'll sell the VW.

Then she raised her head and looked at me. You know, Eddie, you're a strange guy.

I nodded. I never said I wasn't.

I'm not going to let what we've got go to hell over a car, she said. Already, you're very special to me.

When I came to Montana, I said to her, I never thought I'd get into a heavy relationship. It's kinda spooky.

I think I love you, she said.

I think I love you, too, I told her.

269

She nestled deeper into my shoulder. It was a fine fall day, cool and crisp. A slight breeze ruffled her hair against my cheek. I had my arm around her and I guess we looked like something out of one of those Norman Rockwell paintings.

I want to know all about you, Lorry said. I don't know anything. What was your childhood like?

I don't want to get into that kind of stuff, I said. Not now.

She didn't argue, just closed her eyes and let the breeze blow over us under that big Montana sky.

I sat there in the silent VW with her head pressing against my shoulder wondering if this was the karma that Kathleen Kelly told me I'd find here in Montana. Was this the answer to my problem! Was this what I came here for? And what about the future? Could I have a real future—a loving future—with Lorry Haines? A man like me?

Could I?

I started the engine of the VW, then headed back for the Interstate. We would have to live the future hour by hour, day by day.

And the compulsion. What about the killings? Maybe, with Lorry in my life, I could find a way to stop.

Maybe.

As a native Montanan, Lorry knew Great Falls. She was my own personal tour guide, telling me things as we drove.

Got its name, she said, from the Lewis and Clark Expedition when ole Meriwether Lewis walked out of camp one summer morning in 1805, following the sound of a tremendous roar along the river. That's when he discovered what he called The Great Falls of the Missouri. Big dam is there now.

Is it still worth looking at? I asked Lorry.

You bet, she said. It's a sight, lemme tell you.

You know, I told her, I've always had a yen to go white water rafting down the Colorado River, along the Grand Canyon and all.

Sounds like fun. We can do it together, she said.

The scenery around us was postcard perfect. Off to the west the Rockies took a hike into the sky and to the east were vast wheat fields and rolling prairies.

How big is Great Falls? I asked.

Pretty big, for Montana, she said. More than seventy thousand, last time I heard. People just like the location, the way it's set between Glacier and Yellowstone. And the winters are not at all that bad here, because of the chinooks.

The what?

Warm winds that blow down off the slopes of the rockies. You never heard of 'em?

Never, I said.

Now we were into town, with Lorry pointing out various sights as we drove past.

That's the Russell Museum, she said. You know, the famous western artist, Charles M. Russell. He lived here in Great Falls. His paintings are worth a fortune.

I think I've seen some of his stuff, I said.

This would be a nice place to raise kids, Lorry said.

I never wanted kids, I told her, my voice taking on a sharp note. If you're looking to have kids by me, you've got the wrong stud.

Hey, don't take everything so personal, she said. I was just talking about what kind of a place this is. It's a *family* kind of town.

What about you, I asked. Did you ever want children?

I guess every woman wants children at some time—but I don't think I'd make a very good mother, she said.

Maybe not, I said.

We found a motel with a long wooden hitching rail in front and three big plaster horses hitched to it. The place was called (you guessed it) The Hitching Post. Another touch of the Old West.

We booked a room there and spent most of the afternoon having sex.

Lorry was great in bed. I'd never felt so free before when I'd been with a woman. With her, everything was different. Easier. More comfortable. And a whole lot more fun.

We had a TV in our room and Lorry was watching the news when I came out of the bathroom, rubbing my head with a towel. They had a picture of the Big Sky Strangler on the screen. I threw the towel aside and sat down on the bed, staring at the composite drawing, asking myself, does it really look like me? How *much* does it look like me?

I don't know how they expect to catch the guy from that sketch, Lorry said. It could be any one of ten thousand guys. What they need is a big scar on his cheek, or a harelip, or something.

I was calm. Inside me, there was no feeling of connection with the news story.

The anchorwoman was talking about how police throughout Montana were looking for the killer.

How do they know he's still in Montana? I said. The guy could be halfway across the country by now.

Lorry didn't reply. She was listening as the woman reported that authorities figured that the same killer was responsible for another murder. The police had discovered the strangled body of a 12-year-old girl in Dodson, not for from Malta. She'd been dumped in a trash bin behind a drugstore.

When they showed the little girl's photo I jumped from the bed, walked over and snapped off the television set. I was furious and my heart was pumping fast.

Lorry complained. Hey! I was watching that. What's wrong with you? Why did you turn it off?

My hands were fisted. I was half-shouting at her. Because they're lying! That . . . guy they're after . . . he'd *never* kill a 12-year-old!

Lorry stared at me. How do *you* know?

I hesitated. I realized that my sudden anger had put me in a tricky spot with her. I took in a couple of deep breaths to steady myself.

Well . . . because . . . his other victims were all much older. Why would he start killing children? It doesn't fit his pattern.

Lorry shook her head. Who knows what a crazy person is going to do next? she said. I can't understand why you're so upset.

I . . . I just get emotionally involved with this kind of thing. I don't like the way they exploit these deaths.

Murder is news, she said. When a serial killer is on the loose, people deserve to know. They *need* to, for their own self-protection.

What are they gonna do—carry guns around? I asked.

People deserve to know, Lorry insisted. Now can we watch the rest of the news?

Sure, I said, slumping into a chair. I felt exhausted, drained of energy.

I'd have to be more careful around Lorry in the future.

That night I had another dream. Another nightmare. About being down in Mexico (where I've never been) and walking naked over this landscape of dead trees and broken brush—like after an atomic blast, and having one tree look like its head had been ripped off. It had long, clutching arms with dead bark clinging to them like pieces of black skin and one arm had a hand on it, like one of my hands. A strangler's hand. In the dream I stumbled over a rock, and the tree's dead hand closed over my neck. I could feel it tightening around my windpipe and I could feel the sharp-edged bark digging into my skin like razor blades.

And that's when the dream ended.

The next morning we went out to sell the VW. Lorry had a pretty fair idea of what the car was worth, even as old as it was, and she didn't like what the first two used car lots offered her for it.

These VWs can run forever, she told me. This one's in real sharp condition. Engine had a complete overhaul last year. Got another hundred thousand miles in it at least.

Then we saw this lot with big coloured banners and a blinking neon sign:

FRED FARLEY IS FAIR!
TOP DOLLAR FOR YOUR CAR!
YOU CAN TRUST FAIR FREDDY!

Pull in here, Lorry told me.

I did, and by the time I'd cut the engine a tall skinny guy in a dark business suit topped by a white ten-gallon hat comes out of this wooden shack to look at the VW. He's all smiles.

Howdy there, folks! I'm Fred Farley. They call me Fair Freddy.

He didn't impress me much. Just another cheap huckster.

I wandered around the lot looking at the cars he had for sale while Lorry talked to him about the VW. Some of the cars looked okay, but there were plenty of junkers. When I got back to Lorry she was shaking hands with Farley. They both seemed satisfied.

We've made a deal, she told me. Mr Farley says he'll swap even—my VW for the red Mazda pickup. What do you think?

Okay with me, I said.

As she was filling out the paperwork inside the shack I sized up the Mazda. I didn't like the bench-type front seat. Her legs were shorter than mine, which meant that when she drove, my knees would be in my face. And there was a big dent in the front right fender, and quite a bit of rust along the bottom of the driver's door. But I didn't complain. Anything was better than driving Ted Bundy's VW. That's how I thought of it, as *his*. If she'd traded it for a hay wagon I would have kept my mouth shut.

We were moving along the Missouri River and Lorry was driving the pickup. It had more snap than the bug but it was still sluggish. And the front seat *was* uncomfortable.

You look kinda sour, Lorry said. I hope you're not gonna tell me the Boston Strangler drove a Mazda.

I grinned. Lorry could be pretty funny and I admired her sense of humor.

It's not the pickup, I told her. There's nothing wrong with it.

Then what's bugging you?

I'm hungry, I said.

I was, but that wasn't what was bothering me. I'd been fighting back the compulsion all morning. It was spreading inside me, growing like a kind of dark fungus, getting more intense with each passing hour.

I guess that's the way a heroin addict feels when the need for a fix begins to take over his body. The feeling just kind of overwhelms everything else.

What worried me—and still worries me as I write these words—is that instead of lessening after each kill, the compulsion was coming back stronger than before. As if each time I killed someone I was feeding it, making it grow.

For the first time since I came to Montana I wondered if I *could* control this disorder of mine.

Which is really frightening to consider.

We found a cheap, family-type steak house and Lorry ordered a T-bone while I ordered a tuna salad.

Is that all you're going to eat? she asked me. I thought you were hungry.

I am, I told her, but I decided just this week to quit eating dead animals. That's what steak is, you know. A dead cow.

That's crazy! she snapped. Tuna is *fish*. They're animals, too. And they're dead as any cow right there in your salad.

It's not the same, I said. They fill cows with all kinds of chemicals in their food. You can get cancer and heart trouble and all kinds of other diseases from eating meat. And the animal fat is almost pure cholesterol. It's a scientific fact that vegetarians have the best health of anybody. I've been giving the whole thing a lot of thought lately and I've decided not to eat any more steaks or hamburgers or bacon or ham. It's a decision I made.

You're a weird dude, Eddie, she said.

There's nothing weird about not eating meat, I said. A lot of people are becoming vegetarians now. It's in the magazines and newspapers and on the news and everything. I just want to be healthy and live to be a hundred years old.

Don't we all? she said. Well, she added, not actually a hundred. That's too old, and nobody wants to be a walking corpse.

She ordered strawberry ice cream for dessert. As she was eating it she looked up at me. You don't trust me, do you? she said.

Why do you say that?

If you trusted me, you'd tell me what's been bugging you. Ever since we got to Great Falls, something has been bugging you. I got rid of the VW, so it can't be that.

I'm just a little tired, I said. Then I grinned at her, trying for some lightness. I've been in bed a lot, I said, but I haven't been sleeping much.

She grinned back.

And rubbed her hand over my crotch.

We were parked at a spot overlooking the Missouri River. No other cars around. The sky above us was like an immense sheet of black punched through with stars. Below us, we could hear the sound of water going past.

Lorry had her head against my shoulder and I could smell the fresh-washed scent of her hair. I would have been enjoying it, except for what was building up inside me.

The compulsion.

You picked the wrong guy to travel with, I finally said. My voice was soft and sad.

Lorry raised her head to look at me. Her eyes burned like jewels in the darkness. I picked the *right* guy, she said.

If you knew me—really knew me—you wouldn't say that, I told her honestly.

So what should I know about you?

The darkness roiling up inside me was blacker than the sky. A whole universe of pressure was engulfing me, commanding me. I couldn't fight it anymore.

I'm him, I said softly.

Him? She shifted in the seat, sitting up straight. What are you talking about?

The one they're looking for. The one on TV and in the papers. I'm him.

There was a long, strained moment of silence. Lorry's eyes got real intense and I could feel her muscles tighten underneath her clothes. She edged back from me.

Why are you doing this? she asked. Why are you trying to scare me? I don't like it and it's not funny.

I'm not trying to be funny, I said in the darkness.

Her eyes were wide now. She blinked rapidly. This is for *real*?

For real, I said.

You're—

—the Big Sky Strangler. I finished the sentence for her.

Lorry threw open the Mazda door and jumped out. She began to run along the grass toward the main highway, about a half-mile from where we were parked.

She wasn't hard to catch. Most women aren't. They just don't run the way a man does. Besides, I'm fast. I can move like a lizard when I've a mind to. I caught her before she'd gone five hundred yards.

I grabbed her by the throat, my thumbs in place, ready to dig in. She was shaking and sobbing. Killing her would be easy.

But Lorry was a surprising woman. Suddenly she brought up her right knee in a hard, swift arc and got me right in the balls. I doubled over, gasping, as waves of pain rippled through me.

You sick bastard! she screamed. She ran back towards the Mazda.

By the time I got there, still dizzy with pain, she'd managed to start the engine and was about to drive off. I grabbed through the open window, fumbling for the ignition key, as she tried to slap my hands away.

Then she lashed out with a fist, catching me a good one across the face. I felt blood running from my mouth. It tasted salty.

Bastard! Bastard! Bastard! She kept screaming the word at me as I got the door open and dragged her out. I got her arms pinned, but she was kicking wildly.

I really like you, I told her, spinning her around and punching her in the stomach. Her breath puffed out in a grunt as she collapsed forward.

I mean it, I said. I think the two of us share a very special chemistry. And you're great in the sack.

She used the "f" word on me, which kind of ruined things. By then I had my thumbs in her throat. She began clawing at me, but I was a lot stronger and it didn't take long to kill her.

I felt the power.

I was just sorry that it had to be Lorry.

I dumped her in the Missouri River with the idea that she'd be carried to the bottom and that no one would find her body. To make sure, I tied the Mazda's heavy iron tire jack to her waist. I guess I didn't do such a great job of it because when her body hit the water I saw the rope come untied. The tire jack sank while she floated on downriver with the current.

I'd botched the job. I'd been nervous and too hasty and I'd botched it.

I knew one thing: I had to get out of Great Falls. Fast. Before anybody found Lorry Haines.

I drove the Mazda out of town a few miles and left it in a wheat field. I couldn't keep driving it because I didn't know when Lorry's body would be found. When it was—when Lorry's picture was printed in the paper—Fred Farley would remember he'd sold her the Mazda and then the police would be looking for it. Better to be on the safe side and get rid of it early.

I mourned Lorry. I missed her. We'd had a really good relationship, the best of my life up to now. But I'd given in to the compulsion and killed her. I didn't want to do that. I wanted us to have a life together. But I went ahead and killed her anyway.

Which meant I didn't have any real control left at all.

Not any at all.

DAVID STARKEY

Ready

DAVID STARKEY was born in Wytheville, Virginia, and has lived in Virginia all his life—"generally in rural, 'back-woodsy' kinds of places". His first short story was published in *Twisted* No.1 in 1985, since when he has appeared in *Grue, Fantasy Macabre, 2AM, Noctulpa, Deathrealm, Ouroboros, The Mage, Portents* and *Z Miscellaneous*.

His story "W. D." was reprinted in the anthology *Tales By Moonlight II*, and he has fiction upcoming in *Grue, Tales of the Unanticipated, Doppelganger* and *Iniquities*.

Another non-supernatural horror story, "Ready" builds to a truly shocking denouement.

READY

I T DIDN'T ACTUALLY START with the neighbor's dog.
Something was there from the very beginning. Inside. Waiting.
All it needed was the right opportunity.

I've been out of high school for a good while now. And college is
a few years behind me. I lived at home during college, thank God.
Lord, the temptations that lurked on that campus. Thank God I had
the shelter of my own parents' Southern Baptist walls to protect me
from all that.

But now, I'm on my own. As it should be. It's family tradition:
when a boy grows up, he leaves the nest, finds his own place, learns
what it means to be a man standing on his own.

For me, it meant going to work in a town far away. Coming back
to my apartment alone. Channelling persistent urges into writing the
sort of poems that would have killed my mother if she ever saw as
much as half a stanza.

But I'd been keeping myself clean. Living with my thoughts.
Managing to keep myself away from the lure of opportunity—at
least until it moved in right beside me.

He moved in while I was away at work one day. And that same
night, I heard him through my bedroom wall.

He was beating his dog.

I remember breaking out in a cold sweat. My stomach got tight,
and hot, as though I'd just eaten a steaming plate of spicy meat,
and my mouth got dry, and then it filled with saliva, and then it
got dry again.

That first night, I wanted him to quit. I wanted to *make* him quit.
But after the second night, and the third, and he still kept at it, I
grew less and less sure about what I wanted.

I figured he was using his belt, or the dog's leash, from the sound
of things. The wall between my apartment and his was thin, and after
I got home from a day on the automotive assembly line, all I wanted
to do was eat my TV dinner, write a poem or two, drink my sixpack
of Pabst in front of the tube, and go to bed.

That's when he usually started. Generally I'd be lying there in
bed, my eyes wide open, waiting, waiting for him to do it.

Most of the time he would.

I'd hear the sound of a door slam, like he was closing the dog up
inside one of the rooms in his apartment. I could only guess what
room he was closing up, but I figured that all these apartments were
pretty much alike, so I was pretty sure it had to be his bedroom.

"God damn dog," I'd hear him say. And then I'd hear a slap, like
a leather strap hitting flesh, and the dog would yelp.

He usually kept it up about half an hour. Slap! Yelp! Slap! Yelp! "God damn dog!" I'd hear him say. "God damn *stupid* dog!"

By the time he'd quit, it would usually be around 11:30 or so, and my heart would be racing. I'd be practically shivering. I felt like I had intimate knowledge of the most amazing thing in the world, and that it was going on right next door. This terrifyingly amazing monstrous thing. It began to hold an endless and sordid fascination for me. It aroused intense feelings of disgust, and, something else. I wanted to know if the dog bled, for instance. I wanted to know if he hit it hard enough to make it bleed. My stomach would be killing me when he stopped for the night. Hurting real bad.

I'd get out of bed and piss, and chug some Pepto, and sit there at my dining room table 'til the pain eased up a bit. Sometimes I thought about calling the police, or the SPCA. Having them take away that man's poor dog.

But I kept telling myself that I didn't want to get involved in any of it. That guy. His dog. The beating. And anyway, calling the police or the SPCA, that sounded like something some nerdy kid would do. One of those slimy tattletale kind of kids everybody knew in school. One of those creepy wimps that would never *do* anything about a problem himself, but just run and tell the god-damned teacher.

So I didn't call.

What I did was this: I made a decision. I decided that if I wanted to do something about that guy and his dog, then I was going to do it myself.

It was getting pretty rough staying up past midnight most every night and getting up for work at 5:30. And even for those few hours I slept, I didn't sleep well. I tossed and turned, wondering when I was finally gonna do it. Wondering when I was finally gonna get up the nerve to go over there.

I was getting real curious, too. I'd never seen the dog—not once, and I hadn't seen the man either. It was pretty weird, his living right next door and everything. But he'd been living there a full five weeks and I'd never seen either him or his dog.

Yep, I'd have to say I was getting *real* curious.

Was he an old man? Or a young man? Some big stupid jerk with a beer belly hanging over the top of his pants? Or some skinny faggy-looking little elementary school teacher who took out all his frustrations on his poor dog? And was the dog big? Or little? It was hard to tell from just a yelp. But I guess it sounded like a pretty big dog. But something real good-tempered. Something that would take a beating without ever fighting back. A retriever of some kind, maybe.

Labrador or Golden. Or maybe a setter. One of those nice red Irish Setters. They've got a real sweet disposition, or so I've heard. You could probably beat one of those setters for half an hour every night and afterwards it'd come crawling over and lick your hands.

The whole thing was making me kind of sick. Jittery. When my stomach wasn't aching outright, it felt real hollow, real odd. And even though my stomach hurt like hell, I felt hungry most of the time. But food didn't seem to fill me up. I just kept feeling hungry all the time. And I kept getting more and more curious about what that bastard looked like, and what kind of dog he had.

Finally, I couldn't take it any longer. It was Wednesday night. I was half dead. I needed some sleep. And that son-of-a-bitch started in on his goddamn dog.

What was wrong with the *other* people in this place, anyway? Why didn't one of *them* do something? But, after all, his bedroom was right next to mine. So I'm sure I could hear what was going on in there lots better than anybody else. And I knew there was all this fire-wall stuff between the floors; that stuff kept pretty much all the noise from traveling to the rooms above and the rooms below. I was probably the only one in the whole crappy building who knew what he was up to.

More and more, it seemed like it was my responsibility to do something about it. But I kept hesitating and hesitating, holding off, as if I was afraid of something. As if I was afraid I might learn something I'd just as soon not know.

But I really needed some sleep.

And, dammit, I wanted to at least find out what that guy and his dog looked like.

So, that Wednesday night, after he'd been beating the blasted dog for a good solid ten minutes, I jumped out of bed.

I put on my blue jeans and a T-shirt. And my tennis shoes.

And I stomped into the hallway and pounded on his door.

At first he didn't answer. But then I heard him coming toward the door. He walked fast, and when he opened the door, he didn't hesitate. He pulled it the whole way open, all at once.

And he was all smiles.

This nice-looking guy. About twenty-five years old. Tall. Blue eyes. Blonde hair. Mr Normal. Mr All-American.

"Hi," I said. "I'm Mike Turner. Your next door neighbor."

"Hello," he said. He smiled even wider, even warmer, like he recognized an old friend, somebody he could have gone to school with—he looked like he was about the same age as me. He had great teeth, really white. He looked like Mr Success. He was wearing a light gray suit that looked really smart. Great fit.

"I'm Jerry," he said. "Jerry Rose. Come on in. Nice to meet you."

He extended his hand, and I shook it. He had a good grip. Firm. Proper. He looked me right in the eye.

This all seemed too weird for me. It seemed wrong—like I had the wrong guy. This guy didn't seem like a weirdo. He didn't seem like a guy who would beat his dog. I glanced down the hallway to make sure I'd gone to the right apartment, to make sure I hadn't gotten his place mixed up with the one next door. Nope. This was the one, all right.

I stepped inside, and he closed the door behind me. His place was clean, comfortable, normal-looking. White walls with half a dozen watercolor landscapes, a tannish-brown sofa and matching easy chair in the living room, a nice glass-and-dark-wood dinette set in the dining room. House plants in all the right places. My apartment didn't look bad, but his place definitely looked better—classier, if you know what I mean.

"So, Mike," he said. "You're my neighbor, huh?"

"Yeah," I said.

"Up kind of late, aren't you?" he asked.

I saw him glance toward a closed door—it had to be his bedroom door. The layout of everything else I could see was a mirror-image of my own place. His bedroom was bound to be on the wall directly across from my bedroom.

"Yeah," I said. "I know it's kinda late. But I was having a tough time getting to sleep."

"Really," he said. "Hey, I'm sorry about that. You ought to do what I do."

And then he opened the bedroom door.

"Come on in," he said.

Just like that.

"What?" I said.

"In *here*," he said. "I'll show you what you came to see."

I followed him into his bedroom.

The dog was lying in the corner.

"Bingo," I thought. "Golden Retriever."

The dog stood up when we walked in. It stayed in the same spot, standing on top of several big old towels that had been spread across the floor. Its tan fur was streaked with blood. One eye was swollen closed. It breathed in a raspy, whimpering kind of gasp, as if its throat was full of blood and mucus.

Jerry lifted a belt from the top of his chest-of-drawers and handed it to me.

"Go ahead," he told me. "You'll feel lots better. You'll sleep like a baby afterwards. Go on."

I stood looking at him, and at the dog. He picked up the leash. It was bloody, cracked, worn with use.

I felt that hot-steamy-meat feeling in the pit of my stomach. I broke out in a sweat. My mouth got dry.

He struck the dog across the face with the leash. The dog yelped once. But it didn't try to get away. It just stood there.

"Go *on*," Jerry said. "Use the belt."

Water was running from between the lids of the dog's swollen eye. The damn dog looked disgusting. Standing there like that. Not fighting back. Not even trying to get away.

I realized just how easy it would be.

Stupid mutt, I thought. Why didn't it try to get away?

What would it *feel like* to hit a helpless piece of living flesh, I wondered. It wasn't the first time I'd wondered such a thing, I'll readily admit. But to have it made so easy, to have everything I needed right here in front of me . . .

This was one of those opportunities I'd never wanted to actually have, wasn't it? A chance to find something out about myself. A chance to feel something I'd never felt, but had just wondered about, quietly, all by myself, for a hell of a long time.

Still I hesitated.

"Go ahead," said Jerry. "There's plenty of dog for the both of us."

Maybe just once, I thought. Just so I'll know how it makes me feel. Just so I won't ever have to wonder about it again.

I hit it. A hard slap right across its skinny butt.

It yelped once. And stood waiting for more.

I felt strange. Appalled at myself. But fascinated with everything about the situation. I'd done it. I'd inflicted pain for the sheer curiosity of it—for no other reason than I'd finally had the opportunity to do it.

Jerry smiled. He flashed All-American teeth straight and clean and white. "God damn dog," he said.

He hit it again.

And so did I. It yelped. And I hit it again.

We both kept at it for about twenty minutes more.

Until we were both exhausted.

I dropped the belt. Jerry dropped the leash.

The beaten dog sank back to the floor, its mouth oozing saliva onto the blood-spotted towels.

I was shivering. And I had a hardon. I walked out of the bedroom, my hands pressed over the front of my pants to hide my embarrassment. I headed toward the door of Jerry's apartment. Jerry followed me as far as the living room.

"Feel better?" he asked.

I nodded.

"Then come back tomorrow," he said.

I guess I nodded again.

I went back to my apartment.

I closed the door.

I stripped off my clothes and stood in the shower. I jerked myself off, then let the bathroom fill up with steam. I soaped myself three times, and rinsed all the lather away each time. I dried off and went to bed. I think I may have cried a few tears, but I know I slept soundly, as if everything had been a dream.

I worked ten hours on the automotive line the next day. I kept thinking maybe it all really had been a dream. Knocking on Jerry's door. The dog. The belt. The leash. I went home in a daze. I ate a TV dinner. I wrote a filthy sexual poem, drank a sixpack. Stripped for bed.

But I didn't lie down.

Instead I pulled on my blue jeans, a T-shirt. My tennis shoes.

I went to Jerry's apartment, knocked on the door.

He opened it; again he was all smiles. Again he was dressed in a stylish suit—this one was dark gray.

"Mike!" he said. "Welcome! Ready for another round, eh?"

I nodded.

I felt a moment of doubt. Was I ready? What did I expect to get out of tonight? Was I just curious again? Did I wonder how I'd feel about beating a helpless animal for the second night in a row? Would it make me feel any different than I'd felt the first night? Would it make me feel anything at all? Had I really cried last night? Had I wept for the dog? Or myself? For just a moment, I wondered if I'd wept because I'd finally learned that all my old lonely thoughts were who I really was. They weren't harmless little whimsies from some innocuous and secret place destined to remain hidden forever. They were me. They were the stuff I was made of.

"Come on in!" Jerry said.

I walked into his apartment. He closed the door behind me.

I felt a little sick. But less sick than the night before.

As soon as I saw the dog, I picked up the leash. Jerry grabbed his belt.

I hit the dog first; then Jerry hit it. He aimed for the face. He loved to hit its face. I went for everything—its butt, its flanks, its neck, its big bloody nose.

The dog never tried to get away. Never tried to fight back. Its behavior infuriated me. Made me lash it harder. Made me take real pleasure at each and every pathetic yelp.

It was actually difficult to keep myself from kicking its head in.

When we were done, I threw down the belt and got ready to leave. But Jerry stopped me.

"I'm moving out tomorrow," he said. "The dog's yours. Take it with you tonight."

"I don't want it," I said.

"Don't lie to me. You want it. You want it a whole lot."

"But what about you?" I asked. "It's your dog."

"I'll find another," he said. "Go ahead. Take it."

So I scooped it up in my arms. I got its blood on my shirt, the front of my pants. Some of it stuck to the hair on my chest.

I carried it into my bedroom and lowered it onto the bare floor in a corner.

It whimpered once. I gave it a bowl of water. Some scraps of bread. It lapped them up slowly, gratefully, its one open eye looking at me with utter love and devotion. The expression on its pathetic face made me want to whack it a few times. But I just shrugged. I decided it had had enough for one night. Besides, I had a hardon that required immediate attention. When I got in the shower, I realized I had some of the dog's blood on my cock. I came while I was scrubbing it off—it felt like two tons of dynamite exploding.

Then I dried off and went to sleep.

I slept fine.

The next day, I put down a stack of newspapers for it to do its business on. But I've since found out that the damn thing knows how to use the toilet. It's one of those city dogs you hear about, one of those dogs that actually knows how to squat over the fucking toilet. The damn dog's nearly perfect. It's no trouble at all. Can you imagine that? It barely eats; it lies in its corner all day. It shits and pisses in the toilet. And it knows how to take a beating.

Anyhow, I went to work the morning after I brought it home. When I got back that night, I knocked on Jerry's door, just to see. There was no answer.

So I went back to my apartment and ate dinner. I watched TV, wrote a poem, drank a few beers, and beat the dog.

I beat it the next night too. And the next.

It's getting easier every night. Easier to accept everything I've learned about myself. Some nights I wake up crying, though. But not many. Only once during the past week.

I keep thinking some guy's gonna move into Jerry's old apartment. Some guy who'll hear what I'm doing to this poor dog. Some guy who'll think about calling the police or the SPCA. But who'll really want to resolve the problem himself.

Until he knocks on my door late one night and discovers what it is that he really wants.

I feel like all this has just been a warmup, ya know? I feel like once I've gotten rid of this damn dog, I'm gonna give up the bachelor life, find the right woman, pump up her belly with a kid or two.

Funny. Never seemed like I had a place in my heart for a wife and kids. But I feel different now.

I feel ready.

KARL EDWARD WAGNER

The Slug

KARL EDWARD WAGNER has been editing *The Year's Best Horror Stories* since volume VIII, and probably knows more about horror fiction than anyone else working in the genre today.

Recent projects include a graphic novel for DC Comics, *Tell Me, Dark*, with artist Kent Williams; a medical chiller, *The Fourth Seal*; *Satan's Gun*, a horror novel, and the reprinting of the *Year's Best* series as *HorrorStory* in multi-edition hardcovers.

A multiple winner of both the World Fantasy Award and the British Fantasy Award, Wagner reveals in his original afterword to this story in Ellen Datlow's *A Whisper of Blood* that "Every writer—every creative person—lives in dread of those nagging and inane interruptions that break the creative flow. A sentence perfectly crystalized, shattered by a stupid phone call, never regained. A morning filled with inspiration and energy, clogged by an uninvited guest, the day lost. The imaginative is the choice prey of the banal, and uncounted works of excellence have died stillborn thanks to junk phone calls and visits from bored associates.

"After all, a writer doesn't have a real job. Feel free to crash in at any time. Probably wants some company.

"Nothing in this story is in any way a reflection upon this one writer's various friends, nor does it in any way resemble any given actual person or composite of any persons known to the author. It is entirely a fictitious work and purely the product of the author's imagination.

"It has taken me five days to scribble out this afterword.

"There's the door . . ."

M ARTINE WAS HAMMERING AWAY TO THE accompaniment of Lou Reed, tapedeck set at stun, and at first didn't hear the knocking at her studio door. She set aside hammer and chisel, put Lou Reed on hold, and opened the door to discover Keenan Bauduret seated on her deck rail, leaning forward to pound determinedly at her door. The morning sun shone bright and cheery through the veil of pines, and Keenan was shit-faced drunk.

"Martine!" He lurched toward her. "I need a drink!"

"What you need is some coffee." Martine stood her ground. At six feet and change she was three inches taller than Keenan and in far better shape.

"Please! I've got to talk to someone." Keenan's soft brown eyes implored. He was disheveled and unshaven in baggy clothes that once had fit him, and Martine thought of a stray spaniel, damp and dirty, begging to be let in. And Keenan said: "I've just killed someone. I mean, something."

Martine stepped inside. "I can offer gin and orange juice."

"Just the gin."

Keenan Bauduret collapsed onto her wooden rocking chair and mopped at his face with a crumpled linen handkerchief, although the morning was not yet warm. Now he reminded her of Bruce Dern playing a dissolute southern lawyer, complete with out-of-fashion and rumpled suit; but in fact Keenan was a writer, although dissolute and southern to be sure. He was part of that sort of artist/writer colony that the sort of small university town such as Pine Hill attracts. Originally he was from New Orleans, and he was marking time writing mystery novels while he completed work on the Great Southern Novel. At times he taught creative writing for the university's evening college.

Martine had installed a wet bar complete with refrigerator and microwave in a corner of her studio to save the walk back into her house when she entertained here. She sculpted in stone, and the noise and dust were better kept away from her single-bedroom cottage. While Keenan sweated, she looked for glasses and ice.

"Just what was it you said that you'd killed?"

"A slug. A gross, obscene, mammoth, and predatory slug."

"Sounds rather like a job for Orkin. Did you want your gin neat?"

"Just the naked gin."

Martine made herself a very light gin screwdriver and poured a double shot of Tanqueray into Keenan's glass. Her last name was still McFerran, and she had her father's red hair, which she wore in a long ponytail, and his Irish blue eyes and freckled complexion. Her mother was Scottish and claimed that her side of the family was responsible for her daughter's unexpected height. Born in Belfast, Martine had grown up in Pine Hill as a faculty brat after her parents took university posts here to escape the troubles in Northern Ireland. Approaching the further reaches of thirty, Martine was content with her bachelorhood and her sculpture and had no desire to return to Belfast.

"Sure you don't want orange juice?" She handed the glass to Keenan.

Keenan shook his head. "To your very good health." He swallowed half the gin, closed his eyes, leaned back in the rocker and sighed. He did not, as Martine had expected, tip over.

Martine sat down carefully in her prized Windsor chair. She was wearing scuffed Reeboks, faded blue jeans, and a naturally torn university sweatshirt, and she pushed back her sleeves before tasting her drink.

"Now, then," she said, "tell me what really happened."

Keenan studied his gin with the eye of a man who is balancing his need to bolt the rest of it against the impropriety of asking for an immediate refill. Need won.

"Don't get up." He smiled graciously. "I know the way."

Martine watched him slosh another few ounces of gin into his glass, her own mood somewhere between annoyance and concern. She'd known Keenan Bauduret casually for years, well before he'd hit the skids. He was a few years older than she, well read and intelligent, and usually fun to be around. They'd never actually dated, but there were the inevitable meetings at parties and university town cultural events, lunches and dinners and a few drinks after. Keenan had never slept over, nor had she at his cluttered little house. It was that sort of respectful friendship that arises between two lonely people who are content within their self-isolation, venturing forth for nonthreatening companionship without ever sensing the need.

"I've cantelope in the fridge," Martine prompted.

"Thanks. I'm all right." Keenan returned to the rocker. He sipped his gin this time. His hands were no longer shaking. "How well do you know Casper Crowley?"

"Casper the Friendly Ghost?" Martine almost giggled. "Hardly at all. That is, I've met him at parties, but he never has anything to say to anyone. Just stands stuffing himself with chips and hors d'oeuvres—I've even seen him pocket a few beers as he's left. I'm told he's in a family business, but no one seems to know what that business is—and he writes books that no one I know has ever read for publishers no one has heard of. He's so dead dull boring that I always wonder why anyone ever invites him."

"I've seen him at your little gatherings," Keenan accused.

"Well, yes. It's just that I feel sorry for poor boring Casper."

"Exactly." Keenan stabbed a finger and rested his case. "That's what happened to me. You won't mind if I have another drink while I tell you about it?"

Martine sighed mentally and tried not to glance at her watch.

His greatest mistake, said Keenan, was ever to have invited Casper Crowley to drop by in the first place.

It began about two years ago. Keenan was punishing the beer keg at Greg Lafollette's annual birthday bash and pig-picking. He was by no means sober, or he never would have attempted to draw Casper into conversation. It was just that Casper stood there, wrapped in his customary loneliness, mechanically feeding his face with corn chips and salsa, washing it down with great gulps of beer, as expressionless as a carp taking bread crumbs from atop a pool.

"How's it going, Casper?" Keenan asked harmlessly.

Casper shaved his scalp but not his face, and he had bits of salsa in his bushy orange beard. He was wearing a tailored tweed suit whose vest strained desperately to contain his enormous beer gut. He turned his round, bland eyes toward Keenan and replied: "Do you know much about Aztec gods?"

"Not really, I suppose."

"In this book I'm working on," Casper pursued, "I'm trying to establish a link between the Aztecs and Nordic mythology."

"Well, I do have a few of the usual sagas stuck away on my shelves." Keenan was struggling to imagine any such link.

"Then would it be all right if I dropped by your place to look them over?"

And Casper appeared at ten the following morning, while Keenan was drying off from his shower, and he helped himself to coffee and doughnuts while Keenan dressed.

"Hope I'm not in your way." Casper was making a fresh pot of coffee.

"Not at all." Keenan normally worked mornings through the afternoon, and he had a pressing deadline.

But Casper plopped down on his couch and spent the next few hours leafing without visible comprehension through various of Keenan's books, soaking up coffee, and intermittently clearing his throat and swallowing horribly. Keenan no longer felt like working after his guest had finally left. Instead he made himself a fifth rum and Coke and fell asleep watching *I Love Lucy*.

At ten the following morning, Keenan had almost reworked his first sentence of the day when Casper phoned.

"Do you know why a tomcat licks his balls?"

Keenan admitted ignorance.

"Because he can!"

Casper chuckled with enormous relish at his own joke, while Keenan scowled at the phone. "How about going out to get some barbecue for lunch?" Casper then suggested.

"I'm afraid I'm really very busy just now."

"In that case," Casper persisted, "I'll just pick us up some sandwiches and bring them on over."

And he did. And Casper sat on Keenan's couch, wolfing down barbecue sandwiches with the precision of a garbage disposal, dribbling gobbets of sauce and cole slaw down his beard and belly and onto the upholstery. Keenan munched his soggy sandwich, reflecting upon the distinction between the German verbs, *essen* (to eat) and *fressen* (to devour). When Casper at last left, it was late afternoon, and Keenan took a nap that lasted past his usual dinnertime. By then the day had long since slipped away.

He awoke feeling bloated and lethargic the next morning, but he was resolved to make up for lost time. At ten-thirty Casper appeared on his doorstep, carrying a bag of chocolate-covered raspberry jelly doughnuts.

"Do you know how many mice it takes to screw in a light bulb?" Casper asked, helping himself to coffee.

"I'm afraid I don't."

"Two—but they have to be real small!" Jelly spurted down Casper's beard as he guffawed. Keenan had never before heard someone actually guffaw; he'd always assumed it was an exaggerated figure of speech.

Casper left after about two in the afternoon, unsuccessful in his efforts to coax Keenan into sharing a pizza with him. Keenan returned to his desk, but inspiration was dead.

And so the daily routine began.

"Why didn't you just tell him to stay away and let you work?" Martine interrupted.

"Easy enough to say," Keenan groaned. "At first I just felt sorry for him. OK, the guy is lonely—right? Anyway, I really was going to tell him to stop bugging me every day—and then I had my accident."

A rain-slick curve, a telephone pole, and Keenan's venerable VW Beetle was grist for the crusher. Keenan fared rather better, although his left foot would wear a plaster sock for some weeks after.

Casper came over daily with groceries and bottles of beer and rum. "Glad to be of help," he assured Keenan as he engulfed most of a slice of pepperoni-and-mushroom pizza. Sauce obscured his beard. "Must be tough having to hobble around day after day. Still, I'll bet you're getting a lot of writing done."

"Very little," Keenan grudgingly admitted. "Just haven't felt up to it lately."

"Guess you haven't. Hey, do you know what the difference is between a circus and a group of sorority girls out jogging?"

"I give up."

"Well, one is a cunning array of stunts!" Casper chortled and wiped red sauce from his mouth. "Guess I better have another beer after that one!"

Keenan missed one deadline, and then he missed another. He made excuses owing to his accident. Deadlines came around again. The one novel he did manage to finish came back with requests for major revisions. Keenan worked hard at the rewrite, but each new effort was only for the worse. He supposed he ought to cut down on his drinking, but the stress was keeping him awake nights, and he kept having nightmares wherein Casper crouched on his chest and snickered bad jokes and dribbled salsa. His agent sounded concerned, and his editors were losing patience.

"Me," said Casper, "I never have trouble writing. I've always got lots of ideas."

Keenan resisted screaming at the obese hulk who had camped on his sofa throughout the morning. Instead he asked civilly: "Oh? And what are you working on now?"

"A follow-up to my last book—by the way, my publisher really went ape-shit over that one, wants another like it. This time I'm writing one that traces the rise of Nazi Germany to the Druidic rites at Stonehenge."

"You seem to be well versed in the occult," observed Keenan, repressing an urge to vomit.

"I do a lot of research," Casper explained. "Besides, it's in my blood. Did I ever tell you that I'm related to Aleister Crowley?"

"No."

"Well, I am." Casper beamed with secret pride.

"I should have guessed."

"Well, the name, of course."

Keenan had been thinking of other similarities. "Well, I really do need to get some work done now."

"Sure you don't need me to run you somewhere?"

"No, thank you. The ankle is a little sore, but I can get around well enough."

At the door, Casper persisted: "Sure you don't want to go get some barbecue?"

"Very sure."

Casper pointed toward the rusted-out Chevy wagon in Keenan's driveway. "Well, if that heap won't start again, just give me a call."

"I put in a new battery," Keenan said, remembering that the mechanic had warned him about the starter motor. Keenan had bought the clunker for three hundred bucks—from a student. He needed wheels, and wheels were about all that did work on the rust-bucket. His insurance hadn't covered replacement for his antique Beetle.

"Heard you had to return your advance on that Zenith contract."

"Where'd you hear that?" Keenan wanted to use his fists.

"My editor—your old editor—brought it up when we were talking contract on my new book the other day. She said for me to check out how you were getting along. Sounded concerned. But I told her you were doing great, despite all the talk."

"Thanks for that much."

"Hey, you know the difference between a sorority girl and a bowling ball?"

Keenan did not trust himself to speak.

"No? Well, you can't stuff a sorority girl into a bowling ball!"

After the university informed Mr Bauduret that his services would no longer be required as instructor of creative writing at the evening college, Keenan began to sell off his books and a few antiques. It kept the wolves at arm's length, and it paid for six-packs. Editors no longer phoned, and his agent no longer answered his calls.

Casper was sympathetic, and he regularly carried over doughnuts and instant coffee, which he consumed while drinking Keenan's beer.

"Zenith gobbled up *Nazi Druids*," he told Keenan. "They can't wait for more."

The light in Keenan's eyes was not the look of a sane man. "So, what's next?"

"I got an idea. I've discovered a tie-in between flying saucers and the Salem witch burnings."

"They hanged them. Or pressed them. No burnings in this country."

"Whatever. Anyway, I bought a bunch of your old books on the subject at the Book Barn the other day. Guess I won't need to borrow them now."

"Guess not."

"Hey, you want some Mexican for lunch? I'll pay."

"Thank you, but I have some work to do."

"Good to see you're still slugging away."

"Not finished yet."

"Guess some guys don't know when they're licked."

"Guess not."

"Hey"—Caster chugged his beer—"you know what the mating cry of a sorority girl is?"

Keenan gritted his teeth in a hideous grin.

Continued Casper in girlish falsetto: "Oh, I'm so-o-o drunk!" His belly shook with laughter, although he wasn't Santa. "Better have another beer on that one!"

And he sat there on the couch, methodically working his way through Keenan's stock of beer, as slowly mobile and slimy gross as a huge slug feasting its way across the garden. Keenan listened to his snorts and belches, to his puerile and obscene jokes, to his pointless and inane conversation, too drained and too weak to beg him to leave. Instead he swallowed his beer and his bile, and fires of loathing stirred beneath the ashes of his despair.

That night Keenan found the last bottle of rum he'd hidden away against when the shakes came at dawn, and he dug out the vast file of typed pages, containing all the fits and starts and notes and revisions and disconnected chapters that were the entirety of his years' efforts toward the Great Southern Novel.

He had a small patio, surrounded by a neglected rock garden and close-shouldering oak trees, and he heaped an entire bag of charcoal into the barbecue grill that rusted there. Then Keenan sipped from the bottle of Myers's, waiting for the coals to take light. When the coals had reached their peak, Keenan Bauduret fed his manuscript, page by crumpled page, onto the fire; watched each page flame and char, rise in dying ashes into the night.

"That was when I knew I had to kill Casper Crowley."

Martine wasn't certain whether she was meant to laugh now. "Kill Casper? But he was only trying to be your friend! I'm sure you can find a way to ask him to give you your space without hurting his feelings."

Keenan laughed instead. He poured out the last of her gin. "A friend? Casper was a giant grotesque slug! He was a gross leech that sucked out my creative energy! He fed off me and watched over me with secret delight as I wasted away!"

"That's rather strong."

"From the first day the slug showed up on my doorstep, I could never concentrate on my work. When I did manage to write, all I could squeeze out was dead, boring, lifeless drivel. I don't blame my publishers for sending it back!"

Martine sighed, wondering how to express herself. She did rather like Keenan; she certainly felt pity for him now. "Keenan, I don't want to get you upset, but you have been drinking an awful lot this past year or so . . ."

"Upset?" Keenan broke into a wild grin and a worse laugh, then suddenly regained his composure. "No need for me to be upset now. I've killed him."

"And how did you manage that?" Martine was beginning to feel uneasy.

"How do you kill a slug?"

"I thought you said he was a leech."

"They're one and the same."

"No they're not."

"Yes they are. Gross, bloated, slimy things. Anyway, the remedy is the same."

"I'm not sure I'm following you."

"Salt." Keenan seemed in complete control now. "They can't stand salt."

"I see." Martine relaxed and prepared herself for the joke.

Keenan became very matter-of-fact. "Of course, I didn't forget the beer. Slugs are drawn to beer. I bought many six-packs of imported beer. Then I prepared an enormous barbecue feast—chickens, ribs, pork loin. Casper couldn't hold himself back."

"So you pushed his cholesterol over the top, and he died of a massive coronary."

"Slugs can't overeat. It was the beer. He drank and drank and drank some more, and then he passed out on the patio lounge chair. That was my chance."

"A steak through the heart?"

"Salt. I'd bought dozens of bags of rock salt for this. Once Casper was snoring away, I carried them out of my station wagon and ripped them open. Then, before he could awaken, I quickly dumped the whole lot over Casper."

"I'll bet Casper didn't enjoy that."

"He didn't. At first I was afraid he'd break away, but I kept pouring the rock salt over him. He never said a word. He just writhed all about on the lounge chair, flinging his little arms and legs all about, trying to fend off the salt."

Keenan paused and swallowed the last of the gin. He wiped his face and shuddered. "And then he began to shrivel up."

"Shrivel up?"

"The way slugs do when you pour salt on them. Don't you remember? Remember doing it when you were a kid? He just started to shrivel and shrink. And shrink and shrink. Until there was nothing much left. Just a dried-out twist of slime. No bones. Just dried slime."

"I see."

"But the worst part was the look in his eyes, just before they withered on the ends of their stalks. He stared right into my eyes, and I could sense the terrible rage as he died."

"Stalks?"

"Yes. Casper Crowley sort of changed as he shriveled away."

"Well. What did you do then?"

"Very little to clean up. Just dried slime and some clothes. I waited through the night, and this morning I burned it all on the barbecue grill. Wasn't much left, but it sure stank."

Keenan looked at his empty glass, then glanced hopefully at the empty bottle. "So now it's over. I'm free."

"Well," said Martine, ignoring his imploring gaze, "I can certainly see that you've regained your imagination."

"Best be motivating on home now, I guess." Keenan stood up, with rather less stumbling than Martine had anticipated. "Thanks for listening to my strange little story. Guess I didn't expect you to believe it all, but I had to talk to someone."

"Why not drive carefully home and get some sleep," Martine advised, ushering him to the door. "This has certainly been an interesting morning."

Keenan hung on to the door. "Thanks again, Martine. I'll do just that. Hey, what do you say I treat you to Chinese tomorrow for lunch? I really feel a whole lot better after talking to you."

Martine felt panic, then remorse. "Well, I am awfully busy just now, but I guess I can take a break for lunch."

Martine sat back down after Keenan had left. She was seriously troubled, wondering whether she ought to phone Casper Crowley. Clearly Keenan was drinking far too heavily; he might well be harboring some resentment. But harm anyone . . . No way. Just some unfunny attempt at a shaggy dog story. Keenan never could tell jokes.

When she finally did phone Casper Crowley, all she got was his answering machine.

Martine felt strangely lethargic—her morning derailed by Keenan's bursting in with his inane patter. Still, she thought she really should get some work done on her sculpture.

She paused before the almost finished marble, hammer and chisel at ready, her mind utterly devoid of inspiration. She was working on a bust of a young woman—the proverbial artist's self-portrait. Martine squared her shoulders and set chisel to the base of the marble throat.

As the hammer struck, the marble cracked through to the base.

MICHAEL MARSHALL SMITH

The Dark Land

1991 WAS A good year for Michael Marshall Smith. Not only did his story "The Man Who Drew Cats" win the British Fantasy Award for Best Short Story, but he was also presented with the Icarus Award for Best Newcomer.

Smith was born in Knutsford, Cheshire, and grew up in the United States, South Africa and Australia, before returning with his family to England in 1975. His stories have appeared in *Dark Voices 2* and *4*, *Darklands 1* and *2*, and *Best New Horror 2*, and his first novel, *Only Forward*, will be published by HarperCollins in 1993. He is currently working on more short stories, gearing up for a second novel, co-writing a situation comedy for BBC-TV and developing a feature treatment based loosely on the very strange story that follows . . .

FOR WANT OF ANYTHING BETTER TO DO, and in the spirit that keeps my room austerely tidy when there are other things I should be doing, I decided to move my bed. After returning from college I'd redecorated my room, as it had been the same since I'd been about ten, and I'd moved just about everything round except for the bed. I knew it was largely an excuse for not doing anything more constructive but pulled it away from the wall and tried it in another couple of positions.

It was hard work, as one of the legs is rather fragile and the thing had to be virtually lifted off the floor, and after half an hour I was hot and irritated and becoming more and more convinced that its original position had been the optimal, and indeed the only, place to put it. And it was as I struggled to shove it back up against the wall that I began to feel a bit strange. When it was finally back in place I sat down on it, feeling light-headed and a bit ill and I suppose basically I just drifted off to sleep.

I don't know if the bed is part of it in some way. I only mention it because it seems important, and because I guess that it was while I was asleep on it that it all began. After a while I woke up, half-remembering a dream in which I had been doing nothing more than lying on my bed remembering that my parents had said that they were going to extend the wood panelling on the downstairs hall walls. For a few moments I was disorientated, confused by being in the same place in reality as I had been in the dream, and then I drifted off again.

Some time later I awoke again, feeling very sluggish and slightly nauseous. I found it very difficult to haul my mind up from sleep, but eventually stood up and lurched across the room to the sink to get a glass of water, rubbing my eyes and feeling very rough. Maybe I was going down with something. I decided that a cup of tea would be a good idea, and headed out of the bedroom to go downstairs to the kitchen to make one.

As I reached the top of the stairs I remembered the dream about the panelling and wondered vaguely where a strange idea like that could have come from. I'd worked hard for my psychology paper at college, and was fairly confident that Freud hadn't felt that wood panelling was even worth a mention. I trudged downstairs, still feeling a bit strange, my thoughts dislocated and confused.

Then I stopped, open-mouthed, and stared around me. They really *had* extended the panelling. It used to only go about eight feet up the wall, but it now soared right up to the front hall ceiling, which is two floors high. And they'd done it in exactly the same wood as the original panelling: there wasn't a join to be seen. How the hell had they managed that? Come to that, *when* the hell had they managed that? It hadn't been there that morning, both my parents were at work and would be for hours and . . . well, it was just impossible, wasn't it? I reached out and touched the wood, marvelling at how even the grain was the same, and that the new wood looked just as aged as the original, which had been there fifty years.

As I struggled to get my still sluggish mind in gear surprise suddenly gave way to astonishment. Wait a minute, I thought, that isn't right. There hadn't used to be *any* panelling in the hall. It used just to be white walls. Sure, the stairs were panelled in wood, but the walls were just plain white plaster. How the hell could I have forgotten that? What had made me think that the front hall had been panelled, and think it so unquestioningly? I could now remember that I'd recently noticed, sensitised to these things as I was by having recently repainted my room, that the white paint in the hall was rather dirty, especially round the light switches. So what was all this panelling doing here? Where had it come from, and when, for Christ's sake? And why had I been so sure that at least some of it had always been there?

I walked slowly into the kitchen, casting bewildered backward glances at the walls. I heard a soft clinking sound outside and walked to the back door, too puzzled about the front hall to even notice that it was rather late for a milk delivery. The back door, which like the front door opens out onto the driveway, is in a little corridor full of gardening implements, shoes and tools which leads off the kitchen to the garage. I threaded my way through these and wrenched the stiff door open.

As soon as it was open I reeled backwards from the light and unthinkingly crouched just inside the back hall. Then I realised that it wasn't even that bright outside: it was late afternoon and the light was muted, but everything seemed very intense, like colours before a storm. Odd, but not odd enough to throw yourself to the ground over, I thought as I stood up. But it had been the milkman after all, for there was our milk bottle holder with four bottles of milk in it. Only they weren't milk bottles, but large American-style quart containers somehow jammed into slots meant to take pints. And someone had taken the silver tops off.

Something at the edge of my vision caught my attention and I looked up towards the top of the driveway. There, about thirty yards away, were two children, one fat and on a bike, the other slim and standing. I was seized with a sudden irrational fury and started quickly up the drive towards them, convinced that the clinking sound I'd heard was them stealing the tops off the milk.

I had covered scarcely five yards when from behind me someone who'd been at my school walked quickly and inexplicably past me up the drive, staring straight ahead. I couldn't remember his name, had barely known him, in fact. He'd been two or three years older than me, and I'd completely forgotten that he'd existed, but as I stared after him I remembered that he'd been one of the more amiable seniors. I could recall being proud of having some small kind of communication with one of the big boys and how it had made me feel a bit older myself, more a man of the world, less of a kid. And I remembered the way he used to greet my yelling a nickname greeting at him, a half-smile and the raising of an eyebrow.

All this came back with the instantaneous impact of memory, but something wasn't right. He didn't smile at all, or even seem to register that I was there. I felt oddly disturbed and chilled, not by the genuinely strange fact that he was there at all, or that he was wearing school athletic gear when he must have left the school seven years ago, but because he didn't smile and tilt his head back the way he used to. It was so bizarre that I wondered briefly if I was dreaming, but if you can ask yourself the question you always know the answer, and I wasn't.

My attention was distracted on the other side by a reflection in the glass of the window in the back hallway. A man with glasses, a chubby face and blond hair that looked as if it had been cut with a basin seemed to be standing behind me, carrying a bicycle. I whirled round to face where he should have been, but he wasn't there. Then I remembered the kids at the top of the driveway and, seeing that they were still standing motionless, began to shout at them again, needing something to take my bewilderment out on.

Almost immediately a tall slim man in a dark suit came walking down the drive. I don't know if it was a trick of the light in the gathering dusk, but I couldn't seem to fix on his face. In retrospect it was as if an unnatural shadow hung there but at the time my eyes just seemed to slide off it as if it were slippery, or made of ice.

"Stop shouting at them," the man said as he passed me, walking towards the back door. I stared at him open-mouthed. "They're not doing anything wrong. Leave them alone."

The kids took themselves off, the one walking beside the other on the bike, and I turned to the suited man, anxious, for some reason, to placate him, and yet at the same time slightly outraged at his invasion of our property.

"I'm sorry," I said. "It's just, well, I'm a bit thrown. I thought I saw someone I knew in the drive. Did you see him? Sort of wavy brown hair, athletics gear?"

For some reason I thought that the man would say that he had, and that that would make me feel better, but all I got was a curt "No". I was by now looking at his back as he entered the back hallway.

"Shall we go into your old house then?" asked another voice, clearly talking to the suited man, and I saw that someone else was in the back hall: the man with the blond hair and glasses. And he really was carrying a bicycle, for God's sake.

"What?" I said incredulously, and hurried after them, catching a glimpse of the suited man's face. "But it's you . . ." I continued, baffled, as I realised that the man in the suit was the man who had been in athletics gear. The two men walked straight into the kitchen and I followed them, quietly, and seemingly impotently, enraged. *Was* this his old house? Even if it was, wasn't it customary to ask the current occupants if you fancied a visit?

The suited man was by now peering round the kitchen, where for some reason everything looked very messy. He poked at some fried rice I'd left in a frying pan on the stove, or at least I seemed to have left it there, though I wasn't sure when I would have done so. Again I felt the urge to placate and hoped he would eat some, but he just grimaced with distaste and joined the other man at the window looking out onto the drive, hands on hips, his back to me.

"Dear God," he muttered, and the other man grunted in agreement.

I noticed that I'd picked up the milk from outside the back door, and appeared to have spilt some of it on the floor. I tried to clean it up with a piece of kitchen roll which seemed very dirty and yellowed as if with age, my mind aching under the strain of trying to work out what the hell was going on. I felt that there must be some sense to it somewhere, some logic of the situation that I was missing. Even if he had lived here once he had no right to just march in here with his friend like that, but I realised as I continued ineffectively trying to swab up the milk before he noticed it (why?) that there was something far wronger than a mere breach of protocol going on here. The suited man looked about thirty-five, far older then he should have been if he was indeed the man I'd been to school with, and yet far too young to ever have lived here, as between our family and the people we'd bought it from, the house's last 40 years were accounted for. So how the hell could it be his house? There was no way. And was it him anyway? Apart from being too old, it looked like him, but was it actually *him*?

As I straightened up, having done the best I could with the milk, I staggered slightly, feeling very disorientated and strange, my perception both heightened and jumbled at the same time, as if I was very drunk. Everything seemed to have a nightmarish intensity and exaggerated emotional charge, and yet there also seemed to be gaps in what I was perceiving, as if I was only taking in an edited version of what was going on. Things began to appear to jump from one state to another, with the bits in between, the becoming, missed out like a series of jump cuts. I felt hot and dizzy and the kitchen looked small and indescribably messy and the orange paint of the walls seemed to jump in at me beneath a low swaying ceiling. I wondered confusedly if I was seeing the kitchen as they saw it, and then immediately wondered what I meant by that.

All the time they just stood there, turning round occasionally to stare balefully at me, radiating distaste and impatience. Obviously they were waiting for something. But what? What was going on? Noticing I still had the piece of kitchen roll in my hand I stepped over all the rubbish on the floor—what the hell had been going on in this kitchen?—to put it in the overflowing bin. Then, squeezing my temples with my fingers and struggling both to concentrate and to stand upright against the weight of the air I turned towards the men.

"L-look", I stuttered, "what the hell is going on?" and immediately wished I hadn't. There was a pause and then the suited man turned his head very slowly towards me and it kept turning and turning until he was facing me while his body stayed facing the other way. I could feel my stomach trying to crawl away and fought against the gagging. He'd done that deliberately, done it because he knew it would make me want to throw up, and I thought he might just be right.

"Why don't you just shut up?" he snarled, the words squirming from his mouth like rats out of the stomach of something recently dead, and twisted his head slowly back round through 180 degrees until he was looking out onto the drive once more.

Meanwhile, the mess in the kitchen seemed to be getting worse. Every time I looked there were more dirty pans and bits of rubbish and old food on the floor. My head was getting thicker and heavier and felt like it was slipping away from me. I half fell against the fridge and clung to it, almost pulling it off the wall, and began to cry, my tears cutting channels in the thick grime on the fridge door. I dimly remembered that we'd bought a new fridge the week before but they must have changed it because this one looked like something out of the fifties, but it was hard to tell because it was swimming back and forth and there was a lot of white in my eyes and I couldn't see past it. They were both watching me now.

Suddenly a terrible jangling pierced my ear, as if someone were hammering a pencil into it. It happened again and I recognised it first as a sound and not a blow after all, and then as the doorbell. Someone was at the front door.

The two men glanced at each other and then the blond one nodded. The suited man turned to me.

"Do you know what that is?" he asked.

"Yes, it's the front door," I said, trying to please him.

"Yes. So you'd better answer it, hadn't you? Answer the *door*."

"Should I answer it?" I said, stupidly. I just couldn't seem to remember what words meant any more.

"*Yes*," he grated and then picked up a mug, my mug, the mug I came down, I remembered randomly, to put tea in, and hurled it at me. It smashed into the fridge door by my face. I struggled to stand upright, my head aching and ears ringing, hearing a soft crump as a fragment of the mug broke under my foot. Then the doorbell jangled again, its harsh sharpness making me realise how muted sounds had been becoming. I fell rather than stepped towards the kitchen door, sliding across the front of the fridge, my feet tangling in the boxes and cartons that now seemed to cover the filthy floor. I could feel the orange of the walls seeping in through my ears and mouth and kept missing whole seconds as if I was blacking out and coming to like a stroboscope. As I banged into the door and grabbed the handle to hold myself up I heard the blond man say,

"He may not go through. If he does, we wait."

But it didn't mean anything to me. None of it did.

Stepping clumsily over more piles of rubbish I headed for the front door. The chime of the doorbell had pushed the air hard and I could see it coming towards me in waves. Ducking, I slipped on the mat and almost fell into the living room on hands and knees. But it was getting dark in there, I could see, really dark, and I could hear the plants talking. I couldn't catch the words, but they were there, beneath the night sounds and a soft rustling which sounded a hundred yards away. The living room must have grown, I thought groggily, picking myself up and turning myself to the front door as the bell clanged again. It should be about four paces across the hall from the living room door to the front door but I thought it was only going to take one and then it took twenty, past all the panelling and over the huge folds in the mat. And then I had my hand on the doorknob and then the door was open and I stepped out of the house.

"Oh hello Michael. I thought someone must be in, because all the lights were on."

"Wuh?" I said, blinking in the remnants of sunlight, breathless with the feeling of my mind soaring up towards normality like a runaway lift. Then "Sorry?"

"I hope I didn't disturb you?" the woman standing in front of me said, and I now recognised her to be Mrs Steinburg, the woman who brings us our catfood in bulk.

"No, no, that's fine. Fine," I said, looking covertly behind me into the hall, which was solid and unpanelled and four paces wide and led to the living room which was light and about ten yards deep. Good. Think about that later. Deal with the cat woman.

"I've brought your delivery," she said. "Look, are you all right?"

"Yes. I'm fine," I replied, smiling broadly. "I . . . er . . ." I . . . er . . . what? "I . . . er . . . just nodded off for a moment, in the kitchen. I still feel a bit, you know . . ."

"Of course." Mrs Steinburg smiled. I followed her up the drive and heaved the box of catfood out of the back of her van, looking carefully back at the house. There was nothing to see. I thanked her and then carried the box back down the drive as she drove off.

I walked back into the house and shut the front door behind me. I felt absolutely fine. I walked into the kitchen. Normal. It didn't even occur to me to wonder if the two men would still be there. They weren't. I must just have fallen asleep making tea, and then struggled over to the front door to open it while still half asleep. I could remember asking myself if it was a dream and thinking it wasn't but that just showed how wrong you could be, didn't it? It had been unusually vivid, and it was odd how I'd been suddenly awake and all right again as soon as I stepped out of the front door. Odd, and a bit disconcerting. But here I was in the kitchen again and everything was normal, clean and tidy, spick and span, with all the rubbish in the bin and the pans in the right places and the milk in the fridge and a smashed mug on the floor.

Suddenly I didn't feel quite so good. It was my mug, and it was smashed, on the floor, at the bottom of the fridge. Now how had that happened? Maybe I'd fallen asleep holding it (fallen asleep standing up with a mug in my hand? Now how likely was that?), maybe I'd knocked it over waking up and incorporated the sound into my dream (better, better, but where exactly was I supposed to have fallen asleep? Just leaning against the counter, or actually stretched out on it with the kettle as a pillow?). Then I noticed the fridge door.

There was a little dent in it, with a couple of flecks of paint missing. At about head height.

That wasn't good. That wasn't good at all. In fact it felt as if someone had just punched a hole in my chest and poured icy water into it. But everything else was all right, wasn't it? I cleared up the mug and switched the kettle on and while it was boiling wandered into the hall and the living room. Everything was fine, tidy, normal. Super. Back into the kitchen. The same. Great. Apart from a little dent in the fridge door at about head height.

I made my cup of tea, though not in my mug of course, and drank it standing looking out of the kitchen window at the drive, feeling unsettled and nervous, and unsure of what to do with either of those emotions. Even if it had been a dream, it was odd, particularly the way it had fought so hard against melting away. Maybe I was much more tired than I realised. Or maybe I was ill. But I felt fine, physically at least.

I carried the box of catfood into the pantry, unpacked it, and stacked the cans in the corner. Then I switched the kettle on for another cup of tea. Suddenly my heart seemed to stop and before I had time to realise why, the cause repeated itself. A soft chinking noise outside the back door.

I moved quickly to the window and looked out. Nothing. I craned my neck, trying to see round to the back door, but could only see the large pile of firewood that lay to one side of it. The noise again.

Clenching my fists I walked slowly into the back hallway and listened. Silence, except for the sound of blood beating in my ears. My stomach knotting and hands moist with perspiration. Then I grabbed the knob and swung the door open. Stillness. Just a rectangle of late afternoon light, a patch of driveway, a dark hedge waving quietly. I stepped out into the drive.

A very faint crunching noise. And then again. Sounded almost like pebbles rubbing against each other. Again. I looked more closely at the drive, peering at the actual stones, and then noticed that a very small patch about ten yards in front of me appeared to be moving slightly, wriggling, almost. As I watched they stopped, and then the sound came again and another patch, about a yard closer than the first, stirred briefly. As if registering the weight of invisible feet. I was so engrossed that I didn't notice the whistling straight away. When I did, I looked up.

The blond man was back. Standing at the top of the driveway, carrying a bicycle with the wheels slowly spinning in the dusk, whistling the top line of two in perfect harmony, the lower line just the wind. As I stared at him, backing slowly towards the house, the crunching noise got louder and louder and then the suited man was standing with his nose almost touching mine.

"Hello again," he said.

The blond man started down the driveway, smiling.

"Hello again indeed," he said. "Come on, in we go."

Suddenly I realised that the very last thing in the world I should do was let those two back into the house. I leapt through the back door back into the hallway. The suited man, caught by surprise, started forward but I was quick and whipped the door shut in his face and locked it. That felt very good but then he started banging on the door very hard, ridiculously hard, grotesquely hard, and I noticed that to my right the kitchen was getting messy again and the fridge was old and I could barely see out of the window because it was so grimy and a slight flicker made me think that maybe I'd missed

the smallest fraction of a second and I realised that it really hadn't
been a fucking dream and I was back there, and I was back there
because I'd come in through the back door again. As I backed into
the kitchen I tripped and fell, sprawling amongst the cartons and
bacon rind and the dirt and was that puke, for Christ's sake? The
banging on the back door got louder and louder and louder. He was
going to break it. He was going to break the fucking door down. I'd
let them back and they had to come in through the back door. I'd
come in through the wrong door . . .

Suddenly realising what I must do, I scrambled up and kicked my
way through the rubbish towards the door to the front hall. The
fridge door swung open in my way and the inside was dark and
dirty and there was something rotted in there but I slammed it out
of the way, biting hard on my lip to keep my head clear. I had to
get to the front door, I had to open it, step out, and then step back
in again. That was the right door. And I had to do it soon, before
the back door broke and let them in. As I ran out of the kitchen into
the front hall I could already hear a splintering quality to the sound
of the blows. And the back door was about two inches thick.

The hallway was worse than I expected. I came to a halt, at first
unable to even see the front door. Then I thought that I must be
looking in the wrong direction but I wasn't, because there it was
over to the left where it was supposed to be, but the angles were
all wrong and to see it I had to look behind me and to the right,
although when I saw it I could see that it was still over there to the
left. And it looked so close, could it really be less than a yard away,
but when I held my hand out to it I groped into nothing, my hand
still in front of the door when it should have been past it. I stared
wildly around me, disorientated and unsure somehow even of which
way to go. Then the banging behind me got even louder, probably
as the blond man joined in, and this helped marginally to restore my
sense of direction. I found the door again, concentrated hard on its
apparent position and started to walk towards it. I immediately fell
over, because the floor was much lower than I expected, and in
fact must be tilted in some way as one of my legs reached it easily
enough, although it looked flat and level. I pulled myself up onto
my knees and found I was looking at a sort of sloped wall between
the wall and the ceiling, a wall which bent back from the wall and
yet out from the ceiling. And the door was still over there on the
left, although to see it I now had to look straight ahead and up.

Then I noticed another sound beneath the eternal banging and
whirled round to face the direction it was coming from. I found
that I was looking through the living room door and that it gave into
sheer darkness, a darkness which was seeping out into the hallway

like smoke, clinging to the angles in the air like the inside of a dark prism. I heard the noise again and it was a deep rumbling growling far far away in there, almost obscured by the night noises and the sound of vegetation moving in the wind. It didn't seem to be getting any closer but I knew that was because the living room now extended out far beyond, into hundreds and hundreds of miles of dense forest jungle, and as I listened carefully I could hear the gurgling of some dark river far off to the right, mixing with the warm rustling of the breeze in the darkness. It sounded very peaceful and for a moment I was still, transfixed.

Then the sound of a violently splintering crack wrenched me away and I turned my back on the living room and flailed towards where the front door must be. The hall table loomed above me and I thought I could walk upright beneath it but tripped over it trying and fell again, headlong onto the cool floorboards. The mat had moved, no, was moving, sliding slowly up the stairs like a draft and as I rolled over and looked at the ceiling I saw the floor coming towards me, the walls shortening in little jerks. Another splintering thud and now I had no idea which way was up.

As I lay there panting a clear cool waft of air stroked my cheek. At first I thought that it must have come from the living room, although it had been warm in there, but then I remembered rather than saw that I was lying on the floor and that the breeze must be a draught coming under the front door. I must nearly be there. I looked all around me but all I could see was panelling and floor and what was behind me. I closed my eyes and tried to grope for it but it was even worse inside so I opened them again. Then I caught a glimpse of the door, far away, obscured from view round a corner but visible once you knew where to look. On impulse I reached my hand out in not quite the opposite direction and felt it fall upon warm grainy wood. The door, the bloody door. I'd found the front door.

I pulled myself along the floor towards it and tried to stand up. I got no more than a few inches before I fell back down again. I tried again with the same result, feeling as if I was trying to do something very unnatural and bizarre. Again, and this time I reached a semi-crouching position, muscles straining. I started to slump down again but as I did so I threw myself forwards and found myself curled up, my feet a couple of feet from the floor, lying on the door. Forcing my mind not to even try to come to terms with this I groped by my side and found the doorknob. I tried to twist it but the sweat on my hands made them spin uselessly on the shiny metal. I wiped them on my shirt and tried again and this time I got some purchase and heard the catch withdraw as the knob turned. Exultantly I tugged at it as with a tremendous crash the back door finally gave way.

The door wouldn't budge. Panicking, I tried again. Nothing. By peering down the crack I could see that no lock or bolt was impeding it, so why wouldn't it bloody move?

Footsteps in the back hall. Suddenly I realised that I was lying on the door, and trying to pull it towards me against my own weight. Silly me. The footsteps reached the kitchen.

I rolled over off the door onto the wall beside it and reached for the handle but I'd gone too far. As the footsteps came closer, towards the kitchen door into the hall, I scrambled across the slippery wall, grabbed and twisted the doorknob with all my strength. It opened just as they entered the hall and I rolled out through it, fell and landed awkwardly and painfully on something hard and bristly and for a few moments had no clear idea of where or who I was and just lay there fighting for breath.

After some time I sat up slowly. I was sitting on the doormat, my back to the front door. At the top of the drive a passing couple were staring at me curiously. I stood up and smiled, trying to suggest that I often sat there and that they ought to try it as it really was a lot of fun, hoping to God that they hadn't seen me fall there from about two-thirds of the way up the door. They smiled back and carried on walking, mollified or maybe even hurrying off home to try it for themselves, for all I knew. I turned hesitantly back towards the door and looked in.

It had worked. It was all all right again. The mat was on the floor, right angles looked like 90 degrees again and the ceiling was back where it was supposed to be. I stepped back a pace and looked across at the back door. It had been utterly smashed and now looked like little more than an extension of the firewood pile.

I walked back into the hall through the front door, the right door, and shut it behind me. I wandered carefully and quietly into the living room and the kitchen. Everything was fine, everything was normal. Just a nice normal house. If you came in through the right door.

The wrong door was in about a thousand pieces now, of course. I thought about that for some time, with a cup of tea and what felt like my first cigarette in months. Less than an hour had elapsed, I saw with frank disbelief, since I'd first come downstairs.

The wrong door. It was coming in through there that took me to wherever or whatever it was that the house became. Coming in through the front door brought me back to wherever it was that I normally lived. So presumably I was safe so long as I didn't leave the house and come back in through the back door. They couldn't get me.

Presumably. But I didn't like having that door in pieces. The wrong door, the door through which they had to come, was in pieces. Being safe was only part of the problem. I wasn't going to feel *secure* until that portal was well and truly closed. It wasn't precisely clear, however, what I could do about that.

I walked into the back hall and looked nervously out through the wreckage onto the drive. Everything was fine. There was nothing I needed protecting from. But I didn't like it. Did it have to be me who came through it, or what if maybe a falling leaf or even just a soft breeze came inside? Would that be enough? Could I take the risk?

As I stood there indecisively I noticed once more the pile of firewood propped up against the outside wall of the back hall. I probably still wouldn't have thought of it had not a very large proportion of the pile been old thick planks. I looked at the tool shelf on the inside wall and saw a hammer and a big box of good long nails. Then I looked at the wood again.

I could nail the damn thing shut.

I flicked my cigarette butt out onto the drive and rolled up my sleeves. The hammer was big and heavy, which was just as well because when I nailed the planks across the door frame I'd be hammering into solid brickwork. I was going to have to board right the way up but that was all right as there were loads of planks, and if I reinforced it enough it should be well-nigh impregnable. Feeling much better now that I had a way of sealing off the door, I set to work. I may even have hummed.

Kneeling just inside the door, I reached out and began pulling planks in, taking care to select the thickest and least weathered. I judged that I'd need about thirty-five to make the doorway really secured, although that was largely guesswork as I'd never tried to turn the back hall into a fortress before. Getting the planks in was heavy work as I had to stretch out to reach them, and I began to get hot and tired, and anxious to begin the nailing. Outside it was getting darker as the evening began, and the air was very cool and still.

As the pile in the back hall increased in size it became more difficult still, and I had to lean further and further out to reach the next plank, and this made me nervous. I was still inside, my feet were still on the ground in the back hall. I wasn't "coming back in", I was just leaning out and then, well, sort of coming back in but not really, because my feet never left the back hall, did they? But it made me nervous, and I began to work quicker and quicker, perspiration running down my face and arms as, clinging to the doorframe with my left hand, I stretched out to bring the last few boards in. I felt tired and irritated and was dying for a smoke but couldn't take the time: I was anxious to start nailing. Thirty-one, thirty-two, just a couple more. Now the last one I could possibly reach: that would have to be enough. Hooking my left foot behind the frame and gripping it hard with my left hand I stretched out towards the plank, my waving fingers little more than an inch from the end. Just a little further forward: I let my hooking foot slide round slightly, let my fingers slip round half an inch and tried to extend my back as far as it would go. My fingers just scraping the end I tried a last yearning lunge.

And then suddenly a stray thought struck me. Here I was, pulled out as if on some invisible rack: why on earth hadn't I just gone out of the front door, picked up piles of wood and brought them back into the house through the front door? It would have been easier, it would have been quicker, and it wouldn't have involved all this monkeying around at the wrong door. Not that it mattered now, because as it happened even if I didn't get this last plank I'd probably have plenty, but I wouldn't have been so hot and tired and it was also a bit worrying that in my haste I'd been putting myself in needless danger. I'd better slow down, calm down, take a rest.

An unimportant, contemplative thought. But one that distracted me for a fraction of a second too long. As I finally got the tips of my fingers round the plank I realised with horror that my other fingers, the ones on the doorframe, were slipping. I was slowly sliding forwards. Desperately I tried to scrabble with my fingers, but my hands were too sweaty and the doorframe itself was slippery now. I felt the tendons in my hand stretch as I tried to defy my centre of gravity and think my weight backwards, and then suddenly my forehead walloped onto the ground and I was lying flat on my face.

I was up in a second, and I swear to God that both feet never left the hall floor at once. I hurled myself back into the hallway, clutching that last bloody piece of wood without even noticing it.

Panting and almost sobbing with nervous hysteria I crouched in the doorframe, looking out. Everything looked normal. The driveway was quiet, the pebbles were still and there was none of the faint deadening of sound that I associated with the other place. I was furious with myself for having taken the risk, for not having thought to bring them in through the front door, and especially for falling, which had been bloody painful quite apart from anything else. But I hadn't fallen out, not really. I hadn't come back in, as such. The drive was fine, the kitchen was fine. Everything was fine.

Soothed by the sounds of early evening traffic in the distance, my heart gradually slowing down to only about twice its normal rate, I began to feel a bit better and had a quiet cup of tea, perched on the pile of planks. In falling over my right foot had caught the tool shelf and there were nails all over the place, inside and out, but there were plenty left and the ones outside could bloody stay there. I wasn't going to make the same damnfool mistake twice.

314

Gathering up the hammer and a fistful of nails I laid a plank across the door and started work. Getting the nails through the wood and into the masonry was even harder than I'd expected, but in a couple of minutes it was in place, and felt very solid. I heaved another plank into place and set about securing it. This was actually going to work.

After half an hour I was into the swing of it and the wood now reached almost halfway up the doorframe. My arms aching and head ringing from the hammering, which was very loud in the confined space of the back hall, I had a cigarette leaning on the completed section, staring blankly out onto the drive. I was jolted back from reverie by the realisation that a piece of dust or something must have landed in my eye, slightly distorting my vision, and I blinked to remove it. But it didn't go. It didn't hurt, just made a small patch of the drive up near the road look a bit ruffled. I rubbed and shut both eyes individually and discovered with mounting unease that the distortion was present in both.

I stood upright. Something was definitely going on at the top of the drive. The patch still looked ruffled, as if seen through a heat haze, and whichever way I turned my head it stayed in the same place. It was flickering very slightly now too, like a bad quality film print. But the flecks weren't white, they were dark. I rubbed my eyes hard again, but once I'd stopped seeing stars I saw that the effect was still there, and I stared hard at it, trying to discern something that I could interpret. The flecks seemed to organize into broken and shifting vertical lines as I watched, as if something were hidden behind a curtain of rain, rain so coloured as to make up a picture of that patch of the drive. This impression gradually strengthened until it was like looking at one of those plastic strip "doors", where you walk through the hanging strips. It was as if there was one of those at the top of the drive with a patch of driveway pictured on it in living three dimensions, with something moving just the other side of it.

Then suddenly the balance shifted, like one of those drawings made up of black and white dots where if you stare at it long enough you can see a Dalmatian. I dropped to my knees behind the partially completed barrier. Fear was no longer a word I had any use for. They were back.

Standing at the top of the drive, their images somehow both underlying and superimposed on it as if the two were woven together, were the man in the suit and the blond man. They were standing in a frozen and unnatural position, like a freeze-frame in a very old home movie, their faces pallid and washed out, the colouring uneven, the image flickering and dancing in front of my eyes. And still they stood, not there, and yet in some sense there.

As I stared, transfixed, I noticed that the suited man's foot appeared to be moving. It was hard to focus on, and happening bizarrely slowly, but it was moving, gradually leaving the ground. Then, as over the course of several minutes it was raised and then lowered back onto the ground a couple of feet in front of its original position, leaving the man's body leaning slightly forward, I realised what I was seeing. In extraordinary and flickering slow motion, somehow projected onto the drive, the suited man was beginning to walk down towards the house. Except that the image wasn't flickering so much any more, the colours were stronger, and I could no longer see the driveway through them. Somehow they were coming back through. I thought I'd got away with it, but I hadn't. I'd fallen out. Not very far by anyone's standards, but far enough. Far enough to have come back in through the wrong door. And now they were tearing their way back into the world, or hauling me back towards theirs. And very very slowly they were getting closer.

Fighting to stay calm I grabbed a plank, put it into position above the others and nailed it into place. Then another, and another, not pausing for breath or thought. Through the narrowing gap I could see them getting closer and they didn't look anything like two-dimensional photographs any longer and they were moving quicker now too. Then as I leaned towards the kitchen for a plank I saw that there was a single dusty carton on the floor. It had started.

I smacked another plank into place and hammered it down. The suited man and the blond man were now real again, and they were also much closer, though still moving at a weirdly graceful tenth of normal speed. Hammering wildly now, ignoring increasingly frequent whacks on the fingers, I cast occasional monitoring glances aside into the kitchen. The fridge was beginning to look a bit strange, the stark nineties geometry softening, regressing, and the rubbish was gathering. I never saw any of it arrive, but each time I looked there was another piece of cardboard, a few more scraps, one more layer of grime. It had barely started, and was still happening very slowly, maybe because I'd barely fallen out, but it was happening. The house was going over.

And I kept right on hammering. Obviously what I had to do at some point was run to the front door, go out and come back in again, come in through the right door. But that could wait, would have to wait. It was all developing very slowly this time and I still felt completely clear-headed. What I had to do first was seal off the back door, and soon. The two men, always at the vanguard of the change, were well and truly here, and getting closer all the time. I had to make sure that the back door was secure against anything those two could do to it for long enough for me to get to the front door. I had no idea what the front hall would be like by the time I got there and if I left the back door unfinished and got caught up in the front hall trying to get to the door I'd be in real trouble.

So I slammed planks into place as fast as I could. Outside they got steadily closer and inside another carton appeared in the kitchen. As I jammed the last horizontal board into place the suited man and the blond man were only a couple of yards away, now moving at full pace, and I'd barely nailed it in before the first blow crashed into it, bending it and making me leap back with shock. I hurriedly picked up more wood and started to place planks over the barrier in vertical slats and crosses, nailing them in hard, reinforcing and making sure that they were securely fastened to the wall on all sides, furiously hammering and building. After a while I couldn't feel the ache in my back or see the blood on my hands: all I could hear was the beating of the hammer, and all I could see were the heads of the nails as I piled more and more wood onto the barrier. I had wood to spare—I hadn't even needed that last bloody plank—and by the time I finished it was four planks thick in some places, and the reinforcing strips spread several feet either side of the frame. I used the last three pieces as bracing struts, forcing them horizontally across the hallway, one end of each lodged in niches in the barrier, the other jammed tight against the opposite wall.

Finally it was finished and I stood back and looked at it. It looked pretty damn solid.

"Let's see you get through that then, you bastards," I said quietly, half sitting and half collapsing to the ground.

After a moment I noticed how quiet it was. At some point they must have stopped banging against the door. How long ago I had no idea. I'd been making far too much noise to notice, and my ears were still ringing. I put my ear against the barrier and listened. Silence. I lit a cigarette and let tiredness and a blessed feeling of safeness wash over me. The sound of the match striking was slightly muted, but that could've been the ringing in my ears as much as anything and the kitchen looked pretty grubby but no more than that. And I felt fine.

Vaguely wondering what the two outside were up to, whether there was any chance that they might, not realising that I understood about the right door and the wrong door, have given up and be waiting for the change to take its course, I sat and finished my cigarette, actually savouring the feeling of being balanced between two worlds, secure in the knowledge that in a moment I would just walk out that front door and the house would come back and none of it would matter a damn.

Eventually I stood up. I was really going to ache tomorrow, I thought as I stepped into the kitchen, narrowly avoiding a large black spider that scuttled out of one of the cartons. The floor was getting very messy now, with scraps of dried-up rotted meat covered with the corpses of dead maggots and small piles of stuff I really didn't want to look at too closely. Skirting the rubbish I walked over to the door past the now bizarrely misshapen fridge and into the front hall.

The hallway was still clear, and as far as I could see, utterly normal. As I crossed it towards the front door, anxious now to get the whole thing over with, and wondering how I was going to explain the state of the back door to my family, I noticed a very faint tapping sound in the far distance. After a moment it stopped, and then restarted from a slightly different direction. Odd, but scarcely a primary concern. Right now my priority was getting out of that front door before the hall got any stranger.

Feeling like an actor about to bound onto stage, and looking forward very much to looking out onto the real world, I reached out to the doorknob, twisted it and pulled it towards me, smiling.

At first I couldn't take it in. I couldn't understand why instead of the driveway all I could see was brown. Brown flatness. Then as I adjusted my focal length, pulling it in for something much closer than the drive I'd been expecting, I began to realise, because the view looked rather familiar. I'd seen something like it very recently.

It was a barrier. An impregnable wooden barrier nailed across the door into the walls from the outside. Now I knew what they'd been doing as I finished nailing them out. They'd been nailing me in.

I tried everything I could think of against that barrier, my fists, my shoulder, a chair. It was there to stay. I couldn't get out. I couldn't come back in through the right door and for the moment they couldn't get in through the wrong door. A sort of stalemate. But a very poor sort for me, because they were much the stronger and getting more so all the time, because the house was still going over and now I couldn't stop it.

I walked into the kitchen, rubbing my bruised shoulder and thinking furiously. There had to be something I could do, and I had to do it fast. The change was speeding up. Although the hall still looked normal the kitchen was now filthy, and the fifties fridge was back. In the background I could still hear the faint tapping noise. Maybe they were trying to get in through the roof.

I had to get out, had to find a way. Come on, lateral thinking. You leave a house by a door. How else? No other way. You always leave

by a door. But is there any other way you *could* leave? The doors . . .
Christ. The windows. What about the windows? If there was a right
door and a wrong door, maybe there were right and wrong windows
too, and maybe the right ones looked out onto the real world. Maybe,
just maybe, you could smash one and then climb out and then back
in again. Maybe that would work.

I had no idea whether it would or not, I wasn't kidding myself that
I understood anything, and God alone knew where I might land if
I chose the wrong window. Perhaps I'd go out the wrong one and
then be chased round the house by the two maniacs outside as I
tried to find a right window to break back in through. That would
be a barrel of laughs, wouldn't it? That would be just Fun City. But
what choice did I have? Through the square window today, children,
I thought crazily, and ran into the living room, heading for the big
picture window.

I don't know how I could not have made the connection. Maybe
because the taps were so quiet. I just stood in the living room, my
mouth open. This time they were one jump ahead. They'd boarded
up the bloody windows.

I ran into the hall, the dining room, upstairs to the bedrooms.
Every single window was boarded up. I knew where they'd got
the nails from, I'd spilt more then enough when I fell, but how
. . . Then I realised how they'd nailed them in without a hammer,
why the tapping had been so quiet. With sudden sickening clarity
I found I could imagine the suited man clubbing the nails in with
his fists, smashing them in with his forehead and grinning while he
did it. Oh Jesus.

I walked downstairs again. Every single window. Even the ones
that were too small to climb through. Then as I stood in the kitchen
amidst the growing piles, the pounding on the back door started.
There was no way I could get out of the house. I couldn't stop
it. This time it was going over all the way and taking me with it.
And they were going to smash their way in to come along for the
ride. To get me. I listened, watching the rubbish, as the pounding
got louder and louder.

It's still getting louder, and I can tell from the sound that some of
the planks are beginning to give way. The house stopped balancing
long ago, and the change is coming on more quickly. The kitchen
looks like a bomb site and there are an awful lot of spiders in
there now. Eventually I left them to it and came through the
hall into here, only making one or two wrong turnings. Into the
living room.

And that's where I am now, just sitting and waiting. There is nothing I can do about the change, nothing. I can't get out. I can't stop them getting in.

But there is one thing I can do. I'm going to stay here, in the living room. I can see small shadows now, gathering in corners and darting out from under the chairs, and it's quite dark down by the end wall. The wall itself seems less important now, less substantial, less of a barrier. And I think I can hear the sound of running water somewhere far away, and smell the faintest hint of dark and lush vegetation.

I won't let them get me. I'll wait, in the gathering darkness here in the living room, listening to the coming of the night sounds, feeling a soft breeze on my face and sensing the room opening out as the walls shade away, as I sit here quietly in the dark warm air. And then I'll get up and start walking, walking out into the dark land, into the jungle and amidst the trees that stand all around behind the darkness, smelling the greenness that surrounds me and hearing the gentle river off somewhere to the right. And I'll feel happy walking away into the night, and maybe far away I'll meet whatever makes the growling sounds I begin to hear in the distance and we'll sit together by running water and be at peace in the darkness.

DENNIS ETCHISON

When They Gave Us Memory

DENNIS ETCHISON has been described as the best short story writer
in the horror field today. After winning $250 at the age of twelve
for an essay called "What America Means to Me", he made his first
professional sale to *Escapade* in 1961.

Although not a prolific writer, Etchison has contributed to numerous magazines and anthologies, and his short fiction is collected in
The Dark Country, *Red Dreams* and *The Blood Kiss*. He has edited
the anthologies *Cutting Edge*, three volumes of *Masters of Darkness*,
Lord John Ten and *MetaHorror*, and he is the author of the novels
Darkside, *Shadow Man* and the novelisation of John Carpenter's
movie *The Fog*. Under the pseudonym "Jack Martin" he has also
novelised *Halloween II*, *Halloween III* and *Videodrome*.

"When They Gave Us Memory" is a particularly autobiographical
story by the author and a fine example of what he doesn't consider
to be horror fiction. But we do.

H ALFWAY AROUND THE BAY, BEFORE PASSING through the rock, he stopped and listened.

There was only the creaking of masts as sailboats listed back at the docks, straining their ropes and drubbing the pilings where they were moored. That and a distant hissing as water lapped the shore and deposited another layer of broken shells on the sand.

He saw the beach and the pier through the mist, the teenagers with zinc oxide on their noses, the white-legged tourists in walking shorts. No one else, except for the faded statue of an old-fashioned groom or footman in front of the carousel enclosure. The path along the jetty behind him was clear.

Even so, he could not shake the conviction that he was being followed.

He had sensed eyes on him in the restaurant, and the feeling grew when he went down to the pier. At every stand and gift shop he had paused, pretending interest in the souvenirs as he stole glances over his shoulder, but the boards remained empty. Pearly mobiles spinning in Mother Goose's Mall, cotton candy congealing against glass in the Taffy House, postcards curling outside the Fortune Hunter. Nothing else. He tried to let it go.

I should have called first, he thought.

He had hoped to surprise them in Captain Ahab's, their usual lunchtime spot, but the drive was longer than he remembered and he'd arrived late; by then strangers filled every table. Had his parents come early to avoid the noon rush and then gone for a walk? He couldn't imagine his dad sitting any longer than necessary . . .

By now he had covered most of the waterfront, including the pier and the beach. All that was left was the jetty, a stone path that curved out over the bay in a half circle before returning to shore. In order to complete his search he would have to pass through the rock, an ancient landmark left untouched by the harbor's developers except for the installation of a railing where the foothold narrowed and became treacherous.

Now the natural arch loomed before him, dark and dripping with moisture.

He hesitated as a sudden wind moaned within the cavern.

Leaning on a coin-operated telescope, he caught his breath. Here the sea was calm, lapping gently at colonies of mollusks that clung to the slippery stones, at skittering crustaceans that sought purchase on the slick, eroded surfaces. Farther out, however, past the breakers, whitecaps were already forming where the currents merged in the gulf.

He watched one of the whitecaps detach from the tip of a wave, lift and begin to drift inland. Then another, another, flecks of spume breaking loose and taking flight.

They were coming this way.

When he saw that they were gulls, he waved. They swooped closer, poised just above the railing, their sleek wings fully extended.

Then they cawed, zeroing in on him.

He held out his arms to show that he had no food, no bread or leftover bait, but they dropped closer, feathers ruffling as they hovered in a holding pattern. The largest gull beat the air and cawed again. He noticed the sharp beak, the arrow tongue, the beady eyes focused on his empty fingers, and nervously stuffed his hands into his pockets.

The bird cocked its head, opened its beak wider, and shrieked.

What did it see?

He turned.

There was no one else on the jetty. A quarter mile away, the teenagers and tourists were still on the beach. The concession stands on the pier were boarded up now. It appeared that even the carousel was closed; the statue of the groom was no longer there.

When he turned back, the gulls were gone. He caught a last glimpse of their crescent wings pumping away on the horizon.

Ahead, a wave boomed in the cave.

The tide was rising. As plumes of spray settled over him he imagined the jetty awash, the rock path submerged, cutting off his return to land.

There was nothing left to do but go through before the waters rose any higher.

In the center of the arch a circle of diffused light shone through salt spray. The jetty beyond curved landward again so that there seemed to be nothing but endless sea on the other side. The walls of the cave swam with condensation, winking at him as though encrusted with tiny eyes.

He let go of the railing, hunched his shoulders, and walked forward.

Inside, the pounding of the surf was magnified until the pressure against his eardrums reached an all but unbearable level. He reconsidered, but there was no way around the rock. The jetty leading out from shore was less than a yard wide here, with only jagged boulders and the ocean beyond the railing. And the tide was swelling dangerously. Wasn't that a splash of white foam already bobbing above the path behind him?

Between the ebb and flow he heard water draining away, every drop resonating with the force of a pistol shot. He covered his ears but the throbbing was in the bones of his skull. He took his hands away, and almost lost his footing as a deep, bellowing roar sounded directly in front of him.

The cave wall shimmered and expanded, and something huge and formless spilled out over the rail into the circle of light, blocking his way.

A sea lion.

The massive creature reared its head, settled heavily on its haunches, and bellowed again.

He held the rail tightly and stood stock-still.

After a few seconds the animal twitched its glistening gray whiskers and waddled aside to allow passage. Another, smaller shape wriggled wetly in the shadows. It slapped its flippers and cried out hoarsely, as if welcoming him.

He took a breath, measuring his next step.

"Hi," said a voice.

He froze as something cold touched the middle of his back, then came to rest on his shoulder.

"I hope you don't mind," said the voice, barely audible above the pounding.

He spun around too fast. This time he lost his foothold and went sprawling.

A statue looked down at him. It was the groom from the pier. The cutaway jacket now hung in sodden folds. The figure extended a clammy, gloved hand and helped him to his feet.

"I hope you don't mind, but I recognized you right off."

It was not a statue. It was a young man in costume. A mime, he realized, one whose job it must be to stand in front of the carousel for hours at a time without moving a muscle, attracting customers.

He stared incredulously at the young mime. "You've been following me."

"You're Madsen, aren't you?"

"What?"

"Sure you are. From 'As the World Ends'? It's my favorite show! I've been watching it since I was a little boy."

The mime reached under his jacket and brought out a damp piece of paper and a ballpoint pen.

"Would you mind?"

"You've got to be kidding."

The young man blinked through running makeup. The smile faded.

"What's the matter? Too stuck-up to sign autographs for your fans?"

They stood there in the cave, daring each other to back off, as the sea lions barked from the sidelines.

When he finally managed to call from a pay phone, a computerized voice told him that the number he had dialed was no longer in service.

That was impossible. Had it been so long? Only last Christmas he had spoken to them, or was it New Year's? And he had sent his mother something on her birthday, and his father, after the operation. Surely he had done that.

Directory Assistance was unable to help.

Had they taken an unlisted number? That was reasonable, he supposed. Reporters had a way of tracking down relatives for gossipy feature stories; he had learned that the hard way during his first marriage.

He drove out along back streets to the house where he had grown up. The plain stucco one-story had still been his address when he began reading for little theater parts in high school. It was where he had sat up nights memorizing lines in his room, where he had lost his virginity to Carol Moreland while his parents were gone on vacation. After that he had seen them less often as rehearsals kept him away from home except to eat and sleep, until he could afford his own apartment. By his mid-twenties his lifestyle had become something his parents could no longer share or understand.

As he turned the corner he slowed, wondering if this was the right street, after all. The trees were denser and older, their split limbs hanging low over a buckled sidewalk. The houses seemed small and dingy, with cracked driveways and peeling facades. But then he reached the end of the block and recognized the sagging mailbox, the one he had repaired for his dad before moving out.

While maneuvering for a place to park between unfamiliar automobiles, he noticed a sign stuck into the ground at the edge of the property, next to the weathered fence and the oleander bush:

For Sale.

It couldn't be true. But the lawn was parched and overrun with weeds, the screen door rusting, the bare windows clotted with grime. One of the panes had been broken out and left unreplaced. That was not like his dad. It was not like him at all.

He got out of the car and went to the shattered window.

Squinting between the dust and harsh shadows, he saw a torn curtain hanging from a twisted rod, an emptied bookcase. The floor he knew so well was bare, the boards scuffed and warped. Through the kitchen doorway he could make out denuded cupboards and the misaligned geometry of water-damaged linoleum.

He rang the bell at the next house. No one answered there, though when he walked away a pale face withdrew from the front window, as if someone were hiding inside, too frightened of him to open the door.

The post office had no forwarding address.

He was about to give up, when he remembered the real estate company on the sign.

"We don't give out that kind of information," a suspicious woman told him over a cluttered desk.

Don't you recognize me? he thought. Monday through Friday at two o'clock, the most popular show in its time slot? But judging by the mound of papers in front of her, the realtor did not have time to watch afternoon television. Or perhaps she did and mistook him for Madsen, the despicable character he portrayed. Could that be it?

"I'm their son," he explained.

The way he delivered the line he had trouble believing it himself. Even his driver's license would not prove it. He had changed his name years ago.

"Please," he said, allowing his voice to break with a hint of desperation.

"Well," she said, "there *is* a box number. So we can send them the escrow papers. That's all I have. It's the way they wanted it. I'm sorry . . ."

The box number turned out to be a mail drop in Santa Maria that shared space with a parcel delivery service and an instant-printing franchise.

The clerk there was no help. The man refused even to admit that he had a list of names and addresses for those who rented his postal boxes. It was not hard to understand. The one thing such a business had to sell its customers was anonymity.

What else was there to do? He was not ready to quit. It was Saturday and he did not have to be at the studio. He had told Claire he would meet her after the engagement shower tonight, but that was still hours away.

If he did not find them today, what then? A letter? He had come out to tell them the good news in person. They would want to meet his fiancée and her family. There were details to be worked out—the reception, the guest list. He could have his secretary do it all. But his parents deserved to be involved. He owed them that much. He had waited too long already, and the wedding date was closing fast.

"Excuse me," he said again to the man at the counter.

The clerk finished loading a ream of bond paper into the photocopy machine.

"Something else I can do for you?"

"Listen." He felt like a spy attempting to buy secrets behind enemy lines. He took another look at the clerk, the distracted eyes that bulged from the sharp scent of solvent, the ink-stained fingers. "I'll make you an offer. You don't have to tell me anything."

"Right," said the clerk, "I don't."

"All you have to do is take a break." He reached for his wallet. "While you're away, let's say somebody slips behind the counter and gets a peek at your files. By the time you come back I'm gone. You didn't see a thing. How does that sound?"

He took out a twenty and held it casually between two fingers.

"Sounds like you're a cop."

"I'm not."

"Bill collector, then." The clerk's eyes fixed on him. "Are you skip tracing?"

"That's right." He lowered his voice as an old man from the laundromat next door entered and headed for the locked mail compartments, key in hand. He fished out another twenty. "I'm skip tracing. Now can you help me? Or do I get a court order? That would be a lot of trouble. For both of us."

"Then I guess you'll have to get your court order," said the clerk, his back straight, his face steely. "It's hard enough to make a decent living without your kind."

Frustrated, he leaned across the counter. "Okay, I'm not a bill collector. I already told you—I'm looking for my folks. I don't know where they live."

"How come you don't know a thing like that?"

"They moved."

"Sure."

It was no use. He put the money away, defeated.

As he made for the door he passed the old man with the laundry bag, who was fumbling with his letters and relocking his box, one of hundreds of numbered metal compartments set into the wall.

He stopped and faced the clerk again.

"I'll wait, then," he said defiantly. "They have to come in to pick up their mail sooner or later."

The clerk lumbered out from behind the counter. "I don't want you in here. I've seen you before, hanging around."

"You've never seen me in here." You're confused, he thought, like everybody else. I'm not Madsen. "I'm an actor, for God's sake. It's only a part."

"My son was an actor," said the old man.

He was startled by the voice. He looked at the balding head, the

327

stooped posture, the gray skin. It was difficult to believe that anyone could have changed so much.

"*Dad*?" he said.

"I wouldn't have recognized you, son."

"Never in a million years," said his mother.

"No?" He forced a laugh. He had grown the beard three or four years ago, for the show. Didn't they remember?

"Does it itch?" asked his father.

"A little. I guess I don't notice it anymore." He cracked his knuckles and sat back in the Winnebago, then leaned forward again. At his spine was his dad's laundry bag, a pillowcase spilling clothes yet to be folded, socks and underwear and shirts.

"Let me move that for you," said his mother.

"It's all right," he said.

"I used to hang everything up before it wrinkled," she explained. "But we can't do that now. The laundromat is seven blocks, and there's never a place for the RV . . ."

"Don't they let you use the washer and dryer?" He parted the curtains at the back of the motor home's kitchenette, pointing at the apartment complex adjoining the lot where they were parked. "After all, you're paying for this space."

"Oh, we're not renting," said his mother. "You see, the nice couple who manage the building are friends of ours. We don't even have a proper address."

"Retired folks," added his father with a wink. "Like us."

"And there are families with children who need clean clothes every day . . ."

"They can't be that nice," he said. "Jesus, it would be the least they could do."

He saw his mother avert her eyes. I shouldn't have taken the Lord's name in vain, he thought. *Language, young man*, he remembered her saying. He had said much worse when he was a teenager, but those three words from her were always enough; the words, and the catch in her voice, the disappointment. He was filled with regret. He wanted to reach out and take her hands.

He cleared his throat.

"You must be hungry," she said.

"Not really." How ungrateful that must sound. "Unless you are." Then he remembered Claire. "What time's it getting to be?"

"You'll stay?" said his mother.

He checked his watch.

"Let me take you out to dinner," he said.

"Oh, no. The decent places are all so expensive . . ."

328

"Even with our seniors' discount," his father said.

"Don't worry about it. It's my treat."

"We couldn't let you do that," said his mother. "We know how hard it's been."

"What do you mean? I can afford it."

His mother smiled indulgently.

"Don't you believe me?" he said. "Do you know how much they're paying me every week?"

"You have a regular job, then?"

He almost laughed. "Well, I don't know if you can call it that, but— "

"It's all right," said his father.

"What is?"

He did not understand. Unless they, too, had him confused with the character he played on "As the World Ends." It was not possible. Was it?

"You don't believe that soap opera, do you?"

Then he saw the portable television set, its antenna poking out between the cardboard cartons above the trundle bed. It was dusty with disuse. He was relieved, until he realized that they did not even know about the show.

"It must have been hard," his father said, "after you and Carol broke up."

His mother leaned closer. "She was never really one of us, you know."

He blinked. "Carol?" The girl he had gone with in high school. "That was—a long time ago."

"You had to find out for yourself," said his father. "I know how it is."

"I could fix something to eat," said his mother.

"Later." I'll go out and pick up some food, he thought. Soon. Time was running out. Like irregular rows of stones, the tops of parked cars cast lengthening shadows across the apartment complex lot; the motor home's shadow was the longest, extending to the side of the building itself, like the adumbration of something long forgotten whose presence remained inescapable. "Just some coffee for now," he said. "If it's not too much trouble."

His mother busied herself with plastic cups and spoons, heating water on the mini-stove. Above the hissing of a propane flame he heard children roaming free in the hallways between the nearby apartments, finding their own reckless way, making choices the consequences of which would not be felt for years to come. When she sat down with the coffee, she had a book under her arm.

"I'll bet you don't remember this," she said.

"What?"

Then he recognized the slender volume as his junior high school yearbook.

"Mama, please," he said.

"Just you wait, now . . ."

He braced himself for yet another look at his infamous full-page portrait as class president, the one with his hair slicked back in the geeky style of the times, his fly partially unzipped for all the world and posterity to see.

Instead she flipped to the back of the book and the group photos.

"Here."

Each side of the two-page spread contained a pair of homeroom classes. She tapped one of the wide-angle photographs.

"This one."

His mother beamed.

He scanned the back row of the panorama for his own scrubbed features, centered as always among the tallest in his age group. He did not find it. He checked the caption. Yes, it was his old homeroom, the 7-15's. Had he been absent that day?

"Where?"

She laid a finger near the bottom of the page.

Next to her fingernail was the front row, made up of the shortest students, mostly boys. The heads of the thirteen-year-olds were no larger than buckshot. How ridiculously young they looked, dressed in jeans with rolled cuffs and shirts picked out for them by their mothers, grinning toothlessly as though it all mattered.

"I don't— "

She tapped her finger.

There, at the edge of the first row, one little boy stood apart from the rest. He posed with his thumbs hooked in the pockets of his rumpled, ill-fitting denims, his chin stuck out pugnaciously.

Somehow, in that part of his mind where such things were recorded forever, he seemed to recall a similar T-shirt with faded stripes, the short sleeves too tight . . .

But he had never looked like this. His clothes were always pressed. And by then he had already grown to most of his adult height. That was why he had been chosen for the Drama Club, so that he could play older characters.

"Let me see this," he said.

He riffled to the portraits of class officers, found the right page and pressed it flat.

"There. Remember now, Mom?"

"What is it you want to . . .? Oh, yes! Wasn't he the nicest young

330

man? I often wonder what became of him. Maybe if you'd had friends like that . . ."

He took the book away from her.

There was the seventh-grade class president, wearing a letterman's sweater and a world-weary smirk. If you looked closely you could detect the unforgettable half-opened zipper.

Only it was not his face.

It was another boy's.

"And this one . . ." his mother said.

She brought out more yearbooks. He recognized the colors of his school, the dates. And yet each told a different story from the one he remembered. A very different story.

"These books," he said. "Where did you get them?"

"I've saved them all," she said. "They're the only record of the past now."

Whose past? According to these he had never been elected class president, had never served on the student council or edited the school newspaper or starred in the senior play. He had never earned the grade point average that kept him at the top of his class.

"How could you be proud of someone like that?"

"We are," said his father.

"But— "

"You're our only son," his mother said softly. "You're all we have."

He paced the short distance of the Winnebago's interior.

"Let me get this straight," he said. "You don't remember the acting scholarship, the trip to New York, the auditions, the jobs? The reviews?" He had sent them copies, hadn't he? "Then Hollywood and the series, the daytime TV?"

"That was always your dream, I know," said his mother. "You would have done those things if you'd had the opportunity. I'm sure of it. I only wish we could have helped you more."

"Then what *do* you remember? When was the last time I came out to see you, for example?"

"At the old house?" His mother's hands fidgeted. "Let's see. It would be just after you and Carol—had that trouble. And you went away. Not that we blame you. She was a worthless piece of fluff."

"What else? What about *your* lives?"

"Well, after your father's operation there wasn't anything left, of course, even with the Medicare, so . . ."

"So we made the best of it," said his dad. "The same as you. That's life."

"You didn't get the checks?" he said. "I told my secretary to mail them out." I did, he thought, I swear.

"You would have if you could," said his mother. "We know that. But now you're here, and that's all that matters. We always knew you'd come back."

"Do you need a place to stay, son? Just till you get on your feet. There's always room for one more."

"A family has to take care of its own," said his mother.

"Or we're no better than animals," said his father.

His legs began to fail him. His head reeled under the low ceiling and his eyes lost focus in the dimness. He groped for the door at his back.

"Excuse me," was all he could say before he staggered outside.

After six rings he gave up. He lowered the phone.

Just before he let go of the receiver there was a faint click on the other end.

"Post-Production."

He fumbled it back up to his ear. "Marty?"

"Talk to me."

He felt a surge of relief. "Marty, thank God."

"Who's this?"

A tingle in the pit of his stomach, like the feeling in the middle of the night that wakes you up before you know why.

"Who do you think?"

A shuffling on the other end, Marty's voice fading in and out. "Listen, we're up to our assholes here, so— "

"Put me through to Jack."

"Jack's not here. Who am I speaking to?"

He was afraid to say his name. What if Marty did not recognize it?

"Debbie, then. She's there, isn't she?"

"Who?"

"Debbie Conner." My assistant, he thought. Or at least that's the way I remember it.

"You got the wrong extension. Dial again and— "

"Who's in the booth?"

"Nobody."

"Somebody has to be in the booth! Who's directing?"

"There *is* no director," said Marty. "We don't *need* a director. It's Saturday—we're doing sound cues. Bye."

The phone went dead.

He stood by the pay phone, between Beach Boy's Chinese Food and Sinbad's. To the east, new signs broke the skyline like alien coral.

American Diner, Chiporama, Frostie . . . all unrecognizable. When had it happened?

Shaking, he took out another coin.

He could call his agent. Or his accountant. Or his secretary.

But not till Monday morning.

And he could not wait that long.

There was still Claire . . .

But what if she did not know him, either? Was he ready to face that?

Instead he let the receiver slip from his grasp and leafed through the directory.

Marcos, Morehead, Morel . . .

Moreland, Carol.

She was in the book, his old girlfriend. And the address was the same. She was still here. She had never moved.

He could call her . . .

When she answered, what would she say? And what would he say to her? That he had come back to make things right? Was that even possible now? What if she remembered a different past, too—what if it really was too late?

His fingers closed and tore the page out.

He walked on, feeling the boards creak and begin to give way beneath his feet.

HELP KEEP YOUR PIER BEAUTIFUL, warned a sign. PLEASE USE RECEPTACLES.

Without breaking stride he dropped the page into the trash can.

My first love, he thought. So many years ago. And all this time I've told myself I was right to end it. That it was good for both of us to move on, following separate paths. I rationalized that there was more. For me. And for her. I thought she left for the city when I did. I told myself that.

But she didn't have the strength.

Or the recklessness.

People should look after each other. Or we're no better than animals. I did that, didn't I?

No. I went off to find a way, *my* way. Everyone else be damned. And now the score is evening up . . .

He raised his collar and continued walking.

The Playland Arcade was still open. Bright lights, people of every age hunkered over the games: Genesis, Big Choice, Party Animal, Battle Zone, Bad Dudes, Banzai Run, Millionaire, Eight Ball, Forgotten Worlds, The Real Ghostbusters.

He stopped to watch them. They were so intent on the play, as balls were lost in the machinery and points accumulated, to be added up or subtracted at the end, depending upon one's control. He considered going inside. Then he noticed a sign at the entrance:

FAMILY FUN ZONE
BAD LANGUAGE
NO VIOLENCE
LOITERING

He moved on.

Ahead was the old carousel, closed for the night, and opposite it a large unfinished building: FUTURE HOME OF THE MUSEUM OF MARINE MAMMALS. Farther along, at the tip of the pier, only a bait and tackle shop, and beyond that darkness.

Behind him, the waterfront restaurants and shops and street signs pointing the way into a strange town.

I could go back, he thought. But what's left?

What have I done?

I identified with my role, ignoring everything else; that was my mistake. If you do that sort of thing, you become that sort of animal. I was too lost in the game to realize. And now it has come due at last, an empty sum with nothing to draw on. The good eroded by the bad, as if it never existed.

Only this moment.

That was why they gave us memory. Without it everything else falls away, the legacy of the past is trashed and we are left stranded.

The logic is perfect. The future created by the present, the present by the past . . .

But there is one part they don't tell you.

It works retroactively—in both directions.

Now a rumbling sounded directly beneath him, as if the earth were about to open.

It was the tide rolling in, clacking the stones, pounding the boulders and resounding through each fractional inch of the shoreline.

He held the rail.

Out there, he knew, was the rock where something lived, something old, a species out of touch with the mainland and all but forgotten. Were they trapped? Unless someone came to show the way, they would remain there, cut off, until they were finally dragged to shore and installed as curiosities in the marine museum to die.

He wanted to go out there, to be there with them. But the sea was dark, and even the jetty was lost to him now.

A sudden breeze stirred.

He thought he heard a cry drifting in on the waves.

He listened intently, until the cry was no longer distinguishable from any other sound in the night.

Then he shivered as the breeze strafed the pier, swept the boards and returned to the open sea.

The white form of a pelican rose above the breakers and began to circle slowly, its pale wings extended as if anticipating an embrace. As the circle widened to include the pier, it came to rest atop the carousel enclosure.

His eyes followed the line of the roof down to the boardwalk.

Incredibly, the mime was still there. So taken with his role, perhaps, that he was not aware of the hour, unwilling or unable to leave.

You may as well go home now, he thought. It's over.

He walked past, turned and came back, studying the face that was frozen behind a mask of greasepaint.

The mime stared straight ahead, at a spot on the horizon where the sun had gone down.

"Hi."

The mime did not move a muscle.

He cleared his throat and tried again. "Remember? This afternoon. You called me—something. A name. What was it?"

He moved in, closing the distance between them until their faces were inches apart.

"What did you call me?" he said. "I can't remember."

The mime refused to answer.

"Please. I need to know."

They stood there facing each other. Time passed, each second slipping into the next and lost forever. He waited, but there was no response.

J. L. COMEAU

Taking Care of Michael

JUDITH LYNN COMEAU's story "Firebird", a fast-paced blend of police procedural and witchcraft, was one of the best received stories we included in *Best New Horror 2*. She returns in this volume with a much shorter, but no less impressive, contribution.

A full-time writer since 1987, whose interests include aviculture, ancient music, 18th and 19th century English novels, textile arts, anthropology, archaeology, psychology and "all things dark and horrible", her fiction can be found in such anthologies as *The Women Who Walk Through Fire*, *Women of the West*, *The Year's Best Horror Stories: XIX*, *Borderlands 2* and *Hottest Blood*.

She recently completed her first novel, entitled *Haunted Landscapes*.

MICHAEL'S EAR FALLS INTO THE BATHWATER with a loud plunk and I have to remember not to scrub so hard when I wash him. Momma would've had a fit before she got so quiet, but Michael doesn't seem to mind. I blow a sweaty strand of hair away from my forehead and fish around the bottom of the tub with one hand for the lost part. I need my other hand to hold on to Michael. Wouldn't want him to fall under the water, too! I find his ear soon enough and stick it back onto the hole in the side of his head where it came from, but it keeps sliding off back into the water. Finally, I give up and lift Michael into his roller chair where I wipe him dry real good with a big fluffy towel nice and hot from the clothes dryer.

Just think what Momma would say about that ear! She thinks I never do anything right. Michael, he was always the smart one. He made good grades in school and always had lots of friends. Popular, you know? And Michael was always good to me, too, sticking up for me when the other kids laughed at me or called me ugly names and ran away. One time, the kids left me out in the woods holding an empty pillowcase. They said they were going to fan out and drive some kind of animals called "snipes" toward me so I could catch them in the pillowcase. I was real happy that the kids let me play with them and I waited and waited, but the snipes never came and neither did the kids. I found out later that they all laughed and went home. I don't see what was so funny, do you?

Anyway, Michael came into the woods the next day and found me still holding the pillowcase and waiting. He never said a word about the way I'd peed and messed my pants. That's Michael for you. A real prince of a young man, like Momma always used to say.

One day Momma came in my room crying and told me Michael crashed his little red car and was hurt real bad: broke his neck, she said. When they brought him home from the hospital, Michael was in a chair with wheels and couldn't move his arms or legs or talk or anything. He could move his mouth a little, and his eyes, that's all. So Momma took care of Michael, feeding him and bathing him and shaving him and everything. It's too bad about Michael, Momma said all the time. We've got to take care of your brother now.

But then a couple of weeks ago, Momma never got up from the couch after watching *Jeopardy*. She's still there in the front room, sitting on the sofa in front of the television set. She watches the television all day and all night, even when there's nothing on but fuzz and static. Momma never blinks, even though her eyeballs got all dried and crusty. I guess she just got tired from taking care of Michael all the time.

I don't mind taking care of Michael while Momma rests. He's my brother and I'd do anything for him. He's always been good to me and now it's my turn to be good to him.

I'm going to shave Michael's face now. Momma always said she hated whiskers on a man, even before we took Daddy out to the big green park with trees and rocks and buried him in a long box in the ground. I like the sound Daddy's straight razor makes on the leather strop hooked to the bathroom wall. *Whop*, *whop*, *whop*, it goes. It doesn't take long until the blade's sharp enough to split a long black hair I pull out of my own head.

I turn to Michael with a smile, but Michael doesn't smile back because I accidentally slipped and cut off his lips the last time I shaved his face. But I can tell by the way his eyes roll around that he's ready for Daddy's big, sharp razor. This time I'll try not to slice off anything by mistake.

Like Momma always says, "Practice makes perfect." And I'm getting better all the time.

THOMAS TESSIER

The Dreams of Dr Ladybank

THOMAS TESSIER was born in Connecticut, where he currently lives. Educated at University College, Dublin, he spent several years in London working as a freelance journalist and publisher.

Tessier is the author of three volumes of poetry and a trio of plays that were professionally staged, and his novels include *The Fates*, *The Nightwalker*, *Shockwaves*, *Phantom*, *Finishing Touches*, *Secret Strangers* and *The White Gods*. His short fiction has been collected in *The Lady Crossing and Other Tales of Panic*.

The novella which follows proves that Tessier's view of people and the world is becoming, if possible, even bleaker.

A Divine Image

Cruelty has a Human Heart
And Jealousy a Human Face
Terror, the Human Form Divine
And Secrecy, the Human Dress

The Human Dress, is forged Iron
The Human Form, a fiery Forge.
The Human Face, a Furnace seal'd
The Human Heart, its hungry Gorge.

—William Blake

PROLOGUE

"It's an amusing thought, Ian, but . . ."

"Impossible."

"Well, yes."

"Science fiction."

"And weak on the science," Jack said.

"But doesn't the idea itself excite you?"

"Not really. I mean, what's the point? Everyone knows it's a dead end. Besides, even if it were possible, and I'm not for a moment admitting that it is, but if it were, you'd probably wind up with a raving psychotic on your hands, and that's not my idea of fun. Psychotics are very boring people."

"Psychosis is by no means inevitable."

"This is a splendid malt, by the way."

"Help yourself to more."

"Thanks, I will."

"The point you're refusing to acknowledge is the simple fact of communication, establishing once and for all that it really is possible. My God, Jack, that's a huge leap and you know it. You can't deny it."

"And you can't prove it."

"Perhaps I can."

"Well, I'd love to see it."

"What would you say if I told you I've found a suitable mind for the experiment?"

"I'd say she's probably young, impressionable, quite pretty, very malleable, and a great piece of ass."

"Jack."

"But I'm afraid that your getting her in bed and fucking her brains out will not be widely accepted as scientific proof."

"All right, I give up."

"Ah, don't stop now, Ian. I'm enjoying this. I haven't had such a good mix of booze and bullshit since college, when we used to sit up late at night, trying to figure out what the hell an ethic was, and how to get around it. We called those sessions the Utica Club, because that's all we could afford to drink."

"But I'm serious."

"Okay, you're serious, and you've got this, uh . . ."

"Subject."

"Right, subject."

"Two of them, actually," Ian said with a hint of smugness in his tight smile. "Two young men."

"Men, huh? You must be serious."

"Yes, and the fact that there are two of them should provide proof enough to justify continuing the research, don't you think? One might be a fluke, but two different people, who are strangers to each other, who respond and meet and interact *by design*—you would take that seriously, wouldn't you?"

"Sure, but come on, Ian. You can't do that with people. If you could, somebody would have discovered it by now. It's not as if we're completely ignorant of how the brain works. What it can and can't do—and I'll tell you one thing, it can't do that."

"The human brain does generate extremely low frequency radio waves, ELF signals. That's a well-known fact."

"Yes, but you can't do anything with them."

"If you say so."

"Not like you're talking about."

"We'll see."

"So, are these guys patients of yours?"

"No, they're just a couple of losers I met."

"And they agreed to go along with whatever it is you plan to try out on them, this experiment?"

"They don't know anything about it."

"What?"

"That would ruin everything, Jack. If they knew, they would expect, and expectation would contaminate their minds. Of course I haven't told them anything."

"Uh, have *you* ever heard of ethics, Ian?"

"Which one did you have in mind?"

"Oh, the one about not experimenting on people without their knowledge and consent. Seems to me there might even be some kind of a law about that."

"Tsk, tsk."

"What exactly is it you intend to do?"

"Nothing. That's the beauty of it."

"I don't understand."

"I'll just be thinking, Jack. That's all. Thinking of them and perhaps even for them."

"Ah, that's all right. Thinking isn't against the law, not yet anyway. But how will you know if it works?"

"I'm not sure, but I imagine it will become apparent one way or another."

"Well, if it does work, let me handle the legal side of it. Maybe we can sell it to Sony, ha-ha."

"That's a thought."

"I can see it now. Everybody will go around wearing a smart little beanie on their head, with an antenna sticking up. They'd sell like Walkmans—or should it be Walk*men*?"

By the time Jack finally left, after sopping up a good deal more single malt scotch, Doctor Ian Ladybank was almost sorry he had mentioned his little secret. But he had to tell someone, and Jack was the closest thing to a friend he had. You can't stumble across something like that and then not want to shout about it.

Nor was it really a little secret; it was serious, major, an awesome challenge. He was sure it had in fact been discovered by others, in the past, although they might not have understood what it was the way he did. It was a skill, it had limits, and it was suitable only for personal purposes.

Amazing, how it had happened. Doctor Ladybank had given the matter a lot of thought over the years. The brain was his hobby, as well as his vocation. He read everything that came out and he even made a special study of radio science. His obsession wasn't his alone—there were other people active in the field. He was aware, for instance, of the theory that some UFO sightings may be triggered by localized disturbances in the earth's magnetic field that interfered with the wave cycles in the observer's brain. It was a matter of some significance to Doctor Ladybank—although few others seemed to consider it important—that the earth, the planet itself, was constantly broad-casting its own ELF waves, and that they were remarkably similar to those generated by the human brain. He devised his own mental exercises, instructing his mind to do what it had never done before.

All of this led nowhere until a young woman named Shelly had come to see him, not long ago. She thought she was stigmatic and she had the wounds to prove it. Her case was not as interesting as it had seemed at first glance but she was an attractive little creature.

344

In his waiting room, as he was showing her out, Doctor Ladybank suddenly found himself wishing, or willing, that Shelly would reach up and touch her breast. A silly but typical erotic fancy, borne no doubt of mid-afternoon tedium. The girl did not respond, but her boyfriend, who had accompanied her to the office and was standing nearby, absently rubbed his Megadeath T-shirt at the spot where it covered his left nipple. The young man's blank expression indicated complete ignorance.

Stunned, Doctor Ladybank at first could not bring himself to believe what had apparently just taken place. It was too easy to be true. But yes, he had felt a tiny mental spasm at the instant the thought—wish, command, whatever—formed within his mind. Doctor Ladybank was flushed with a sense of accomplishment, happy as a boy who suddenly flicks his wrist in precisely the right way and at last manages to skip a rock across water.

He stood by the window in his office a few minutes later and watched Shelly and her boyfriend walk away down the street. When they were almost out of sight, Doctor Ladybank had a parting idea for them—and sure enough, the boyfriend's hand swung around to pat Shelly's ass. That evening Doctor Ladybank thought about the boyfriend again. *You need to talk to me. Urgently.* Less than a minute later, the telephone rang. He was Alvin Doolittle, but he preferred the nickname Snake.

The other one was sent to Doctor Ladybank, like many of his cases, by the juvenile court. Tony Delgado was only sixteen, but he had his own apartment, a trick pad near the river in the south end of the city. It was a decrepit neighborhood, full of rotting old tenements and abandoned factories, a tidal basin of foundered lives, but it provided all the tolerance and anonymity needed for Tony to practice his trade.

Doctor Ladybank quickly sized the boy up as innately Machian in affect. What Tony possessed was not quite a mind, but more of a constantly shifting panorama of received images and sensations. He learned little but survived, thanks to an underlying canniness that for nearly three years had helped him dodge both the law and the retribution of the streets. A minor stupidity had led him to juvenile court, which promply fobbed him off on Doctor Ladybank, who within a quarter of an hour had the youth uttering numbers in German while tugging at his earlobes.

It was a discovery that should be important. It should give Doctor Ladybank power, fame, wealth—all the usual prizes. The only trouble was, he didn't know how to take the next step. What to do with this fantastic skill. How could he present it in such a way that would satisfy the scientific community? He could make videotapes of sessions with Snake and Tony, inducing all kinds of bizarre and unlikely behavior, but that would prove nothing. Not the least of Doctor Ladybank's problems was the painful fact that this skill of his simply didn't work with most people. He tried it with everyone he met now, but the original poor fools were the only two in the plus column. In spite of the odds against it, he was dogged by a fear that both of them really were flukes. Maybe it was just a freak of nature, devoid of any principle or broader application. But even if that were so, there was still a measure of personal satisfaction in what he was doing.

And it was early days yet. Doctor Ladybank was sure that he would learn much more as he pursued his experiment, and sooner or later the ultimate answers would come to him.

I

Tony Delgado thought he understood the problem. This Pied Piper, to give him a name, had a special kind of radio that he used to beam his infernal messages into Tony's brain. It had been going on for a couple of weeks now, and the situation was only getting worse. Tony had tried to catch the Pied Piper several times before he realized that it was impossible. The Pied Piper was only about six inches tall, and could appear or disappear at will. Many times he was heard, not seen. There was no way Tony could get a hold of the little demon.

Tony was running out of possibilities. He had gone to Dom's Connection, the largest electronics store in the city, but they told him they didn't have any kind of jamming device that would do what he wanted. They suggested that he consider buying a good radio or stereo system, and just play loud music whenever he was bothered. But Tony had already tried that with the boombox he owned, and it didn't work. Static-ridden, distorted perhaps, the Pied Piper still got into Tony's head.

Now Tony had another idea. He rooted through the underwear in the top drawer of his bureau, and came up with the stiletto he had acquired somewhere along the line. It was his best weapon in the awkward moments that occasionally arose, not so much for use as for display. In Tony's chosen line of work it was sometimes necessary to introduce a deterrent factor, that slight touch of intimidation that prevents serious trouble, and the stiletto had never failed to chill a tricky customer. He was pleased to find that it hadn't lost any of its sharpness, though for the task he had in mind now all he would require was the very fine tip of the gleaming blade.

Tony Delgado lived in a small apartment in the heart of the south end. He was sixteen, and had been on his own for the best part of a year now. He had a perfect body, which he took care of religiously because it was his bread and butter. At five-ten, he was neither too tall nor too short. His physique was slender and boyish, and he avoided the muscular look, but he exercised enough to maintain a body texture that was both supple and firm.

He had one good room, the large one where he entertained his customers. Tony had invested a lot in that room, setting it up for the fantasy scenarios that were his trademark. He sometimes had to discourage mushy johns who wanted to use his personal bed or to stay all night. He preferred it that way, keeping the rest of his place, and life, off-limits. Tony's bedroom was small and cluttered, the kitchen bug-infested. The bathroom was modest but clean, and one way or another it saw a lot of use.

The trouble started more than a month ago. Tony had always been successful at avoiding the police until then. He had picked up a john at a bar in the neighborhood, but when they got outside the asshole lost his nerve. A patrol car happened to pass by as Tony was kicking in the rocker panel on the man's shiny new car. It should have come to nothing. The asshole naturally refused to press charges. However, Tony then made the unfortunate mistake of giving the cop a hard time, even shoving him away once. Since he was still a minor, Tony was sent to juvenile court, where some drip of a judge gave him a boring lecture and then ordered him to see a psychiatrist.

What a joke that turned out to be. For one thing, the guy had a funny name, Lady-something. Ladybug would be right, Tony thought, because the shrink was the crazy one. He was straight, and even beautiful, but as the interview went on Tony began to feel like he was stuck with a creep. It was no one thing the guy did that bothered him, just a very uncomfortable feeling that got stronger all the time. Tony had never experienced anything like that, and he had met some strange people.

In the end, the shrink talked pure nonsense. He told Tony to watch out for the bright lights, bright colors, and, most of all, bright flowers. What kind of shit was that? Tony decided Doctor Ladybug was in bigger trouble than he was, and he nodded his head politely, agreeing with everything the shrink said.

It must have been the smart thing to do, because he was sent home to his mother, no additional sessions required. He was free of any legal obligations. Tony was back at work in his apartment that same night.

Tony's mother understood nothing. For thirty years she had worked at a dry-cleaning shop, and still did. Some people argued that the fumes were dangerous, and Mrs Delgado did get headaches regularly, but it was steady work and there was a lot to be said for seniority.

She believed anything Tony told her. He was her youngest child, born when she thought her body was past all that. And he was the best when it came to calling her, visiting and giving her little gifts. So kind and considerate. She didn't like the fact that he lived away from her when he was still so young, but there was nothing she could do about it. Kids grow up quicker today, they do what they want, and Tony didn't have a father around to lay down the law. But at least the boy was good to her, and he lived less than a mile away.

So his first brush with the law had come to nothing, and his mother still lived in happy ignorance of his activities, but Tony faced other problems. AIDS had claimed or scared off some of his top customers, and to keep his income up he was forced to cruise the bars more often. That multiplied both his legal and medical risks. So far he remained clean, but business was tough, and getting tougher every week.

He had also developed a taste for coke. The good stuff, not that crack shit. But it cost money, and Tony was also convinced that it was one of the reasons he was so jumpy of late. However, these drawbacks were not enough to curb his appetite. They were simply new factors to bear in mind.

Worst of all, the Pied Piper had entered his life. At first Tony thought he was imagining things, or that it was some kind of weird side-effect of the drug. He would glimpse a trick of light or a play of shadows, but it was always on the other side of the room, and he always caught it out of the corner of his eye. When he turned to look carefully, there was nothing to see.

Then there were the sounds. Tony began to think of them as messages of some kind, though he never really understood them at all. They were like bubbles of noise that burst open deep inside his head. There was always a lot of static with it, which is how Tony finally cottoned on to the possibility that the Pied Piper was broadcasting to him. It was possible to pick out a few words now and then, sometimes a phrase or two, but none of it ever made any sense. Tony did get a certain feeling of urgency, and that only aggravated his distress.

Soon enough, the little man emerged tauntingly, letting Tony see him clearly—if only for a brief instant at a time. Now, a day never passed without one appearance, usually more. He never actually said anything, and his expression was always blank. The little fucker was a constant torment, even when he wasn't there. The only positive thing was that so far he hadn't turned up when there was a customer present.

Tony went into the bathroom and turned on the light around the mirror. He stood close to it, opened his mouth and found his targets. Tony's teeth were not perfect. Over the years he had accumulated a few plastic or composite fillings. They were okay, he figured. He wanted the two larger ones that were made of lead or silver, some kind of metal. It seemed obvious to him that the Pied Piper was using those fillings as built-in receivers for his transmissions. The metal picked up the beam and relayed it along the nerves in Tony's jawbone on to the center of his brain. So, if he could just get rid of those two fillings he might solve his problem. He had called three different dentists, but they seemed to think it was a set-up for a lawsuit, and turned him down cold. The only alternative was to do it himself.

It wasn't easy. At least he could get at the two fillings and still see what he was doing, but for the longest time the tip of the blade found no hold. Tony grew frustrated, then angry as the knife slipped off the tooth and jabbed his gums. He tasted a little of his own blood when he swallowed. His open mouth filled with saliva too fast, and some of it trickled down his windpipe, setting off a violent but useless coughing jag. Tony's eyes were bleary as he tried to refocus on the tooth. He was beginning to think it was an impossible chore, but then the point of the blade finally lodged in some tiny crevice for a second. It slipped off almost at once, but he was encouraged, and several tries later he found the spot again. Tony worked it carefully, digging the tip into the gap and trying to expand it. As long as the metal blade touched the metal filling it jangled the nerves in his tooth like a constant electrical charge, but he would endure that to get rid of the Pied Piper. Any pain would be worth suffering if it would end the daily nightmare visitations.

Tony's eyes continued to blur with tears and his jaw ached, but he was making progress. Now he had gouged enough of a crack to be able to use the knife as a lever. But whenever he relaxed or became careless, the knife would pop loose again and stab Tony in the gum or on the roof of the mouth. The saliva that spilled out on his chin was distinctly pink. Worst of all, the goddamn metal filling seemed to be welded to the goddamn tooth. No matter how hard he pried at it, there was barely any movement.

"Come on, you fuck," Tony whined. "You're killing me."

Then he screamed and dropped the knife as he reached for the wall to hold himself against as a blast of pain shot through his entire body. The knife clattered in the sink. This is too much, he thought as he reached for it with trembling fingers. But then he discovered that the filling was loose. Yeah, he could move it with his tongue. It was still hooked in there, but when he poked it repeatedly it felt like it was rattling in place. Gasping for breath, Tony forced himself to re-insert the knife.

"*Ein, zwei, drei . . .*"

He increased the pressure, and the pain blossomed, weakening him so much that all the strength in his body seemed to be flying out of his pores. One last shove—the filling was at last torn free, but the knife blade scraped a bloody furrow across the roof of Tony's mouth at the same time. He nearly swallowed the jagged filling but managed to spit it into the sink. It bounced around like a deformed marble before coming to rest. Tony was dizzy and drained, and the hole in his tooth felt enormous, but he had done it. One down, one to go. He washed his mouth out, and then sat on the toilet lid for a few minutes to rest.

The second filling seemed to take longer, probably because he had little patience left. His arms and neck ached, along with his jaw, but somehow the pain bothered him less. Tony pushed on, desperate to finish the job, and eventually he was rewarded when the second filling slid off his tongue and joined the first one in the sink. He felt an enormous sense of satisfaction, freedom and accomplishment. He took the two lumps of twisted metal into the kitchen, opened the window, and threw them as far as he could out in the weed-choked, trash-strewn backyard.

Tony rinsed his mouth again, this time with warm salty water to stop the bleeding. Then he poured a large scotch, to remove the bad taste and soothe his nerves. He sat down in his one good room and sipped the drink carefully. God, he was still shaking. His arms and legs felt so weak. He let his tongue dance over the two holes in his teeth. They were huge. The edges were so sharp he would have to be careful not to cut his tongue on them.

But no dentist could refuse him now. Two fillings fell out when he was eating. Tough pizza crust, say. Or peanuts, or when he bit into a steak. It didn't matter what. That kind of thing happened all the time. Tony would insist they be replaced with plastic or porcelain fillings, anything but metal.

He smiled faintly as he sloshed the whiskey around in his mouth. It stung his exposed nerves, but he knew that it was also beginning to deaden them. The pain was fading deliciously.

Zzzzzt.

Oh no, no.

Zzzzzt.

Tony put the drink down on the table because he was afraid he might drop it. This can't be happening. He looked around the room nervously. A glimmer of movement, then gone. A shadow that passed in an instant, as if a bird had flown by the window. Then the static cleared up beautifully.

—Ah, that's much better.

The words blared inside Tony's trapped mind.
—You can really hear me now, can't you!

II

"*Hic, haec, hoc.*"
"Say what?" The bartender looked puzzled, wary.
"What?"
"You said something to me?"
"No," Snake replied. "I didn't say nothing to nobody."
"You want another beer?"
"Yeah, I want another beer," Snake said, his voice brimming with defiance. "And a clean glass."

The bartender brought the drink and the glass, withdrew some money from the small pile of cash in front of Snake, and muttered to himself in Spanish as he turned away. Lousy greaseball, Snake thought as he inspected the new glass. I'm sitting here, minding my own business, having a quiet beer, and this asshole has to get on my case. Say what? Say, fuck you, bro.

At least tonight Snake knew what he was doing in this place. He was waiting for the whore, Toni. Last night he had no idea at all why he had come there. The El Greco was a pisshole of a bar, buried in the unfriendly depths of the south end. But Snake went out last night, leaving Shelly behind alone and cursing, and he'd come straight across the river to this dump. He hated the place. It had the terrible smell of food you'd never want to eat, and it was full of jabbering spics. They all had the same look on their faces too, mean and vaguely pissed off, as if every damned one of them had to go through life with a splinter up his dick.

They wouldn't bother him, though, because Snake was wearing the colors. Sure, they could beat the living shit out of him if they wanted to, but they knew he'd be back sooner or later with thirty of the hardest fuckers around who would trash the El Greco, along with every spic they could get their hands on. Nor did it matter that Snake was no longer exactly in good standing as a member of the Legion of the Lost; he wore the colors, and that was all that counted in a situation like this. The colors commanded respect, or at least fear—which wasn't very different.

Last night he sat in the same place at the bar for nearly an hour, wondering what the hell he was doing there and why he could not bring himself to leave. It was odd, but then some odd things had been happening to Snake lately. Headaches, for one, the kind that ordinary painkillers didn't cure. And, according to Shelly, he was talking to himself more and more. But that was crazy. It stood to reason that a man can't go around talking to himself and not know it. Could he? What about that latest incident, the one with the bartender a few minutes ago? No, it was impossible. In a noisy place like this, the bartender made a mistake.

Besides, Shelly had her own problems. She'd gone quite pale and spotty in recent weeks. She also scratched herself a lot, so much so in fact that it had reached the point where she had these ugly open wounds in her hands and feet and on her body. Then, as if that weren't enough, she decided they were the marks of Christ on the Cross. Snake had to take her to the doctor, who sent them along to a shrink. Dumb fucking bitch. He ought to sell her off to an out-of-state gang, but the way she was now, her sales value was scraping along the bottom. Shelly was so bad that he didn't even want to touch her anymore—unless he had to hit her.

Maybe that was why Snake had come to the El Greco, to meet a new piece of ass. He had accomplished that much last night, when Toni sat down beside him and they got to talking. She was a fine item, all right. Cute fanny, long legs, pretty face. She could be a bit fuller up front, but Snake had never been all that keen on big tits. He liked women lean and—snaky.

It didn't bother him that she was a spic. Somehow, that was okay in a woman. Toni's creamy skin was such a pleasant contrast to Shelly's newsprint surface. And the eyes—deep, round, warm and brown, with flecks of gold. Snake couldn't remember the last time he'd looked closely at Shelly's eyes, but now he thought of them as washed-out blue peas adrift in a pinkish-white glaze. No question, Toni was an exotic gem in comparison.

It did bother him, however, that she was a whore. He didn't care how many men she fucked. The problem was that he lacked the money to buy her talents. Even if he had it, it would go against the grain for Snake to spend it on something he'd always managed to get for free.

He and Toni were eventually able to work out a deal based on non-cash considerations. She liked coke, and she needed Demerol. Snake had experience and helpful contacts in the field. He was strictly minor league, but he did know how to cut himself an edge in such transactions. It was one of the many ways in which he cobbled together an erratic income.

"Darling."

"Hey, babe." Snake smiled as Toni edged close to him at the bar. "You look great."

"Buy me a drink."

"Sure. What'll you have?"

"You forgot already. Tsk, tsk."

"Yeah, well . . . What was it again?"

"Red Death on the rocks."

"Right."

As there were no other barstools free, Snake gave Toni his. He signalled the bartender. Toni looked fantastic in a clinging black minidress. Snake could hardly take his eyes off her legs, but he did turn away long enough to watch the bartender carefully when he took the money for Toni's drink.

"You can take your sunglasses off."

"I like the dark," she replied.

"It's dark enough in this dump."

Toni sipped her drink. "Do you have something for me?"

"I told you I would."

"I know what you told me, but do you have it?"

"Of course I do."

"You're a darling. What is it?"

Snake leaned close to her. "God, you smell great."

"What do you have?" Toni repeated with an edge in her voice. "What do you have for me?"

"Demerol."

"Beautiful." Toni relaxed and smiled at him. "There is one thing I have to tell you."

"Yeah? What's that?"

"It's the wrong time to use my little pussy."

"That don't bother me, babe," Snake declared proudly. "In the Legion of the Lost we don't just poke bloody cunts, we hunker right down and eat 'em."

"Really?" Toni gave a dramatic shudder. "Sounds icky. And it would bother me, darling. But you know, I really have a great ass, and I'm sure you'd love it."

"Yeah, it looks good, and I bet it feels like velvet," Snake said. "But I ain't no butt-fucker."

"So there are some things the Legion of the Lost won't do," Toni said sarcastically.

"Damn right."

"Oh well. I guess— "

"Read my mind," Snake told her.

"I give great head."

"Right. You better, babe."

"How many pills do you have?"

"Put it this way. You owe me five blow jobs."

Toni looked rather disappointed. "But darling, you will be able to get more, won't you?"

"What do you do, eat 'em like candy?"

"I'm in pain," Toni said resentfully.

"You need somebody to look after you," Snake pointed out, a clever idea forming in his mind. Blow jobs every night. A great source of income. He would move her out of the south end and put her to work making real money, no more of this back alley boffing for bucks. "Yeah, somebody who'll take good care of you."

"I take care of myself."

"I mean a regular guy."

"I've got a hundred regular guys, darling."

"To protect you," Snake clarified firmly.

"I've never needed protection."

"That just means you're overdue for trouble."

"Oh." Toni didn't seem to care for what Snake had in mind, but then her face moved slightly as if she had just felt a twinge of pain, and then she smiled up at him. "Oh dear."

"Yeah, but don't worry about it, babe," Snake told her with a wide grin. "Now that I'm here you'll be all right. I'll take care of you and you'll take care of me, right?"

"You might decide you don't want me," Toni said. She had a peculiar smile on her face. "When you get to know me."

Snake laughed. "Oh, I'll want you, babe, you can be sure of that. Matter of fact, I want you right now."

Toni discreetly slipped her hand between Snake's legs.

"Mmm, so you do."

"Come on, let's go."

"Your old lady must not be treating you right."

"What old lady?"

"I can tell, darling."

"Yeah, well, she's on the way out," Snake said. "She just don't know it yet."

"No one ever does."

"Come on," Snake said anxiously.

"Let me finish my drink," Toni insisted calmly. "Besides, I can see that you like standing in the middle of a crowd of people and having me touch you this way. It's nice, isn't it?"

"Jesus, babe."

But she was right.

III

—Greetings, plasmodium.

"Hey, I've been looking for you."

354

—Stand by.

"Where are you?"

—Here.

"I can't see you."

—You can hear me.

"Come on out, man. Let me see you."

Tony had a large mayonnaise jar. If he could just get his hands on the Pied Piper long enough to shove him into the jar and screw the cap on . . . Into the trash . . . Into the landfill . . . But, only after Tony hammered a few nail holes in the cap and then steamed the brain-eating son of a bitch alive over a pot of boiling water for a couple of hours.

But maybe Tony wouldn't throw him away. Maybe he'd put the jar on a shelf in the living room and let his johns goggle at it. What the hell is that, they'd ask. Souvenir from the Caribbean, he'd tell them with a straight face. My voodoo chile.

—Slime.

"Where the hell are you?"

—Everywhere.

"Yeah? Where's that?"

—In your head.

"That's what I have to talk to you about," Tony said. "You have to let me call a dentist and get an appointment, because my jaw is killing me all the time now."

—No.

"I can't take it anymore."

—No.

"Fuck, man, why the fuck not?"

—He'll see what you did to your teeth and he'll think that you're crazy.

"I *am* crazy."

—He'll get them to lock you up.

"I'm locked up here most of the time, talking to myself."

—I am always with you.

"Then come on out and let me see you."

—See!

Suddenly Tony couldn't see anything but the Pied Piper. It was as if he were inside Tony's eyeballs, peering into his brain. He had an evil grin on his twisted face, and now his filthy hands came up and started scratching at the inner lining of Tony's eyes in an effort to shred through the membrane. Scraping, ripping, peeling the cells away with ridged fingernails that were as sharp as razorblades.

The pain was excruciating. Tony slid off the chair and fell to his knees on the floor, holding his head in his hands. He was too weak to scream, it felt like the breath had been sucked from his lungs. One hand groped blindly toward the small brown bottle on the coffee table. Tony had tried all the regular store-bought painkillers, but none of them helped. Finally he had scored some Demerol from a beautiful idiot named Snake, his new friend. The Demerol was fantastic, although it never really lasted quite long enough. Now Tony had just a few left.

—No.

The muscles in Tony's arm went dead. His fingers fumbled at the brown bottle but could not grip it. *Please*, came the whimper from the back of his skull. *Please let me*—but a shrill racket overwhelmed his feeble thought.

—Sorry.

Tony began to beat his head against the floor.

—So you want the people downstairs to come up and find you like this? They'll call a doctor and he'll decide you're crazy. He'll have them lock you away forever.

Tony continued to bang his head on the hardwood floor in an effort to knock himself unconscious.

—Listen.

Tony could no longer lift his head; it rested face down in a smear of blood. But the pain had let up, and his brain began the laborious process of forming clear thoughts again. His breathing came back in short, shallow gasps.

—You can have your pill.

Tony tried to reach for the bottle, but couldn't.

—Not yet. Only when you have listened to what you must do for me.

"Yes."

—And accept.

The air was thin and liquid. It had a raw, unpleasant edge that reminded Tony of grain alcohol.

"What is it?"

—You must bring someone here.

"Who?"

—Someone you trust.

"I don't trust anybody, man."

—Nevertheless.

"How can I, with you hanging around?"

Business had fallen right off the table ever since the Pied Piper had taken over Tony's life. He couldn't dare bring anyone home when he no longer had control of the situation. He had to go out at night all the time now, hustling quick tricks in toilets and alleys for prices he would have laughed at a couple of months ago. Tony's whole world had shriveled around him like the skin on a rotten corpse.

—You can.

"Can I take money from him?"

—Yes.

"And do my job?"

—That is what you must do.

"I get it," Tony said, smiling faintly. "You can't see me when I'm outside, and you want to watch. Right?" For once the Pied Piper was silent. Tony chuckled. "That's okay, man, that's cool. But you have to understand." His voice took on a pleading tone again as he pushed himself over onto his side. "I can't go on living like this. It just won't work."

—Leave the living to me, plasmodium.

"I mean it, man. I'm dying in my socks. People will come to see what's the matter, why I'm not in touch. My family, like that, you know what I mean."

—Then deal with them.

"I can't handle it."

—Why not?

"I just can't. I'm afraid."

—Of what?

"You . . ."

—But, I'm you.

"The fuck you are," Tony protested. "I'm sick. I hurt all the time now. The only way I can face people is in the dark, and it's all because of you. *Not me*, I'm the one you're doing it to, and maybe I should be locked away somewhere. Maybe that'd be the best thing."

—Nonsense.

"You're killing me. Day by day, you're killing me."

—Ingrate.

"Come here, you little shit."

Tony had regained a slight measure of strength by now, so he lunged in the direction of where he thought the Pied Piper might be, but his fingers grasped empty air. The demon was gone. Tony knew it at once from the sudden lightness he felt, the release of his mind.

It was the worst attack yet. Tony's heart banged inside his chest, weak but frantic, and his skin was slick with sweat. His arms trembled, nearly buckling, as he made an effort to sit up on the floor. He looked at the thin patch of blood on the hardwood and felt a terrible anticipation of his own doom. This is how he would die, like an animal. Like trash, like slime, unseen, all but invisible, stepped on, rubbed away, a smear, a tiny stain on the street.

Tony crawled up into the chair. He saw the brown bottle of Demerol, but he no longer felt the need for any. Save them. The ache in his jaw was dull and distant. If only he could manage to grab the Demerol and get it down his throat in the minute before the Pied Piper got a hold of him. It was the only thing that did seem to keep the demon from getting through, at least for a short while. But he would have to carry a loose pill all the time, or else have one installed in a special socket in his teeth, like some of the Nazis. Come to think of it, the holes were already there, waiting to be custom-fitted.

He needed more Demerol, that was the main thing. Enough to keep him safe day and night. It was so damn good, so much better than coke or weed or anything else he'd ever tried. Better even than sex. So what if it turned him into a placid addict, lolling about like a zombie? Anything was better than having that fucker inside his brain.

Tonight he would see Snake again, and he would make sure the guy was sufficiently motivated to get more Demerol. There was no way Tony could live without it now.

He noticed the mayonnaise jar on the floor, and it puzzled him for a moment. He picked it up and looked at it. The strands of mayonnaise left inside had turned into a greenish-black slime. Slime, the Pied Piper had called him.

Plasmodium. That was a word Tony knew for certain he didn't know and had never heard before. Until today. Where did it come from? Impossible. Unless the Pied Piper was real.

The pain began to swell like an infernal orchestra in Tony's head, and he reached for the brown bottle.

IV

"Where y'goin'?"

Snake looked over his shoulder. Shelly was still on the old couch, which sagged nearly to the floor. She looked like she was sampling coffins and had found one that suited her. She had been lying there most of the day. She was out of it, brain-blitzed on those pills the shrink had prescribed for her. Shelly discovered happiness when she doubled the original dosage and now she didn't scratch herself so much. She was also a lot easier for Snake to handle, although his feelings for her did not improve. Snake was hooked on Toni.

"Out," he replied curtly.

"Out where?"

"Fuck you."

Shelly struggled to push herself up on one elbow. It wasn't a pretty sight. Scrawny arms and legs. A whining, watery voice that came from a face resembling a tombstone. She also broadcast an odor that would pit steel. He looked away from her and put on his Legion of the Lost leather jacket.

"Snake . . ."

"Don't wait up."

Twenty minutes later Snake parked his beat-up Dodge Colt on South Freedom, hurried around the corner and entered the El Greco bar. The usual do-nothing crowd was on hand, drinking, yammering over the soccer table and sticking their chests out at each other like animals. Snake hated them all. They seemed to smirk at him and laugh to themselves whenever he came in, but not one of them had the balls to take him on because they knew he'd kick the shit out of them. Snake knew about spic fighting abilities—they were game little roosters, but hit them in the body and they all break up like a sack of sticks.

Toni was there too, as she knew she damn well better be. It hadn't taken him long to straighten her out on that score. Snake was not to be kept waiting, not for one minute. You have to make sure a whore knows her place and toes the line, otherwise she'll piss all over you. Snake was pleased, but didn't show it, though he did tell her she looked sexy when she came and wrapped her arm around his waist. They got drinks and sat down at the far end of the bar, away from the crowd. Unfortunately, the El Greco didn't run to booths or tables.

Toni smiled, gave him little kisses, murmured in his ear and touched him secretly, but for all that she seemed tense and edgy. Her face was drawn and she toyed with her drink nervously.

"What's the matter, babe?"

"I'm in pain," she said.

"Drink your drink, and have another."

"You know what I mean."

"Relax."

"You got more?"

"Sure," Snake said.

"How much?"

"Jesus, you are jumpy tonight. Enough, okay? I have enough for you."

Toni settled down a little and stroked his thigh gratefully. Nice. Snake was pleased, but not entirely happy. His efforts to advance the situation in the last ten days had so far failed. He loved the blow jobs in his car, parked in a dark lot, and he knew he had a hold on Toni, but his control over her was only partial. She had agreed to consider working exclusively for him, but still would not commit to it. Snake's dream of free sex *and* free money hovered just beyond his reach. For the moment.

"But," he said quietly.

"What?" Toni's face tensed immediately. "But what?"

"I'm not happy."

"Why?"

"Take those sunglasses off."

"Pretend I'm a stranger, hot for you, and— "

"Take 'em off," Snake demanded. "It's dark enough here."

"Okay." Toni removed the shades and blinked, wincing. Then she smiled at him. "Whatever you want, darling."

"That's better."

"Besides, I'm hot for you anyway, you know."

"Yeah, well." Snake tried to look cool, but it wasn't easy to ignore her hand between his legs. "Listen to me."

"What's the matter?"

"I want you working for me."

"I know, but— "

"You don't belong down in this part of town. I can take you to better places, fix you up with guys that have more money. You can pull a ton, and I'll take care of everything. Everything you need, I'll get it for you."

"Sounds good," Toni said in a neutral tone of voice. "Maybe we could do that, but I'm not ready for it yet."

"No? We could leave right now, head on up to the Green Door and bag a half-dozen yuppies in no time."

"But not tonight, darling. I don't feel too good."

Snake shrugged his shoulders as if it didn't bother him one way or the other, but the expression on his face tightened.

"There's something else."

"What?"

"I'm getting kind of tired of doing it in the car."

"Oh."

"Don't worry, babe. You're great. But I'd like to go back to your place, where we can take a little more time and really do it right. Slow and sweet, you know?"

Toni looked unhappy. Snake knew he was walking a fine line. She had already made it clear to him that she didn't bring anyone home, that it "wasn't convenient" for some reason which she would not specify. If he pushed her too hard, she might decide to drop him and take her chances with somebody else. Whores know so many people. It might take her a few days, but sooner or later she'd find another source of coke and Demerol, and Snake would be left out in the cold, Toni was too valuable to lose. It wasn't often that you found such a hot young thing, such an unusual beauty who really could perform. Toni was a sizzler.

But damn it, if Snake was going to be her one supplier, then he was entitled to more than he was getting. She didn't even let him touch her hardly at all, aside from a little ass-grabbing and an occasional brush with her nubby tits. Snake wanted more, much more. He wanted to roll around naked with her on a bed, to watch her strip, to splash around together in a bubble bath—the kind of things he did with Shelly, when she was human. Toni was great when she put her nose to the grindstone, but Snake was determined to strike a better deal.

"Darling, I will take you back to my place, and we'll have a wonderful time—many wonderful times."

"All right."

"But," Toni said, holding her hand up, "I have to get myself organized first."

"What the fuck does that mean?"

"I told you, I'm suffering the most monumental pain, from my dental problems. That's why I need the medicine."

"Right," Snake said wearily. He knew better than to ask why she didn't just get her dentist to write a prescription. She was a no-hope junkie whore, and it wasn't hard to figure out what the future had in store for her, but at least he had found her while she was young and still had a lot of tread. She was worth taking a certain amount of bullshit to keep. "How long will that be?"

"Next week."

"Really?"

Her eyes danced vaguely, avoiding him. "I hope."

"Jesus, babe."

"You poor darling," she said soothingly, caressing him again discreetly. "I'll make it up to you, just wait and see. I will, I really will. We'll have the most fantastic time together. And in the meantime, I'll suck your brains out, I'll drink you dry."

Talk like that dazed Snake. "God, you make me hot," he told her. "Let's get out of here."

"First."

Business first, was what she meant. Snake expected that and had prepared for it. In his pockets he had two packets of pills, a larger quantity in case Toni met either or both of his demands, and a smaller number if she turned him down. It was time to yank the leash. Snake slipped her the packet containing half a dozen Demerols. Without looking at it, her eyes widened in alarm.

"That's all?"

"'Fraid so, babe."

"Why?"

"Recession. Supply and demand. Things are tight. Remember when I told you it'd be a lot easier if we worked together?"

Toni was trying to look stern, but it didn't suit her. "You know I can find other sources," she said.

"It isn't wise to take business away from the Legion," Snake countered, falling back on his last serious threat. Not that the Legion gave a damn about him. However, Toni didn't know that, so the threat was as good as real. "It makes 'em want to go out and kick somebody's face in, that kind of thing."

"All I want is a little time," Toni said pleadingly.

"What I just gave you is a little time."

Toni sighed unhappily. "All right."

"Now, let's go out to the car."

V

Tony couldn't stand it anymore. The pain was too much for him to bear. Three days ago he had finally gone to a dentist and had his teeth filled with some kind of plastic. It was a hideous session, lasting hours. The dentist obviously thought that Tony was crazy because of what he had done to his teeth, and for not removing his sunglasses. It cost a lot, and since Tony was not a regular patient and had no dental coverage he was obliged to fork over the money in advance. That was smart on the dentist's part, as Tony never would have bothered if he knew the fillings weren't going to work. They didn't.

At first he thought it was just a matter of time before the pain wore off for good, but after three days it was clearly there to stay. Perhaps he should have had new metal fillings installed to interfere with the Pied Piper's broadcasts, but the originals hadn't really done the job, and it now seemed likely that Tony's teeth had little if anything to do with the strength or weakness of the torment he experienced.

He hadn't actually seen the Pied Piper in some time now, but the messages still came through several times a day. They meant little to Tony, aside from the sheer pain and terror they caused him. It had reached the point where he spent most of his time in bed or on the couch, weak from the last onslaught, trembling with dread in anticipation of the next one.

The pain usually subsided at night, and Tony would go out to eat and then hustle up some work. He tried to do what the demon voice wanted. He brought several customers back to his place and performed magnificently. They were cheap bums who didn't deserve such royal treatment but Tony would do whatever it took to please the Pied Piper. When the voice returned, however, it was always dissatisfied, and the agony continued.

Worse, Tony hadn't seen Snake since the night before he went to the dentist. He needed more Demerol, huge amounts, to get him through each day and make life somewhat bearable. Tony stabbed a glossy fingernail at the ice in his drink. It looked as if Snake would not appear at the El Greco tonight. That was bad, because Tony was completely out of Demerol. It had occurred to him that unless he got some he might kill himself tomorrow—assuming the Pied Piper would let him. Tony didn't know what to do. He left the bar, planning to return later. In the meantime, he would hit a few other places and see if he could find Snake.

The bastard was jerking his chain, that's what it was. Tony wouldn't work for him, wouldn't take him home for a long night of sex. Well, there was a problem. Somehow, Snake had yet to grasp the fact that Tony was at least nominally male. Tony could work the straight side of the street, but that was nerve-wracking, and he had no appetite for it. Nor could he bring Snake home, as it wouldn't be long before the Lost Legionnaire noticed some little something taped flat between Tony's legs.

Tony pulled a couple of quick tricks in his wanderings, but he didn't find Snake. He eventually found himself crossing the bridge into Riverside. It was a poor working-class neighbourhood, virtually identical to the south end but for the fact that there were very few blacks or Hispanics in Riverside. It was for the most part unknown territory to Tony, but for some reason he felt he was heading in the right direction.

He tried a few bars along the way, looking in, then turning to leave immediately. Tony had long ago developed an ability to recognize places where he was sure to get beaten up.

He had to work out something with Snake. He could tell him the truth, and probably get beaten up for that, but at least it would clear the air. The charade couldn't go on much longer, and it might be better to get it over with sooner than later. But he had to have something to appease Snake. A share of Tony's income from gays—that might do it. Why not? It was the same kind of deal Snake wanted, except that Tony would be working his regular beat, not the cashladen yuppie straights at the Green Door. The money might be less but it was still money for nothing. And Tony would have his steady supply of coke and Demerol. Yeah, it might just work out.

Nonetheless, Tony shuddered at the prospect of confronting Snake with the truth. Was it really necessary? Tony had enough cash on him now to buy a few days' worth of pills. Do that, just pay for the medicine, take it and go. No sex, no promises. Keep it strictly on a business footing. And if Snake insists on more? Tell him it's that time of the month. No, Tony remembered he had done that only a week or two ago. Vaginal fungus? Snake might want to eat it. Tell him you've got the clap, and you're out of action for a while. Head, yes; anything else, no.

The rattletrap Dodge Colt—there it was. Tony was amazed. He had found Snake. Almost. The car was parked in front of an aged triple-decker. On one side of the house there was a vacant lot, then a bakery and some more shops. On the other side, there was a diner, now closed, and a bar that Tony had already checked. Across the street, nothing likely. It had to be this apartment house. But which of the three apartments?

Tony started on the ground floor. He pushed the doorbell, but it didn't ring. He was about to knock when, through the side window, he caught sight of an elderly man sitting in an armchair in the front room. Doubtful. Tony went up the battered stairs. The light was mercifully dim, a single hanging bulb nearly burned out, and the air was permeated with the compressed smell of stale cooking—decades of it. The apartment on the second floor was dark and the screen door was locked. Tony caught his breath, and then continued on to the top floor. Lights, a dull noise inside. Tony knocked. Nothing. He knocked again, louder. Still no sign of a response. He knocked hard enough to hurt his knuckles.

"Yeah."

The voice was faint and distant, but Tony was certain he had heard it. He tried the door, and it opened. He entered a narrow hallway. It was dark, but light came through an archway ahead on the right. Tony took a few steps and stood, looking into a drab living room. There was a girl on the couch.

"You must be the little woman."

"Who're you?"

"I'm looking for Snake."

"He's out."

"Where?"

"I don't know."

"His car is out front," Tony said. "Would he be somewhere in the neighbourhood?"

"He went with Crabs."

"What?"

"Crabs. His friend."

"Oh." Tony felt uncomfortable talking across the room. He moved closer to the pathetic girl, who made no effort to get up. She was squeezing her fingers strangely. "Are you okay?"

"No. I'm out of medicine and I'm all fucked up."

"So am I."

Without thinking about it, Tony went to the couch and sat on the edge of it beside the girl. She looked awful.

"That's a pretty dress."

"Thank you." Tony glanced at the girl's hands again and was shocked to see that she was digging her nails into the palms, and blood was oozing between her fingers. She was gouging out a hole in the center of each hand. "What're you doing?" Tony cried in a voice strangled with alarm.

"It's Jesus," the girl said. "Jesus is in me."

"Jesus?"

"These are His wounds." The girl's eyes were brighter now, lit with enthusiasm. "Look at my feet."

Tony turned his head and glanced back. "Oh my God."

"Yes, yes."

"Honey, let me— "

"And look here."

Before Tony could do or say anything, the girl yanked up her T-shirt, revealing a pancake breast. That's not much bigger than mine, Tony thought. Then he noticed the running sore in the side of the girl's body, about the size of a silver dollar. The skin around it was streaked with dried blood. She must have picked at it for hours, days. It was terrible to see, but also fascinating and even exciting. Tony felt as if he'd walked into this girl's dream.

"Nobody believes me," she said sadly.

"I do," Tony found himself saying.

"You do?"

"Yes. I do."

The girl smiled. "You're so pretty."

"When is Snake coming home?"

"I never know."

Tony's eyes drifted helplessly back to the bloody wound near the girl's breast. The skin had not been allowed to form a scab. The wound has the wet, puckered look of a vagina, Tony thought in a fog of wonder. You have two of them and I don't even have one. He couldn't keep from smiling.

"Put your hand in," the girl said. "Just like they did with the Lord Jesus. Go on. Please."

"My hand won't fit."

"Your finger then."

Tony hesitated, but then was astonished to see his hand move toward the girl's body. His middle finger slid effortlessly into the moist wound. It terrified him to picture the long artificial nail, hard and sharp, pushing deeper into the girl's body, but he didn't stop until the finger was in all the way.

"Tell me your name."

"Shelly." Then, "No. *Jesus.*"

Tony felt as if he had plugged into a chaos of heat, turmoil and liquid. Shelly's body quaked violently, her eyes shining, an unfathomable expression on her face. Pain and peace, maybe. Her hands clutched Tony's arm, pressing it harder to her body.

The next thing he knew, he was in a squalid kitchen, washing his hands in a stream of tepid tap-water. Roaches huddled in the gap between the backsplash and the crumbling plaster wall, but he ignored them. Tony's mind couldn't seem to focus on anything for more than a second or two, and now the pain was starting to seep back in at the edges.

Where was Snake? But that didn't matter. Go away. Get out of here. Now. You can always kill yourself tomorrow, but if you stay here they'll come, and they'll think you're crazy. And then they'll lock you up, and it'll be too late to do anything.

In the living room, Shelly was still. Her eyes followed him as he approached. He imagined the faintest smile on her face, or maybe it was actually there. At the edge of his vision, where he could not quite look, he knew that Shelly had inserted her finger into the wound. Her hand twisted and poked. There was a lot of bright red, and it was spreading, but Tony looked away. Then he left as quickly as he could.

ENTR'ACTE

Doctor Ladybank chatted with Jack and his wife, Gloria, for a few minutes, and then took his drink out onto the terrace. The party was in full swing, and it was a little too hot and crowded inside for him. The evening air was pleasantly cool, sweet with a mix of fragrances from Gloria's flower garden. Nice woman, was Gloria. A bit too nice for a rogue like Jack, but they seemed to get along and had been together for years.

Doctor Ladybank normally didn't care for social gatherings, mingling with a lot of strangers, making forced conversation, but every now and then Jack threw a good old-fashioned cocktail party that simply couldn't be missed. This one came at a particularly good time. Doctor Ladybank needed a break. He'd been giving too much of himself to his experiment lately.

It didn't tire him, it wasn't stressful, there were no nasty side effects at all as far as he could tell. But it was utterly irresistible!

In just a few short weeks he had become thoroughly caught up in the lives of his two subjects. He resented any time spent away from them. Work, eating, sleeping—the bulk of his normal activities had faded into dullness.

There were many problems yet to be resolved. First, was the lack of quality time with Tony and Snake. It was often difficult to get through to them, especially at night. When Tony went out, Doctor Ladybank almost always lost contact. The same applied to Snake. It was not an absolute rule, however. There were several times when he did reach them at night, including a few important moments. Doctor Ladybank had no idea whether that was because of the intensity of his concentration or merely the configuration of their surroundings.

By now he had a rough idea of the range of his effect on the two young men. It went from basically annoying them to generally influencing their behavior, and peaked at substantial control of their thoughts and emotions. It was dazzling, but also somewhat perplexing. He could hurt them, to the point of unconsciousness, but he had not yet learned how to make them laugh or feel sudden moments of spontaneous pleasure. Doctor Ladybank regretted that, as both Tony and Snake were doing so much for him, and they lived such unrewarding lives. But he didn't regret it very much; there was no place for sentiment in science.

Feedback was bliss. That was perhaps the most exciting part of Doctor Ladybank's discovery. How would he know if his efforts were really working? In practice, he found that he just knew, he sensed it somehow, without knowing quite how he knew. It was not as if he "heard" Delgado answering him, for instance. But Doctor Ladybank's thoughts and directives flowed intuitively, as if they were in fact conversing on some new level, and thus, when he held either of them in the strongest contact he was aware of what they were doing, how they responded and what his own next words should be. To Doctor Ladybank it didn't qualify as vicarious experience but there was certainly an intellectual thrill in it.

It was a bitter disappointment to him that in the four weeks since he had happened on the technique, as he thought of it, he had not found anyone else receptive to it. That was definitely a puzzle, apparently defying the laws of chance and probability.

The greatest mystery, though, was at the heart of the whole experiment. To what degree did he affect their behavior? Was it mostly his doing, or was he just providing an added mental shove, urging them along paths they would have taken anyway? So far, it was impossible to know for sure.

A mosquito buzzed close to his eye. Doctor Ladybank went in

and got another drink. He was buttonholed by Margaret Zuvella, a lawyer with the Public Defender's office. She didn't fit in with Jack's corporate law crowd but she was young and very attractive, which made her an ideal party guest. Doctor Ladybank had met her on one of his court-appointed cases, and they'd encountered each other a few times since. What a subject she'd make, he couldn't help thinking. But when he tried the technique, it had no effect whatsoever on her. Sad. They chatted about a nineteen-year-old pyromaniac they had both tried, and failed, to keep out of prison a few months ago.

"He set a fire in the library," Margaret said with obvious delight. "Then he got the prison laundry."

"Splendid. Troy's a determined lad."

At that moment Jack horned in, looking loose and well-oiled, but not at all tipsy.

"Maggie," he said, smirking like someone about to explain an inside joke. "I have to warn you."

"About what?"

"Ian here. You better watch out. He can make you take your clothes off right here, in a room full of people."

A tendril of dismay uncoiled in Doctor Ladybank's mind.

"Really," Margaret said, smiling. "How can he do that?"

Jack tapped his forehead. "Brain waves. He beams them over to your brain and makes you do whatever he wants."

"Jack." Doctor Ladybank forced himself to chuckle and shake his head dismissively.

"I'd love to see it," Margaret said.

"Honestly," Jack continued. "Ian is conducting experiments on a couple of people, doing just that. How's it going, by the way, Ian? Got them jumping through hoops yet?"

"You're not," Margaret said.

"Of course not," Doctor Ladybank replied. "Jack and I were laying waste to a bottle of malt last month, and we were talking about clairvoyance, telepathy, that kind of thing. It was just a load of idle speculation, that's all."

"Ah." Margaret nodded.

"Oh, Ian, come on now," Jack protested. "You were damn well serious about it. I wasn't, but you were."

The silly crock was pushing it. Doctor Ladybank was shaken, but he maintained an expression of placid indulgence.

"It was the whiskey talking," he told Margaret. "Then, and now, in Jack's case, I'm afraid."

"I see."

Jack gave up, and the three of them laughed politely.

368

"I still think it's a good idea," Jack said as he started to leave in search of others on whom he could shower bonhomie.

"What is?" Margaret asked.

"If Ian gets you to take your clothes off."

"Jack, go away," she told him, trying to suppress a giggle. "Go away and behave yourself."

Yes, Doctor Ladybank thought. Go away, Jack.

VI

For once in his life something had gone right. If he hadn't been in the right place at the right time the cops would have put the collar on him in a flash. They knew him, they'd busted him a couple of times in the last few years, though never for anything too serious. Yeah, they'd love to hang some hard time on his ass if they could, but Snake was covered.

It was a minor miracle, looking back. Half of his life, it sometimes seemed, was spent in transit, scraping around, looking for this guy or that, hanging out—unaccountable time witnessed by nobody who would ever remember. But on the night Shelly died, Snake fortunately had been with or seen by other people for every minute of the hours in question. More amazing, they all stood up for him when it counted.

He and Crabs had gone to Rudy's early that evening. The two of them teamed up to monopolize the pool table for several hours, winning drinks until nearly midnight. Then they decided to go to a nightclub called Ravens, on the other side of town. They were turned away at the door and exchanged mean stares with—of all people—a cop moonlighting as a bouncer. Snake and Crabs were both known to the cop; he'd thrown them out of Ravens a couple of months earlier. Retreating across the road to Cher's Plus Two, a titty bar favored by area bikers, Snake and Crabs met a number of other people they knew. They stayed until closing time, two a.m. By then they were in such good spirits that they decided to drink a nightcap or two at Snake's place. Instead, they found the dead body and promptly called the police.

What a way to go, Snake thought as he drove aimlessly around town. Shelly. She had her good side, a while back. But to die like that, to carve a hole in yourself with your own fingernails, and bleed to death . . . Jesus. It was enough to make Snake wonder how he had put up with her for so long. She must have been stone cold loco, so far off the wall that she couldn't even see it. To tell the truth, however, he had never imagined she was that sick. Weird, sure, and the laziest damn thing on earth. But not sicko sick. Maybe Snake should have paid more attention to that shrink who saw Shelly. Maybe they all missed something then.

Oh well. It was over now. Any residual feelings that Snake might have had for Shelly disappeared when he learned that he, as her common-law husband, had to pay to dispose of her remains. If she had any relatives, he didn't know who or where they might be, and she didn't leave much more than a pile of dirty clothes. She lived light and went fast, amen. Snake didn't hesitate to choose the cheapest available cremation (the "Bake 'n Shake," according to Crabs). Shelly's ashes were in the jar on the seat beside him now. It was time to find somewhere nice for her.

The ocean was too far away. A babbling brook would be nice, but then Snake considered the fact that any moving waters in this old mill city were bound to be thoroughly polluted. What about a park? Open air, a quiet setting, flowers—shit, he could strew her ashes right in a flowerbed. That would be perfect. But then again, it wasn't so easy. The two or three city parks Snake knew of had pretty much gone to seed, neglected, overgrown, dangerous. The best one was adjacent to the public library, and it wasn't so bad, but even there the winos used the flowerbeds as a toilet and a parade of fags stalked the shrubbery.

It wasn't as if Shelly deserved a spot in Arlington National Cemetery, but Snake felt obliged to do the best he could. He hadn't been much help to Shelly in what turned out to be her last weeks alive. Plus, she had spared him the aggravation of throwing her out, so he figured that he owed her something.

There it was! Snake knew he'd found the ideal place for her as soon as he drove around the bend in the road and saw the green expanse of a fairway in the distance. The city golf course. She would like it, he had no doubt. All he had to do now was find an attractive little spot off to the side somewhere, maybe beneath a birch tree in the rough. Hell, there might even be a clear brook in a place like this.

Snake parked the car along an open stretch of the road, took the container of ashes and walked quickly through the weedy grass toward the fairway. It was the tail-end of dusk, so if he didn't find a place soon he'd end up dumping her in the dark.

There was a foursome a hundred yards away, but they were on the way in, their backs to Snake. He jogged across the fairway. The woods on the other side looked promising, but when he reached them he found the ground unsuitable. More tall grass, rocks, and bare dirt where paths had been worn. At least at the library she would have had flowers. Damn it all anyway. He was looking for the kind of scene they put on greeting cards and in Disney films, but this was just a bunch of useless country-type land.

Snake pushed on. A few minutes later he came out on the far side of the woods, and he was startled by the sudden change. He was in someone's backyard. Nice looking house, must have cost an awful lot. Beautiful grounds, too. Snake hadn't tried burglary, but this would be the kind of place to start with if he ever felt like having a go.

He had other business now. His eyes had settled on a lovely rock garden just a few yards away. Snake hurried across the lawn to it. Oh yes, the perfect resting place for Shelly. There were cascades of delicate flowers, clusters of blue, purple and white, not much pink or red. Just the colors you saw at funerals, Snake thought as he bent over and started to scoop out a hollow in the rich soil. You'll love it here, kid. The kind of folks who live in a place like this will take real good care of you, or at least the garden around you.

"What do you think you're doing?"

Snake jumped upright. He had been about to unscrew the cap of the jar containing Shelly's ashes, but now he froze, gaping at the middle-aged man who stood ten feet away, hands on hips. Must have seen me from the house, Snake thought uselessly. He wasn't worried about having been discovered by the homeowner, but he was puzzled. The guy was a stranger, and yet seemed familiar. Snake could turn and run, and he knew he'd get away easily, but somehow the urge to flee had been transformed into curiosity.

"Who are you," the man demanded, his voice more threatening, "and what do you want?"

"Hey, Jack." Snake was surprised to hear himself say that. "How the hell are you, Jack?"

The man's head clicked back a notch. Then he stepped closer and peered at Snake.

"I don't know you."

"Sure you do, Jack. We used to hang out at the Utica Club, remember? *Agricola, agricolae, agricolorum.* Right? *Hic, haec, hoc, ad hoc,* in hock around the clock with bock beer."

Even in the gathering darkness, Snake could see the man's eyes widen as he tried to digest what he'd heard. Snake couldn't help him. He had no idea.

"Get out of here this instant."

"Jack, lighten up."

"I'll call the police."

"Why don't you crack open a bottle of Glen Grant? We can sit down and talk twat, just like the old days."

The man tottered, then turned stiffly toward the house.

"Jack, Jack . . ."

Snake scooped up a rock and caught the man easily. The rock crushed the back of his skull, creating a wreath of pinkish-grey jelly around the edges of the impact. The man grunted once, the last of his breath forced out of him. He hit the lawn and didn't move again.

Snake pulled the body over onto its back. Now the wife will have to sell this place, he thought. Who knows what'll happen to the rock garden? The new owners might well dig it up and plow it under. That wouldn't be right. You're going to get a real fancy burial, Shelly. Elegant casket, expensive plot. Can't beat it.

He unscrewed the jar, forced the man's mouth open, and began to pour the ashes down the throat. It soon filled. Snake tamped the coarse powder down with his fingertips. Believe me, Jack, if you saw Shelly at her best you *would* want to eat her. That would have been when she was about fifteen.

The cheeks bulged, Snake noticed when he was finished. Jack the Chipmunk. Best I could do. Time to take a *haec*.

So long, kid.

VII

Tony washed down the Demerol with a gulp of Red Death on the rocks. Behind the shades, his eyes watered slightly, but he felt his body steadying. That was mental, since he knew it would take a good five minutes before serenity began to kick in and all was right with the world again . . . for a while.

"You look happy, darling."

"I buried Shelly."

"Maybe that's it. Where did you put her?"

"Somewhere out in the countryside," Snake said with a vague wave of the hand, as if he'd suddenly lost interest in the topic. "It's a pretty place."

"I'm sure it is."

Tony had heard about it only last night around this time, as they were sitting on the very same two barstools at the El Greco. It was boring. Tony didn't want to listen to another word about the stupid cunt who'd bled herself to death, but Snake was having a hard time putting it behind him. He kept pulling away from it, and then sinking back, like a car stuck in a rut. It was morbid, as well as incredibly tiresome.

Tony had his own uneasy feelings about Shelly. He imagined he had met her—or was it a dream? Anyhow, he had this picture of her in his mind, like he could see her dying. It was probably because

Snake had given such a graphic description of what Shelly looked like when he found her. And it had stayed in Tony's head, making him feel very uncomfortable.

Part of the problem was that Snake kept him jangled up in a state of constant uncertainty, dishing out the pills in ones and twos like candy. Wouldn't sell a quantity, even though Tony had the cash. Snake wanted other things, and so he was making a move for absolute control. It was clear and simple, but Tony had yet to figure out a worthwhile response to it. Shelly's death was a minor week-long distraction that didn't really change anything in Tony's life.

The easiest thing, of course, would be to stop using Demerol or coke, period. Then Tony would be able to kiss Snake goodbye, and how sweet that would be. The big clod had lost any semblance of attractiveness he might have possessed. Not that he was ever anything but a trick and a supplier as far as Tony was concerned. The game was fun at first, but now Snake's mean and demanding way of treating Tony most of the time was simply unbearable.

And how could he get off the drugs? That was impossible, at least in Tony's present condition. They weren't drugs, they were medicine. They kept him alive. Whether that was a good idea was another matter, but as long as he wanted to survive all the pain and mental interference, he had to have his medicine.

Zzzzt.

Oh God, no. Not now, not here. Tony had a terrible fear of the Pied Piper getting through to him in a public place. Even if it was only the El Greco, where some pretty weird things happened from time to time.

Zzzzt.

Fucker. Get lost. Ignore him. But that never worked. The demon had continued to haunt and hurt Tony everyday over the past week, never letting up for long. The Demerol helped, but it was by no means a perfect immunity. All it did was keep the agony in moderate check for a while, so that Tony remained just this side of suicidal. The Pied Piper still got through.

—Plasmodium. Found you.

"Be right back, darling," Tony said to Snake. "I've got to make a trip to the little girl's room."

"Yeah," Snake muttered.

Tony slid off the barstool, wobbled for a second on his high heels, and then clattered quickly across the linoleum. Thank God the pisser was vacant. Tony shut the door and leaned against it, pressing his head to the blotchy particleboard.

—I want him.

"Fuck off."

—You heard me.

"For what?"

—Bring him home.

"It won't work with him. He's straight."

—Do it, slime.

"Listen, when he sees my *cojones* he'll go crazy. He'll tear them off and shove 'em down— "

Tony went blind and sagged to the damp floor, too stunned to make a sound as pain exploded throughout his body, abrading every cell in his nervous system. It felt as if sonic booms were being triggered inside his brain and the plates of his skull were about to crack open at the seams.

Yes, yes, okay. He couldn't even get the words out, but the torture died down immediately. Tony found that he could breathe again, he could think, he could see the slick of scummy water his face rested in on the floor. He was theoretically still alive, a fact of dubious value. Why is this happening? Why are you doing this to me?

—Because you are slime.

You got that right. "But you're me, right? That's what you said a while back, fucker. If I'm slime, so are you."

Silence. Relief. Goddamn, Tony thought as he struggled to his feet, I shut him up. I shut the Pied Piper up. At least for a minute or two. Turned him right off. Tony gripped the sink to steady himself and then looked in the mirror. His face was grimy and wet from the floor. He washed himself and applied some fresh make-up, regaining a little composure in the process.

It was no good. The Pied Piper was gone for now, but he had delivered his message. Tony had to bring Snake home tonight, and whatever happened from that point on—would happen. Might even be better if Snake did go berserk and kill him. That would put a stop to all this misery. He could see the newspaper stories. An anguished biker tricked by a transvestite—Snake might have to transfer to the Foreign Legion to live that one down. Meanwhile, Tony's tearful mother wouldn't believe a word they said about him and his queer life. She'd hand out pictures of him as a choirboy and talk about the perfume he gave her last Mother's Day (because she was still young and pretty).

Why the fuck not? Who the fuck cares anyway? When you live in the shadow of the curb, where else do you expect to die? Grab the best chance that has come along in years. If you don't, that little demon fucker will just come back and eat at you, rip away at you, until you do what he wants. Get it over.

Besides, Tony knew that the column inches, however lurid and distasteful, would be a kind of comfort to his mother. Maybe not right away, but in the long term. A front-page murder story was better than no obituary at all.

VIII

The place was a dump on the outside, but the living room was nice enough. In a spooky kind of way. The shades were drawn and the only light came from a large floor lamp with a fringed shade that cast the room in a soft golden glow. The air was humid and warm, but it had a sweet scent that added an exotic, mysterious touch, and the furniture was comfortable. It wasn't the way he'd fix up a room, but Snake decided that he liked it as he sat back in a big armchair.

Toni was on edge, nervous as a high school girl on her first date. What a riot. Snake wasn't going to make it any easier for her. Why should he? This was his payoff. He was going to enjoy every minute of it. On the way there from the bar Snake gave her explicit instructions. He was to be treated like a king, she was to wait on him, pamper him, baby him, indulge him, humor him, and above all, she was to tease him to the max. He couldn't wait for that to start. This was going to be the greatest damn fuck Snake had ever had, the one he'd dreamed of for years.

The whore looked good, real good. Her hair was quite short, and it was brushed and slicked back in a striking fashion, and it looked so wet you'd think she had just this minute stepped out of the shower. Tonight her dress was almost elegant, not at all the usual trashy glitter.

She wore a white blouse that hung loosely on her flattish upper body, and a long wrap-around skirt that had a nice way of parting to flash her terrific legs when she walked. Toni was somewhat on the tall side, a sort of slum-pussy version of Jamie Lee Curtis without the front porch.

"What would you like to drink?"

Better already, Snake thought. Just being there had changed her tone of voice. Gone was the bar room hustle, replaced by such a sweet desire to please—God, he loved it. Toni was standing beside the chair, close to him. Snake liked that too. He placed a hand on her leg, just behind the knee, savoring the firm flesh beneath the fabric of her skirt. It was one of his favorite sexy spots on a woman's body. You could feel those wires—no, what the hell are they called, tendons, sinews?—that run all up and down the leg. Neat.

"Do you want a drink, darling, or . . . not?"

"Mmmm."

Snake's hand slid higher, taking the skirt with it, but Toni stepped

aside gracefully, escaping his reach. As she did so, she contrived to
flap the front of her skirt open briefly. Very nice little move, Snake
thought appreciatively.

"Well?"

"Got any bourbon?" he asked.

"Of course."

"Okay, let's have a large glass of bourbon, on the rocks and with
a splash of water."

"*Ein, zwei, drei.*"

"Huh?"

"What?"

"What'd you say?"

"I said it's on the way."

"Okay. Fine."

A little weird, but what the hell. Snake already had a good buzz
on, so nothing was going to bother him. As long as Toni did her
part. From where he was sitting he could see her in the tiny kitchen,
pouring the drinks. At that moment, she put the bottle down and bent
over. She opened her skirt and fiddled around with the catch on her
garter. It took a moment for the significance of the navy blue ribbon
and the bare skin to register. Oh Jesus, she's wearing stockings, Snake
realized with joy. And now she's showing me. Man, this is just like
being in the foreplay part of a porn movie. Scenes like this were the
best—the teasing, the slow seduction—even better than the wild sex
that would follow soon enough. But now Snake wasn't just another
jerk-off watching the picture; he was starring in it.

The bourbon was good and there was plenty of it in the heavy
crystal tumbler Toni brought him. She sipped a pale liquid from a
glass about the size and shape of a lipstick holder.

"What's that?"

"Cointreau," she told him.

"Oh yeah." None of that Red Death shit here. She was doing it
all right, no question. "Nice stuff."

"Snake?"

"Yeah?"

"Do you have any metal fillings?"

"Metal—what?"

"Metal fillings in your teeth. Lead, silver, like that."

"Oh, sure. Lots. I've got a regular scrapyard in my mouth,
everything but gold. Why?"

"Do you get much static?"

"Just from people who don't know better," he replied with a quick
laugh. "But I soon straighten them out."

"So . . . You don't hear anything?"

"Like what?" Like, what the hell is this all about?

"A voice."

"Just yours and mine, babe." Snake sounded calm, but he was beginning to worry. She looked nervous, close to panic, in spite of the fact that she was sitting on the couch, drink in hand, her thigh tantalyzingly visible. "Hey, relax."

As if on cue, Toni said, "Whatever they want."

"What?"

"Whatever they want."

"Who?"

"Men."

"Oh." This was an abrupt shift, but it was definitely a lot more promising, so he went with it. "Such as?"

"Come on my face. Come in my mouth."

Her voice was stiff, and her eyes seemed to be fixed on some remote inner point. However, Snake now thought he understood the game. She was going to tell him about the things she did. Dirty talk to turn him on. It was a little more open and blunt than he would have liked, but he was prepared to cut her some slack if it had the desired effect.

"That's pretty normal," he told her.

"Ride my ass."

"Some do like that. Not me, but some do."

"Tie me up. Blindfold me."

"Uh-hunh."

"Hurt me."

"Not too bad, I hope."

"Piss on me. Shit on me."

"Aw, Jeez." That was exactly the kind of stuff Snake didn't want to hear. How the hell could he lick her body now, with that stuck in his mind? "Where? On your back or stomach," Snake said hopefully. "Right?"

"And my chest. And face. And mouth."

"That really drags me down, babe." The script had gone into some other movie. Snake was not happy. The only thing that kept him from clocking her on the jaw was the fact that he didn't want to give up yet. There was still a chance Toni would snap out of her robot stare and get back on track. "I wouldn't treat you bad like that," he said. "I'd treat you like a queen."

Toni suddenly began laughing. Snake didn't understand, but he smiled at the improvement in her manner. She appeared to be much more relaxed again. He also liked that foxy look in her eye as she tuned in to him.

"Darling, would you really be a good boy?"

"Sure."

"I want you to do something for me."

"What?"

"Promise not to peek? Promise not to touch where you're not supposed to?"

"Well, I don't get it."

"Put your drink on the floor and sit forward on your seat."

"Okay."

When Snake did what she told him, Toni got off the couch and carefully stepped up onto the coffee table, inches from his face. Hey, hey, hey, Snake thought. This is more like it.

"Here," Toni said, handing him her glass of Cointreau. "I'd like you to rub it into my skin. Just the bare skin now, and you must behave yourself."

"*O-kay.*"

Snake splashed the liqueur on his hand and then placed the small glass on the table. Toni pulled her skirt open, and cupped one hand modestly over her panties. The sight of that navy blue underwear against her golden skin was fantastic. Snake lovingly stroked her upper thighs, above the stocking tops.

"Mmmm . . ."

"Your hand is in the way," he dared.

"You don't touch there. Understand?"

"Yes."

"That's good. You're a good boy, aren't you?"

"Yes."

"And you're doing a good job. What does it smell like? You can put your face closer."

Snake went so far as to put his face between her thighs, his cheeks touching her. His forehead bumped against her hand. Toni didn't stop him.

"Oranges."

"Right." Now her fingers gently pushed his face away. "The back, too. Don't forget the back."

Snake poured the last of the Cointreau in his hand, and Toni turned slightly on the table. She pulled the skirt higher, so he had a clear view of the flimsy blue fabric stretched tightly over her ass. He rubbed the back of her legs gently and slowly, while his eyes were locked on target just above. Toni's other hand was still planted on her crotch, so deeply that her fingers curved up in sight from behind. Odd, but Snake barely gave it a thought as he had other things on his mind. His hand inevitably slid up and grazed her firm round bottom. She let him do that until he began to squeeze it energetically, insinuating his fingers beneath her panties, and then she spun around.

"I told you to behave."

"Oops."

"Never mind, you did a good job."

Toni stepped down from the coffee table and took her spot on the couch again. Snake took his drink from the floor and slurped a major mouthful. He smiled at her and let his eyes drift slowly along the length of her body, stretched out on the couch. As if responding to his gaze, one of her knees pushed up so the flap of her skirt fell away.

"Did you hear that?" she asked.

"What?"

"The voice."

"No." She was still a little crazy, he thought. "You hear voices, you better see the Doc."

"Which doctor?"

"The witch doctor, yeah," Snake said with a laugh. "Hell, I don't know. Go to a shrink, babe."

His eyes were on her legs and he didn't feel like discussing anything else. Toni's arm had fallen casually across her crotch, another peekaboo move that tickled Snake, and her thumb rolled in a small arc on her upper thigh. Lightly, back and forth. It was mildly hypnotic, very arousing.

"Tell me about him," she said.

"Who?"

"Your doctor."

"I don't have one."

"But you know one."

"No, I— "

Snake hesitated. Well, he did know one. Technically. He'd met Shelly's shrink, back a month or two ago. But he didn't know the man, in fact he couldn't even remember the guy's name.

As if to encourage Snake, Toni now stretched out completely on her back and raised both knees up straight. Then she let them loll open and she rubbed herself in a slowly escalating rhythm as her body squirmed with pleasure. Snake didn't know what he could say, but he didn't want to stop the show. He was caught up in it almost as much as Toni was.

"The Doc is okay."

"Yeah . . ."

"The Doc is good."

"Yeah . . ."

"He'll take care of you, but you have to trust him."

"Yeah . . ."

"And do what he tells you."

"*Yeah.*"

Her knees drove toward her chest, her hands worked in a last frenzied rush.

"I wish I could tell you his name."

"YEAAAAAAAHH!"

Her body rocked convulsively, then turned rigid. She puffed air in short bursts. You momma, Snake thought. He nearly missed his mouth as he tried to take a drink with his eyes frozen on the girl. You hot little whore momma, that was better than a sexpic. The way she had done it with her clothes still on somehow made it that much more real. It was like peeking through the window next door and watching your teen queen neighbor engage in self-service fun. Snake had a hard-on, and he was clean out of words.

Toni rolled over onto her belly, her skirt rumpled and still showing a lot of leg. Her face was pressed to the couch, her one visible eye peering brightly at Snake. There was the faintest of smiles at the corner of her mouth.

"You like to watch."

"Hey." Snake shrugged with a grin.

"You do, and you like to have someone do it for you. That's okay, darling, that's cool."

"Well, not always . . ."

"I'll do it for you. Special, because you're special."

"So are you, babe."

"Come on with me."

Snake followed her into the bathroom. It was dark, and Toni didn't turn on the light. Instead, she pulled the door so it was almost shut, allowing only the slightest illumination to filter in from the living room. She had Snake stand facing the bathtub and told him to unbuckle his belt and unzip his pants. She was right behind him, speaking in a low soft voice, caressing his back.

"Grab hold of the shower bar," she directed. "That's right, that's it. Now close your eyes and imagine you're in a luxurious hotel room somewhere, maybe Paris, or Rio. You're high up, maybe forty floors, and the view is fantastic. You stand at the window and gaze out at the spectacular scene. It's night, and it's like a dream, just being there. The city is far, far below, but it's all lit up like a million shiny jewels. Now, a young woman comes into the room. Women always come to you, so you don't even turn around, you just know she's there. For you. She comes right to you, her hands flowing over your body. You still don't turn, you watch the city below and you let her love you— "

Her hands snaking around him, finding his nipples, squeezing them through his shirt, then planing down, snagging his pants and taking them to the floor. Her face to the small of his back, her hands gliding up the front of his thighs. She takes his cock in one hand, cups his balls with the other, tightening her grip with expert care as her face burrows into his backside. She licks and explores until she finds the puckered rim.

"Ohhh-aaaah . . ."

She tongues it delicately while her hands play him in front, the pace of her movements increasing steadily. Snake heaves with anticipation, his body shaking beyond his control, and she knows he is about to come. Her tongue plunges deeply into him.

"Oooooh-Gaaaaaahd . . ."

He shoots off. Little spattering sounds from the porcelain tub, but they're almost lost in the noisy rush of breath above. Snake can hardly hold himself up by the shower bar, he's so weak and dazed by this onslaught of pleasure. He still can't believe it, what she did to him. So good.

"Toni . . ."

She had backed away from him a little. When he glanced over his shoulder at her he caught sight of the swift movement, but he didn't understand it. Then he felt it, and it was the last thing he felt. The stiletto blade punctured his spine, paralyzing him. The tip snapped off, but she kept hammering the broken blade into his body, up and down, between the ribs, into his flabby midriff, blood blossoming in a spray of grey roses, his hands slipping off the shower bar, the slow dizzy fall through hot buzzing air, and still it came at him, that knife, *bam bam bam bam bam bam*, arcing at him, fixing him for all time, his shiny metal transport to the end of the night, *bam bam bam bam bam*, out of the grey, the gloom and the shadows and into the perfect no pain the perfect no night the perfect no light the perfect the

IX

silence was terrifying.

Tony was shaking so violently that he had to hold onto the sink and the wall to keep from falling to the bathroom floor. He hit the switch and the ceiling light went on. It was temporarily blinding, since Tony didn't have his shades, and he whimpered in pain. The floor was covered with blood—such a vibrant red—he could see that much as he squinted through his tears. Tony breathed deeply, sucking air in an effort to hold off panic.

Snake was in the tub. Tony had pushed him into it when he saw that the guy was about to keel over backwards on top of him. Now the only thing he could think to do was to leave him there in peace.

He's draining, Tony told himself. Let him drain. It was the best place for him.

But then what? He couldn't move a big body like that on his own, and he certainly couldn't get it out of this building or the neighborhood without being seen. Not even in the middle of the night. Impossible. This is bad, bad, bad. He hazarded a glance in the mirror. A savage stared back.

"What now?"

Nothing. The little shit. Tony noticed his stiletto on the floor, and saw for the first time that the tip was broken. Where was the other piece? The way his life was going, that would turn out to be the one little thing that landed him on Death Row. The two hundred-plus pounds of incriminatingly dead meat lying in the tub suddenly seemed as vast as a continent, and somewhere in that land mass was a vital scrap of metal. He had to find it and then get rid of it.

Tony edged closer to the bathtub. Jesus, why did he have to stab the guy so many times? But why did he ever have to stab him at all? Dead, Snake looked merely pathetic. A nobody. Just one more poor stiff who wanted to live, and be loved by somebody, but who never quite got a handle on his life. Not all that different from me, Tony thought.

But, on to business. Tony picked up the stiletto and washed it under the tap in the sink. Then he wrapped it tightly in the hand towel, wiping it several times to make sure he didn't leave a fingerprint on it, and carried it into the kitchen. He dug up a plastic supermarket bag and put the knife in it, towel and all. He rolled it into a tidy little parcel, squeezing out as much air as he could, and he used the loop handles to bind it with several knots. He set it aside on the counter.

Tony wasn't ready for the next step yet, so he changed into jeans and a T-shirt, put on his sunglasses and had a large drink to settle his nerves. He didn't feel better, but at least he was somewhat calmer.

The silence was truly awful. Tony thought he could hear the cells beginning to turn rotten in Snake's body. Snake had become a factory, a death mill where billions of tiny forces worked away nonstop at the process of decay. Snake was sliming out, so there was no time to waste.

He mopped up the blood on the bathroom floor, and then began the awkward job of removing Snake's clothes. Why? It seemed the thing to do. In the pockets of Snake's cheap black pants he came across a wallet containing thirty-two dollars, and a medicine jar that held fifty Demerol pills. Fifty of them! To think I almost felt sorry for you, you cheap bastard. I'm in good shape now, he thought gleefully. Tony burned the driver's license along with a few other papers in the kitchen sink, wiped Snake's wallet clean, and buried it in an empty milk carton in his garbage bag. He put Snake's clothes in another bag.

So far, so easy. Three ordinary parcels to throw away. But what about the big parcel in the bathtub? Tony needed help. The Pied Piper had gotten him into this mess, so where was he? Not a peep. The little fucker. I'll bring him here fast. Tony got on his knees and smashed his forehead against the kitchen floor. It worked immediately.

—Slime.

"Jesus, man." He struggled to his feet. The pain wasn't so bad but black spots peppered his vision for a moment. "You can't take me to a certain point and then leave me there alone."

—I can do anything.

"Then get rid of the guy in the bathtub."

—That's your problem.

"I might as well call the cops," Tony said. It was a bluff, and not a very good one, but it had just occurred to him that the Pied Piper needed him, or wanted him, in some way. He reappeared the minute Tony banged his head on the floor. For the moment, at least, it seemed to give Tony a slight amount of leverage. "I'll tell them he was a trick, and he turned nasty and pulled a knife, and I had to defend myself."

—That's the ticket.

The quick mockery worried Tony. "Why not?"

—You defended yourself by stabbing him all those times in the back?

"Well . . ."

—Remove the body, plasmodium.

"How do I do that?"

—Piecework.

"No way, man, no way. I'd rather call the cops, and take my chances that way."

—Yes?

"You bet yes. I'll do it right now."

Tony turned toward the telephone, but froze, and then sagged against the wall. It was as if invisible hands were wringing his liver, and at the same time a tiny neon worm burned like acid in the depths of his ear, eating its way into his brain.

—Yes?

". . . No . . ."

—I own your mind, which means I own your body. Listen and hear, boy. I can make the acid pour into your stomach all day, I can dump adrenalin into your blood till your heart shivers so bad it knots up and can't send oxygen to your brain, I can bleed your eyes and ears. I can make your nose run so much you'll drown in your own snot. I can cover you with sores, I can make your skin itch so much you'll scratch it to bloody shreds, and I can bloat your balls so they're as big and foul as rotten apples, or I can make them as small and hard as orange pips. I can squash them, I can make you piss hot acid and ground glass, I can make your lips peel off like layers of parchment, and your muscles turn to mush. I can make you chew up your tongue and spit out the bits. I can turn the marrow in your bones to lava, I can fill your mouth with fungus and raise hordes of maggots in your arsehole. And believe me, I can keep you ticking along this way forever. Yes?

". . . yes . . ."

—Good little plasmodium. Now get to work. Use the Ginsu steak knives you got from that nig-nog limousine driver. They're tacky, but they'll do the job.

"You know everything in my life?"

—Your life is mine.

Then he was gone. Tony obediently got the steak knives and took them, along with every spare plastic bag he could find, into the bathroom. The pasty bulk of flesh was still there.

"Sorry man, but you're already dead."

Tony made a few tentative slices at one elbow, and promptly threw up all over the corpse. Jesus mother's tit, he'd never get through this. He made sure that the drain was fully open, turned on the cold shower and pulled the curtain around the tub. While Snake was being sluiced down, Tony went to the sink to pat water on his own face and rinse his mouth out. Then he took a Demerol, figuring it would help him through the ordeal.

A few minutes later, he hummed as he cut loose Snake's left forearm. The elbows and knees were trouble enough with all those wires to saw, but the shoulders were much worse, far messier. At least the head was easy. By then, however, Tony had filled every plastic bag he had. He would get more tomorrow, but for now the only thing he could find to put Snake's head in was the spaghetti pot his mother had given him. It had a lid. Tony squirted some wash-up liquid in with the head and added water until the pot was nearly full, hoping the detergent would delay the inevitable rot and stench. He placed the covered pot on the stove, where it did not seem too conspicuous.

He did as much as he could, eight plastic-wrapped items, the head in the pot and the torso still floating in the tub. When he woke up the next morning, Tony had to have a shower. He couldn't stand the feeling of dried blood on him, dried scum, and the bits of Snake's flesh that had lodged beneath his fingernails. He had fallen asleep as soon as the last package was taped up. The only way he could have his shower was if he had it with the torso too, since there was nowhere to put it. Reluctantly, that's what Tony did, heaving the ghastly thing as far back in the tub as possible and then standing directly under the showerhead. He had to clear the drain a couple of times, as it got clogged with greasy chunks of gristle and meat. Tony showered quickly, then sat on the edge of the tub and cleaned between his toes with running water.

As he had done the night before, he filled the tub until the torso floated, and sprinkled pine-scented kitchen cleanser on it. To be on the safe side, he added two-thirds of a bottle of Canoe, the last of his rubbing alcohol (which was also useful in certain sexual scenarios) and a blue toilet tablet. That should keep the smell down for a while.

Sleep had refreshed him somewhat. Tony didn't need the Pied Piper to tell him what he had to do. Fortunately it was overcast outside. He put on his sunglasses and went to the supermarket to buy the largest and heaviest trash bags they had. He also bought a couple of rolls of sticky packing tape, more detergent, rubber gloves, alcohol and disinfectant. The store's fluorescent lights were getting to him, even with his sunglasses on, so he picked up a pair of mirrored clipons that helped considerably.

Tony had a couple of ideas. He now thought he knew the best way to get rid of the torso, and in the back of his mind he had a rough notion of how to escape the torments of the Pied Piper once and for all. But he would have to approach it carefully when the time came, never quite letting his thoughts settle on it, or else the demon might tune in and foil the attempt.

It was a long day, taking four trips in all. A piece of arm and a piece of leg each time. He carried them in a gym bag, and he dropped them in litterbaskets, dumpsters, anywhere reasonably safe, where they were unlikely to be noticed and opened. He even managed to slip one forearm into the trash bin at Burger Billy's, along with the remains of his lunch. By the end of the afternoon Tony was exhausted from all the walking he had done, but he also felt enormously relieved that much of Snake was scattered around the center of the city. Out of my life.

Tony examined the trunk of Snake's car, to make sure it had enough room for the torso. Some people fill a trunk with garbage and then just leave it there, God only knows why. Snake's trunk had a well-worn spare tire, a jack and some small tools, and the puzzler: a beat-up copy of Elvis's *Blue Hawaii* album. Good place to keep your record collection, Snake. Tony parked the car right in front of his building.

He had a drink, though he didn't need it to relax. He felt serene, almost—*almost* in some kind of control of his life once more. Tony had sailed through this horrible day, popping Demerol whenever the wave seemed to falter.

What day was it anyway? Sunday. Time? A little after six in the evening. Good, perfect. People were eating, and in a few minutes they'd sit back to watch *60 Minutes*. There would not be many cops on patrol at this in-between hour.

Wearing the rubber gloves, Tony somehow got the torso into a large heavy-duty garbage bag. He knotted and taped it, then slid it into another one. Was a third bag necessary? Why not? There was no point in taking chances. Tony wiped a thin streak of scum from the outer plastic when he finished, and dragged the big sack into the living room. He removed the rubber gloves and carefully put bandaids on his fingertips. With the torso, at least, there would be no prints on the bags.

Now. No need to carry it, even if he could. Tony looked up and down the hallway outside his apartment. All clear, nobody in sight, no sounds of activity. Tony tugged the garbage bag by its plastic loop handles, dragging the load into the hall. He locked his apartment, and then pulled the sack to the top of the stairs. Still no one about. Gripping the loop handles firmly, he tipped the torso over the edge and followed behind, letting it bump down the stairs but holding it so that it didn't bounce noisily out of control. It was like walking the dog, Tony thought with a smile. No sweat. When he got to the ground floor he stepped over the bag and was about to drag it to the front door when Leo Jenks emerged from his apartment. He was okay, a middle-aged man who delivered bread for a local bakery, but Tony wasn't at all happy to see him at that moment.

"Hey, Tony."

"Leo, how's it going?"

"Good, and you?"

"Okay. Just cleaning up."

"Yeah? Whaddaya got there?"

"Newspapers and magazines. You want 'em?"

Jesus, don't get cute.

"Not unless it's *Penthouse* or *Playboy*," Leo said with a sly grin. Like everyone in the building, Leo knew Tony was gay.

"'Fraid not."

"The stuff piles up, huh?"

"Sure does."

"Let me give you a hand," Leo said, bending to reach for one end of the garbage bag.

"No, don't bother, Leo. It's too clumsy to handle that way, but no trouble to drag, you know? Just leave the front door open for me, will you?"

"Yeah, sure. See you, Tony."

"Yeah, thanks."

Fuck me pink, Tony thought when Leo was gone. If he had got his hands on it he'd have known right away that it wasn't a bunch of newspapers and magazines. But it was no time to stand around, worrying about a near-miss. Tony hauled the sack outside to the edge of the curb as quickly as he could.

"Jesus," he groaned, heaving it up and into the car. Fucker must have weighed a quarter of a ton. Tony banged the trunk shut and allowed himself a casual glance around. The old geezer next door was sitting on his front stoop, but he was busy playing with his grandson. There were other people on the street, but none of them seemed to be watching Tony. He straightened his sunglasses, got into the car and drove away.

"All *right*."

With the window rolled down and the radio playing, it wasn't bad at all, especially since the humidity had fallen. Tony liked driving but he seldom got the chance to do any, so it was a treat for him to be out like this—in spite of the load he had in the trunk. He cruised through the neighborhood, then headed into the center of town. He circled The Green, drove out to the east side and checked the action along the commercial strip leading to the mall. Nothing much happening. Well, of course. It was a Sunday night, and that's the way it's supposed to be. Quiet.

By nine o'clock Tony was ready to get it done. Better to do it while there was still some light in the sky. He drifted north into the woody hills near the highway, on the outskirts of town. There were few houses on these side roads that zig-zagged up the steep valley walls. A power company sub-station. A junkyard. A landfill transfer depot. Not much else. Aha, there it was, just what Tony was looking for: a clearing off to the side where folks dumped unwanted items. He stopped the car and got out.

Nothing, only trees for a hundred yards in either direction. Tony listened carefully, but there was no sound of an approaching car. On the ground: an abandoned sofa, several bald tires, rusty wheel hubs, a corroded hand-wringer washing machine, and the best sight of all, plenty of garbage bags similar to the one Tony had.

People. Makes you wonder, Tony thought with a smile. There was a junkyard down the road, *and* a landfill station. They could bring their rubbish to either place, but no, they've got to throw it here, along this nice woody stretch of land.

Tony opened the trunk and took extra care not to rip the bag as he pulled it out. He dragged it across some of the other bags on the ground. Still no cars coming. He left the package behind a dirty but unscarred vinyl clothes hamper that had no doubt been discarded because of its ugly design.

Sorry, Snake. We had our moments, one or two.

The pot on the stove was a shock. For some reason, Tony had blanked it right out of his mind. But there it was. Okay, so he still had work to do. Tomorrow he would dispose of Snake's head, and then he would deal with the Pied Piper.

X

The windowshade appeared to be on fire, which meant it was extremely bright outside. The sun has no mercy, he thought. Men have no mercy—not much anyway, and not often. Everything was supposed to be better now, but it wasn't. Tony thought two days had passed, but it might have been three.

Where was his brain? The sun beat him, the moon laughed at him, nothing worked. He found it hard to keep track of anything. So much time, thousands of minutes, had been spent sitting still, trying to think, trying to focus his mind. Trying to find it.

The Pied Piper had got him once—or was it twice? Hard to be sure. The Demerol helped and Tony had found some silence, but the demon voice jarred him from sleep, pried open his brain when his guard was down. No mercy.

—Open a vein.

"Fuck you."

—Get it over with. Best thing.

Like that, juiced with spasms of pain meant to keep Tony in line. But he was learning. The Pied Piper couldn't be there all the time. Even in a fog of Demerol, Tony managed to organize his thoughts into a rough plan. There wasn't much chance it would do any good, but it was worth a try. Anything was better than going along with this shadow-life, twitching between drugs and torture, barely able to function.

He remembered how he had at first been plagued with a lot of static and garbled bits of words. That had been bad enough, but not nearly as bad as the clear reception he had been getting ever since he removed his metal fillings. The metal had not aided the broadcast, as Tony originally believed, but instead had actually interfered with it, at least a little. So, a lot of metal would block out the Pied Piper completely. Maybe.

The spaghetti pot was taken, unfortunately. Tony put on his doubled sunglasses and ventured outside. The glare was so fierce that his eyes were seared with pain from light leaking in at the sides, and he was nearly blind before he even got to the corner. The supermarket was three blocks away, too far to go. Tony dived into the cool, dark interior of the Sparta Mart, a neighborhood shop that carried groceries and a few basic items. Mrs Bandana, the wife of the owner, sold a lottery ticket to another customer and then directed her indifference to Tony.

"You got any aluminium foil?"

"Bottom left," she replied curtly, pointing toward the rear of the store.

Tony took two overpriced boxes. He also found some rolls of masking tape, which he figured should not be as harsh on his skin as the sticky packing tape he had at home. He paid, and insisted on being given a plastic bag to carry his purchases. Tony needed it for Snake's head. Steeling himself to face the glare outside, he ran all the way back to his apartment.

He put the pot in the kitchen sink and removed the lid. The smell was horrendous. He turned on the hot water and let it pour over the head, gradually rinsing away most of the muck. At least there were no worms crawling through the eyes and mouth, nor any other nightmare surprises that Tony had feared. When the water finally ran clear, he dumped the head into the sink and put the pot aside on the counter.

You don't look so bad now, he thought. What was your name? Alvin Doolittle, according to the driver's license. How the hell could a person with a name like that ever get into the Legion of the Lost? Snake sounded better. In fact, he looked better dead than alive. A bit rubbery, but the color had washed out nicely. The skin had the bleached look of white marble, Tony thought, or a fish's belly. There was no sign of trauma in Snake's face. He looked calm, an admirable quality.

Something Snake had said. The Doc this, the Doc that, trust the Doc, do what the Doc says. Hard to tell if it meant anything at all, since the whole scene had been mad, sick. But Snake told him to go see a shrink, and that seemed important. Tony had been sent to a shrink by the court, the weird guy with the weird name. All my troubles started after that. Maybe he can help.

—Easy, slime.

Tony shuddered. "Go away."

—Poor little plasmodium.

"The Doc'll take care of you."

—Maybe I am the Doc.

Jesus, that was a thought. "Are you?"

—You've got two heads now. You tell me.

"I'll find out, one way or the other."

—Will you indeed?

"Believe it."

But the demon was gone, his parting shot a raucous laughter that erupted in Tony's head. It took a moment to clear. Oh yes, I'll kill you, he thought bitterly. If he could just get to see that shrink again, he might find an answer.

Tony took a large, empty trash bag and dropped Snake's head into it. Then he rolled the black plastic tightly, taping it to form a rough ball. When he was satisfied with his work, Tony put the head in the Sparta Mart bag and then picked it up by the loop handles. There. He looked like anybody carrying home a nice big cabbage or honeydew melon from the market.

—Die, you slime.

"Oh fuck . . ."

—Lie down and I'll help you die. It'll be easy, it won't hurt at all. Lie down. Now.

"No, no . . ."

But Tony could feel the demon taking hold of him. The blood in his veins felt like broken glass, slashing him apart, churning his insides into a massive hemorrhage. As he started to fall, he grabbed the box of aluminium foil from the counter, ripped it open and fumbled to unroll a length of it. He hit the floor, rapidly losing strength. He couldn't even tear the foil, but he did yank enough of it out of the box to pull over his head—and suddenly the Pied Piper was silenced. Not completely gone, for Tony could still sense his presence, but substantially muffled. He pressed the aluminum foil to his skull, adjusting it to fit more tightly, and then he waited anxiously. Was the demon voice merely toying with him, allowing Tony to think he had won, before unleashing the final assault? It would be just like the sadistic bastard to do that.

But nothing happened, and Tony gradually became aware of a distant, very faint static buzz. There you are, little buddy. A minor irritation, nothing more. No pain. No words. No torture. Tony laughed out loud, shocked with relief and joy.

"It works! It works!"

Now you know you can beat the guy, Tony told himself. It's always something simple, easy to overlook or misunderstand. Like the common cold that wiped out the Martians in that old movie.

Less than an hour later Tony was ready to go. You look like a crazy, he thought sadly as he checked himself for the last time in the bathroom mirror. But that didn't really matter because he would be walking through the south end, where half the people out on the street looked damaged one way or another. Maybe he should have kept Snake's car, instead of abandoning it in the lot at the train station. No, the car was a major risk. He'd done the best thing he could with it. Now Tony would just have to walk, and if people stared—let them.

Tony had fashioned an aluminum foil skullcap, which he kept in place with an ordinary headband. For extra safety he had tied a couple of dozen thin foil strips to the headband, making a long fringe that hung down as far as his jaw on both sides, and around the back.

It would be better to wait until evening, but he was anxious to get rid of Snake's head. Besides, Doctor Ladybank wouldn't be at his office later. Now that the Pied Piper couldn't reach him, Tony was full of good ideas. He'd looked up psychiatrists in the Yellow Pages, and discovered an Ian Ladybank. His office address was in the center of the city. That was the shrink Tony had been sent to, no doubt about it. He called to make sure that Ladybank would be in all afternoon, but he didn't give his name or ask for an appointment. It seemed a safe bet that when he walked in with this headgear they'd lead him right to the shrink.

Tony's doubled sunglasses did a pretty good job, but all the light leaking in at both sides was enough to wear him down fast, so he taped the shades to his face with masking tape, overlapping the strips until he had built up a thick screen that tapered down across each of his cheeks. That should do it, he thought. Block out most of the unwanted light and you'll be okay. He could hear the Pied Piper still clamoring to get in, but faint and far away. Oddly, it was good to know the demon hadn't vanished.

Tony walked a couple of blocks with no difficulty. The tape worked fine, his eyes were still okay. No sweat. Well, no, that wasn't exactly true. It was a hot day, very humid, and Tony was perspiring already. But that was a minor inconvenience. He felt good for the first time in ages.

Was he the only person on earth being tormented by the Pied Piper, or were there others? Strange, how Tony had felt a sudden urge to ask Snake if he heard the voice. A very strange thing to do—you just don't ask other people if they hear any mysterious voices. It didn't matter, because Snake had so much metal in his head that he most likely wouldn't hear anything even if the Pied Piper did broadcast to him.

That old movie came to mind again. Was it possible that the Pied Piper was really a Martian, or some other alien? Could this be part of a plan to take over human minds, Tony wondered. Drive us crazy, turn us into slaves? *Because*, he thought, if the voice came from me, if it was all just my own craziness, then how could the aluminum foil work? So the voice had to come from someone or something outside. Ordinary people can't do that, but perhaps it was a top-secret government project. Or aliens. Tony had seen a few stories in the newstand rags about this kind of thing, and he had always laughed them in the past. But this was now. He knew a lot more, from bitter experience. Anything was possible.

What about Doctor Ladybank? The Doc. Was he in on it? Why did Tony feel drawn to see the man today? For help. But the Doc hadn't helped him at all last time. Just gave him some bullshit about watching out for—bright lights and colors. Jesus, maybe I was hypnotized, Tony thought. Maybe that's what this is about. If that's it, I'll kill him. Right there in his office.

How good it felt to be able to use his brain again! It had been so long since his thoughts weren't cluttered or twisted with the Pied Piper's invasive tactics. Tony felt human again.

But he was beginning to think he had make a mistake. He was approaching the center of the city and he still hadn't gotten rid of Snake's head. It was partly due to the fact that Tony had not found a suitable place to dispose of it, but even more because he was simply attracting too much attention. People—every rotten one of them—were stopping in their tracks to gawk at him as he walked along the street. How could he dump his parcel with a big audience on hand? Somebody would step up to open the bag at once and then they'd all grab him before he could get away.

To make matters worse, the aluminum foil skullcap and fringe were magnifying the heat and frying his brain. Tony was sweating like a pig now. He stopped abruptly and went into the department store he had almost passed. The air-conditioning came as a great relief. He wandered around for a few minutes, imagining that all the security people in the place were watching him.

Shit! What if they demanded to inspect his bag? He couldn't very well refuse, they'd just hold him until the cops came. Tony began to tremble with fear. Then he saw what he needed. He kept his shopping bag clutched tightly in one hand, and he went to the counter in the sports department. He paid for a New York Yankees baseball cap, which he put on immediately. It sat snugly on the aluminum foil. The clerk appeared to be in shock, but handed him his change and receipt without a word. Tony then strolled out of the store as if he hadn't a care in the world.

Brilliant idea, he thought. The fringe was still hanging in plain view, and there was all that tape on his cheeks, but he now felt somewhat less conspicuous. It would be a lot better if Tony could do away with the fringe, but that was too risky. If he let the Pied Piper back in, he'd never be free again. Maybe he could do without the fringe, maybe the skullcap was sufficient to block out the Pied Piper, but Tony wasn't about to take a chance.

Burger Billy's was crowded. Tony was pleased to see that he was indeed drawing fewer stares, thanks to the baseball cap, but there were still people watching him. He didn't feel comfortable enough to drop Snake's head in the trash bin, so he turned around and left the fast food restaurant.

The public library. That was the place. There was a large litter barrel (disguised as a piece of mod sculpture) in front of the library. Tony had already tossed one of Snake's feet into it and the newspapers had made no mention of its having been found. Best of all, it was located in the middle of a long sidewalk that went from the curb to the library, which sat back a distance from the street. That meant he could time it so that there was no one nearby when he walked past and dropped the dead man's head in the artsy-fartsy opening of the litter barrel. In spite of the heat, he pushed on in a hurry.

One more block, Tony thought. Then the park. He was sticky with sweat, tired but determined. I'm going to treat myself when this is over. A quick warm bath, followed by a long cool shower. Broil a T-bone steak, wash it down with that bottle of bubbly the TWA steward had given him, do a couple of lines and hit the bars. But tonight it would be for fun, not work.

"Hey, fuckhead."

Tony was only a little way into the park when the half dozen or so teenagers descended on him. Assholes, every one. They had nothing better to do with their time than hassle the elderly, the drifters and the gays who lingered in the park. Anyone they felt they could pester without comeback. They closed around Tony like an evil cloak, taunting him, shoving him, flicking fingers at his Yankee cap, snatching at the plastic bag.

"Fuck off, you little shits."

"Eat shit, fuckhead."

Some of them were a year or two older than he was, but that didn't matter. Tony strode on toward the library, poking elbows at anybody who got too close. They answered by bumping him, and then he was tripped. As he fell, cursing them loudly, he was hit on the head and his hat went flying. The aluminum foil skullcap was knocked loose. Oh Jesus, no. He clamped his hands on it and tried to adjust the headband. Somebody was yanking at the strips of foil that hung across Tony's face.

"Nice hair, asshole."

"What's in the bag?"

"Open it."

The kids were already pulling at the tightly wrapped parcel. Tony jumped up and lunged for it, but they pushed him down again. He had been sweating so much that the masking tape wouldn't stick to his cheeks anymore. Light flooded in, burning his eyes. Tony shrieked at them and swung out with his fists, but he didn't make contact. In return, he was pummeled from all sides. The doubled sunglasses were ripped from his face.

Tony fell to his knees, hands clapped tightly over his eyes. I'm okay, I'm okay, he tried to convince himself. But he already knew from the shouts and screams that they had discovered what he had in the bag. Now he was being kicked and punched, and when he tried to ward off the blows he was hit in the stomach so hard his eyes opened briefly. The color purple ravaged him—he was in a flowerbed full of violets.

Tony screamed.

"No! Don't touch that, not that! Please don't— "

But they did. They were ready to take his mug shot, and one of the cops calmly reached up and pulled off that stupid aluminum foil thing he had on his head.

Zzzzzt.

EPILOGUE

Life isn't disappointing, but people so often are. They may raise your hopes for a while, but sooner or later they'll let you down. People are . . . Doctor Ladybank pondered the matter for a few moments, seeking to find the right word. Yes, he had it.

People are unworthy.

He was not entirely sure what they were unworthy of, but the point seemed irrefutable. It was difficult to follow every train of thought to the end of the line when you were drowning in a sea of disillusionment. The gift—for that was how Doctor Ladybank now regarded it, not as a skill or a technique—was apparently gone. Radio silence. Day and night he tried to tune in someone, anyone, but he found no one.

What happened? Doctor Ladybank wasn't sure. For a few days after Tony Delgado's arrest, the boy could still be reached. But then he began to fade gradually, and after a month he disappeared altogether. It was not the effect of buildings and metalwork and power lines, or

Doctor Ladybank never would have managed to reach across the city in the first place. Nor could it be a matter of distance, as he had driven the fifty-plus miles to the Bartholomew Forensic Institute, part of the state hospital for the criminally insane, where Delgado was being held pending trial. He parked in the visitor's lot and sat there for an hour, trying feverishly to regain contact with the boy. Nothing.

Doctor Ladybank wondered if the failure was his. But he did the same things with his mind, he hadn't forgotten how it worked, anymore than you can forget how to ride a bicycle. Of course, it may have been a gigantic fluke, a scientific peculiarity that had its brief moment and then passed. But Doctor Ladybank could not believe that. He still had faith in his gift. All he had to do, he told himself, was persist. It would come back to him. And he would connect. Believe. Persist.

His favourite theory about this temporary failure centered on the inadequacy of his two subjects. Snake had always been tricky to handle, a dim prospect. Doctor Ladybank had never enjoyed the same intimacy of mind with Snake that he had with Tony. To steer him out to Jack's backyard and then get him over the hump—that was like composing the *Gurre-Lieder*. Delgado, on the other hand, was ravishing in his openness and malleability. Great potential, unlimited opportunity. But something had gone wrong, and Doctor Ladybank feared that he had gone too far with the boy. Now parts of Delgado's brain had simply shut down and were incapable of any mental reception. How else to explain it?

Of course, terrible things had happened. But no, don't say that. Terrible is an emotive word that has no meaning. It would be more accurate to say that unfortunate things had happened. He couldn't explain it, but it was hardly all his doing. When minds meet and interact in such a pioneering way the results are almost certain to be unexpected. Two minds adrift in each other, it was like—and here Doctor Ladybank took comfort in the persistence of the musical metaphor—a vast orchestra lost in the aleatoric reaches of the night.

Besides, Snake and Tony were hardly innocents.

Fuck it, as they would say.

Doctor Ladybank stared at the papers in front of him, but he couldn't see the words. It was that time of day, when he usually summarized his notes on the patients he'd seen, but his mind just wouldn't focus. Such boring and squalid lives that people insist on living . . . Doctor Ladybank was glad when the phone warbled.

"Margaret Zuvella on the line for you."

I remember the bristol, but the face escapes me.

"Yes, put her through." Pause, click. "Hello, Maggie?"

"Hi, Ian. How are you?"

"Fine, thanks, and you?"

"Busy as usual, but bearing up."

Doctor Ladybank gave the obligatory chuckle. "Now, what can I do for you on this rainy Tuesday?"

"I was hoping you'd agree to examine a client of mine. He's indigent, of course, so it'll be at the usual lousy state rates. But he's convinced you can help."

"Oh? What case is it?"

"State versus Anthony Delgado."

"Ah."

"You know him, you saw him a while back on another case. He seems like a major league fuck-up, but what do I know? The state experts are picking his brain now, which is why we need you."

"Yes."

"Yes, you remember him? Or yes, you'll examine him?"

"Both."

"Ian, you're a doll."

Not really—but Doctor Ladybank didn't say that. The tide had come in, his boat was lifted off the sand, and he was sailing again. The time would come, he knew beyond the slightest doubt, when he would make contact, and *connect*, with some other person. When that happened, Doctor Ladybank would progress with the gift, exploring new territory, achieving the unimaginable.

But for now, thanks be to the void, he had a chance to learn more from one of his mistakes. Perhaps even to save it.

Tony smiled when he saw Doctor Ladybank's fountain pen, one of those fat expensive jobs. In happier times he'd had a couple of well-off tricks who used that kind of pen. Check-writers with skinny dicks.

They were in a small consulting room at Bartholomew. It was painted the mandatory institutional shade of pastel green, and it was stuffy from a lack of air-conditioning, but it was as good as heaven—compared to the ward in which Tony was kept. The guard stood outside the door, keeping an eye on them through the sturdy wire-and-glass window. Doctor Ladybank had brought Tony a carton of cigarettes from Maggie. Tony had never smoked before, but in a ward full of wackos it seemed a perfectly natural, even healthy thing to do.

The questions were stupid and boring, but Tony tried to give polite answers. There was something eerie and unreal about this. After so much time, he was still unsure of Doctor Ladybank's true role in what had gone down. Had he been directly involved in all of Tony's suffering? Was he partially responsible for the bleak future Tony faced? It seemed unlikely, because the same man was now trying to construct a "demon voice" insanity defence so that Tony would be spared hard prison time. Not that he relished the prospect of an indefinite committal to the nuthouse.

"One problem," Doctor Ladybank said, "is your assertion that the voice stopped communicating with you."

"Yeah, it did."

"When did that happen?"

"When I was still in the city jail," Tony said. "It took me a couple of weeks, maybe more, to get rid of it."

"You stopped the voice?"

"That's right."

"And how did you accomplish that?"

"By banging my head on the bars and the cement floor," Tony explained proudly. "See, it really bothered him when I banged my head on the floor at my apartment. He said the people downstairs would put the cops on me. But I figured, maybe he was afraid I'd shake up the works." Tony tapped the side of his head. "So that he couldn't get to me anymore. In jail, I had the time to try it out, to do it everyday, as much as I could take. And it actually worked. I could feel him getting weaker, and finally I couldn't hear him at all anymore. If I'd only done that at the beginning, I'd have saved myself—my life."

"I see." Doctor Ladybank put his pen down. "Do you have to continue this behavior, banging your head, in order to— "

"Hell, no," Tony cut in. "It did the job, and that's it. I never got a kick out of knocking myself senseless, you know. I'm not crazy. I just . . . went through *something* crazy. And I'll tell you this too: he's still out there, man. I know he is."

"Yes. Now, tell me— "

"Doc, I have a question for you."

"Yes?"

"Why did you tell me about bright lights and colors?"

"Pardon?"

"The first time you saw me," Tony said, leaning forward, his arms on the table. "You gave me some line about watching out for bright lights and bright colors."

"I'm sure I didn't," Doctor Ladybank insisted.

"Yeah, you did. It sounded weird at the time, and I didn't give it much thought. But later, when the voice came and all the trouble really started, lights and colors began to hurt me. They got so bad I had to wear sunglasses and dark clip-ons. But I was still in agony." Tony paused. "Why did you do that?"

"I can assure you I did no such— "

"What was it, some kind of test? Or were you just having a little fun with me?"

"Anthony, you won't help your case this way."

Doctor Ladybank was trying to sound calm, but he was clearly flustered. His cheeks had more color now and his eyes cast about evasively as he droned on about Tony's "willful and naive attempt to embellish the delusion," and other uptown bullshit.

"Doc," Tony interrupted. "I'm a whore. Maybe that's why I can always tell when I'm being jived. I thought it was the CIA, or aliens from space, or that I was just crazy. I doubted it was you, I really did. Until now."

"I'll speak with your attorney."

Doctor Ladybank was trying to look annoyed. He shuffled the papers on the table, picked up his pen and began to write. As if Tony were no longer there, and had indeed ceased to exist.

Writing about me. The subject. That's what you were doing. You weren't trying to read my mind, Tony thought, you were trying to write it, to script my life like a dream or some kind of movie in your mind.

"Plasmodium."

Doctor Ladybank looked up sharply when Tony spoke the word. A ghost of a smile formed around the psychiatrist's eyes, seeming to say *I cannot be hurt by you.*

The baleful, haunting expression on the man's face triggered a profound claustrophobia in Tony. It felt as if the world, the universe itself, and every cell in his brain, was shutting down, blinking off, closing forever, and all that would be left was his sense of awareness—perpetual awareness of the dark around him. The room itself was being blotted out.

Write this!

Tony snatched the fat pen from Doctor Ladybank's fingers and in a single swift motion rammed it nib-first through the shrink's right eye. He pushed it as far into the demon brain as he could, and then sat back, experiencing a remarkable sense of clarity and peace of mind.

Doctor Ladybank's mouth opened slightly. Otherwise, he did not move. His left eye was still open, glistening sightlessly. He appeared to be considering the matter.

NINA KIRIKI HOFFMAN

Zits

NINA KIRIKI HOFFMAN resides in Eugene, Oregon, with three cats and a mannequin. She is fast gaining a reputation as a short story writer with appearances in *Asimov's*, *Analog*, *The Magazine of Fantasy & Science Fiction*, *Aboriginal*, *Pulphouse*, *Alfred Hitchcock's Mystery Magazine*, *Weird Tales* (she was a featured author), and such anthologies as *Doom City*, *Greystone Bay*, *Shadows 8* and *9* and *The Ultimate Werewolf*. She has also appeared in several volumes of Datlow and Windling's *The Year's Best Fantasy and Horror* and Karl Edward Wagner's *Year's Best Horror*.

Two collections of her short fiction have so far been published, *Author's Choice Monthly 14: Legacy of Fire* (Pulphouse Publishing) and *Courting Disasters and Other Strange Affinities* (Wildside Press). She collaborated with Tad Williams on the young adult fantasy *Child of An Ancient City*, and has a horror novella, *Unmasking*, coming from Axolotl Press.

There are far too many child abuse stories being published in the horror field today, and most of them merely exploit their given theme. "Zits" is a welcome exception. It may be short, but it certainly packs an emotional punch.

O NCE I READ A BOOK WHERE they put the jewels in the teddy bear's stomach. A lot of people were chasing that teddy bear but the kids and the police got it in the end and when they sliced him open, there were all those colored jewels, sparkling and shining and promising everything.

You have to dig deepest to find the best secrets, my daddy said, burying his in me.

Some secrets you don't want to keep.

The worst zits are the red ones where you can't see any white. You press them and the white doesn't pop out. You have to dig around with a needle to find the white under the blood, because until you get the pearly white out the sore won't heal no matter how many times you pull the scab off. And you've only got so much time in front of the mirror in the morning. If you leave the red zits alone and go to school then they get really big and everybody can see the pearl under the skin and they make jokes. Pizza face. Balloon factory.

It's always dark when he comes in. I used to have a night light, but when I turned thirteen a year ago, he said, "Now you're a teenager. You're all grown up, and you don't need that little light anymore. That's for scared little kids."

It's always dark when the door opens, so I see the light from down in the front hall, faint and yellow, leaving a giant fuzzy shadow of him dark across the ceiling. Then he slips inside and the light goes away again, and that's when I stop hearing myself, no breathing, no blood moving through my ears to let me know my heart's still beating. I hear the click of the door closing, and I hear his feet as they slap the hardwood floor and pad across the rag rug by my bed, and I smell his soap and his aftershave and a little hint of Mom's perfume because he's been lying close to her.

I never move after I hear the door click shut.

By the time he reaches the bed his breathing is harsher and louder than it ever is during the day. He lifts the sheet and the blanket and the spread. The linen whispers against itself. The cold air goose bumples across my arms and legs.

I am asleep, I tell myself. I am a piece of stone. I am dead. I don't breathe and I don't move. I can't.

I have been lying on my back, my arms and legs straight, locked tight. He turns me away from him and bends my hips and knees and slides in behind me and pulls my nightie out of his way.

I used to sit on his lap. It used to stay flat.

I don't move, but he moves me, and he moves around me and in me.

I click my brain off, because tomorrow I'll have to kiss him good-bye at the breakfast table, just like Mom does.

When he's finished and I am messy, he whispers that if I ever tell Mom about this her heart will break and she'll die. If I ever tell anybody else they might tell Mom and her heart will break and she'll die.

He leaves. After a long time, my brain clicks back on, and I get up and shower and change the sheets and go back to bed and drop into sleep like it was a cliff I fell over.

My heart breaks, and I don't die.

When a zit gets big enough, you can pop it.

I've been sharpening a knitting needle on a whetstone I found in a drawer in the kitchen. This zit is one of the red ones. It's not big enough yet, even though the bleeding stopped three months ago. I don't want to wait for it to show. Though sometimes I think about the pearl forming in there, and wonder if it is worth more than I am.

I think I'll slide the needle in through my belly button tonight, before he gets here.

STEPHEN JONES & KIM NEWMAN

Necrology: 1991

I N 1991, DEATH CLAIMED far too many writers, artists, performers and technicians who made significant contributions to the horror, science fiction and fantasy genres . . .

AUTHORS/ARTISTS

Screenwriter **Richard Maibum** died on January 1st after a short illness. He was 81. Best known for his scripts for such James Bond extravaganzas as *Dr No, From Russia With Love, Goldfinger, Thunderball, On Her Majesty's Secret Service, Diamonds Are Forever, The Man With the Golden Gun, The Spy Who Loved Me, For Your Eyes Only, Octopussy, The Living Daylights* and *License to Kill*, he also adapted Ian Fleming's *Chitty Chitty Bang Bang* for the screen.

Everett Freeman, who scripted *The Secret Life of Walter Mitty* starring Danny Kaye and Boris Karloff, died on January 24th from renal failure. He was 79.

Leo Katcher, who co-scripted the remake of *M* (1951), died from a heart attack on February 27th, aged 79.

Author **Michael Hardwick** died on March 4th. He continued the adventures of Sherlock Holmes (until restrained by the Conan Doyle estate), and together with his wife, Mollie, novelised the 1970 movie, *The Private Life of Sherlock Holmes*.

Ian McLellan Hunter, who was blacklisted by Hollywood in the 1950s and still won an Oscar under a "front" name for his script for *Roman Holiday*, died on March 5th. He also won an Emmy for his TV adaptation of *Dr Jekyll & Mr Hyde*.

Television and film writer Morton Fine died from cancer on March 7th, aged 74. His many credits include *I Spy*, *The Pawnbroker*, *The Fool Killer* and *The Alfred Hitchcock Hour*.

Author John Bellairs died on March 8th of cardiovascular disease, aged 53. His books, primarily aimed at children, and often illustrated by Edward Gorey, include *The Face in the Frost*, *The House With a Clock in Its Walls* (adapted for television), *The Figure in the Shadows*, *The Mummy the Will and the Crypt*, *The Dark Secret of Weatherend* and *The Mansion in the Mist*.

Lyricist Howard Ashman, whose credits include both the stage and film version of *Little Shop of Horrors*, *The Little Mermaid*, *Aladdin* and a musical version of Kurt Vonnegut's *God Bless You, Mr Rosewater*, died from AIDS on March 14th. He was 40, and won a posthumous Academy Award for the title song from Disney's *Beauty and the Beast*.

The same day saw the death of Sarah Gourley (Sadie) Shaw, well-known science fiction fan and wife of SF writer Bob Shaw, apparently from liver failure.

Graham Greene, author of *The Third Man* and *The Quiet American*, died from a blood disease on April 3rd, aged 86. A relative of Robert Louis Stevenson, his acclaimed body of work included a few science fiction and ghost stories and such film adaptations as *The Third Man*, *Ministry of Fear* and *This Gun for Hire*.

George T. Delacorte, pulp and comics publisher and founder of the Dell Publishing imprint, died on April 4th, aged 97. A philanthropist in later life, he gave New York City the Alice in Wonderland bronze statues in Central Park.

Maurice Binder, who created the distinctive title sequences for fourteen James Bond movies, died on April 9th from lung cancer. He also created the credits for *Damn Yankees*, *The Private Life of Sherlock Holmes*, *Repulsion*, *Bedazzled*, *The Mouse That Roared* and the 1979 version of *Dracula*.

Playwright and scriptwriter Michael Pertwee (brother of Dr Who Jon) died on April 17th, aged 74. His films include *A Funny Thing Happened on the Way to the Forum*, *Mouse on the Moon*, *Salt and Pepper* and *One More Time*.

Holocaust survivor Jerzy Kosinski, author of *The Painted Bird* and *Being There*, died from an apparent suicide on May 3rd. He was 57. He had been despondent over failing health and an inability to write.

Editor and publisher **Clarence Paget** died on May 18th, four days after lapsing into a coma following a stroke. He was 82. As chief editor at Pan Books, Paget created *The Pan Book of Horror Stories* in 1959, working closely with the series' editor, Herbert van Thal. Following the latter's death, Paget continued the series himself, editing volumes 26–30, and he co-edited the 30th anniversary volume, *Dark Voices: The Best from the Pan Book of Horror Stories* in 1990.

Author **Sharon Baker**, aged 53, died on June 4th from pancreatic cancer. Her first novel, *Quarreling, They Met the Dragon*, appeared in 1984, followed by *Journey to Membliar* and *Burning Tears of Sassurum*. She also contributed to J. N. Williamson's *How To Write Tales of Horror, Fantasy & Science Fiction*, and a poem appeared posthumously in *Now We Are Sick*.

Science fiction artist **Roger Stine** died on June 17th of kidney and liver failure after being hospitalized for two weeks. He was 39. Stine, who turned freelance in 1976, did a number of covers for *Cinefantastique* magazine, plus artwork for *Shayol, Asimov's, Heavy Metal, Oui, National Lampoon*, DC Comics' *Star Trek* series, paperback publishers and games companies. He won an Edgar for his Sherlock Holmes frontispiece, "The Three Pipe Problem".

Distinguished Yiddish writer and Nobel Prize winner **Isaac Bashevis Singer** died on July 24th, aged 87, after suffering several strokes. His acclaimed books include *Gimpel the Fool and Other Stories, The Seance and Other Stories, Satan in Goray* and *The Magician of Lubin*, and he was a contributor to Kirby McCauley's landmark *Dark Forces* anthology.

Writer/producer **Oliver Drake** died August 5th after a long illness, aged 88. He wrote numerous westerns (such as *Riders of the Whispering Skull*) and was associate producer of the last in Universal's Kharis series, *The Mummy's Curse* (1944).

Underground comics artist **Rick Griffin**, aged 47, died from head injuries on August 17th, following a motorcycle accident. His work appeared in *Zap Comix* and others, and on album covers for Jimi Hendrix, Grateful Dead, Jefferson Airplane etc.

American movie poster artist **Reynold Brown** died on August 24th after a long illness. He was 73. Brown's distinctive artwork for such posters as *Creature from the Black Lagoon, This Island Earth, The Incredible Shrinking Man, The Time Machine, Masque of the Red Death* and *Attack of the 50ft Woman*, amongst others, was profiled in the March 1988 issue of *Cinefantastique* magazine.

Dorothy and **Howard Dimsdale** used sleeping pills to kill themselves in a suicide pact on August 27th. She was in her 60s, he was 78. He wrote the scripts for *The Living Ghost, Somewhere in the Night* and *Abbott and Costello Meet Captain Kidd*, and was blacklisted in the 1950s.

Author **Gerry Davis** died from cancer on August 31st, aged 61. He was story editor on BBC's *Dr Who*, created the *Doomwatch* TV series, and co-scripted the 1980 movie *The Final Countdown*. His novels include *Mutant 59: The Plastic Eaters, Brainrack, The Dynostar Menace* (with Kit Pedler) and several *Dr Who* novelisations.

Actor turned author **Thomas Tryon** died from cancer on September 4th, aged 65. After starring in such movies as *Moon Pilot* and *I Married a Monster from Outer Space*, he became a bestselling writer with *The Other* (filmed in 1972 from his own screenplay), *Harvest Home* (turned into a TV mini-series), *Lady, Crowned Heads, Night of the Moonbow, The Wings of Morning* and *Kingdom Come*.

Composer **Alex North** died on September 8th from pancreatic cancer, aged 81. His many movie scores include *Spartacus, Cleopatra, Shanks, Dragonslayer, Shoes of the Fisherman, The Bad Seed* and *The Blue Bird*. He also wrote "Unchained Melody", which was featured in *Ghost*.

Theodore Seuss Geisel (aka Dr Seuss) died September 24th, aged 87. He was the author and illustrator of such perennial children's favourites as *Dr T, How the Grinch Stole Christmas* (recorded by Boris Karloff), *The Cat in the Hat, Green Eggs and Ham, Horton Hears a Who!, How the Lorax was Lifted* and *Beenill*. He created more than forty books, which have been translated into twenty different languages and sold well over 200 million copies worldwide. He also won three Oscars in the 1940s and '50s, and in 1984 was awarded the Pulitzer Prize for his contributions to children's literature.

Movie publicist **Scott Holton** died of AIDS on September 27th, aged 52. His many credits include *2010, Quest for Fire, Invaders from Mars* (1985) and *Leatherface: The Texas Chainsaw Massacre III*.

Lyricist **David Huddleston** died from a heart attack on September 28th, aged 73. His credits include the Disney movies *Robin Hood* and *The Aristocats*.

Thaddeus E. ("Ted") **Dikty** died of a heart attack on October 11th, aged 71. In 1948 he created Shasta Publishers (with Melvin Korshak) to publish the famous *Checklist of Fantastic Literature* and several other major books in the SF field. After editing a number of anthologies, he formed the publishing house Fax Collectors Editions in 1972 and, later, Starmont House. He is survived by his wife, bestselling writer Julian May.

Russian science fiction author **Arkady Strugatsky** died on October 14th in Moscow, aged 66. He often collaborated with his younger brother, Boris, and the first novel to appear under their byline was

Country of the Purple Clouds in 1959. Other books include *The Far Rainbow, The Final Circle of Paradise, Hard Way to Be a God, The Ugly Swans, Roadside Picnic* (filmed as *Stalker*) and *The Snail on the Slope*. The Strugatskys were frequently in trouble with the Soviet authorities, who objected to the political content of their books.

Henry Wilson ("Heck") **Allen**, who wrote some of the all-time best Tex Avery cartoons (*Screwball Squirral, Swing Shift Cinderella, Uncle Tom's Cabana* etc.) died October 26th from pneumonia. He was 79.

Photographic archivist **John Kobal** died from AIDS on October 28th. He was 51.

Czechoslovakian-born publishing magnate **Robert Maxwell** died under mysterious circumstances on his yacht near the Canary Islands on November 5th, aged 68. His worldwide multi-media empire was in severe financial trouble and it has been speculated that he could have taken his own life. Maxwell's extensive holdings included the UK's Macmillan Publishing Group and its many subsidiary companies, the *New York Daily News* and several British newspapers.

Robert Kaufman, who scripted *Dr Goldfoot and the Bikini Machine* and *Love At First Bite*, died from a heart attack on November 21st, aged 60.

Lead singer of Queen, **Freddie Mercury**, died from AIDS on November 26th, aged 45. His music can be heard in *Flash Gordon* (1980), the 1984 reworking of *Metropolis*, and *Highlander*.

ACTORS/ACTRESSES

Actor **Berry Kroeger** died from kidney failure on January 4th, aged 78. On radio he had the lead in *The Falcon*, starred in *Inner Sanctum* and was on Orson Welles's *Mercury Theatre of the Air*. He often played a villain in such films as *Black Magic, Atlantis the Lost Continent, Chamber of Horrors, The Incredible 2-Headed Transplant, Nightmare in Wax, The Mephisto Waltz* and *Demon Seed*, and on TV in *Lights Out, Inner Sanctum, Thriller, The Man from UNCLE* and *Get Smart*.

John Eckhardt (aka Johnny Eck), "the living half-boy", who appeared in Tod Browning's classic *Freaks* (1932) died of heart failure on January 5th. He was 82.

Veteran character actor **Keye Luke** died on January 16th from a stroke, aged 86. He portrayed No. 1 son, Lee Chan, in many of the best Charlie Chan movies (such as *Charlie Chan at the Opera*) and in the series crossover, *Mr Moto's Gamble*, and he appeared as the faithful Kato in the serials *The Green Hornet* and *The Green Hornet Strikes Again*. His many other credits include *Mad Love*, *Invisible Agent*, *How Dooo You Do*, *Lost City of the Jungle*, *Project X*, *Gremlins*, *Gremlins 2* and *Alice*. On TV he appeared in *The Cat Creature* and *Star Trek*, and he was a regular on *Kung Fu*.

Another of the original munchkins from *The Wizard of Oz*, **Nita Krebs**, died of an apparent heart attack on January 18th, aged 85. The 3' 8" tall actress was also featured in the 1938 western, *The Terror of Tiny Town*.

The same day saw the death of **Lillian Bond**, aged 83, who starred in the *The Old Dark House* (1932) with Boris Karloff, as well as *The Picture of Dorian Gray*, *Man in the Attic* and *The Maze*.

Leading man **Glenn Langan** died January 19th from cancer. He was 73. His credits include *The Return of Doctor X*, *Hangover Square*, *The Amazing Colossal Man*, *The Andromeda Strain*, *Mutiny in Outer Space* and *Women of the Prehistoric Planet*.

Character actor **John McIntire** died from emphysema and cancer on January 30th, aged 83. His numerous credits include *Francis*, *I've Lived Before*, *Psycho*, *Herbie Rides Again*, *Cloak & Dagger*, the TV movie *Goliath Awaits* and such shows as *Alfred Hitchcock Presents*, *Twilight Zone*, *Fantasy Island* and *The Incredible Hulk*.

Jean Rogers, who portrayed Dale Arden in the '30s serials *Flash Gordon* and *Flash Gordon's Trip to Mars*, died on February 24th, aged 74.

Eileen Sherman, who appeared in such 1920s serials as *The Great Radium Mystery*, *The Diamond Queen* and *Terror Trail*, died on March 15th. She was 93.

Gloria Holden who portrayed Countess Maria Zaleska, the title character in *Dracula's Daughter*, died from a heart attack on March 22nd. She was 82. Her other films include *Miracles for Sale*, *The Corsican Brothers*, *Strange Holiday* and *Dodge City*.

Veteran character actor **Aldo Ray**, aged 64, died on March 27th from complications due to throat cancer and pneumonia. Among his many low-budget credits are *The Power*, *Psychic Killer*, *Haunts*, *The Lucifer Complex*, *Human Experiments*, *The Centerfold Girls*, *Haunted*, *Bog*, *Nightstalker*, *Mongrel*, *Vultures*, *Evils of the Night*, *Biohazard*, *Prison Ship Starslammer*, *Frankenstein's Great Aunt Tillie*, *Night Shadow*, *Don't Go Near the Park*, *The Secret of NIMH* and *Shock'em Dead*.

Also on March 27th, **Ralph Bates**, who during the 1970s looked as if he was being groomed to be the new Cushing or Lee at Hammer Films, died from cancer, aged 50. His credits include *Taste the Blood of Dracula*, *Horror of Frankenstein*, *Dr Jekyll &*

Sister Hyde, Persecution, Fear in the Night, Lust for a Vampire, Devil Within Her and TV's *Moonbase 3*.

7' 2" actor **Kevin Peter Hall**, who starred in the movie and TV series *Harry and the Hendersons* and also appeared as the alien in *Predator* and *Predator 2*, died from pneumonia on April 10th, aged 35.

Ken Curtis, who starred in *The Killer Shrews* and produced both that movie and *The Giant Gila Monster*, died April 27th, aged 74. He also appeared as Festus in *Gunsmoke* and in many classic John Ford westerns.

Veteran British character actor **Wilfred Hyde-White** died from congestive heart failure on May 6th, aged 87. He co-starred as Dr Goodfellow in the 1980s TV series, *Buck Rogers*, and his numerous film credits include *Murder By Rope, The Third Man, The Ghosts of Berkeley Square, Ten Little Indians* (1965), *Chamber of Horrors, Skullduggery, The Million Eyes of Su-Muru, The Cat and the Canary* (1977), *King Solomon's Treasure*, the TV movies *Fear No Evil* (1969) and *Ritual of Evil*, and the pilot for *Battlestar Galactica*.

Character actor **Ronald Lacey** died on May 15th from cancer. He was 55. His many credits include *Raiders of the Lost Ark, Dance of the Vampires, Crucible of Terror, Gawain and the Green Knight, The Final Programme, The Hound of the Baskervilles* (1983), *The Adventures of Buckaroo Banzai Across the 8th Dimension, Sword of the Valiant, Into the Darkness, Red Sonja, Disciple of Death, Firefox* and the 1987 TV version of *The Sign of Four*. He often turned up as a villain on TV in *The Avengers, The New Avengers, Randall and Hopkirk (Deceased), Blake's 7* etc.

Australian actress **Coral Browne** died from cancer on May 29th, aged 77. Her second husband was Vincent Price, who she met on *Theatre of Blood*, and her other credits include *Dreamchild, The Ruling Class, Dr Crippen* and the short-lived TV series with Price, *Time Express*.

Jazz diva **Bertice Reading** died from a stroke on June 10th, after collapsing during rehearsals for *Notre Dame*, a musical version of *The Hunchback of Notre Dame*. She was 54, and also appeared in the musical movie version of *Little Shop of Horrors*.

Distinguished stage actress **Dame Peggy Ashcroft** died June 14th from a stroke, aged 83. Her film credits include *The Wandering Jew* (1933) and the 1935 version of *The 39 Steps*. She won an Oscar and BAFTA Award for her supporting role in *A Passage to India*.

Producer/actor and Founder of London's Mermaid Theatre, **Lord Miles of Blackfriars** (aka Sir Bernard Miles) died the same day, aged 83. His movie appearances include *Midnight at Madam Tussaud's,*

Great Expectations, Moby Dick, The Man Who Knew Too Much (1956), *tom thumb* and *Heavens Above.*

1940s leading lady, **Joan Caulfield,** also died on the 14th, aged 69. She was menaced by a homicidal Claude Rains in *The Unsuspected* (1947).

Ronald Allen, best known for his recurring roll in the British TV soap *Crossroads* and the *Comic Strip Presents* series, died on June 18th from cancer, aged 56. His film credits include *The Projected Man* and *The Fiend* (aka *Beware the Brethren*).

American leading actress **Jean Arthur** (aka Gladys Greene) died on June 19th from heart failure, aged 90. Her movie career spanned three decades and includes *The Mysterious Dr Fu Manchu* (1929), *The Return of Dr Fu Manchu, Mr Deeds Goes to Town, Mr Smith Goes to Washington* and *Shane.*

Actor and producer **Michael Landon** (aka Michael Orowitz) died from liver and pancreatic cancer on July 1st, aged 54. The star of the hit TV series *Bonanza, Little House on the Prairie* and *Highway to Heaven,* he made his debut in the title role of *I Was a Teenage Werewolf* (1957).

American leading lady **Lee Remick** died from cancer on July 2nd. She was 55. Her movie credits include *Anatomy of a Murder, Experiment in Terror, No Way to Treat a Lady, The Omen* and *The Medusa Touch.*

Character actress **Mildred Dunnock** died on July 5th, aged 90. Among her many film appearances are *Kiss of Death, The Trouble With Harry, What Ever Happened to Aunt Alice?* and d the 1975 remake of *The Spiral Staircase.*

Hammer veteran **Thorley Walters** died on July 6th, aged 78, after a long illness. His credits include *The Phantom of the Opera* (1962), *Dracula Prince of Darkness, Frankenstein Created Woman, Frankenstein Must Be Destroyed, Vampire Circus, The Man Who Haunted Himself, Trog, The People That Time Forgot* and TV's *The Avengers.*

James Franciscus died from emphysema on July 8th, aged 57. He starred in *The Valley of Gwangi, Marooned, Beneath the Planet of the Apes, Cat O'Nine Tails, Killer Fish, Great White* and the TV movie *Night Slaves.*

Actor and American quiz show host **Bert Convy** died from cancer on July 15th, aged 56. His movie credits include the Corman cult classic *A Bucket of Blood, Hero At Large,* the made-for-TV *Man in the Santa Claus Suit* and the 1971 remake of *Death Takes a Holiday.*

Emmy and Tony Ward-winning actress **Collen Dewhurst** died from cancer on August 22nd, aged 67. She appeared in *When a*

Stranger Calls, Final Assignment, The Dead Zone and *The Boy Who Could Fly,* amongst other movies.

British actor **Alan Wheatley**, best-known as the Sheriff of Nottingham in the 1950s TV series *Robin Hood,* died from a heart attack on August 30th, aged 84. He portrayed Sherlock Holmes on radio and television, and his movie credits include *The Diamond Wizard,* Hammer's *Spaceways, Shadow of the Cat* and *A Jolly Bad Fellow* (aka *They All Died Laughing*).

Brad Davis died from AIDS on September 9th, aged 41. He starred in such movies as *Midnight Express, The Curious Case of the Campus Corpse* and *Song of Darkness Song of Light,* and on TV in *Twilight Zone, Hitchhiker* and *Alfred Hitchcock Presents.*

Veteran character actor **John Hoyt** (aka John Hoystradt) died from cancer on September 15th. He was 87. Hoyt's many genre roles—often playing a scientist—include *When Worlds Collide, Lost Continent, The Black Castle, Attack of the Puppet People, Curse of the Undead, The Man With X-Ray Eyes, Two On a Guillotine, The Time Travellers* and *Flesh Gordon,* as well as numerous TV shows. He was also the Enterprise's original doctor in the *Star Trek* pilot, "The Menagerie".

Dwarf actor and newspaper seller **Angelo Rossito** died from complications during surgery on September 21st, aged 83. He was discovered by John Barrymore and featured as a character in Nathanael West's *Day of the Locust.* His long career included such films as *Seven Footprints to Satan* (1929), *Freaks, Spooks Run Wild, The Corpse Vanishes, Scared to Death, Mr Wong in Chinatown, Mesa of Lost Women, Carousel, The Magic Sword, Dracula vs. Frankenstein, From a Whisper to a Scream* (aka *The Offspring*), *Galaxina* and *Mad Max Beyond Thunderdome.*

Lady Oona Chaplin died on September 27th, aged 66. She was the widow of Charlie, the daughter of Eugene O'Neill and the mother of Geraldine.

David Gale, who portrayed the evil Dr Hill in *Re-Animator* and *Bride of Re-Animator,* died of a heart attack while working in an Off-Broadway play in early October. Gale, who was becoming something of a cult star, also appeared in *The Brain* and *Syngenor.*

Actor **Thalmus Rasulala** died from a heart attack/leukaemia on October 9th, aged 55. His movies include *Blacula, Dick and Marge Save the World, Friday Foster, The Slams* and *New Jack City.*

Comedian **Redd Foxx** died from a heart attack after falling ill at the White House on October 11th. He was 68, and his film credits include *Ghost of a Chance.*

Veteran character actor **Regis Toomey** died on October 12th, aged 93. His numerous films include *Murder By the Clock, One Frightened*

Night, The Phantom Creeps, Murder in the Blue Room, The Bishop's Wife, Mighty Joe Young, Voyage to the Bottom of the Sea and TV's *The Phantom of Hollywood.*

British actor **Donald Huston** died October 13th, aged 67. He played Dr Watson in *A Study in Terror,* also appeared in Hammer's *Maniac* (1963), *Tales That Witness Madness, Clash of the Titans* and portrayed David Caulder in the 1973 TV series *Moonbase 3.*

Knigh Dhiegh, best-known for his role as the evil Wo Fat in *Hawaii Five-O,* died on October 25th, aged 75. He also appeared on TV in *The Girl from UNCLE, Wild Wild West, Fantasy Island, Mission Impossible, Kung Fu,* and in such movies as *The Manchurian Candidate, Seconds, The Destructors* and *The Mephisto Waltz.*

Donald Churchill, who portrayed Dr Watson in the 1983 version of *The Hound of the Baskervilles,* died from an apparent heart attack on October 29, aged 60. He also appeared in the SF movie, *Spaceflight IC-1.*

Hollywood leading man **Fred MacMurray** died from pneumonia on November 5th, aged 83. His many movies include *Double Indemnity, Murder He Says, Where Do We Go From Here?, The Shaggy Dog, The Absent-Minded Professor, Son of Flubber, Charlie and the Angel, The Swarm* and TV's *Beyond the Bermuda Triangle.* He is survived by his second wife, actress June Haver.

American leading lady **Gene Tierney** died from emphysema on November 6th, aged 70. Tierney, who suffered a mental breakdown in 1955 and spent several years in and out of hospital, starred in *Laura, Heaven Can Wait* (1943), *The Ghost and Mrs Muir, Leave Her to Heaven, Dragonwyck, Whirlpool* and TV's *Daughter of the Mind,* amongst others.

French-Italian actor-singer **Yves Montand** (aka Ivo Levi), once described by Marilyn Monroe as "the most exciting man in the world", died from a heart attack on November 9th. He was 70. Married to actress Simone Signoret for 37 years, Montand's films include *The Wages of Fear* (1953), *The Witches of Salem, Is Paris Burning?, Z, On a Clear Day You Can See Forever* and *Mr Freedom.*

Former teen idol **Christopher Hayes** died from a heart attack on November 12th. His age was kept secret. He appeared in *The Computer Wore Tennis Shoes, The Dark, Body Double* and *Star Trek III: The Search for Spock.*

Distinctive-looking actor **Reggie Nalder** (aka Alfred Reg Natzler) died on November 19th from bone cancer. He was aged somewhere around 80. He played many menacing roles in *The Man Who Knew Too Much* (1956), *The Manchurian Candidate, The Bird With the Crystal Plumage, Dracula's Dog, Salem's Lot* (as Barlow, the vampire), *Mark of the Devil, Mark of the Devil II, The Dead*

Don't Die, Dracula Sucks (under a pseudonym), *The Devil and Max Devlin* and *Fellini's Casanova*, amongst others.

Polish-born character actor and father of Nastassja, **Klaus Kinski** (aka Nikolaus Gunthar Nakazynski), died from apparently natural causes on November 23rd. He was 65. Kinski appeared in literally hundreds of movies, including many westerns, Edgar Wallace mysteries and horror thrillers. Just a few titles include *The Avenger, Dead Eyes of London* (1961), *The Door With Seven Locks, Dr Mabuse vs. Scotland Yard, Jules Verne's Rocket to the Moon, The Million Eyes of Su-Muru, Circus of Fear, Web of the Spider* (as Poe), *Count Dracula* (as Renfield), *Justine* (as De Sade), *The Creature With the Blue Hand, Venom, Nosferatu the Vampyre, Vampire in Venice, Android, Creature, Star Knight, Crawlspace, Timestalkers, Aguirre Wrath of God* and *Fitzcarraldo*.

Eleanor Audley, who supplied the voice of the Wicked Stepmother in Disney's *Cinderella* and Maleficent in *Sleeping Beauty*, died on November 25th, aged 86.

American leading man **Ralph Bellamy** died on November 29th after a long illness. He was 87. His many credits include *Before Midnight, The Man Who Lived Twice, The Wolf Man, Ghost of Frankenstein, Rosemary's Baby, The Immortal, Something Evil, Search For the Gods, Oh God!, The Clone Master, Space, Billion Dollar Threat* and *Amazon Women on the Moon*.

FILM/TV TECHNICIANS

Edward A. Blatt, who directed the 1944 fantasy *Between Two Worlds*, died on his birthday, February 5th, aged 88.

Bernard Burton, who was associate producer on *The Beast from 20,000 Fathoms*, died on February 26th, aged 92.

George Sherman, who directed more than 100 westerns—many starring John Wayne—died on March 15th from heart and kidney failure, aged 82. His other credits include *The Lady and the Monster, The Crime Doctor's Courage, The Wizard of Baghdad, The Secret of the Whistler, The Bandit of Sherwood Forest* and *Panic Button*.

Samuel G. Gallu, who directed *Theatre of Death* starring Christopher Lee, died on March 27th from prostate cancer. He was 73.

Producer **George J. Morgan**, who was an associate of Ray Dennis Steckler, died from cancer on March 28th, aged 77. His credits include such Steckler-related projects as *The Incredibly Strange Creatures Who Stopped Living and Became Mixed-Up Zombies*!!?,

The Rat Pfink a Boo Boo and *The Lemon Grove Kids Meet the Monsters*.

Writer and 3-D expert **Milton Gunzberg** died on April 6th from cancer, aged 81. His credits include *Bwana Devil* and *House of Wax*.

Oscar-winning producer/director **David Lean** died on April 16th, aged 83. He began his film career as an editor (*Secret of the Loch*) before directing such classics as *Blithe Spirit*, *Great Expectations* (1945) and *The Sound Barrier*, amongst others. At the time of his death, Lean was working on an adaptation of Joseph Conrad's *Nostromo*.

Director **Don Siegel**, aged 78, died on April 20th after a long illness. His films include the original *Invasion of the Body Snatchers* (1956), *The Beguiled* and *Dirty Harry*, amongst others. As an actor, he appeared in the 1978 remake of *Invasion of the Body Snatchers* and *Play Misty for Me*.

TV producer **William Dozier** died on April 23rd, aged 83, following a stroke. His many credits include the 1960s *Batman* series (and movie), *The Green Hornet* and *Twilight Zone*.

Steve Broidy, once described by producer Albert Zugsmith as "the worst man I know in the business", died April 29th from a heart attack. He was 86. From 1945 to 65, Broidy was President of Monogram/Allied Artists, where he oversaw such series as *Charlie Chan*, *Bomba the Jungle Boy and the Dead End Kids*, as well as some of Bela Lugosi's worst movies.

Veteran special effects expert, **Roy Seawright**, died on April 30th, aged 85. His credits include *Topper Takes a Trip*, *Topper Returns* and *One Million BC*

Director **Richard Thorpe** died May 1st, aged 95. Among his many films are *The Fatal Warning*, *King of the Kongo* (with Karloff), *Murder at Dawn*, *Night Must Fall* (1937), *Strange People*, several of the best Weissmuller Tarzan adventures, and *Jailhouse Rock*.

Production executive **Dennis Crosby** died on May 4th, aged 56. He was the second of Bing's sons to commit suicide.

Joy Batchelor, wife of John Halas and partner in the animation company Halas and Batchelor, died on May 14th after a long illness. She wrote and directed the 1954 version of Orwell's *Animal Farm*.

Leading Filippino film-maker **Lino Brocka** was killed in a car accident on May 22nd. He was 51. Brocka's career began working with Eddie Romero as a script supervisor on the *Blood Island* movies.

Director, art director and special effects wizard **Eugene Lourié** died on May 26th from heart failure. He was aged 89. Lourié worked with Jean Renoir on such movies as *La Bete Humaine, Regle de Jeu* and *Grande Illusion*, before moving to Hollywood for Chaplin's *Limelight, Confessions of an Opium Eater, Shock Corridor, Crack in the World, What's the Matter With Helen?, Burnt Offerings*, and the TV movies *Haunts of the Very Rich* and *Death Takes a Holiday*. As a director, he was responsible for *The Beast from 20,000 Fathoms, Gorgo, The Colossus of New York* and *The Giant Behemoth*.

Low budget writer/director **Andy Milligan** died from AIDS on June 3rd, aged 62. Milligan's cult movies include *The Naked Witch, The Ghastly Ones, Bloodthirsty Butchers, Torture Dungeon, The Rats Are Coming! The Werewolves Are Here!, The Man With Two Heads, Legacy of Horror, The Body Beneath, Garu the Mad Monk, Blood, Carnage, The Degenerates* and *The Weirdo*.

Screenwriter/producer **Milton Subotsky** died June 27th from heart disease. He was 70. After writing the scripts for such TV shows as *Lights Out, Danger, Suspense, The Clock* and *Mr I. Magination*, he teamed up with financier Max J. Rosenberg to make *Rock, Rock, Rock* (1956). The team moved to Britain to make *City of the Dead* (1960) and the 1964 production *Dr Terror's House of Horrors* led to the formation of Amicus Productions. Second only to Hammer during the 1960s and '70s, Amicus produced a string of successful horror and science fiction films, many also scripted by Subotsky: *Dr Who and the Daleks, The Skull, Torture Garden, Scream and Scream Again, The House That Dripped Blood, Tales from the Crypt* and *The Land That Time Forgot*, amongst many others. He also produced *The Uncanny, Dominique, The Monster Club* and the TV mini-series *The Martian Chronicles*. Subotsky is credited on several movies based on Stephen King stories, the most recent being *The Lawnmower Man* (1992).

Ben Chapman died of heart failure on July 8th, aged 83. He was the associate producer on *Donovan's Brain* and also donned the Gill Man costume for the land scenes in *The Creature from the Black Lagoon*.

TV director **Murray Golden** died August 5th following complications from a stroke. He was 79 and his many credits include episodes of *Star Trek, Get Smart, The Time Tunnel* and *The Invaders*.

Academy Award-winning director **Frank Capra** died on September 3rd, aged 94. His many classic movies include *Lost Horizon* (1937), *Arsenic and Old Lace, It's A Wonderful Life* and his last, *Pocketful of Miracles* (1961).

STEPHEN JONES & KIM NEWMAN

Writer/producer/director **Chuck Vincent** died September 23rd, aged 51. Best known for his porno movies, such as *American Tickler*, *Hollywood Hot Tubs*, *Slammer Girls* and *Sex Crimes 2084*, he also made horror films such as *Bad Blood* and *If Looks Could Kill*.

Star Trek creator **Gene Roddenberry**, aged 70, died from cardiac arrest caused by a massive bloodclot on October 24th. A pilot for Pan Am and a sergeant with the LA Police Department, he began writing for TV in the 1950s. The pilot for *Star Trek* was aired in September 1966 and the series ran for 79 episodes. Roddenberry also produced such unsuccessful pilot shows as *Spectre*, *The Questor Tapes*, *Planet Earth* and *Genesis II*, executive produced *Star Trek: The Next Generation*, and was creative consultant on the six *Star Trek* movies. He is survived by his wife, Majel Leigh Hudec, who played Nurse Chapel on *Star Trek* under the stage name Majel Barrett.

Film and TV producer **Irwin Allen** died from a heart attack on November 2nd, aged 75. He created such series as *Voyage to the Bottom of the Sea*, *Lost in Space*, *Land of the Giants* and *The Time Tunnel*, the TV films *City Beneath the Sea* and *Time Travellers*, and the mini-series *The Amazing Captain Nemo* and *Alice in Wonderland*. His movie credits include *The Story of Mankind*, the 1960 remake of *The Lost World*, *Voyage to the Bottom of the Sea*, *Five Weeks in a Balloon*, *The Poseidon Adventure*, *The Towering Inferno*, *The Swarm*, *Beyond the Poseidon Adventure* and *When Time Ran Out*.

British stage and screen director **Tony Richardson** died from AIDS on November 14th, aged 63. His films include *A Taste of Honey*, *Tom Jones*, *The Loved One*, *Hamlet* (1969) and the 1990 TV version of *The Phantom of the Opera*.

Daniel Mann, who directed *Our Man Flint* and *Willard*, died from heart failure on November 21st, aged 79.

Oscar-winning *Batman* designer **Anton Furst**, aged 47, committed suicide on November 24th by jumping from the seventh floor of a Los Angeles building. A pioneer of laser-based special effects, his other credits include *Star Wars*, *Superman*, *Alien*, *Moonraker*, *Outland*, *Company of Wolves*, *Full Metal Jacket*, *High Spirits* and the Planet Hollywood restaurant in New York. Furst, who was set to design and direct *Midknight* starring Michael Jackson, had been under treatment for alcohol problems and was suffering from depression.

Writer/director/producer and sometimes collaborator with Curtis Harrington, **George Edwards**, died from cancer on November 26th, aged 67. His film credits include *Queen of Blood*, *Games*, *How Awful About Allan*, *What's the Matter with Helen?*, *Frogs*, *The Killing Kind*, *Legend of Hell House*, *The Attic*, *Evil Spirits* and *Ruby*.

Gene Milford, who won an Oscar for editing *Lost Horizon* (1937), died on December 23rd, aged 89. His other credits include *On the Waterfront, Countdown* and *Wait Until Dark*.